Praise for Mary Freeman's
DEVIL'S TRUMPET

"Interesting characters, a sharp puzzle, gardening details, and not one, but two romances make *Devil's Trumpet* a scintillating mystery debut. Rachel O'Connor is an engaging character, definitely worthy of a series. The pace is lively and the story intriguing. What more could anyone ask for in a mystery?"

—*Romantic Times*

"Mary Freeman evokes for us the dark goings-on in and around the charming gardens of the mythical town of Blossom, Oregon. We can't relax until the landscaper heroine, Rachel O'Connor, unearths the solution to some very nasty murders."

—*Ann Ripley, author of The Garden Tour Affair*

"Mary Freeman writes as though she has known these townspeople all their lives . . . [*Devil's Trumpet*] kept me guessing till the end. I would love this story to become a series."

—*Literary Times*

"Music, gardening, herbs, and old hurts combine perfectly in this enjoyable debut novel."

—*Mystery Time & Rhyme*

"A very good amateur sleuth mystery. Readers will like the characters and the serpentine plot filled to the max with red herrings."

—*Midwest Book Review*

BLEEDING
HEART

Mary Freeman

BERKLEY PRIME CRIME, NEW YORK

BLEEDING HEART

A Berkley Prime Crime Book / published by arrangement with the author

PRINTING HISTORY
Berkley Prime Crime edition / September 2000

The Penguin Putnam Inc. World Wide Web site address is
http://www.penguinputnam.com

ISBN: 0-425-17669-X

Berkley Prime Crime Books are published
by The Berkley Publishing Group,
a division of Penguin Putnam Inc.,
375 Hudson Street, New York, New York 10014.
The name BERKLEY PRIME CRIME and the BERKLEY PRIME CRIME
design are trademarks belonging to Penguin Putnam Inc.

PRINTED IN THE UNITED STATES OF AMERICA

10 9 8 7 6 5 4 3 2 1

For Paul and Debbie
Who are Wrigley-Cross Books

ACKNOWLEDGMENTS

I'd like to thank Richard Morris, who was a police officer, is a mystery lover, and tries very hard to keep me from making too many procedural mistakes.

I'd also like to express my enormous gratitude to the staff and tireless volunteers of the Leach Botanical Garden who were ever helpful. Although there is absolutely no relationship between my character Eloise Johnston and Lila Leach, I have tried to render the garden faithfully, in spite of the fictional neglect I've imposed on it. The very beautifully maintained Leach Botanical Garden is open to the public at 6704 S.E. 122nd Avenue, Portland, Oregon 97236.

CHAPTER

1

Beck didn't talk.

Which made the drive from the Columbia River town of Blossom to Portland seem rather longer than it should, and gave Rachel O'Connor plenty of time to question the wisdom of taking a landscaping job so far from home. But her young landscaping business near Hood River wasn't yet paying all the bills, and Eloise Johnston had offered a lucrative job, restoring the overgrown grounds of her home. Her friend Sandy—who was working for the property owner—had insisted that Rachel would love the job. Considering that Eloise Johnston and her late husband were prominent botanists, Rachel decided that she would have agreed to at least look at the job even if it had been clear out on the Oregon coast. Well, maybe not, she thought as she dodged a semi rig whose driver seemed to think he was piloting a Ferarri.

"Why don't you talk?" Rachel asked Beck as she negotiated—finally—the exit that would take them into southeast Portland.

After another few moments of silence, Beck dragged his gaze from a vista of weedy fields and the new concrete warehouses that were springing up east of Portland. He turned his mild blue eyes in her direction. "I talk." He tugged at his thick braid.

End of conversation. At least he had put a shirt on for the trip. Usually he looked like a refugee from the sixties; shirtless, his gray-streaked blond hair woven into a thick braid, strings of beads around his neck. He was quite a sight for most prospective clients. But for all his garb, he was only a few years older than she—barely into his thirties. Rachel sighed. If she were alone, she could listen to the radio. But the radio seemed to make Beck uncomfortable, no matter which station she tuned in to. Beck was odd. He lived alone, in a remote cabin in the woods above Blossom, accompanied by a vast number of black cats. There he worked miracles with wood. Gentle and very quiet, he was artist more than artisan, even when all he was building was a garden shed.

Beck was simply . . . Beck.

Rachel shook her head as she exited the freeway onto crowded 181st Avenue. Not for the first time, she wondered if she had made a mistake bringing him along. But Mrs. Johnston had mentioned several construction projects, and she needed Beck's input for her estimate. She just hoped that this woman was tolerant of the unusual. Rachel glanced at the scribbled directions she'd pinned to the notepad mounted on her pickup's dashboard. They had left the brief and welcome sunshine behind as they neared Portland, and now traveled beneath a low ceiling of gray cloud. This had been one of the coldest and wettest springs on record. Her uncle had been worrying incessantly about the budding pear trees on the family orchard.

"I haven't been out to the property yet." She spoke determinedly to the silent Beck. "Mrs. Johnston isn't very young. But she sounded nice. I hope . . . I mean . . ." Rachel gave up. You couldn't exactly ask Beck to act normal.

He didn't say anything, but when he looked at her, there was a suspicious twinkle in his gray eyes, as if he knew very well what she found herself unable to say. Rachel let her breath out in a gusty sigh of exasperation, once more wondering just who the real Beck was, if maybe the beads and braid and black cats were nothing more than a private and elaborate joke on the stolid rest of society. Shaking her head, she waited through a red light, then turned down Powell to 122nd Avenue, following Sandy's directions, penned in her looping, high-school script. The wide street narrowed abruptly, becoming winding and very rural, dropping sharply down through dense firs to a wide creek. Just before the bridge, a pair of huge iron gates stood open on either side of an asphalt driveway. Red rust streaked the bars, although the weeds had been kept cut at their base, suggesting that they were actually closed once in a while.

Rachel turned onto the narrow lane, and that turned into a circular drive in front of a peeling, white-painted house and garage, joined by a brick breezeway. The steep roof of the garage nearly touched the sharp slope of the hillside behind it, and ferns sprouted lushly in the gutters. Tall firs overhung the house and yard, shading it for much of the day. This early in the summer, a riot of lush growth covered the slope above the house and the bank that led down to the creek. Rachel picked out hydrangea, spirea, and a struggling rhododendron. The hillside had been planted to shrubs before the weeds took over. She swallowed, realizing the enormity of the job, if the entire property had been allowed to get to this state.

She would certainly be able to give her weeding crew a few hours. The filtered light in the clearing gave the scene a rain-forest feel. Rachel parked next to the front patio, beneath an impressive stand of black bamboo. She got out but didn't go up the steps to the front door right away, instead going over to admire the dark gleaming bamboo stems that soared twenty-five feet high, and to peer over the bank. The clump had spread down the bank to the creek, but morning glory twined heavily up many of the slender shoots, and stinging nettle grew thickly along the bank, along with a breathtaking variety of native and nonnative ferns. There was a path down there, she was pretty sure, although you could hardly make it out at all anymore.

Stone steps wound down from the house to the creek, visible here and there through clumps of invasive geranium. More flagstone-and-brick pathway peeped from the lush growth in the wetland strip between the water and the sharp bank. Dried mud and strands of dead weeds snagged in the salmonberry canes suggested that the spring floods had covered the path at least once this year. A fat mallard drake preened himself on a carved stone bench beneath an enormous cedar. Not too long ago, Rachel thought, this had been a lovely place. It would take an army, she thought. A small one but . . .

"Rachel! You're early!" Her friend Sandy's bright soprano interrupted her glum reverie.

"I'm impressed." Rachel turned around as her blond friend skipped down the steps to the driveway. "I'm not sure if I'm impressed more with the weeds or the original plants."

"Now come on." Sandy tossed her curls indignantly. "It's a wonderful place. You haven't even seen things yet."

"Oh, I'm not really grumbling." Rachel wrinkled her nose. "I'm just afraid I'm going to have to bid this so high that your boss will faint on the spot. But I can see why you told me I'd like this place." She sighed, imagining what it would look like cared for and restored. "Oh, look! Camellias!" She pointed up at the overgrown slope above the house where a few late blossoms in shades of crimson and pink glowed like jewels among the tangle of greenery. "That's quite a bed of them. I've heard of the Johnstons, you know." She nodded at the old house. "They were good friends of my botany professor in college."

"How cool." Sandy's eyes strayed toward the drive. "Be sure to tell Eloise. You'll like her," she said absently. "Oh, dear." She made a face. "You brought *him* with you."

"Beck?" Rachel turned to look for him. He had gotten out of the truck and wandered down the lane toward the road. At the moment he stood beneath a huge fir, his face turned up to the tree. Lips moving as if he was talking to

himself, he ran his fingers sensuously across the rough bark.
"Sandy, he's harmless." Rachel rolled her eyes. "He's odd,
but he wouldn't hurt a fly. And he's the best."

"*You* say he's harmless." Sandy gave her a dark look.
"He was in the army, remember? I heard that he got strange
after he was in the Gulf War. Maybe he killed people.
Maybe he could do it again one day." She crossed her arms.
"I always worry about you—working with him like you
do."

"Relax." Rachel put her arm around her friend and
hugged her. "So where is Mrs. Johnston?" She changed the
subject. "And how did you get this job as her biographer,
anyway?"

"She was out back working on the rock garden last time
I saw her. No matter what the doctor says, she still goes
out and weeds every day." Sandy gave Beck one final
doubting glance. "Eloise is a fantastic person. Until her
heart really started giving her trouble, she did nearly all the
work around here, and I guess it looked really good. It's
just killing her, how the place is going downhill. That's
why I told her about you." Sandy's eyes sparkled once
more, Beck obviously forgotten for the moment. "You
know, she's going to leave the garden to a conservation
group, and she's determined to get it back into shape before
they take over. Isn't that wonderful of her? And remember
Mrs. Gittings?"

"Our high-school English teacher?" Rachel nodded as
she followed Sandy around the front of the house on the
concrete terrace. The thick clumps of bamboo whispered in
the breeze. "She wanted you to grow up and be a best-
selling author, if I remember right."

"Not really." Sandy laughed and made a face, but her
blue eyes sparkled. "Although I actually did start writing a
book in her class. I made eight chapters before I quit. Anyway, it turns out she knows Eloise. I guess she and Carl—
Eloise's husband—lived in Blossom for a few years."

"Really?"

"They had some kind of contract with the forest service—doing tree surveys or something. It was years and years ago, back when they were first married. Then they started their book about Northwest botany and lived all over Oregon and Washington."

"I never knew they lived in Blossom. Small world," Rachel said thoughtfully. Apparently nobody in the town considered two of the world's most famous botanists to be celebrities, she thought. But then, botany wasn't exactly a high-profile career. They had rounded the corner of the house and now found themselves on a large brick patio. A double set of glass doors opened into the house, and through them Rachel caught a glimpse of a long room paneled in dark pine. Oriental carpets covered the center of the plank floor, and mission-style furniture filled the room. Vases stood on nearly every table, filled with trusses of camellia and rhododendron blossoms, arranged dramatically with late narcissus and white tulips. The bright blossoms punctuated the rather dark and heavy effect of paneling, carpeting, and furniture, softening the masculine effect of the decor.

She turned away from the house just as a figure emerged from the small building at the far end of the patio. Tall and lanky, with a thick knot of snowy white hair gathered at the back of her neck, Eloise Johnston wore a man's work jeans, boots, and a plaid flannel shirt open at the neck to show the top of a cotton undershirt beneath. "You must be Sandy's friend, the gardener," she said in a clear, alto voice. "I'm so glad to meet you. And I apologize for the jungle." Smile lines crinkled her weathered face as she crossed the bricks to offer Rachel her hand.

Her movements didn't match her robust attire. Her steps hesitated a bit, and when she clasped Rachel's hand in her startlingly firm grip, Rachel realized that she was very thin. Her bones jutted beneath her translucent skin, masked by the bulk of her clothing. "I'm glad to meet you, too," Rachel said, thinking that the woman's eyes were decades younger than her body. "I met your husband once. He was a guest lecturer for my Botany 310 class. He gave a seminar on native prairie grass ecology that I still remember. He was wonderful. And your place is lovely."

"You can see beyond the neglect, then, my dear." Eloise's hazel eyes twinkled. "This is about all I can keep up with these days." She gestured with a dirt-encrusted trowel toward the steep rock garden above the house and patio. "Carl was indeed a wonderful teacher. Unlike me." She laughed. "I have no patience with students. I kept telling him that he should teach, but he loved our fieldwork. I think that's part of the reason he spent so much time on the gardens here," she said thoughtfully. "It brought that part of our lives home. He would be disappointed to see it like this. But he's dead, and I don't believe that such trivial human emotions continue beyond the grave," she went on briskly. "I suppose Sandy told you that I'm leaving this place to the Northwest Garden Conservancy? It's a private organization formed for the express purpose of preserving the garden. It does not yet have much financial support. That is why I intend to fund the restoration effort myself." She took Rachel's elbow and steered her back toward the house. "Roger Tourelle—he's the head of the Conservancy—is planning to hold a public grand opening event in just over a month. So, as you see, I need you to begin work very soon."

"Well, we can talk about what you want," Rachel murmured. Eloise wasn't simply being polite, she realized. The elderly woman clearly needed Rachel's support, and Rachel could feel her weakness. She stumbled once, and as she caught herself, Rachel stifled a murmur of surprise. Eloise Johnston seemed nearly weightless—a papery husk of a woman who could blow away in a strong gust of wind.

The glass doors swung open as they approached. "Oh, Eloise. There you are." A young woman dressed in stone-washed jeans and a camp shirt leaned through them, her expression anxious. "This strange guy is wandering around outside." She looked at Rachel and raised an eyebrow. "Is he with you?" She sounded accusing.

"Uh . . . that's Beck." Rachel's cheeks warmed. "He's

the carpenter I told you about on the phone," she explained to Eloise. "He won't agree to take a job until he visits the site. He's really very good," she went on quickly. "He's just kind of . . . unusual. I hope he didn't startle you," she said to the young woman in the doorway.

"Gosh, no." She laughed. "He doesn't exactly look dangerous. Just kind of weird." She had a flawless oval face with tilted hazel eyes flecked with green, and a slender build that cost Rachel a twinge of jealousy. But it was her expression rather than her beauty that caught Rachel's attention. Those agate-colored eyes held a weary mix of wisdom and wariness tinged with something like cynicism. They were old eyes, Rachel thought. They were older than Eloise's eyes, never mind her young-twenties face.

"Well, I'm looking forward to meeting this paragon of woodworking, my dear." Eloise smiled. "Whatever his demeanor. April, this is Rachel. Rachel, April is my right arm. And my legs at times," she said with a laugh. "I couldn't get along here by myself without her."

"You really could, you know." April laughed, too. "I feel as if I should pay you to live here."

"Nonsense." Eloise took her arm with a naturalness that concealed her real need for support. "The house has never been so clean and well organized. I was never much of a housekeeper," she confided to Rachel as she led them all through the dark living room and into the small entry hall. "That's why I liked living in a tent. As for cooking . . ." She laughed. "Be glad April made lunch and not I. Poor Carl did most of the cooking. It was an act of self-preservation, I believe. Although we ate plenty of peanut butter sandwiches and canned soup." Her laugh chimed, as young as her eyes. "I can at least scramble eggs. If I have to. Why don't you go collect your carpenter, my dear, and we'll all take a walk about the property?"

"I'll do that," Rachel said, and exited through the front door. Of course, Beck was nowhere to be seen. Letting her breath out in an exasperated sigh, because he could be anywhere on the property, Rachel walked along the drive, sweeping the woods on either side with narrowed eyes. Sometimes Beck was a trial. No, amend that, she thought grimly. He was always a trial, with his fears of the Evil One, his personal bogeyman. It wasn't at all unusual for him to refuse a job because the Evil One was hovering about. But his work—when he did choose to take a job— made any difficulty worthwhile. When he had built a deck for the mayor of Blossom, the grain in the individual planks of the decking had formed a unified whole, like a picture that the eye couldn't quite make out, but the mind recognized. That deck had been featured in a prominent Northwest magazine, along with a mention of her company, Rain Country Landscaping.

Her exasperation growing, Rachel planted her fists on her hips. "Beck!" She scanned the slope above the drive. "Where *are* you?" Movement caught her eye, and he appeared from behind the slender trunk of a witch hazel. Quite a few witch hazel dotted the slope. Their yellow blooms would stand out in the early spring, along with the golden catkins of filbert and alder. "Mrs. Johnston wants to show us around," she called up to him.

He came skipping down a barely visible path of riverstone steps set in the steep hillside. His gray braid swung with his movement, and as he got closer, Rachel realized that he was smiling, his blue eyes shining like summer sky. That startled her. Other than a shy smile now and again, Beck seemed utterly solemn. "I take it you approve?" Rachel answered his smile, relieved.

"There's love here," he said happily. "I can build for this place. No problem."

"No Evil One?" Rachel asked, and then bit her lip, because you didn't joke about the Evil One with Beck.

For a moment his expression sobered, and he tilted his head as if to listen. "Not now," he said.

"Good, good. They're waiting for us." She changed the subject quickly, gesturing to where Eloise Johnston, April, and Sandy stood clustered by the small brick breezeway that separated the garage from the main house. Beck strode over to them without hesitation. He always reminded Rachel of a blue heron wading through a pond, with his long legs and rather gawky movements. To her amazement and dismay, he stopped directly in front of Eloise, took her hand, bowed, and kissed the back of it.

"You have done a beautiful thing here," he murmured as he released her.

"Thank you." Eloise returned his bow without the slightest sign of discomposure. "We have tried."

"You shouldn't take that guy out in public," Sandy whispered, nudging Rachel. She raised her eyes to the cloudy sky. "Honestly. He should be on a leash."

"Shall we go?" Eloise Johnston offered her arm to Beck, and, to Rachel's utter amazement, he took it with another small bow. Beck did not touch people casually, but there they went, strolling off toward a flight of moss-grown and tilting stone steps that led up behind the garage, Beck's head bent down to the older woman's murmur of conversation as if they were old-fashioned lovers, stepping out together, and the care with which he guided her up the crooked flight was obvious.

"I'm not kidding," Sandy said, shaking her head. "You better chaperon them, girl, or he'll blow it for you yet." She rolled her eyes again. "I'd better get back to work on those tapes she made for me yesterday evening. If you want me, I'm downstairs in the office." Giving Rachel another look, she disappeared into the house.

"I think he's kind of sweet, actually." April nodded at the couple ahead of them. "Strange, yeah, but I dunno. Honest, I guess. He doesn't seem phony, at least. We talked for a few minutes—I saw him up where the irises grow. There's a ceanothus blooming there—a Persian lilac, you know? Oh, yeah, you're a gardener, I forgot." She smiled. "Anyway, he's nice. Come on." She tugged on Rachel's arm. "You should stick close and listen. She knows everything about this place—all the plants, the trees, *everything*. It still blows me away to listen to her. I mean, you probably know all this stuff, but before I came here, I didn't know a crocus from a dicentra—a bleeding heart. Now I know so much, I think I could get a job at a nursery."

"Well, she and her husband were very famous botanists." Rachel hurried along at April's side. "She ought to know a lot."

"So I found out. She's sure something." April slowed as they caught up, her attention on her employer, with just a hint of worry in her expression. "Eloise, are you getting too tired?"

"Not at all, dear." She smiled down at them. "I'm being very adequately helped, thank you. We'll stop and catch our breath here, though. We planted a number of penstemon here. They are hard to find at the moment," she said regretfully. "A little farther up, we put in quite a variety of hellebore, both orientalis and foetidus. The blooms are quite lovely in winter, especially when the witch hazels and alders begin to flower."

They moved on, more slowly now, Rachel noticed, climbing the long slope above the house. Here and there, Eloise showed Beck where she wanted a bench or a small shelter. Mostly he nodded. Once or twice he argued with her, and one time they compromised on a bench set some twenty yards farther along the trail, beneath a huge fir, instead of a shelter. Rachel and April trailed in their wake. April kept a close eye on her employer. Rachel found herself constantly distracted by the amazing variety of native and nonnative species that lurked beneath rampant weeds. Many had been grouped by family, so that the various genera and species could be compared easily. The weeds needed to be cleared, and the paths had been badly eroded by winter rains. Some species had probably disappeared, but some might be replaced from specialty nurseries like Rhinehoffer's—nurseries that offered native plants, shrubs, and trees.

"I want the old greenhouse repaired." Eloise pointed to a structure that wasn't much more than a metal frame and fragments of broken glass. "And the Stone House. We bought it from the old man who lived there the year before

Carl died. I told Roger that he could rent it or find a live-in caretaker to occupy it. The neighborhood children have, alas, broken most of the windows and the greenhouse glass. I can never catch them at it." She looked sad. "I'd like to see it useful again. Carl started so many of our seeds and cuttings there."

"I can take care of the greenhouse," Rachel said, "but you'll have to hire a contractor for the house."

"Oh, of course, dear." Eloise dimpled. "I didn't expect you to do remodeling, too."

Rachel smiled, but she wasn't really listening. From the corner of her eye she had glimpsed movement in the gaping windows of the old house, but now that she was staring at it, nothing moved. *Of course. Kids,* she thought. *Smoking cigarettes, or worse.* Playing in a ruin the way she and Jeff and Sandy and Bill had played in the old ruined house that Jeff now lived in. But in spite of her explanation, the hairs at the back of her neck still prickled as she turned her back on the house. The dank twilight on this cloudy day filled the ground beneath the tall trees with eerie twilight.

"The paths must be designed with large numbers of people in mind," Eloise went on blithely. She began to lead them downward, through a thicket of salal and native huckleberry. "I want them accessible to the disabled, of course. And I do realize that it will require quite a lot of labor to clear the weeds and the dead brush." She turned a sharp eye on Rachel. "Can you do all this? Hire the people? You can guarantee that it will be done?"

"Yes, I can." Rachel hesitated, because in spite of all the difficulties involved, she wanted this job. She wanted to return this garden to what it had been. Local history—human past, expressed in old buildings, tools, and household items—fascinated her. "You might be better off to get some estimates from Portland firms." She spoke reluctantly. "They wouldn't have the kind of commute that I have, they would use local labor, and they could probably give you a better estimate."

"I don't want somebody simply because they are cheap."

Eloise Johnston gently disengaged herself from Beck's arm and stood very straight. Below her, ferns swayed in the gutters of the garage, where it nearly touched the rock-garden slope, and the bamboo stems along the creekbank swayed gracefully in the wind. "This place was our life together—Carl's and my own. I want somebody good. I did some research on you, you know." Her eyes twinkled. "I had April drive me to your town. We stopped in at a lovely little café near the river, and I asked the woman who owned it if she knew you."

That would be Joy Markham at the Bread Box, Rachel thought.

"She said I should just go look, and sent me out to an old hotel, whose grounds you have been working on. She told me they had been abandoned for decades when you took the job on." Eloise smiled gently at Rachel. "Carl and I stayed at the Columbia River Inn many many years ago. I was impressed, dear. You didn't use the grounds as a chance to do what you wanted to do. You truly restored them to what they once were. That was, I think, as much an act of love as an act of business."

"I couldn't improve on the original design," Rachel murmured, blushing.

"Oh, I think you improved a few things here and there. But what I am saying is that I know what I want, you see. I want you."

"I . . . I'm flattered." The Columbia River Inn had been her first big project, and after the elderly owner had been murdered, it had become her personal tribute to him to finish the restoration he had planned, for his heir. "I would like very much to do this for you."

"Then it's settled." Eloise's smile twinkled in the cloudy light. "Let's go down before it begins to rain again. We will have some tea. You can make up a formal estimate for the restoration of the upper slope and the creek wetlands, and their paths, the rebuilding of the greenhouse, and general improvements. And of course, Mr. Beck, I'll need your estimate for the wooden structures."

"She does that," Beck said as he slipped his arm beneath hers again. "She pays me enough."

Rachel noticed that Eloise's pace had slowed considerably as they descended the path behind the house. Her steps faltered more and more, and April's expression became increasingly anxious as they neared the bottom. As they reached the final steps that led to the drive, Eloise halted, swaying a little, her breathing a harsh rasp. Without a word, Beck picked her up, lifting her in his arms as if she weighed no more than a child. "Where?" he asked her gently.

"You may put me on the sofa in the living room," Eloise said with a gasp. "We can have our tea in there, if you wouldn't mind, April. I'm quite fine. Just a little overtired."

"This way," April said briskly, and led the way down the steps and into the house. There Beck deposited his burden on the dark leather seat of the mission sofa with surprising tenderness. Without a word he collected two brightly upholstered pillows from the chairs and tucked them beneath the elderly woman's shoulders.

"I'll bring the tea in here," April said.

"That's fine, dear," Eloise murmured. "Would you answer the phone if it rings? I'm expecting a call, but I don't believe that I'll jump up and rush for the phone just now."

"Sure," April said. "I'll have the tea in a minute."

"I'll help you," said Beck, and vanished into the rear of the house in her wake.

"Your carpenter is very nice," Eloise murmured. "Would you step downstairs and let Sandy know that we'll be having tea? I could use a moment or two to rest."

"All right," Rachel said. The botanist did not look good. Her color was pale, and her lips and eyelids had a faintly bluish cast. The hems of her jeans had slipped upward on her legs, and Rachel realized that her ankles were swollen. She wore heavy tights that had a functional medical look to them, but the flesh above her boot tops still bulged over the leather. "Would you like a pillow under your feet?" she asked.

Eloise opened her eyes and looked at her feet. "If you

wouldn't mind taking my boots off for me, that would be nice," she said. "I'll just put my feet up on top of the sofa arm. It's the bad heart that makes them swell," she said. "It was worse before I started taking medicine. Thank you, dear." She sighed and closed her eyes as Rachel unlaced and removed her worn and obviously well-used boots. "Now run along downstairs, please."

Without another word, Rachel withdrew. She heard the murmur of voices from the kitchen as she reached the entry hall, and April's tinkling laugh. She and Beck were obviously getting along just fine. Smiling, she descended the steps. The downstairs office had obviously been Carl and Eloise's library. Bookshelves lined the walls from floor to ceiling, and a couple of worn recliners stood beneath reading lamps. A wide desk stood before the big front window that overlooked the creek. A computer and printer took center stage, and a clear space had been created around the keyboard. Other than that area, papers cluttered the surface in tall, precarious stacks. Leaning forward in front of the screen, Sandy's fingers danced over the keyboard as she listened with earphones to a small microcassette recorder.

As Rachel entered the room, she paused, thumbed off the recorder, and straightened, shaking her head. "Wow," she said softly.

"Interesting stuff?" Rachel came up beside her. "Eloise is serving tea."

"I could use some tea, and it's more interesting than you'd guess." Sandy stretched, touched a couple of keys on the computer, and removed a disk from the machine. "I'll take this home and finish today's session there. I always worry that Eloise will forget she's recorded something and tape right over the stuff I haven't transcribed. And we're almost finished." She slipped the tape out of the recorder and dropped it into her pocket. "There are a few skeletons in her closet," she said thoughtfully. "It might make a best-seller. Did you know that she and Carl were close friends of Robert Claymore and his wife? Back when they farmed pears, south of Blossom?"

"Our state representative's parents? No, I didn't know that." Rachel counted back. "Our Favorite Son must have been a kid back then."

"I guess he was in high school. And he lived with the Johnstons for a year after his parents were killed."

"Small world," Rachel said. "I never remember him mentioning the Johnstons, but he doesn't really talk about his childhood much in his campaigns." She shrugged.

"Well, it's going to be a best-seller in Blossom, I'll bet. Brrr," Sandy said as she reached the top of the stairs. "That's a cold draft. Who left the door open?"

In the main room, one of the double glass doors that led out onto the patio from the living room stood ajar. Eloise sat upright on the sofa, her arms wrapped around herself, an expression of undeniable pain on her face as she stared out at the yard.

"What's wrong? Eloise?" Sandy hurried into the room. "Are you all right? Did someone come in here?"

"A ghost." The elderly woman turned a frail smile on them. "Ghosts visit us old folks. Will you close the door, please?" She shivered. "The wind blew it open."

The wind wore muddy shoes, Rachel discovered as she closed and latched the multipaned doors. "Did April or Beck go out this way?" she asked sharply.

"Did I go out where?" April appeared behind them with a platter of cookies and small sandwiches in her hands. Beside her, Beck carried a tray laden with a large dark brown teapot and various cups, saucers, and silverware.

"Are you sure nobody came in here, Eloise?" Sandy eyed the elderly woman suspiciously.

"You don't need to shout, dear. I am not deaf." Eloise raised one eyebrow. "I told you it was a ghost. You discover that the world is populated more and more by ghosts as you get older. One day in the not too distant future, I will be among them. They don't frighten me."

Beck stalked past Rachel and into the room, moving with the stiff posture of a wary dog. For a moment he stood still, his head tilted as if listening. Then he abruptly set the tray of tea things down on the long low coffee table.

"You should introduce me next time." April set down her platter. "I've never met a ghost." She began to pour tea and hand out cups and plates of sandwiches and Vienna Finger cookies, and everyone relaxed. Except for Beck. He accepted a cup of tea and a plate with sandwiches and cookies from April, but he perched awkwardly on the edge of a chair and didn't touch the food. Rachel hoped hard and long that the Evil One wasn't about to mess up a very nice beginning here.

Sandy and Rachel finished their tea quickly, because it was obvious that the elderly woman was very tired. Rachel particularly wanted to get back to Blossom before it got too late. She had made a dinner date with Jeff Price, Blossom's young and sometimes controversial chief of police.

"I would like you to write up a formal estimate and contract as soon as possible," Eloise addressed her from the sofa. "After all, time is short at my age." She gave Rachel a wan smile. "It is never a good idea to put anything off. How soon may I expect it?"

"It will take me a couple of days to figure everything out," Rachel said slowly. Estimates were the part of the job she liked least. It always seemed like such a fine line between charging a client so much that they went elsewhere, or leaving yourself with such a narrow margin of profit that the most minor disaster pushed the job into the loss column.

"Don't worry too much about the money." The elderly woman gave her a shrewd glance. "I'm not quibbling about cost, remember? I want the property restored to what it used to be, and I want you to do it. That much I can pay for. The Conservancy will take it from there—but this is my memorial to Carl, and to our sixty years together." Her eyes softened and blurred with memory. "Realize that it is a memorial to us both. I don't want to skimp on it, dear."

"I'll start working on the estimate tonight. I promise." Rachel stood and smiled down at the botanist. "I'll call you if I have any questions."

"You do that." Eloise nodded. "I'm not going anywhere."

Rachel and the still-silent Beck took their leave. The lowering clouds had turned the afternoon into a premature twilight, and the wind gusted restlessly in the tops of the cedars. More rain was coming. Rachel sighed, more tired of rain than she had ever been in her life. Mount Hood and the Cascades still lay buried beneath a record snowpack. Two days of warm rain could cause disastrous flooding as the snow melted precipitously. The damp wind was cold enough tonight. Rachel shivered, thinking it felt like March rather than May. "Let's go home," she told Beck. "Before it pours."

Beck hesitated for a moment as Rachel slid behind the wheel, his eyes on the house as he leaned against the open truck door, his expression troubled. "The Evil One has looked here," he murmured as he finally slid onto the seat. "I am afraid."

Oh, no, not this, not now. Rachel closed her eyes briefly. "Maybe the Evil One will go away," she said feebly as she turned the truck around in the circular drive. The first drops of rain spattered the windshield as she spoke, and a sudden gust of wind tossed the branches of the trees.

"Maybe," Beck said.

Branches clawed at the truck as she eased down the drive to the main road, and in spite of herself, Rachel shivered.

CHAPTER

2

The drive back to Hood River was just as silent as the trip out. Although there was a difference, Rachel noticed as she negotiated her way around a triple-trailer rig just outside of Bonneville. Beck was smiling. It was a gentle, pensive smile that softened the usually wary reserve of his lean face. Rachel felt reassured. His actual invocation of the Evil One's name had made her worry that he would refuse the job after all. When he did that, no amount of coaxing or storming could change his mind.

They made good time, once they left the Portland rush-hour traffic behind. Sandy had left with them, and for a brief time Rachel tried to keep her friend in sight. But Sandy drove her little Honda as if it was a Ferrari. She reminded Rachel of Joshua, her mother's new husband, when he was driving his MG. Although her mother was just as bad when she got behind the wheel of a fast car. Rachel smiled. Not what you'd expect from a woman her age. She gave up on Sandy and settled for making another try with the radio, turned low to a news station. This time, Beck seemed oblivious.

She left the highway at the Blossom exit and drove

through town, on out to Beck's dirt road far up the side of the Gorge. It was dry enough that she could make it clear back to his cabin and well-kept shop without putting the truck into four-wheel drive. His cats were waiting for him, at least ten, she guessed, all black and wild as bobcats. Beck got out of the truck and tugged at his braid. "Tell me when you want me," he said.

"I should have the estimate in two or three days." Rachel leaned out her window, which caused four or five cats to duck for cover. "Can you make some drawings for Eloise? Do you remember all the things she wanted?"

"I remember." Beck gave her a gentle smile. "I don't need to do the drawings for Eloise."

"For me, then, okay?" Rachel sighed. "I have to decide how much money to charge her for what you're going to do."

"I know." He gave her another smile. "I'll do them tonight."

"I'll come get them. Thanks!" Rachel waved and reversed, backing the truck around in the narrow parking area. As she pulled back into the dirt lane, she looked in her rearview mirror to watch Beck walk across the small clearing toward his tiny cabin. Black cats trooped behind him as if he were a pied piper of cats. She smiled, wondering how her feline housemate Peter would react to Beck. He wasn't black, after all. It would be an interesting experiment.

She drove back into town, fumbling for her dark glasses as the last rays of the setting sun slanted through the windshield. The planters along the few blocks of Blossom's Main Street were coming along nicely, especially the big ones in front of City Hall, Rachel noted with satisfaction. Her young Guatemalan assistant, Julio, had a contract with the city to maintain them—his first contract for the yard-maintenance business he had started for himself early this year. She missed him on the days he couldn't work for her. As she braked to turn onto Pine Street, toward home, a waving figure caught her eye. She pulled over to the curb and leaned out the window. "Joylinn, hi!" she greeted her friend, and the owner of the Bread Box Bakery. "I guess I have you to thank for my new job. Eloise Johnston said she did her reference research in the Bread Box."

"I remember her. She was in last week." Joylinn tossed back her thick ginger-colored hair, and shifted the cloth shopping bag she was carrying to her other hand. "Good for you—and for her. It sounded like just your sort of job."

"It is." Rachel laughed. "I just wish it was closer to home."

"Well, the Portland landscapers are willing to come out here and take your business. It's about time you took back a little of theirs."

"Come on." Rachel shook her head. "I haven't lost too much business that way."

"So how come Joshua didn't go into Portland with your mother?" Joylinn rummaged in her bag. "I thought those two were joined at the hip. Here." She pulled out a plastic bag full of darkly glazed rolls. "This is too heavy to carry. Lighten the load for me, will you?"

"Hazlenut rolls? You bet I'll help you out, girl." Rachel made a theatrical grab for the bag and clutched it to her as they both laughed. "If Mom went to Portland, she didn't say anything to me. Are you sure Joshua didn't go with her?"

"I'm sure." Joylinn shrugged. "She stopped in for coffee and a roll this morning, and said something about shopping, and Joshua not wanting to go . . ." Joylinn paused, then gave Rachel a sideways look. "She seemed kind of . . . upset. I'm being a busybody, I know. But I don't think I've ever seen your mother get in a flap about anything."

"She doesn't," Rachel said thoughtfully. Except for the time Rachel's uncle had been suspected of murdering a city councilman. Other than that, she was the anchor of calm in any family storm. "I've probably got a message from her on my machine. I hope nothing is wrong with the family back East." Her mother's vast conglomeration of relatives lived in New York and New Jersey, and alternately Miami, and her mother kept in close touch with them all.

They had visited the New York family—as Rachel had dubbed them—once a year on Rosh Hashanah before her father had died. The visit had always had the feeling of a Large Affair, and although the family was warmly welcoming, Rachel had always felt like an outsider there. Her cousins had a language and shared experience that baffled her as much as her life on a pear orchard baffled them. It was only in New York that she had felt more the child of her Irish father than of her Jewish mother. That feeling had made her uncomfortable, although she always had fun playing with her cousins. It was one of the few things that she had never shared with her mother. "She didn't say anything about flying to New York, did she?"

"Nope." Joylinn shrugged and hefted her bag. "She just said she wanted to do a little shopping in Portland for a day or two. And now I've been gossiping enough. I'd better finish my bread deliveries." She fished a white bakery sack from her heavy bag. "Would you give this to your landlady for me, please? It'll save me a stop. Tell her she can pay me next time."

"Sure." A little disquieted by Joylinn's report on her mother, Rachel took the bag. "I'll let you know what's going on, when I find out."

"You don't have to." Joylinn made a face. "It's her business, not mine. I feel guilty for even saying anything." She waved and started off down the street, swinging her bag. "Stop by for coffee tomorrow," she called back. "I'm trying out a new recipe. I need tasters."

"I'll be there!" Smiling, Rachel put the truck into gear and drove on up the street to the little cul-de-sac off Third Avenue, where she occupied the upstairs apartment of her landlady's tall Victorian-style house.

Mrs. Frey was out among her beloved roses, a small garden sprayer in one hand, a pair of shears in the other. "The cold wet spring this year just played heck with these poor things." She clucked her tongue as she repositioned her large straw garden hat on her head. Today's model sported a wreath of seashells, small starfish, and brightly striped plastic fish. Rachel sometimes wondered if her landlady had an entire room devoted to her collection of garden hats—perhaps with a mirrored wall, where she could inspect her reflection while making her daily choice.

"Well, there will be plenty of water for irrigation, anyway," she said gaily as she started up the outside stairs, which led to her upstairs apartment. "The snowpack is still way above normal for this time of year."

"Hmph. I could do with a little less snowpack and a lot more hot weather. Black spot is just eating up my Abe Lincoln." Mrs. Frey sniffed and tugged at her hat again. "They say it's that *La Niña* effect—all because of global warming. But if you ask me, it's those satellites we keep sending up there. It's got to mess up the weather—all that junk up in space. You have company, dear," she said, and wandered back into her rose bed, still grumbling about weather and satellites.

Company. Rachel smiled as she took the stairs two at a time. Usually Peter, her scruffy ex-stray cat, met her on the landing, complaining about her tardy appearance (she was *always* tardy). He wasn't waiting for her today. The door was unlocked. Rachel went in to find Jeff Price stretched out on her futon sofa, reading her most recent copy of *Fine Gardening* magazine. Peter sat companionably on the back of the sofa in his usual spot, although he sprang to his feet the minute Rachel entered and began to complain loudly.

"I knew there was a reason I gave you a key." Rachel skirted the low table to give him a kiss. "It was so you could let my cat in."

"He likes me. That's new." Jeff sat up grinning, yawned, then scooped her into his lap. "I think it's because I fed him tuna. I think I may do something like the flagstone-and-gravel terrace they show in this issue. On the west side of the house. What do you think?"

"Tuna? Are you crazy?" Rachel rolled her eyes in mock despair. "He'll never put up with mere cat food again. I'll have to move to Los Angeles and landscape for the rich

and famous just to support him. And the west side is going
to be hot in the afternoon. The shadow of those cedars will
miss it by yards. You'll have to use it for breakfast only."

"So I'll put in shade trees. You can pick them out. And
no way you run off to LA." Jeff buried his face against her
neck and nuzzled her until she started giggling and finally
pushed him away. "I brought you a present." Grinning, he
reached down beside the sofa. "I was over in The Dalles,
having a talk with Rourke, the chief of police there. I took
the long way home, through Dufur and ran into the remnants of a weekend barn sale. The elderly woman who was
cleaning up let me look around. There were some neat old
things still left."

"I bet you impressed her when you didn't ask for auto
tools." Rachel tried to peer over the arm of the sofa. "So
what did you get?"

"Tools, actually, but not automotive." He laughed and
blocked her view. "She was, however, a little surprised that
I knew what a frow was, and that I had actually used one
to split cedar shakes for my roof. She says the young buy
everything, and that's what's wrong with the country. Her
dead husband carved the handle himself. It was gorgeous."
He nodded. "She made me take the rest of his tools, too.
Nice stuff. He had adzes, scythes—that kind of thing."

"Can I borrow some?" She made a grab for his arm. "I'm
dying of curiosity," she said plaintively.

"I thought you might like this." He produced a shallow
bowl and handed it to her. Thinner than modern china, a
painted rim of flowers and leaves had faded over the years.
It was very old.

"It's lovely." Rachel turned it carefully, studying the
hand-painted border. "Where did it come from?"

"She thought it came over from Poland with her husband's grandmother. She wasn't sure. But I guess it made
the trip from Ellis Island to The Dalles. Actually there were
two of them. She gave them to me."

"Because you cared that her husband had carved the handles for his tools."

"I appreciated them." He smiled. "They're damn good handles. I've got the other bowl on my table." He touched the rim lightly. "So did you get the job in Portland?"

"Yes, I got the job." Rachel set the bowl carefully on her small table. "It's a huge job. The place is amazing. They collected plants all their lives and put them in there. But it's pretty neglected." She shook her head. "There's a lot to do. It's going to be the biggest contract I've ever taken." She gave Jeff a crooked smile. "Tell you the truth—I'm a little scared. She's donating it to some sort of private conservancy. It'll get a lot of public attention."

"That's good." Jeff took her hand. "You deserve the attention. Just do what you do. Everyone loves your work. Our mayor is proud as a peacock over that backyard of his. I think he's going to demand that we hold Council meetings out there." He grinned. "Big isn't diffferent. It just pays more."

"That it sure will," she said fervently. "The money might even impress Uncle Jack. No—nothing but a successful orchard would impress him, but oh well." She made a face and jumped to her feet. "So let's go celebrate this big scary job. I take it you're not on duty." She eyed his jeans and open denim shirt. He had the lean build of a runner, with the tawny skin tone and dark eyes that he'd inherited from a Paiute grandmother. As Blossom's youngest chief of police ever, appointed by the equally young and controversial mayor of Blossom, Jeff had worked hard and done a good job for the town. "And then again," Rachel said softly, "we could have a late dinner." She gave him an arch look. "All of a sudden I'm not that hungry."

"That sounds lovely." Jeff reached for her hand, raised her palm to his lips, kissed it slowly and sensuously, then released it. "But I think you'd better listen to your answering machine first."

Forget it, she started to say, but something in his tone stopped her. Nodding, she went over to the machine. Two messages. The first—not surprisingly—was a message from her mother. Unexpectedly monotone, it informed her

that her mother was going to Portland for a day of shopping
and would be back the following day. They had planned to
have lunch tomorrow, but they'd have to reschedule. Rachel frowned as she listened, remembering her conversation
with Joylinn. The other message was from Joshua.

"Rachel, I'd like to have dinner with you tonight. I'm
sure your mother told you that she's spending the night in
Portland. Or maybe she didn't . . ." There was a pause.
"You're probably busy but . . . I really would like to get
together. If you can do it."

Joshua sounded . . . tense.

"I was here when he called." Jeff came up behind her.
"It was just a few minutes ago."

"What is going on?" Fists on her hips, Rachel glared at
the machine. "First Joylinn tells me Mom was upset today . . . Then this."

"Dinner tomorrow night?" Jeff tugged gently on a lock
of her hair. "Your stepfather sounds like he needs to talk
to you."

"He does, doesn't he?" Rachel sighed and leaned against
Jeff. "I guess I'd better call him. And to be honest, I really
should spend the rest of the evening working on the estimate for the Johnston job. Eloise really wants to get things
finalized."

"Never keep a client waiting. Tomorrow for sure, okay?"

"It's a date."

"Can I borrow this?" Jeff snagged the magazine he'd
been reading on his way to the door. "Maybe I won't put
it on the west side of the house, after all."

"Sure. I've got a special discount for design consultations
this week." She gave him a sweet smile, wishing briefly
and intensely that Joshua hadn't decided he needed to talk
tonight. "It's a very limited offer."

"I hope so." He leaned down to kiss her, and for a moment everything, including Joshua, receded into a state of
nonimportance. Then he pulled away and tweaked her hair
again. "See you tomorrow," he said. "Good night."

"Thank you so much for the bowl," she said as he trotted

down the steep stairs. "I'll see you tomorrow." She leaned on the railing until he had disappeared down the street into the thick twilight, vanishing in the direction of downtown and City Hall, and the offices of the Blossom City Police. Peter came up behind her and very delicately pricked her ankle with his claws. "You got fed, cat." She scooped him up and carried him inside. "Tuna, yet!" But Peter was having none of that. He squirmed free and bounded onto the back of the sofa to sulk and wash off every trace of her touch. Rachel laughed and went to call Joshua. Stepfather, Jeff had called him. A twinge of guilt pricked her as she dialed his number. She couldn't think of Joshua as anything but . . . Joshua. Not stepfather. He wasn't her father. Her father was dead. He wasn't even a surrogate father. He was . . . Joshua. Her mother's husband.

He answered on the second ring and sounded unexpectedly relieved to hear from her. "Why don't you come out here," he suggested. "I'll ply you with salmon in lettuce sauce for your troubles. And a very good Chardonnay. I really didn't disrupt your evening?"

"Hey, I feel quite adequately bribed," Rachel said. Well, it was only partly a lie. One of Joshua's hobbies was gourmet cooking. "Can I bring anything? Oh—the rolls!" She had put the bag down on the table by the door and had utterly forgotten them. "I've got some of Joylinn's hazelnut rolls."

"By all means bring them," Joshua said. "I am not in Joylinn's class as a baker. See you in a little bit."

Stifling a last pang of regret, she left the sulking Peter to full possession of the sofa. The drive to the house where her mother and Joshua lived wound up the side of the Gorge through rows of old pear trees, whose thick, gnarled trunks attested to their age. This time of year, new green leaves unfurled on the dark branches. The thickening twilight turned the clustered leaves dark and glossy and hid the tiny green fruit. In spite of the cold winter there had been few frost warnings during bloom. Blossom had been spared too many nights of thick smog from the smudge pots, and the fruit had set heavily. With a little market luck, the O'Connor orchard should make a decent profit this year. Not that you could ever count on market luck.

Rachel braked at the far side of a sharp curve, then turned onto the wide asphalt drive that led to the house. She parked in front of the wide double garage. It faced northwest, turned away from the rest of the house, which turned its face to the northeast for a spectacular view of the Columbia River, and the hills of Washington state on the far side. The last of the light was fading as she parked her truck. Joshua had turned on the outside lights, and Rachel paused at the top of the steps that led up from the parking area, eyes on the sweeping slope of the grounds.

This place had been her first major landscaping job, back before her mother had ever met Joshua. The builder had bulldozed off the old pear trees that had once grown there and sold Joshua a house on a bare slope. Her mother had met Joshua because of that job. Rachel smiled, because at the time she had been unhappy with her mother's growing relationship with Joshua. Well, that had certainly changed. She paused, examining the grounds, pleased to see that after two years the plantings were really beginning to fill in. She made a mental note to herself to come back when she had a free afternoon and replace a native wild currant that was not doing well. The ailing ribes made a noticeable hole in an otherwise balanced mass planting at the far side of the small terraced lawn.

Deciding to replace it with a fragrant native mock orange, she followed the brick-and-gravel path around to the wide deck on the northeast side of the house. Beck hadn't built this. The house had been completed before Joshua had hired her. Too bad, she thought as she climbed the wide plank steps that led up to it. It was good, but Beck would have made it art.

"I was watching you." Joshua stood in the open French doors that led from the deck into the spacious kitchen area. "Standing there looking at your handiwork, you made me think of an artist contemplating her canvas."

"Well, I don't know about artist." Rachel laughed and accepted the glass of Chardonnay Joshua was holding out. "But it's coming along nicely. Julio is doing a good job for you. Of course."

"I feel as if I underpay him." Joshua ushered her through the door and into the huge kitchen. "But when I try to pay him more, he won't take it."

"He's terribly honest." Rachel sniffed luxuriously. "Dinner smells wonderful!"

"It's just a rice pilaf with pine nuts so far." Joshua refilled his own glass from the bottle on the counter. "You know, I'm seriously thinking about putting in a greenhouse. I'd love to offer you a salad with arugula tonight, but I'd have to go to Hood River to get the arugula. Know anybody who builds greenhouses?"

"I don't, but the Rhinehoffers might. They put in a new greenhouse when they expanded the nursery last year." Rachel perched herself on one of the elegantly casual chairs that formed a small conversation group at one end of the huge, tiled kitchen. The small wooden table and chairs— just right for a casual supper or breakfast—and the intimate group of chairs and small end table turned the kitchen into the true heart of the rambling house.

If the kitchen was the heart of the house, Joshua was its soul. A retired surgeon, he presided over food and relaxed hospitality, a solid chunk of a man, his belly flat from his morning runs and afternoon workouts, his balding head nimbused by graying hair that always had a rumpled look to it. He could take charge of a situation in a moment, quietly and completely. But he had a genuine warmth to him that Rachel liked enormously.

Her mother had found a good person.

"Just let me get this fish cooked, and we're there." Joshua bustled about the big island in the center of the kitchen. Garlic sizzled in olive oil in the big sauté pan, and he carefully laid two thick salmon fillets in the hot oil. It smelled heavenly. As he waited for the fish to cook, he heated the bright green sauce in a smaller pan.

"Let me do something."

"It's all ready. Except for the fish. You could put the salads on the table. They're in the fridge." He gestured at the big commercial refrigerator built into one wall.

Rachel removed two plates of a carefully arranged spinach, mushroom, and red onion salad topped with toasted walnuts, and dressed them with the fresh vinaigrette Joshua handed her in a thick porcelain bowl. By the time she had them on the table, Joshua had served up two plates of perfectly cooked fish, topped with a dollop of the green sauce and a mound of fragrant pilaf. A handful of steamed baby carrots completed the plate.

"I always think I should bring my camera." Rachel smiled as Joshua refilled her glass from a new bottle of the Chardonnay. "I could sell the pictures to *Gourmet* magazine."

"Well, I hope it tastes good. Here's to good growing things." Joshua lifted his glass to hers, but he looked distracted in spite of his smile.

Tense.

Rachel cut into her fish and raised her eyebrows in appreciation of the delicate sauce, flavored with shallots. "I would never have thought of cooking lettuce," she said.

"Oh, solid-bodied lettuces like romaine are good cooked." Joshua picked bits of salmon from his fillet, then sipped at his wine. "Remind me to serve you braised heart of romaine as a side dish sometime."

"I will," Rachel said. The hazelnut rolls—savory rather than sweet—went perfectly with the meal. Joshua offered more wine, but Rachel declined. The Chardonnay was good, but she was feeling it after her long day. "I've got to drive home," she said.

"You could stay here." Joshua filled his own glass, spilling a few drops onto the polished oak tabletop. "The guest room is always available." He set the bottle back down and leaned back in his chair. He had barely touched his food, and a flush stained his cheeks, even though his hand was steady as he reached for his glass.

"Joshua, is something wrong?" Rachel set down her fork.

"I . . . I don't know." Joshua began to pick the golden pine nuts from his pilaf, piling them carefully at the side of his plate. "Did you think I was too old . . . when I asked your mother to marry me?"

The question caught Rachel off guard. She paused, a forkful of pilaf at her lips, and she set it back down on her plate. She opened her mouth to say something positive and reassuring, but there was an edge of desperation to Joshua that made her reject the platitudes. "No," she said. "I never thought you were too old. I just thought you weren't my father. I got over that," she said softly, and reached for his hand.

He took it and squeezed hard, but the anxious expression on his face didn't moderate. "She's so full of life," he murmured. "That's part of why I love her. She'll be young when she's eighty. She makes me feel young, too. But sometimes . . ." He pushed his plate away, picked up his wineglass, then set it down with a small thump. "I feel like I drag her down. She could do better."

"No!" The syllable burst from Rachel, a truth that surprised her as much as the volume surprised Joshua. "You *are* right for her," Rachel went on, fumbling for the words she needed. "I . . . I was jealous for my father, for a while. But you were right two years ago when you told me that what you and she shared wasn't what they had, that it was different, and just as wonderful."

"I don't know anymore." Joshua stood and reached to pick up their plates. "I believed that, but . . . Deborah just seems. . . . I don't know. Unhappy, I think. Just lately." He paused, his hands full of dirty dishes. "I thought . . . maybe she'd said something to you. I'm not asking you to betray any confidences," he added hastily. "I just wondered . . . if I'm doing something wrong. Not enough? Something?"

"No," Rachel whispered, Joylinn's conversation ringing in her ears. "Mom hasn't said a word to me to make me think she's not terribly in love with you."

"Maybe." He carried the dishes to the sink and began to

make coffee in the glass French-press pot that Deborah had given to him as a present the year before. "Maybe we did rush into marriage too fast," he said as he poured simmering water over the fragrant grounds in the pot. "But if there's one thing I've learned at my age, it's not to wait. If you hesitate too long, you spend too much time on regrets for what might have been." He sighed as he poured out two small cups of steaming coffee. "Your mother said she felt the same way, but maybe . . . Maybe I assumed too much. It's so easy to do when you're head over heels in love."

"No." Rachel got up from the table. "If something's bothering her, it's not you, I'm sure of it. Shall we take our coffee outside? There are stars."

"Better get your jacket." Joshua carried the coffee out to the glass-and-wrought-iron table on the deck. Rachel shrugged into her jacket and followed him.

He was right about it being chilly, Rachel noticed, although he didn't put on a jacket himself. The wind had picked up and blew briskly down the Gorge, still edged with cold from the snow-covered mountains. A million stars spangled the sky. She hunted for Orion, her favorite constellation, but he had vanished below the western horizon. He wouldn't command in the night sky until next winter.

She had grown up living by the rhythm of the seasons. Perhaps that was one reason she'd felt so out of place with her clock-driven cousins back East. Rachel reached for her coffee, settling herself on a teak bench that stood against the house at one end of the deck, out of the wind. Growers lived by blossom time, fruit set, harvest, pruning. The constellations clocked the slow rotation of the year. She sipped the rich, bitter brew in her cup, filled with a sudden contentment. It was still true, mostly, that she lived by the seasons. Joshua stood with his back to her, leaning on the rail that edged the high end of the deck, his untasted coffee cooling on the rail beside him.

"I'll talk to Mom when she gets back from Portland," Rachel said.

"No." He lifted a hand to soften the sharp syllable. "I'm not asking you to mediate. That's not why I asked you to dinner." He turned to face her, leaning against the railing with his back to the dark gulf of the Columbia's huge gash. "I just . . . I guess I just wanted to get a feel for what you thought."

"I think you're wrong." Rachel finished her coffee and stood. She crossed the deck to take his hands. He had small, strong hands, with small fingers. Surgeons were supposed to have long fingers. Like pianists. She had read that somewhere, but from what her mother had told her, Joshua had been a very good surgeon.

"I want to tweak the landscaping here a bit," she told him. "I might come by tomorrow afternoon."

"I'll be around." He gave her a faint smile that didn't erase the shadows in his eyes. "Thanks for listening."

"Thanks for a wonderful dinner. And you *are* wrong." She stood on tiptoe to kiss him on the side of the mouth. "My mother is very deeply in love with you. I know it."

"I hope you're right." Joshua lifted a hand to her as she crossed the deck and left by the stairs. A gust of wind snatched at her hair as she went down the steps to the parking area, tossing it into her eyes. She brushed it back impatiently, wishing once more that she had thick long hair like Joylinn's or something she could manage, like Sandy. Joshua still stood on the deck, his hands planted on the railing. She waved, but he seemed to be staring out at the invisible river and didn't see.

CHAPTER

3

The phone's shrill bleat prodded Rachel out of sleep. She rolled over, tangled in the shreds of a dream, reaching first for the alarm clock beside her bed, annoyed because she hadn't meant to set it, had meant to sleep in a bit before getting back to work on the Johnston estimate. Another shrill peal banished the last remnants of sleep and sent her bolting out of bed. Wet, gray, predawn light seeped through the window. Early. Very early. Heart racing with premonitions of disaster, she snatched the instrument from its cradle. "Hello? Hello!"

"My dear, I'm so sorry. I woke you."

"That . . . that's fine. I would have been up in a minute." Adrenaline ebbing from her bloodstream, Rachel strove to identify the voice. "I'm sorry, who is this?"

"Oh, excuse me. It's Eloise. You visited yesterday. You were preparing an estimate."

"Oh, yes. Sorry," Rachel apologized again, hoping this kind of early-morning call wasn't going to become a pattern. "I was up late working on it." She yawned uncontrollably, covering the phone with one hand. Very late, actually. "I'm afraid I'm not finished yet. I was going to spend the day on it."

"My dear, I have a tremendous favor to ask of you." Eloise hesitated. "It's an imposition, and you can say no, of course. But I feel . . . My dear, at my age, one does not wait to accomplish a goal."

Her echo of Joshua's words last night made Rachel straighten. "Is something wrong?"

"No, dear, or yes, perhaps, but nothing I can do anything about." The botanist laughed. "I'm eighty-six, and I'm feeling it this morning. I would like to get our contract finalized as soon as possible. With my heart trouble, I never know if I'll see another sunrise or not." Her tone was matter-of-fact. "This job is important to me. I don't want to wait."

"Well, I made a good start last night." Rachel spoke slowly, trying to guess how much longer it would take her to work through all the numbers. "If I can spend the day on it, I should be able to give it to you by tomorrow."

"I'm not sure I want to wait that long." Eloise's sigh whispered over the line. "How would you feel about coming out here today, and we can figure out a rough estimate of the cost together? I am happy to err on the side of too generous. As I've told you, I want this project to be completed, dear. Money is not a concern to me at this point. I have more than enough to complete the job, I'm sure."

"I . . . I suppose I could do that." Rachel winced, thinking of what her lawyer would have to say about this kind of agreement. "But I don't want to overcharge you, and I don't want to lose money, so I have to take a lot of things into account. I haven't seen Beck's drawings yet or checked on the availability of some of the plants we'd need. I'd really rather wait."

"I need to do this today." Eloise sounded as if she'd made up her mind.

Rachel swallowed a sigh. "I suppose we could do it," she said reluctantly, "but I'll have to build in a reasonable margin for unexpected complications." And Gladys, her lawyer, would probably fire her as a client if she ever got wind of this.

"I certainly understand. You need to protect yourself, but we'll build that into the agreement. You see, I trust you. Can you come this afternoon and stay for dinner?" Eloise sounded relieved. "I have a couple of appointments this morning, so I won't be able to talk with you until late this afternoon. I would enjoy your company, and I don't want you to feel rushed. We can take as much time as we need, so that you don't come out short-changed."

"I suppose I could do that." Rachel suppressed a moment of indecision. She wanted desperately to talk with her mother—to find out just what was going on between her and Joshua. But on the other hand, this job was huge—the largest project she'd undertaken yet, and one that might net her some very nice publicity in the Portland Metro area. Publicity would help a lot, she thought. A lot of the Portland couples who built vacation or retirement homes out here contracted with a Portland landscaper before they even looked for local alternatives. "I'll be there," she said. "What time would you like me to come by?"

"How about three o'clock? Thank you very much." Eloise hung up.

Slowly Rachel replaced the phone and reached for her bathrobe. Well, she thought. Accommodating client demands was part of running a service-oriented business. She sighed, hoping she didn't regret this rushed contract later on. Peter was on his usual perch outside her window, on the narrow sill two stories above the ground. The sky was gray, spitting rain, promising yet another wet day to prolong this damp, gray spring that didn't seem to want to quit. Peter glowered at her through the glass, letting her know that he had risked life and limb to save himself from imminent starvation.

"You could always wait at the front door." Laughing, Rachel lifted the sash. "I beat you this morning. I was already up."

Peter hopped neatly onto the floor and stalked into the

kitchen, his tail erect. Smiling, Rachel shook out her down comforter and made up the bed. In the kitchen, she started the coffee and finally got down the cat food for the impatient Peter. "You have a full bowl of dry food," she reminded him as she opened the can. Peter gave her an unblinking green stare.

"Okay, here's breakfast." She dumped the food out onto a plate and set it on the floor. Deciding that she wasn't going to work hard enough for an egg breakfast, she got down a box of corn flakes and filled a bowl. The coffee had finished dripping, and she poured herself a cup.

By the time she had finished breakfast, washed her face, dressed, and cleaned up the kitchen, the morning had reached a civilized hour. She let Peter out, making a face at the windy gray morning. Portland weather, she thought. The front had pushed up the Gorge during the night, bringing gusty cold wind and spitting rain. This was March weather, she thought in disgust. Not at all normal for May. Puddles in the driveway testified to considerable late-night rain. Closing the door on the unseasonable weather, she returned to the kitchen and dialed her mother's cell phone.

"Hello?" Her mother answered on the third ring.

"It's me, Rachel." She leaned against the countertop. "Are you still in Portland?"

"I'm almost home, actually. And since I'm on the highway doing about sixty, we'd better make this a brief chat," her mother said briskly.

She sounded cheerful. Too cheerful? Rachel shook her head, thinking that she was reading all kinds of things into an ordinary conversation. "Are you going to be back in Blossom soon? Can we have an early lunch or late breakfast or whatever?"

"Is something wrong, dear?" Her mother sounded unexpectedly cautious.

"No," Rachel said quickly. "I haven't seen you for a while, that's all."

"At least thirty-six hours," her mother interrupted dryly.

"How about the Bread Box for coffee and a cinnamon roll at say . . . ten?"

"And I was going to say that I wanted to tell you about this new job. See you then." Frowning, Rachel hung up. She had a couple of hours to work on her estimate. She glanced at her watch and headed for her office—an old farmhouse kitchen table she'd found in a barn. It and her computer occupied a generous corner of the main room.

The job was much harder to estimate than anything she had undertaken before. There were a lot of things to consider—including the rare and unusual nature of the species that would need to be replaced, and the necessity to comply with city and state codes for a public access facility. By nine o'clock, Rachel had a headache and the worst attack of insecurity she'd experienced since the day she decided to go into business for herself. Deciding she needed to let things settle in her brain for a while, she collected her notes and calculations and slipped them into a folder to take down to Portland. She called Jeff at City Hall, only to learn that he was out of the office. So she left a message on his answering machine, telling him about Eloise's call and her unexpected trip to Portland. She picked up her folder of notes and trotted down the outside stairs. The rain had stopped, although it was still gray and gusty. Mrs. Frey was out in her front yard, scrubbing algae from her birdbath with a toilet brush. Today's hat sported huge orange and red poppies, and tied with a red scarf beneath her chin— which was a good thing, Rachel thought, or the hat would be on its way to the Columbia even now.

Mrs. Frey greeted her with a litany of Peter's latest transgressions against her beloved chickadees. But Rachel noticed the saucer of milk set out on the back step. Milk for the chickadees? Smiling, Rachel drove through town to the Bread Box, thinking that if she ever moved, Peter's absence would break her landlady's heart.

The Bread Box was nearly deserted this time of day. The morning coffee-break crowd had filtered out, and the lunch rush hadn't yet begun. Rachel shook out her wind-arranged

hair as she came through the door and sniffed hungrily.
"Celia's on her break," Joylinn called from the kitchen.
"Grab yourself some coffee. I'll be right with you."

"Well, Rachel." The door opened with a gust of wind
that riffled the paper napkins in a wicker basket on the
coffee bar. "Fancy meeting you here."

"Hi, Mayor." Rachel turned to greet Phil Ventura, Blossom's young and controversial mayor. "How's the yard
looking?"

"Lovely. I can't wait until we get some real summer so
I can start throwing parties on the deck." He crossed to the
coffee bar and leaned an elbow on the slate top. "I framed
those magazine photos, by the way. That may be my one
moment of public glory." He grinned. "Can I buy you a
latte?"

"I hear you're going to hold Council meetings out there.
Make it a cappuccino and you're on." Rachel perched on
one of the tall, wrought-iron stools beside him. "What's
up?"

"I've pulled off a coup. Well, to be honest, it just fell
into my lap, but I'll happily take the credit." Ventura
laughed and greeted Joylinn as she appeared to take their
orders. "I got a call from our esteemed state representative
and native son, Paul Claymore, this morning. That alone is
a first." He chuckled. "Claymore won't usually give me the
time of day. Anyway, he says he wants to hold a one-day
public forum on the new state pesticide laws, and he asked
about using the high school here. That's quite a nice nod
to Blossom."

"Paul Claymore, here?" Rachel reached for the small
white cup of foamy cappuccino that Joylinn had just placed
in front of her. "Why here instead of Hood River?"

"Good question." Ventura shrugged and reached for his
latte. "I sure didn't argue. Maybe he's looking for a lot of
grass-roots support next election."

"He doesn't need to look too hard around here." Rachel
put her cup down and licked foam from her upper lip. "My
uncle and a lot of other orchardists think he walks on water

since he defeated that farm-labor wage bill."

"The business will be nice for the town." Joylinn set a plate of crusty rolls down between them. "These are some new experimental cheese rolls. On the house."

"Mmm. Mushrooms!" Rachel took a huge bite, regretting her earlier corn flakes briefly. "And plenty of cheese. They're a winner, girl. I expect to see them on the menu from now on."

"I second the motion." Ventura ate his roll ravenously. "I think I'll serve them to Claymore. Maybe he'll speak to me after that."

"It still seems odd that he chose Blossom for this wing-ding." Rachel glanced at her watch. "It's going to be awfully crowded if everybody shows up."

"I've got to run. I'm about to be late for an appointment." The mayor swallowed the last of his second roll with a gulp and picked up his half-finished latte. "I'll bring the cup back later," he called to Joylinn as he left. He met Rachel's mother in the doorway, nearly bumping into her, and said something that made them both laugh.

"So how are you?" Deborah O'Connor breezed over to the table, running her fingers through her dark curly hair that was as yet only marked with a few strands of silver. "Tea for me, please, Joylinn. I've had my coffee today. Make it the oolong." She sat down in the chair Ventura had just vacated. "So what's up, sweetheart?"

"I'm not sure." Rachel hesitated as Joylinn brought her mother a white china pot full of steeping tea, a small strainer in its own dish, and a thick porcelain mug. Her mother peeked into the teapot, waiting for the tea to finish steeping. She had a petite figure, which, together with her hair, made her seem years younger than she was. Too young for Joshua? Rachel shook her head. But . . . there were new, tight lines around her mother's eyes.

"I'm thinking about going back East to visit the family for a while." Her mother poured a golden stream of tea through the strainer and into her cup. "My cousin Miriam is worried that Mort is getting Alzheimer's. Me, I don't think he's any more forgetful than usual, but, hey, if she needs a little support . . ." Deborah peered at the scatter of dark leaves in the silver mesh of the strainer. "I'll probably stay a month. Maybe a little more."

"You're going to drag poor Joshua away from his beloved kitchen for a month?" Rachel asked lightly.

"Oh, he'd be bored." Her mother replaced the strainer carefully in its saucer. "He says that my family reminds him too much of his own family. He won't want to go."

"Yes, he will."

"Well, we'll see." Her mother wouldn't meet her eyes.

"Mom?" Rachel hesitated. "Is . . . something wrong?"

"No." Her mother still wouldn't look at her. "What makes you ask? Oh, gosh, it's late." She set down her cup and stood. "I wasn't keeping track of the time. I've got to run."

"Run where?" Rachel demanded, but her mother was already on her way to the door.

By the time Rachel fumbled out her wallet, left money for her cappuccino, her mother's tea, and a generous tip, her mother had vanished. Clenching her teeth, Rachel climbed into her truck and drove slowly through town, watching for her mother on the sidewalks, or for her mother's blue MG—the car Joshua had given her for her birthday the year before. She didn't see it or her mother. Finally she drove out to the house. Nobody was home. Rachel vented a little of her frustration by digging up the dying ribes. She'd go out to the Rhinehoffer nursery tomorrow and pick out a new specimen, she decided. Joshua liked the bright pink flowers of the native currant. Although she dawdled a while longer, cleaning up the tools and her hands, neither Joshua nor her mother showed up.

Finally, it was time to head for Portland if she was going to keep her appointment with Eloise. The drive to Portland seemed even longer this time, in spite of the blaring radio. Worries about her mother fluttered in her head like bats, and no matter how much she tried, she couldn't banish them. Her mother didn't act this way. She just . . . didn't.

By the time she drove through the sagging metal gates of the Johnston house, she had still failed to find any reason for her mother's behavior. April Gerard appeared at the front door almost immediately, as if she'd been watching out the window for Rachel. "That's so nice of you to come back out here." She came down the stairs to meet Rachel in the parking area. "When Eloise gets fixed on something, you can just forget changing her mind." She rolled her eyes. "Talk about stubborn. I told her she's going to live to be a hundred for sure, but no, she's got to take care of all this right now." She paused for breath. "Beck didn't come with you?" She sounded suddenly shy.

"Not this time." Rachel pretended not to see the disappointment on the young woman's face. Beck had obviously made quite the impression on her. "He'll practically live here while he's working," she said quickly.

"Oh, good." April positively glowed. "I really like him."

Obviously. Rachel managed to conceal her surprise. "He's a sweet man," she said cautiously. "But he's rather . . . unique. And he's pretty . . . obsessive when he's working." To put it mildly. She would never have guessed that this attractive young woman would have any interest in Beck, with his necklace of hand-carved wooden beads, his gray braid, and strange manners. She shook her head. "Is Sandy here today?"

"No, she only comes down on Mondays."

"My dear. Thank you so much for humoring an old woman." Eloise appeared in the doorway that led into the dining room, leaning on a carved wooden cane. "I wrote everything down that I want you to do. We can get right to work."

"I'll do my best," Rachel said as she followed the elderly woman into the dining room. "Hopefully we can work something out, but I still think a day or two wouldn't delay the job at all."

"I just want to get it done," Eloise said stubbornly.

A long teakwood table took up the center of the room. A wall of windows opened onto the brick patio outside.

Beyond the bricks, a dogwood tree stood at the edge of the grassy yard. A few early blossoms had unfurled among the new green leaves. It was a lovely specimen.

"As I was sitting here this morning, I got to thinking that it would be nice to have a bench built beneath that tree." Eloise looked outside. "It's always shady at that end of the grass. Visitors could sit there and rest, after they'd toured the gardens up on the hillside. It's very pleasant there on summer afternoons, and you have a nice view of the rock garden."

Rachel suppressed a sigh. This was just what she feared would happen, she thought grimly. They would sign a contract today, then Eloise would keep on having good ideas, keep on asking for a new path here, a new bench there. . . . Little things. She had learned a couple of tough lessons about how fast those little things could eat up any profit to be made on a job.

"Well, we can add it in right now," she said, sitting down in the high-backed chair Eloise indicated, and opening the portfolio she'd brought in from the truck. "But once we sign a contract, we can't add any new things, okay? Are you sure you wouldn't like a week to think this over?" Outside, without warning, rain began to pound down, raising a faint mist above the bricks. The branches of the cedars and firs tossed in a sudden gust of wind.

"What a nice day to be inside," Eloise said cheerfully. She snapped on the overhead chandelier, bathing the table in warm golden light. "Here." She lifted two sheets of lined notebook paper from the table and set them gently in front of Rachel. "This is the list of what I want you to do. The irrigation lines will need to be replaced. They leak dreadfully, and they're quite old. I wasn't even thinking about them when I showed you around yesterday. But now I have thought of everything. I couldn't sleep last night, so I had plenty of time to consider the garden. Decide what you think it will cost, and be very generous," she admonished. "As I told you, I am not asking you to take a risk. We could increase your money later, if we need to, but if I

have died," she said tranquilly, "you will be stuck with
what we decide on today. I expect you to protect yourself."

"I'll do my best," Rachel murmured, admonishing herself
that she was making a big mistake and should simply refuse, get in her truck, and come back with a real estimate
in a day or two.

By then, Eloise could have found three or four other
landscapers willing to take this job.

Sighing audibly, acknowledging how much she wanted
to restore this garden, she bent over the list. Most of it they
had discussed—weed and restore the small gardens she and
her husband had created to showcase their extensive collection of native and nonnative plants, replacing defunct
specimens whenever possible. Repair and gravel the me-
andering paths that crisscrossed the property, rendering
many of them handicap accessible. Prune and restore the
existing shrubs and trees, and remove some dangerously
rotted ones. Eloise had listed the benches and shelters that
she wanted Beck to build separately. Fortunately, Rachel
had a good idea of what Beck charged for his projects. The
irrigation lines would add considerably to her estimate.

Biting her lip, Rachel settled down to calculate the hours
required for the various tasks and to figure how large a crew
she'd have to hire. It was far too much work for just herself
and Julio to handle, even if he hadn't been devoting part
of his time to his newborn landscape-maintenance business.

Outside, the rain descended steadily, running off the
bricks in sheets and drizzling in silver streams from the
overloaded gutters. Eloise Johnston sat upright in the chair
beside Rachel, her expression tranquil, her hands folded on
her lap. "Carl and I camped in this kind of weather on so
many of our collecting trips." Her smile softened the with-
ered planes of her face, giving Rachel a brief glimpse of
her youth. "It was such an adventure. It was always an
adventure. We'd set up our tent and climb inside, and it
was our little protected world. We'd lie there together, talking, sleeping, listening for the rain to end. It was its own
time. There was no impatience. We were simply *there*, and

what time passed for the rest of the world had no meaning for us." She turned a gentle smile on Rachel. "I've wondered sometimes if it wouldn't have been easier if I had married someone that I really didn't care for. We would have grown apart, and when he died, I would only have grieved for a while." Her smile deepened, sparkling in her eyes like sunlight on a deep pool. "But then I would never have had that endless rain time." She got slowly and painfully to her feet. "I wish you that kind of love someday, my young woman. But perhaps it can no longer happen in our modern world. Perhaps we no longer have time for rain and love." She shook her head and touched Rachel's dark curls lightly. "I hope you find the time." She turned abruptly and tottered out of the room.

April came in a few minutes later with a teapot and a plate of sandwiches on a tray. "Eloise went to lie down." She set the tray on the table, frowning. "She didn't sleep well last night, and she says she doesn't feel well. I hope nothing's wrong."

"She seemed sad." Rachel poured herself tea, wrinkling her nose very slightly at the strong mint aroma of the pale liquor.

"You don't like mint tea, do you?" April gave her a half smile. "Sorry. I should have asked."

"That's okay. I don't *hate* it. I just grew up with a mother who didn't brew oolong, she brewed Tie-Guan-Yin or Se Chung oolong. It has warped my mind about herb teas. Although she likes them." Rachel laughed and reached for a sandwich. Outside, the cloudy daylight was thickening into true dusk. "Is it that late?" She stretched, winced, and gave a rueful laugh. "I guess it is. I guess I was concentrating."

"We usually eat late." April picked up the teapot and cup. "That's why I brought you the food. What kind of tea do you like? We have everything, I think." She laughed. "We have jars of leaves on the shelf that I can't even identify. No labels, and they don't smell like much."

"How about plain old black tea? Just not Lipton's."

"We've got oolong. That's black, isn't it?"

"Yes, it is. That'll do just fine, thank you," Rachel said.

"One oolong coming up." April balanced the cup deftly on top of the pot and swept out of the room like an experienced waitress. She was back with a fresh pot in a few minutes, only this time she carried two cups. "Eloise didn't take her nap after all." She placed the pot on a wooden trivet and set out the cups. A moment later, the tap of Eloise's cane sounded on the plank floor, and she hobbled into the room.

"Our ramble yesterday has taken its toll, I'm afraid." The botanist lowered herself into a chair. She had put on a long, heather gray cardigan with bagging pockets. A notepad, pens, a package of tissues, and other assorted items contributed to the bulging of the pockets. "How are you coming along?"

"Well, I'm still not close enough to give you hard numbers yet," Rachel demurred. The numbers would be very big if she did everything the elderly woman wanted. The labor costs alone would be immense.

"Will this cover everything I want, do you think?" Eloise had pulled a battered leather checkbook from her pocket, and now extracted a single loose check from its pages. She laid it in front of Rachel.

Rachel opened her mouth. Closed it. The check had been made out to Rain Country Landscaping in a fine spidery script.

It was for one hundred and eighty thousand dollars.

"I . . . that's more than enough. It . . . it's too much," Rachel stammered.

"Then you can do an extra fine job without skimping." Eloise nodded, satisfied. "If I remember odd jobs that I forgot to mention, I will tell you. When I have used up my money, you will tell me. Agreed?"

"I think . . . you need to wait. I can give you better numbers than that." The size of the check made her breathless.

"I think we will sign the contract tonight." Eloise nodded briskly. "If you're still feeling that you're overpaid by the end of the project, by all means donate any excess to the garden. The Conservancy will need money. But this way I can be certain that if I . . ." She hesitated. "If I die in my sleep tonight, the project will go forward." She pronounced the words precisely, without emotion.

"You're not going to die tonight or any night soon." April glared at her from the doorway. "That's a bad attitude. I keep telling you."

"That's acceptance, dear." Eloise smiled gently up at her. "Acceptance is not the same thing as resignation. Do not confuse the two."

"Whatever." April tossed her head, still angry. "I'm going to go work on dinner." She stomped off in the direction of the kitchen.

"Death makes the young so nervous," Eloise murmured with a fond smile in April's direction. "I believe they think it might be contagious. Does it make you nervous?" She turned to Rachel, one eyebrow lifting. "Or is it simply the money?"

"It's the money," Rachel answered without pause. She had become a little too intimate with death recently, thank you. Death didn't frighten her—it just made her angry. It was so rarely fair. "I feel dishonest taking that much."

"I am asking you to take it as a favor to me. Because I am all too aware of how fragile life is. And I want this garden restored to what Carl and I made it. Don't you understand?" she asked Rachel gently. "This was our tent, where we listened to rain together. It is a memorial—not to Carl, but to our love. I want to know that it is finished, even if I am not here to see it. Here." She pulled a folded sheet of paper from her pocket and handed it to Rachel. "I have spent enough time with lawyers lately to know how complicated these guardians of the legal system like to make things. But I've also spent enough time with them to know that you don't always need a lawyer to make a contract." She laid the page in front of Rachel.

Rachel scanned the lines. *Rachel O'Connor, doing business as Rain Country Landscaping, agrees to complete the*

*following list of jobs on the property at 6704 SE 122nd
Avenue, in Portland, Oregon, in a timely fashion, for the
sum of one hundred and eighty thousand dollars.* Beneath
this, she had drawn in lines for three signatures.

"April, will you come in here, please?" Eloise raised her
voice, but judging from April's immediate appearance, she
must have been right outside the door. Listening? Rachel
wondered.

"Will you witness our signatures, my dear? No, wait a
moment." She stopped April as the young woman fished a
pen from the pocket of the faded apron she was wearing.
"We have to sign first. Then you." She took the pen from
April and penned a precise signature across the bottom of
the page. Silently she handed the pen to Rachel, who took
a deep breath, said a prayer that she wouldn't regret this,
and scrawled her own name in her slanted and hurried
script. Finally, she handed the pen to April, who added her
own name in the small, looping, upright script of a high-
school student.

Her lawyer, Rachel thought grimly, would probably kill
her for this. She didn't believe in casual contracts.

"Well, that's that." Beaming, Eloise folded the contract
and handed it to April. "Just take this downstairs and make
a copy on the machine, would you, dear? We both need
one. You can put mine on my desk, and give the original
back to Rachel." As April vanished into the lower level,
Eloise got unsteadily to her feet. "This is a key to the
house—I do lock up when we are gone, and you might
need to use the phone or the bathroom while you're working here." She handed over a small brass door key. "Now,
if you'll be so kind . . ." She offered Rachel her arm. "I
believe I'll take that nap now. Tell April that if I'm asleep
at suppertime, she can leave something cold for me on the
bureau." She gave Rachel a twinkling smile as they made
their slow way down the hall to the back of the house.

Rachel gathered up her papers. Outside, it was fully dark,
and wind began to howl around the house, rattling the windows and spraying the west wall of the house with wind-

driven bullets of rain. The sound of the wind in the tall firs and cedars was like the noise of a rushing river.

"I think the creek is going to flood tonight." April appeared in the doorway with the copies in her hands. "Here. This is the original." She handed the signed sheets to Rachel. "They're predicting a couple of inches of rain at least. Eloise says the house never floods. I'm glad. They're saying that the Willamette could flood Portland, like it did a few years ago. I guess the warm rain is really melting all that snow in the mountains."

"It's late for this kind of rain, isn't it? I mean, even for Portland." Rachel slipped her bundled papers into the portfolio.

"Yeah, it is." April hesitated. "Eloise said she was going to invite you to stay the night, but you're finished with the contract thing, right? And I don't think Eloise's going to get up again tonight. When she goes to lie down this late, it's usually until morning. Are you going to leave?"

"I was thinking about it." Rachel glanced at her watch. It wasn't that late. She could be home at a reasonable time.

"It's going to be an ugly drive, with all that rain coming down." April sounded wistful. "I've got lamb chops for dinner. And green beans. Fresh ones. Eloise only eats fresh vegetables, and she taught me how to do them okay." She tilted her head. "Why not stay and go back in the morning, when it's not raining?"

Rachel looked at her. "It must get kind of lonely here, with only Eloise for company."

"Well, sometimes." April looked away. "But I don't mind. I hate to leave her alone, and she doesn't have a lot of visitors. Except her sons, and they don't come by very often. I've been reading." She smiled. "I didn't read much in school—it seemed like too much work. But here . . . there's so much *stuff* in books." Her smile widened. "But, yeah, I'd like company tonight." She clasped her arms as if she was chilly. "It's so noisy when the wind blows like this—the trees, the house creaking . . ."

"I'll stay." Rachel smiled. "Why not?"

"Great." April grinned. "Come on back into the kitchen, and I'll broil the chops. Everything's ready to cook. There's a bottle of white wine in the 'fridge, too," she said as she led Rachel back into the big kitchen. The white wooden cupboards and elderly white appliances gave the kitchen an outdated but not quite antique feel. Rachel perched on a stool with a glass of California Semillion and watched April toss sliced green beans into a pot to steam and slide three thick lamb chops beneath the broiler in the old gas stove. Outside, the wind continued to shake the house and wrench at the eaves.

"I'm glad you're here." April glanced nervously out into the darkness. "It scares me when it's really windy like this. A big tree came down last fall. One could fall on the house anytime."

"Those trees have stood here for a long time," Rachel soothed her, "and the ground is drying out. It's when the soil is saturated with water that you have to worry the most."

"Glad to hear that." April turned the meat over and slid it back beneath the broiler flame. "Almost done." She began to set the small table and a black-lacquered tray with thick white stoneware. "I always take a tray up to her room when she goes to bed early like this," the young woman explained. "She usually wakes up about midnight or so. She *likes* storms." She jumped as something thumped against the side of the house.

"A branch," Rachel reassured her. "The firs shed limbs in the wind. I'll do the table."

"Okay." April took the chops out of the oven and set the pan on the stove top. "Tell me about Beck," she said as she began to drain the beans.

"I don't know much about him." Rachel set out woven place mats and matching napkins, silverware, and the heavy plates. "He must have been pretty quiet as a kid. I know he joined the military—the air force, I think—right out of high school. I've heard that he got sent to the Gulf War, but he never talks about it, so I don't know for sure. He's fantastic with wood—a true artisan."

"He's different." April paused with a strainer full of steaming beans, her eyes on the water dripping into the porcelain sink. "Strange, I guess. But he's so *honest*. I've never met a person who really says what he's thinking. I don't think you could make that man lie." She smiled to herself, then dumped the beans into a willowware bowl. "Everybody lies," she said. "No wonder he lives off by himself." She turned abruptly to set the bowl on the table.

Downstairs, something banged sharply, and there was a muffled crash. Rachel and April both started. "The office," April said. She and Rachel stared at each other.

"We'd better go look." Rachel got reluctantly to her feet, the hair prickling on the back of her neck. Which was silly, she thought. Why would somebody choose tonight to burglarize the house? Why now?

"I guess so." Equally reluctant, April joined her in the hallway. "I'm so glad you're here," she murmured.

This is the point in a horror movie where the lights would go out, Rachel thought grimly. She glanced at the wall sconce that lighted the stairs, relieved by its steady yellow glow. Slowly the two women descended the stairs. A cool draft brushed their cheeks, and paper rustled in the dark cavern of the downstairs. "The door blew open," April announced with profound relief. "It does that. The latch is bad."

Nice security here. Rachel's hand brushed a wall switch in the hall at the bottom of the stairs, and she snapped it on. The light made them blink, and Rachel nearly stumbled. The office door—overlooking the creek—had indeed blown open. Maybe, Rachel thought grimly as she crossed the room to close it. The bottom pane of glass—the one just above the lock—had cracked across, and the bottom section lay in two pieces on the floor. Rain and wind swept through the opening, dampening the faded Oriental carpet and swirling papers off the desk beneath the window. The computer screen glowed faintly.

Something about the computer looked wrong, but Rachel wasn't sure what it was. *Screen saver,* she thought. *Most people use a screen saver that features some kind of moving image.* Eloise's screen glowed dully, devoid of any image. Rachel pushed the door closed and turned the bolt lock.

"I guess the glass broke when it slammed open." April bent to pick up the pieces and deposit them carefully in the wastebasket. "Eloise must have opened it and forgotten to lock it."

Maybe. Rachel looked at the damp rug, remembering that open door yesterday. She started to say something about Eloise's ghost, but didn't. All of a sudden, down here in the dim basement, with the sound of wind howling, it didn't seem like a good subject to bring up. "Is anything missing?" She surveyed the paper-strewn desk.

"Who could tell?" April laughed as she retrieved scattered sheets of paper. "I don't think so." She looked around as she laid the papers down. "There was a box of manuscript here—her book. But Sandy took that home with her, I guess." She shrugged. "If anybody was going to steal anything, it would be the computer, you know? That door blows open all the time, if it isn't locked."

She was being paranoid, Rachel decided, as they hunted for cardboard and tape and temporarily patched the broken pane. Upstairs, they reheated their dinner in the microwave and ate, talking about the property, and Beck, and the history of the house, until Rachel began to yawn. She had had a late night last night.

April showed her upstairs to a small bedroom to the right of the narrow upstairs landing. A twin four-poster bed with a pieced quilt covering it took up most of the space. The rest was occupied by a tall oak bureau and a rocking chair beneath the window. Rachel peered out, just able to make out the brick patio by the light of the single outside flood mounted on the house.

"Sleep well," April said cheerfully. "The bathroom is on the landing here, and I put out some clean towels for you,

and a new toothbrush. I get up early, so there'll probably
be coffee ready in the morning."

"Good night," Rachel said. She had meant to call Jeff
tonight, but it was late. She glanced at her watch. He'd
probably be asleep already. She went into the bathroom and
began to get ready for bed.

CHAPTER

4

An earthquake that startled Rachel from sleep became hands shaking her frantically. Rachel bolted upright, squinting in the overhead light, heart pounding as she struggled for an instant to recognize the strange wallpaper and the unfamiliar colors of the quilt that covered her.

"Rachel, wake up! She's gone!"

April. The Johnston house. Orientation returned. "What's wrong?" Rachel gasped, disturbed by April's white face and disheveled hair.

"Eloise is gone. She's not in the house." April scrubbed at her face with her hands. "I . . . I stayed up late reading and took her tray up on my way to bed. Her bed . . . it wasn't even slept in. Why would she go outside on a night like this? It's pouring." She grabbed the quilt, as if ready to tug it and Rachel bodily off the bed. "I should have checked earlier. I should have just looked in on her."

"Are you sure she's not in the bathroom or downstairs or something?" Rachel scrambled out of bed and began to pull on her clothes. "She could have fallen. She could be unconscious."

"I looked. I looked everywhere." Breathless, April hovered in the doorway. "She has to be outside."

Rachel thought of the open office door and frowned, then winced as another fierce gust of wind shook the house. "Does she sometimes . . . wander?"

"No," April said fiercely. "She's not senile, if that's what you mean. If she goes somewhere, she means to go there."

"Let's go look for her again—inside." Rachel took April firmly by the arm as the young woman opened her mouth to protest. "Two sets of eyes are better than one. Once we've double-checked, *then* we can panic."

"She's not inside." April gave her a brief sullen look. "We're wasting time."

"We're not in the middle of a wilderness area." Rachel forced herself to keep a reasonable tone, although she was definitely feeling uneasy herself. The open office door bothered her, and the intruder yesterday had been no ghost, no matter what Eloise had chosen to say. "If Eloise wandered outside and got confused in the storm, she can't go far. And it's not freezing cold. She'll be fine. Wet, but fine."

"I told you—she doesn't get confused." April's expression had gone from sullen to grim. "And there's the creek, remember? It's got to be high by now. And it's right down the steps from the front driveway."

True, Rachel thought with a brief chill. "Let's hope she didn't go anywhere."

They hurried through the house—Rachel in the lead, April radiating impatience behind her. Eloise's room was indeed empty, with no sign that the elderly woman had spent much time there this evening. A bedside lamp on a nightstand beside the four-poster bed was unlit. The covers had been turned down—pastel sheets smoothed down over the white comforter with the perfection of a catalogue ad. A neatly folded blanket sat in the precise center of a teakwood chest at the foot of the bed, and a chair with a needlepoint seat stood exactly between the two windows. The dinner tray, set crookedly on the bureau beside the door, looked jarringly askew in the precise room. Even the lithographs of native plants on the walls were perfectly aligned.

This is a woman who believes passionately in order, Rachel thought distractedly. Her desire to restore the garden before passing it on to the Conservancy suddenly made more sense. Eloise certainly was not there. She wasn't in any other room in the house, either. The office door was still locked, and so was the front door, but Eloise certainly had a key. Rachel glanced at her watch as they peered into closets and behind furniture. It was one o'clock. If Eloise had left the house immediately after going up to her room—while Rachel and April were talking in the kitchen—she had had four hours to wander.

Why? And where? How far could she get? Rachel shook her head as they climbed the stairs up from the office. She had barely had the strength to show them around the property yesterday. "Do you have two flashlights? I have one in my truck," she said, as April shook her head. She got it, while April retrieved a small dim flash from the pantry, and they began to search.

April led her down the stone steps to the creekside path first. Rachel lagged behind the younger woman, cautious on the slick, mossy slabs. Below them, muddy water the color of coffee with cream submerged the stone path along the river and washed inches deep around the stone bench. A metal footbridge cleared the high water by a good two feet, raised on supports above the flood. Water churned beneath it, streaked with foam. Wind-driven rain found its way down the neck of her jacket and soaked her jeans. Rachel shivered as the beam of her flash caught a tangle of tree branches hurrying by on the brown torrent. Surely not . . .

April's wordless cry turned the water seeping down her neck to ice. At the same moment, the younger woman's flashlight winked out. Frightened now, Rachel ran down the last few steps, her own strong flash beam sweeping the wind-shaken weeds, the muddy churn of the swollen creak. She feared that April had fallen in, but a moment later she gasped with relief as her flash picked out April's green rain jacket. As the young woman crouched ankle deep in swirling water, just downstream of the flooded bench, Rachel's chill increased as she caught a glimpse of pale blue among the muddy weeds. Eloise had been wearing a blue sweater.

Heart racing, she splashed over to April. She was cradling Eloise's limp body in her arms. Muddy water saturated Eloise's hair and clothes, and a strand of dead weed adorned her collar like a bizarre necklace.

"She was on her face," April cried. "In the water. She fell down and drowned. Maybe hit her head on the bench."

Rachel leaned over the younger woman, wondering if she was in shock, thinking numbly that she was a little bit in shock herself as she pressed her fingers against the botanist's neck. If there was a pulse, she couldn't feel it. The flesh felt cold and rubbery beneath Rachel's chilled fingers. "Go call 911," she said to April with a gasp. "I'll try to get her breathing." Saying a small prayer of thanks that she had taken a refresher course in CPR last winter, she rolled the elderly woman onto her back and hauled her higher up the bank, thinking numbly that she seemed much heavier now that she was dead. April had already vanished, and the wind covered the sound of her departure. Rachel dismissed her, slid her arm beneath the woman's neck, and leaned down to begin mouth-to-mouth resuscitation.

Nothing blocked Eloise's airway. The cold, clammy kiss of her hair and skin registered dimly as Rachel breathed, compressed her chest, and breathed again, counting, counting. Her shoulders hurt, her arms were tired, April didn't return, and it began to feel as if she was going to do this all night. And the water was still rising, soaking through her jeans, wetting her buttocks and lapping around Eloise's inert body. Dizzily Rachel thought about trying to move her higher, but the bank was steep from there on up to the driveway, and if she stopped, maybe . . .

She jumped and shrieked as someone suddenly grabbed her arm. Someone was saying something that she couldn't hear over the sound of wind and water, and then a uniformed man was hauling her firmly but gently away from Eloise's inert body. He was saying something, and he wore

a paramedic's uniform. *They'll take over,* Rachel thought
dizzily, or maybe he said it. Light dazzled her eyes, and
she stumbled as he handed her over to another man. The
gray fog in her brain was clearing. The second man shined
a light in front of her feet. It reflected on gleaming water,
and as she watched a clump of soggy brown leaves whirl
by, she began to notice the cold.

". . . look like you're about to pass out." The voice was
gravelly, but kind. "Up here. Sit down. . . ." The light swam
away from her, across the muddy water.

She followed the light, stumbling, held up incredibly by
the hand on her arm. Then the ground butted her in the
backside, and the man was pushing her head down gently
toward her raised knees. Specks of light and dark swam
like wandering minnows through her vision. The cold
soaked through her like water through a dry sponge, chill-
ing the marrow of her bones. The first shiver shuddered
through her, then another, and another, building in breathtaking intensity until she was shaking all over, her teeth
rattling, even when she clenched them together. "Is s-s-she
dead?" she managed to force out.

"Don't know yet," the man growled gently. "Here." A
blanket settled around her shoulders. It didn't help, seemed
to trap the freezing cold inside her flesh. "If you can stand
up, we'll get you back to the house. Warm you up."

Warm. A marvelous thought. She was colder than the
air, could feel cold radiating out into the air, like the chill
seeping from a block of ice. She struggled to her feet, felt
the officer's arm go around her. Slowly, stumbling over the
tiniest twig, she made her way back to the steps and up the
endless climb to the driveway. April appeared beside her,
trying to tug the blanket up around her shoulders. The yellow light from the door, glowing through the slanting rain,
looked like heaven to Rachel.

Inside, April helped her take off her sodden rain jacket
and shoes. Wrapped in the blanket, her bare feet frozen and
with almost no feeling, Rachel hobbled into the living room
and sank onto the sofa.

"I made some bouillon." April pressed a steaming mug into Rachel's hands. "Eloise . . ." Her voice faltered, and she looked at the man with an almost frightened air. "Eloise always drank bouillon when she got cold. I . . . I'll go make some coffee."

"Thank you." The man turned a piercing gaze on Rachel as April fled the room. He peered out from beneath a pair of grizzled ginger eyebrows. "Can you tell me what happened this evening?"

"Who are you?" Rachel asked numbly. "A policeman?"

"Yep." He reached beneath his jacket, his disconcertingly direct gaze now fixed on Rachel. "Detective Lieutenant Spiros." He offered her a policeman's badge and ID.

Homicide. Rachel stared at him, her sluggish mind trying to process this. He was a very red redhead, although gray dulled the color. His skin was so pale that it seemed cave-creature white, and his hazel eyes could almost be called gold. Green flecks glinted in them as he studied Rachel, waiting without impatience.

"I'm Rachel O . . . O'Connor," she managed to say at last. She drank some more of the scalding hot bouillon, the racking shivers beginning to subside at last. "You're with Homicide," she said blankly. "You shouldn't be here."

"You're observant." Without hurry, Lieutenant Spiros pulled a notebook from his pocket. "I'd like to hear what happened this evening. But first I'd like a few pieces of information."

"Why is Homicide involved?" Rachel set down her cup. "Was Eloise . . . ?"

"I heard the call on the radio." Spiros spoke impatiently. "I was nearby."

He was lying. Rachel was sure of it and had absolutely no reason for her conviction. But he was. Mechanically she answered his questions. She told him who she was and where she lived, then started in on her account of how she had ended up being here this evening. Lieutenant Spiros listened, asking almost no questions, simply scribbling down the occasional terse note. It made her nervous, so she kept on talking into that crackling silence, adding details to what she had told him, watching his pen move or remain still on the lined pages of his notebook.

Finally, he looked up at her. "You say the office door was open. So you think someone opened it?"

"I . . . I sort of thought so. There was the terrace door yesterday. Eloise said something about seeing a ghost, but someone was there. I saw footprints on the rug." When he made no answer, she studied his face for skepticism, thinking that her assertion sounded lame to her right now. *Hysterical*, she thought. *You sound hysterical.* "She could have just forgotten to lock the office door," she said slowly. "That's what April thought." She tilted her head, studying his silent profile. "You're good at this, aren't you?" she murmured. "Just keep quiet and let people talk."

This earned her a brief glint of amusement in those unreadable eyes.

"How come you're really here?" she said. "I know Homicide detectives don't answer this kind of call."

"Do you know that now?" He gave her a long, narrow look. "As a matter of fact, I knew Eloise. Years ago." Spiros studied his notebook for a moment or two. "Right now, I'm interested in tonight. So you and April were together the whole evening? She was never out of your sight? Not at all?"

This guy wasn't going to give anything away. "I don't think so," Rachel ventured. The evening was getting hard to remember. "No. I'm sure she wasn't. We were in the kitchen while she cooked, and then we ate dinner. She was with me until I went to bed. That was about eleven," she added when he said nothing.

Rachel tried unsuccessfully to stifle a yawn. Outside it was getting light. The rain had stopped, and a bird began a tentative morning song. "It was about one when April woke me up. I looked at my watch." She yawned again. "We looked for Eloise together." She waited, but he still didn't say anything. "I guess April goes to bed late," she said. "She said she was reading and took a tray up to Eloise's room on her way to bed. It was there on the bureau. I guess Eloise wakes up in the middle of the night sometimes and eats then."

"Who made the decision to look along the creek?"

"April." Rachel gave the lieutenant a sharp look and received a benign stare in return. "She knows the paths around here. I don't." When he didn't say anything, she frowned. "It was just kind of random, you know? It wasn't like April said, 'Let's look here.' We just both kind of headed for the creekside path. After all—that had to be the most dangerous place she could be. We were going to look everywhere eventually."

"But you found her right away." Spiros closed his notebook and stood.

"Yes, we did." Rachel stood also, feeling unexpectedly defensive. "So what? The creekbank was the most dangerous place she might be. Of course we looked there first."

Spiros gave her a genial smile. "I'm going to have a word with Miss Gerard now. I'd appreciate it if you wouldn't leave just yet."

"Fine." Rachel yawned, then grimaced at the clammy feel of her damp jeans. "Wish I'd brought a change of clothes," she muttered. Spiros had disappeared into the kitchen. He was shorter than she, with the wiry build of a runner or a wrestler, although his pale skin made her guess that he kept that athletic build through a gym rather than at some outdoor form of exercise. The gray in his vivid hair made her guess his age to be late forties or early fifties. At the doorway to the kitchen, he paused and glanced back at her. "Did Ms. Johnston ever mention any letters?" he asked, as if as an afterthought.

"Letters?" Rachel blinked at him. "What kind of letters?"

But Spiros merely nodded, and went on into the kitchen.

The lieutenant is definitely not a talkative person, Rachel thought. *Letters?* She crossed to the front door and looked out.

Two paramedics maneuvered a wheeled stretcher across the driveway. The sky was clearing, and the first rays of

sun glinted on the puddles. The day promised to be lovely.
As Rachel was about to retreat inside to the warmth of her
blanket once more, a familiar car turned into the driveway.
Sandy! Rachel stepped out onto the patio as her friend
parked and leapt from her car. She stared in horror at the
ambulance, then hurried up the steps. "Oh, poor Eloise.
Every time I came out here, I kept expecting to find her
gone." Her blue eyes brimmed with sympathy. "How awful
for you to be here. And how did you get so wet? And
muddy?" Her eyes widened as she registered Rachel's condition.

"Eloise wandered outside and got lost last night." Rachel
rubbed at the gooseflesh on her arms and retreated inside
with Sandy. "April and I went looking for her. She was . . .
dead when we found her."

"Hello. And who might you be?"

Sandy whirled at the lieutenant's gravelly voice.

"Sandy, this is Lieutenant Spiros." Rachel wrapped the
blanket around herself again. "He's . . . investigating Eloise's death."

"Investigating . . . ?" Sandy said faintly. "Why? Didn't
she have a heart attack?"

"So what was your relationship to Mrs. Johnston?" Spiros had his notebook out and his benign expression in place.

"I was working on her autobiography with her." Sandy
lifted her chin. "I wasn't even supposed to be here today—I
work at the bank this afternoon—but she called me late last
night and said she had a special tape for me. She wanted
me to get it right away and really wouldn't take no for an
answer." Sandy shook her head. "She was really kind
of . . . weird about it. So I told her I would, but I'd have to
come out here first thing, because I'm supposed to be at
work at one o'clock, and . . . I don't know . . ." Her rapid
narrative faltered. "What do I do now? I don't know if I
should even go on with the project." She swallowed. "It's
not real yet, I guess. That she's not . . . that she's not here.
But she already has a publisher and everything."

"Tapes?" Spiros pocketed his notebook, looking interested at last. "Where would they be?"

"In the office." Sandy led the way downstairs, turning frequent and curious glances on the detective. "She was recording her memoirs, and then I put them together, and edited them. It took a lot of editing." She made a face. "Eloise was like my grandmother. She had a good memory, but things didn't exactly come back to her in chronological order. We were working on the years when she and Carl lived in Blossom, while their children were young. She sort of saved that for last, I guess. I don't think they had a happy time there."

"Really?" Spiros gave her an unexpectedly sharp look. "Why do you think so?"

"I don't know. The fact that she didn't talk about it, I guess. What's with the doorknob?" A plastic bag covered the knob of the office door, held in place by a rubber band.

"Prints," Spiros said.

"The door was open?" Sandy glanced at it as she crossed the room to the cluttered desk. "It was locked when I left yesterday. She never went out that way. Have you told her sons? That she's dead? She had three children, but the daughter died. It was while they lived in Blossom," Sandy chattered on, her face pale. "Maybe that's why she wouldn't talk about it. Because her daughter died there."

"Did she?" Something hard in Spiros's tone made Rachel look at him, but his expression was as bland as ever. "Wait!" He caught Sandy's wrist as she reached for a microcasette recorder on the desk. He pulled a red cowboy bandanna from his pocket, picked up the recorder with this unexpectedly colorful aid, and snapped open the tape compartment. "No tape." He closed the machine and put it down. "Are you sure a tape was supposed to be here?"

"That's what she said. That's weird. She was really insistent that I come out and get it today. She always leaves the tapes with the recorder." She started to reach for the scatter of papers on the desk, then snatched her hand back at Spiros's glare. "Why would somebody steal the tape?"

"Can you tell if anything else is missing?" Spiros eyed the desk.

"I . . . I don't know. Something." Sandy had clasped her hands behind her back like a child contemplating a display of untouchable candy. "I think . . . Oh, my God." She clasped her hands, paling. "The manuscript is gone. The whole thing. It was here—in a box. Right here. But it's all in the computer. Why would anybody take the printout?" Automatically she reached for the keyboard, and flinched as Spiros's hand closed over her wrist.

"Not yet." He eased her away from the desk. "So her memoirs are gone." That piercing golden gaze fixed itself on Sandy's round face. "Is there anything in there that someone might not want to see in print?"

"No. Nothing." Sandy shook her head so vigorously that her blond curls bobbed around her face. "It's all about how she and Carl collected plants all over—the people they met, the places they camped, Carl's years as a teacher—that kind of thing. Kind of boring, actually." She made a face. "Why would anybody care?"

"Do you know what was on the missing tape?"

"No." Sandy shrugged. "Stuff about her years in Blossom, I guess. That's all we had left to cover."

Spiros grunted and ushered them back upstairs. "If you'd just wait here," he said, and vanished through the front door.

"What is going on?" Sandy turned wide eyes on Rachel. "Did somebody really break in here? And did they . . ." She broke off and shivered. "Did they murder Eloise?" she whispered.

"I don't know." Rachel wrapped herself in the blanket again, wishing she had another cup of bouillon, or better yet, some real breakfast. "I don't know what's going on here. Lieutenant Spiros said something about letters."

"Somebody threatened to kill Eloise." April came into the room. "I made coffee, and I've got bagels that aren't too stale. If you want something to eat."

"She was getting death threats?" Rachel followed April into the kitchen.

"That's awful," Sandy said indignantly. "Who would do that? And why?"

"They were weird. They just said she was going to die." April made a face. "She got two of them. I wanted her to tell the police, but she didn't believe they were a real threat." April took down three mugs from the cupboard. "I swiped one from the trash and called the police. They weren't too interested, so I called this newspaper guy I know. She was mad. I thought she was going to fire me when the reporter showed up," April said grimly. "But someone had to know."

"Reporters." Sandy rolled her eyes. "I bet she was mad. She hates the newspapers."

"It made the paper—about her and the Conservancy. They even mentioned her memoirs. Actually, it was good publicity for her project. Nobody really remembered her or her husband, you know? Which wasn't right." April poured coffee for all of them. "Cream? There's sugar in that tin." She opened the refrigerator and took out a carton of Half & Half, a block of cream cheese, and a jar of homemade jam. "I think some people donated money to the Conservancy because of the story. But she was really mad at me. I wouldn't have done it if I'd known she'd get so upset." She shook her head. "How come she hated reporters so much?"

She had piled the bagels on a stoneware plate. Sandy reached for one and began to spread a thick layer of cream cheese on it. "I skipped breakfast to come down here. I think it was because of her daughter's death. I guess the newspeople made her life miserable." She scooped up a dark purple mound of jam, spread it on the bagel, and took a bite. "Yum!"

"Eloise made it from salal berries and wild elderberry." April sipped at her coffee. "She never told me she had a daughter who died."

Rachel had been watching the young woman closely. In

spite of her light tone, her knuckles gleamed as she clutched her coffee cup, and her face looked taut and fearful. "He's just doing his job," she said softly.

"Spiros?" April gave her a startled, wary look. "He sure is." Bitterness edged her tone, and she gulped at her coffee. "They make up their minds in about a minute, you know? Then they don't change 'em."

"Who does?" Sandy asked innocently.

"I think you and I wear about the same size." April pretended she hadn't heard the question as she eyed Rachel. "You want to borrow a pair of jeans and a sweatshirt? You look like you're freezing."

"I would love some dry clothes." Leaving Sandy drinking coffee and eating her bagel in the kitchen, they went back to April's room. It was remarkably spare—furniture and bedding that obviously belonged to the house, and two framed photographs of blooming hellebore and wild ginger on the walls. Other than toilet articles on the tall walnut dresser, and a few clothes hanging in the closet, the room could have simply been a guest room, used for a single night and vacated again. No pictures, no books, no letters cluttered any surface. An alarm clock stood on the night stand, next to a Tiffany-shaded lamp and a small personal radio–cassette player.

Rachel gratefully accepted a pair of stonewashed jeans and a heavy fleece sweatshirt from April. "Dry socks?" April fished in the top drawer of the dresser. "Anything else?"

"This will be bliss, thank you." Rachel began to strip off her wet jeans. "How long have you worked for Eloise?"

"Two years." April turned to stare through the window at the stone wall below the rising slope of rock garden behind the house. "I wish . . ." She broke off, shook her head. "If you need anything else, help yourself." She left the room, closing the door softly behind her.

Rachel dressed, bundling her wet clothes up in her jeans. The dry clothes felt like heaven, although the jeans were a bit snug for her wide-hipped build. By the time she padded back to the kitchen, Spiros was there, talking to Sandy.

"We've dusted everything," he was telling her. "Why don't you go check on Ms. Johnston's manuscript—the file on the computer. I'd like a copy of it."

"You're talking nearly three hundred pages, but okay. The laser printer is fast." Sandy put her empty cup and plate in the sink and led the way back downstairs. Seating herself in front of the computer, she frowned, then touched a key. "That's weird." She turned the machine off, then back on. White printing scrolled briefly across the screen, then vanished. A blinking cursor and a C> prompt appeared at the top of the screen. "Something's wrong." Sandy touched a couple of keys. "Windows should have come right up. Was April playing with this?" she asked accusingly.

"No, I didn't touch anything," April said from the doorway behind them. "I'd never touch Eloise's computer."

"Somebody did something. Or maybe lightning struck the pole or something." Sandy switched the computer off and on once again, to no avail. "I don't know what's wrong!"

"So now we have no manuscript at all," Spiros said pleasantly.

"What?" Sandy got slowly to her feet, her expression worried. "Who would do that? There's nothing in there to bother anyone. And what's the publisher going to say?"

"Maybe a computer expert could recover the files," Rachel suggested.

"You sound like you know your way around computers." Spiros's smile was genial.

"Enough to know that if you delete things by accident, you can usually get them back." Rachel met his golden stare, feeling defensive again. There was a prying, piercing attention behind Spiros's bland manner that was really beginning to irritate her.

"I think we're finished here." Spiros nodded abruptly. "You can go back to Blossom if you want." He reached into his pocket and handed business cards to both Rachel and Sandy. "If you think of anything that might help, call this number any time." He turned slowly to offer a third card to April. "You weren't planning on going anywhere for the next few days, were you?"

"No." April's voice was barely audible, and she kept her eyes stubbornly on her shoes. "I don't have anywhere to go."

The girl was terrified, Rachel realized. "Why don't you take my number, too." She offered one of her cards to April. "If you need anything, or it just gets scary being here by yourself, give me a call. I could come out and spend a night." She was aware of Spiros's thoughtful stare. She straightened her shoulders. "And don't forget—I have a contract to restore the grounds. So I'll be around."

April's sullen expression didn't change, and she didn't look at Rachel, but she took the card. She didn't put it in her pocket, though. It lay on her lax palm with the lieutenant's.

"Besides," Rachel went on, "I need to return your clothes."

April finally looked up, her eyes alive with shadows. "No rush," she murmured, then turned and fled up the stairs.

"She's weird." Sandy climbed the stairs with Rachel, leaving Spiros behind, talking into his cell phone. "I've never really trusted her. Eloise would never say how she came to hire her." She paused at the top of the stairs. "Were you serious about working here?" Her blond eyebrows rose into perfect arches. "I mean . . . Eloise . . ." She made a vague gesture with her hand.

"Eloise wanted the work done, we signed a contract, and she paid me." Rachel patted the wallet in her pocket. "I'm going to do what she wanted."

"I hope you can." Sandy paused at her car. The ambulance had left, but one marked and one unmarked police car were still parked along the creek side of the lane. "I wonder who sent those letters. You know, I'd put my money on her older son." Sandy tossed her head. "Alan. He's a stockbroker or something and has a ton of money, but he got really bent out of shape when she decided to leave the property to that nature group. I mean—you can't really blame him for that, but still—he's a jerk."

"Maybe that's why she didn't turn the letters over to the police. Maybe she recognized her son as their author." Rachel shaded her eyes as the sun emerged from the wet clouds. The bright sunshine glittered on every drop of water, spangling the sodden woodland with glittering light.

"My gosh it's late. I'd better run." Sandy slid into her car. "Dad is involved in organizing Paul Claymore's visit, did I tell you? He invited Claymore to a big community reception, and guess what? Claymore accepted! Guess who gets to clean the house and organize the food?" She laughed. "Not that I mind getting a chance to visit with our esteemed State Representative. Maybe he'll hire me to write his autobiography when he gets elected president." She smiled and started the car. "You're invited to the reception. I'll let you know the details as soon as I know them. Consider yourself invited." With a wave, she turned around in the circular driveway and vanished in the direction of the freeway.

Rachel climbed into her truck and started the engine. Less than eighteen hours earlier, she had arrived there to work on a garden design for a client. Shaking her head, she turned the truck around. As she left, she glanced in her rearview mirror to find April standing on the front terrace, staring intently after her.

CHAPTER

5

In spite of her short night, Rachel wasn't at all sleepy on the drive back. Vivid snapshots from the night—Eloise's crumpled form and April's drawn and frightened face—circled restlessly through her brain. Everything around her seemed sharp-edged, almost too bright and clear. As she passed two lumbering truck-and-trailer rigs near Troutdale, she caught a snapshot glimpse of a car passing westward on the far side of the median barrier. The blue sports car with its scarf-headed driver registered on her brain in a strobing instant. Her mother. Rachel was sure of it.

On her way to shop in Portland, Rachel told herself. But she had been there only yesterday. Her mother rarely drove in to Portland by herself. She and Joshua went into town often, to spend the night at the small apartment loft her husband still rented in northwest Portland. Two solo trips to the city in two days was . . . unusual. No, it was odd. She was wrong about the car, she told herself sternly. It hadn't been her mother at all.

Only it had.

In what seemed like no time, she reached the exit for Blossom and left the interstate. The utter normality of the late-morning streets cast the events of the rainy horrible night into stark and jarring relief in her mind. As she passed City Hall, automatically checking the planters out front, a tall figure waved her down. Jeff. She pulled over to the curb and tried for a smile as he came around to her side of the truck. "Hey," she said.

"You look tired." He tilted his head, a briefly worried expression on his face. "Are you okay?"

"I don't know." She related a brief synopsis of her wild night, watching his eyebrows first rise, then draw together in concern.

"Girl, I don't know if I want to let you out of my sight." Worry in his dark eyes belied his smile. "Good thing you weren't down in that office when somebody busted in for the memoirs. Who did you say was handling the investigation?"

"Lieutenant something. I can't remember his name." Rachel shivered, briefly cold. "But he's from Homicide. Wait." She pulled out her wallet. "He gave me his card."

"Homicide?" Jeff gave her a skeptical look. "Are you sure?"

"Drat! I don't know where I put it." She thumbed through the contents of her wallet once more. "He definitely said Homicide, but he was only there by accident. I don't know." She shook her head. "I thought he was lying when he said that. He had red hair, and this kind of gravelly voice. April—Eloise's live-in caretaker—said she'd been getting death threats. She said that Eloise wouldn't give the letters to the police, so she did. Maybe he was there because of that."

"Maybe." Jeff's tone was noncommittal. Well, I'm glad you're out of it." He leaned down to kiss her lightly. "I'll sleep better knowing you're not down there." He straightened, eyes on her face. "Okay, what is it?"

"Uh . . . I'm not quite out of it." She avoided his narrowed stare. "I'm going to do what she paid me to do. It was important to her. The Conservancy group that formed to take over the property probably can't afford that kind of

renovation. She had a contract with me, but if I back out
of it, I bet the heirs won't spend a dime on the place. From
what Sandy told me, they're not happy about Mom giving
away the property as it is."

"Great. Just great." Jeff looked away, his fists briefly
clenched. "All right." He let his breath out in an explosive
sigh. "I know better than to even try to talk you out of it.
It may take me a while, but I do learn. When you've got
that stubborn look on your face, I might as well save my
breath."

"You're right," Rachel said demurely. "I'll be careful."

"You don't have to look so sweetly pleased with yourself, dammit." Jeff glowered. "And you better be careful.
If Portland Homicide is involved, you need to think a little
bit about what that might mean."

"I really did mean it." She met his dark stare. "I got . . .
scared tonight. Someone was there. And Eloise died, even
if nobody murdered her. And I liked her. And we talked
and laughed and then . . . she was dead." She looked away,
feeling the shivering threaten again. "I don't think I'll ever
get used to death," she said softly.

"You don't want to." Jeff leaned through the window to
caress her hair gently. "But I do want you to be careful.
Something seems very wrong here. I worry about you. A
lot."

"The burglar took the manuscript and erased the files on
the computer. Why should he bother me for weeding and
hoeing? And I'll be using Julio on the job. He's better than
a Rottweiler."

"If he wasn't so young, I'd be jealous." Jeff tugged on
a lock of her hair. "But he's certainly protective. I feel a
little bit better. But remember," he said seriously, "crimi-
nals don't always behave logically. I think I'm going to
have a talk with the lieutenant who's running the investigation. Meanwhile, I was just on my way to lunch." He
straightened. "Interested?"

"Yes." Her stomach rumbled a willing assent. "I sort of
didn't think about breakfast."

"I bet not. Why not park here, and we'll walk over to the Bread Box." He opened the door for her. "And you're buying. Since you're going to give me all those gray hairs."

Rachel stepped back to study him, smiling. "A little gray in that inky black would make you look distinguished. It would give you an air of maturity," she said with an almost straight face.

Jeff grunted, then scooped her up and slung her over his shoulder, ignoring her shrill yelp of protest. "Put me down," she tried to say, but she was laughing so hard that she couldn't get the words out. "What . . . what are people going to think?" She gasped. Two elderly women exiting Sally's Antiques on the corner of Main and Cedar stopped short and gave them a dubious stare.

"Oh, great. It's my landlady and her sister." Rachel buried her face against Jeff's back as Mrs. Frey waved enthusiastically. Her sister said something that Rachel couldn't catch, and both women broke into cackling laughter. "I'll never hear the end of this," she groaned. "If you haul me into the Bread Box like this, Joylinn will laugh so hard that she'll probably drop a tray on some tourist's head, and they'll sue, and she'll lose the shop, and it'll be all your fault."

"Actually, I think it would be your fault for provoking me." Jeff stopped as they reached the corner and set her on her feet. "But I wouldn't want to upset Joylinn. Besides . . ." He fanned himself. "It's too hot to carry you all the way there."

"Is that a backhanded way of saying I need to lose a few pounds?" She made a face at him. "And I bet we made Mrs. Frey's day."

"I hope her days aren't *that* boring. And I'd rather you kept your pounds where they are. They look quite fine to me." Jeff untangled a snarl in her hair. "There. You look civilized again. Shall we?" He offered her his arm with a quirky formality that made her smile.

"I'm still having a salad for lunch. Thank you, sir." She took his arm with a flourish, and they promenaded through the doors together, drawing at least a couple of amused glances from patrons.

The dining room was nearly full, even though it was a weekday. Joylinn's reputation had been steadily growing, and her bakery had been written up more than once in various Northwest travel magazines and newspapers. Not only did she bring in a steady flow of tourists and Hood River folk, but a goodly number of Blossom residents had switched their lunchtime loyalties from the Homestyle Cafe to the Bread Box. Which hadn't endeared Joylinn to Stan Bellamy, who owned the Homestyle. All the tables on the deck that had once been a loading dock were full, so they took a table inside, as close to the huge, floor-to-ceiling windows as possible. The two sets of wide doors that led onto the dock were both open, and a gentle breeze found its way inside, bringing the scents of river and summer on its cool breath.

Celia, Joylinn's longtime waitress and sometime–assistant baker, appeared at their table to take their order and fill their glasses with ice water. Rachel ordered a salad, as she had promised, and flicked droplets of water at Jeff when he grinned. He ordered the day's special—a grilled salmon sandwich on one of Joylinn's famous rolls, topped with ginger mayonnaise. Rachel dug into her salad dutifully when it arrived.

"Joylinn sent these along." Celia set a wicker basket of rolls down in the middle of the table. "She said she made too many this morning." With a wink, Celia departed.

"Joylinn caters to all my weaknesses." Rachel rolled her eyes and reached for one of the warm, fragrant rolls. "Since when has that woman ever made too many of anything?"

"Cheese," Jeff announced through a mouthful of bread. "And fennel seed. This is new." He finished the butter roll in a few quick bites.

"You already have bread with your sandwich." Rachel snatched the basket over to her side of the table. The banter with Jeff and the sun sparkling on the Columbia's blue-gray water outside were rapidly dispelling the last of the morning's shadows. She forked up more of her salad, guarding the rolls, smiling at Jeff's chuckle.

"Hey." He nodded toward the street door. "There's Julio. Is he looking for you?"

"I don't know." Rachel turned to wave. Julio waved back and threaded his way between chairs to their table.

"I am looking for your mother, *Senorita* Boss-Lady. *Senor* . . ." He nodded a greeting to Jeff. "I thought she might be here to eat lunch. I am worried."

"Worried?" Rachel put down her fork. "Why?"

"We have the class on this morning, every week." He frowned, his glance sweeping the dock, as if she might be out there after all. "The English class?"

"Oh, yeah." Rachel nodded. Her mother had talked the tiny local library into turning an office into a small classroom and meeting space. She and Julio taught English classes there once a week. Their students were the itinerant and resident local farm workers, most of whom were from Mexico. Julio was there not only to translate as needed, but also as a reassurance to the workers, who were shy about signing up for anything official. Not all of them were in the country legally.

Julio was good at it, her mother had told Rachel. She wasn't surprised. In the nearly three years he had worked for her, he had gone from stumbling pidgin English to speaking it nearly as smoothly as if he had been born in the area. His drive to succeed impressed her. And it had also surprised Rachel to discover that he had learned Spanish as a second language, that English was his third acquisition. At home he and his sister and brother-in-law spoke the language used in their native town in Guatemala. Spanish was for the government officials, he had told her once, and for visits to the city.

"I forgot it was today," Rachel said slowly, thinking of that blue MG zipping past her on the freeway. "I . . . think she had to go into Portland today. She must have forgotten, too."

"She has never forgotten before." Julio's dark eyes brooded. "I am worried for her."

"Do you have her cell-phone number?" Jeff frowned.

"I called her." Julio nodded. "The phone was not . . ." He paused, searching briefly for the word he wanted. "It did not work."

"Sometimes she forgets to turn it on in the morning," Rachel said lightly. "She'll feel terrible when she realizes she missed the class. Did you have a lot of people?"

"Ten." He nodded. "Many of them come each class. Some of them . . ." He shrugged and made a gesture with his hand. "They come once. Twice. Then not for a while. Then they come every time. Or not. It is a good class," he said with quiet satisfaction. "Many people ask questions about many things."

"Do you want to have lunch with us?" Jeff asked as Celia approached. "You're welcome."

"No, thank you, *Senor*." Julio got to his feet, smiling. "I have yards to clean today. I have a new one." He turned a sparkling smile on Rachel. "The lady who wanted a lake in her backyard, do you remember?"

"Oh, her." Rachel groaned and rolled her eyes. A retired account executive from Portland, the woman had asked for a pond in her small backyard, deep enough for her to use as a soaking pool. She wanted a Japanese garden effect— rocks and sand and carefully trained trees. Unfortunately for her, the house was situated atop a vein of basalt that lay only a couple of feet below the soil level. She had been very unwilling to believe that it wasn't feasible to carve a deep pool out of solid rock. "I'm amazed she'll have any-thing to do with either of us," Rachel said. "I kept expecting my first malpractice suit."

"She is happy with her little stream and her little trees." Julio grinned. "She tells the people who visit that it is her garden—she designed it."

"Oh, right." Rachel rolled her eyes. "It took me a week to convince her to let me do the miniature garden design."

"She tips." Julio nodded decisively. "And she is never

there when I come." He grinned broadly. "She is a good client."

"I'm glad." Rachel smiled. "I've got a job for you, if you have the time. Can I stop by this evening and talk to you about it?"

"Oh, *sí*." He grinned widely. "I will be home. I will tell my sister." He waved and made his way out of the building, wiry and graceful as he wove between the tables.

"He's going to end up with a bigger business than me." Rachel sighed theatrically. "I'm going to miss him when he doesn't have time to work for me anymore."

"He sure deserves to succeed." Jeff finished his sandwich and glanced at his watch. "I hate to rush this, but I've got to get back. Our honored mayor wanted to see me this afternoon. I think we're going to have to hire another officer. The price of the tourist trade, I guess." He made a face. "We need a full-time traffic cop. At least in the summer and on holiday weekends."

"More stoplights." Rachel rolled her eyes. "That'll make the no-more-taxes contingent—like my uncle—scream."

"Well, we wouldn't want them to get bored." Jeff reached for his wallet as Rachel pushed her chair back. "Not that that's likely, so long as Phil Ventura is mayor."

"Hey, I'm paying, remember?" Rachel dropped money plus a tip on the table a moment before Jeff got his wallet out. "Phil does keep life lively around here."

"That he does." Jeff laughed. Blossom's young mayor, Phillip Ventura, saw Blossom's future in the recent influx of tourists and retirees, which put him in frequent conflict with some of the conservative growers in the area—and one time had put him in personal danger.

As they left the restaurant, Rachel found that her recovering spirits had been dampened by Julio's words, and all her earlier worry about her mother returned. Subdued, she left Jeff at the steps of City Hall and made her way to the bank, in the next block. Sandy was behind the high marble counter helping a customer when Rachel entered. She finished with a smile, watched the grower turn away, then waved to Rachel.

"I still can't believe it," she said breathlessly. "That Eloise is . . . dead." She lowered her voice. "Have you heard anything more from that Lieutenant Spiros? About whether she was . . . she was murdered," Sandy whispered.

Spiros, Rachel thought with annoyance. *That's his name.* "It's only been a few hours," Rachel said calmly. Sandy's breathless excitement over anything and everything, no matter how minor, was legend. She made a startling contrast to her stolid and practical husband, Bill Daris. Sort of like a bouncing helium balloon anchored by a rock, Rachel thought with an internal smile. They balanced each other well. "I don't think he'll tell me anything anyway. I'll probably hear from him only if he has more questions to ask." She pushed the check Eloise had written to her across the counter. "I'd better deposit this right away."

"Wow." Sandy's eyes widened as she picked up the pale blue rectangle of paper. "I mean . . ." She shuffled her feet and gave Rachel a worried look. "That's a lot of money. And Eloise is . . ." She bit her lip, nose wrinkling as she frowned. "I'm not sure what to do about this. I've never had this kind of thing happen before. I'd better go ask. Hang on." With an apologetic shrug, she vanished into the office behind her.

Rachel leaned against the cool marble counter thinking about her mother on the highway to Portland, with her cell phone turned off, not showing up for her class with Julio. Worrying. She straightened with a sigh as Sandy returned to the counter.

"Can't do it, girl." Sandy made a sympathetic face. "The boss called the bank, and they told him that the account has been frozen. I guess you'll have to wait until it gets unfrozen."

"Frozen?" Rachel looked at her blankly. "How come?"

"Don't ask me." Sandy shrugged. She edged the check toward Rachel with one finger. "I just add and subtract. Nobody tells anybody anything." She pouted. "It's probably one of those probate things that'll get sorted out eventually. Don't worry about it."

But she did worry. It didn't sound like a "probate thing," as Sandy had put it. Not this soon. Rachel folded the check carefully into her wallet. "I'm going to have a talk with the bank people myself and find out what's going on." She sighed. "I'd better call the the Conservancy people, too, if I can find a phone number. They might be able to speed things along."

"Well, maybe I can add one bright note to the day." Sandy smiled. "The social event of the year—the reception for our esteemed representative, Paul Claymore, will take place at Dad's house tomorrow night. It's all planned." Her eyes sparkled. "It'll be so cool. The mayor is coming, and Mr. Wilkins, and the Van Orns, since they have the biggest orchard around here and know him anyway, and I guess gave him a lot of money when he ran for the seat. Would you believe his aide faxed me a list of people to invite? I'd never heard of any of them." She rolled her eyes. "The only problem is the timing, but I already panicked and called Joylinn, and she told me not to worry, so I'm not." She giggled. "I guess I'm just the caterer's assistant, but hey, it'll be fun. Joylinn's so *calm* about it all. Maybe I'll talk her into moving to Washington, and we'll go into business together." Her laugh chimed through the bank, and she covered her mouth hastily, casting a guilty glance back toward the office. "We're going to get started right after work. It's going to be one of those elegant, casual buffets you see in *Sunset* magazine—oh, it'll be so *cool*!"

"Wow, I'm impressed. And flattered." Rachel grinned. "Bet I wasn't on the list the aide faxed."

"You weren't." Sandy made a face. "But Jeff was, so you get to come as his guest. And I would have invited you anyway," she said loyally. "I'm so excited!"

Rachel laughed, waved, and exited the bank. Nothing could spoil Sandy's good spirits for long, she thought with a smile. Death, catastrophe . . . They cast a brief shadow, like a passing cloud, and then the sun shone again for her friend. As she walked down the street to City Hall, where she'd parked her truck, she caught sight of Joshua coming out of the hardware store.

"I want somebody to design a faucet that never drips," he complained. "Oh, well, at least I get to refresh my rusty plumbing skills." He hefted a paper sack that clanked faintly. "Although I wish the darned thing had at least given me more than three years before it started to leak!"

"I hate plumbing." Rachel shuddered. "Which always makes me wonder why I went into landscaping, with all the sprinkler systems and drip irrigation." She smiled at his quick laugh. "So where's my esteemed mother today? I was going to invite her to lunch, but I couldn't find her." *Small fib*, she thought with a twinge of guilt. *Nothing major.*

"She teaches an English class over at the library, remember? Doesn't your assistant help with it? Anyway, she doesn't get through until one o'clock most days. Or later. She's giving a couple of her students some extra help."

"Oh," Rachel said. "I . . . I forgot." The ballooning lie made her tongue stumble, and she blushed. A veil of deception had begun to form about her mother like a tissue of clammy fog. It bothered her a lot. "Well, I'd better get going," she said quickly. "I've got a lot to do."

"Me, I've got plumbing to do," Joshua said with a heavy sigh. Lifting his hand in a cheerful wave, he strode off up the street. Stabbed by brief guilt, Rachel climbed into her truck and headed home.

This is not your business, girl, she admonished herself fiercely as she drove. *It is your mother's life. Not yours. If she doesn't want to let you in on whatever's going on, then you stay out.* Good advice, she figured as she parked in the gravel drive beside the tall white house. She hoped she could follow it.

Peter waited on the railing of her entry stairway, his tail twitching as he watched a couple of finches flutter about Mrs. Frey's bird feeder out back. The phone began to ring inside as Rachel reached him. Muttering a curse under her breath, she sprinted up the steep stairway, fumbling the key into the lock. Peter darted past her and leaped onto the sofa back as she charged across the room and snatched the phone from its cradle. The buzz of a dial tone greeted her. "Damn." She dropped the instrument, telling herself that it was only a sales call, and she had an answering machine, but she couldn't help feeling that it had been important, that it had been her mother.

The phone rang again. She picked it up on the first ring, ignoring Peter's glare. "Rain Country Landscaping. Rachel speaking."

"Rachel O'Connor, right? We've never met, but my name is Roger Tourelle. I'm with the Northwest Garden Conservancy. Eloise Johnston gave me your number."

"Oh, I'm so glad you called." Rachel hesitated. "Do you know . . . ?"

"I'm devastated. It's terrible news. I just found out. A police detective called me. He told me you found her. You and the young woman who lived there with her. How awful for you both," Tourelle rushed on. "And I gather that they think there was foul play involved. . . . How *terrible*! And how terrible for you."

Foul play. Well, Homicide had been there. "It was pretty awful," Rachel said slowly. "I didn't know . . . What kind of foul play do you mean?" She reached for a can of cat food, cold all over again. "Or are you talking about the threatening letters?"

"Oh, those." Tourelle sounded grim. "The paper had fun with that, and it really upset poor Eloise. The police didn't take it seriously at the time, of course. They don't take much seriously, do they? Never mind. I just can't take this all in." Tourelle rushed on. "Everything was going so well, our open house was all planned, but it won't be the same without her. She was so very excited about what we were going to do together. Actually we'll have to cancel the open house." He sighed. "I can't see either of her sons paying for the renovations, and we don't yet have the funding."

"I can still do the landscaping work." Rachel opened a can of catfood and dumped it onto a plate. "We signed a contract last night. She gave me a check even." She hesitated. "Although the bank won't honor it yet. I'll have to wait until that gets straightened out."

"She signed a contract? And paid you? Bless her." Tourelle sounded surprised. "I must tell you that's totally out of character. Eloise was a careful woman who dotted every *i*, and crossed every *t* before committing her signature to anything. That's why I at least don't have to worry about the bequest. It's ironclad."

Rachel wondered if he thought Eloise's sons would dispute it. Sounded like it, she thought. "Well, I'll keep in touch. As soon as the check is cashed, I can get started."

"I am so relieved. I can't tell you . . . Good thing I didn't cancel the open house yet." His enthusiasm matched Sandy's. "We need the exposure so desperately."

"I'll need the money for labor and materials, if you want me to have the place ready for your open house," Rachel interjected.

"Oh, yes. I'm sure the bank account problem is just a legal formality. And I'm sure you'll be done in plenty of time. Eloise said so many good things about you. We'll keep in touch."

"But I can't . . ."

Tourelle had hung up.

Feeling as if someone had dumped a large bucket of water over her head, Rachel slowly replaced the receiver. "You have indeed met your match, Sandy," she said out loud. But she didn't laugh. There was no guarantee that she could get the money in time to pay for the labor and irrigation supplies that the renovation would require. It sure couldn't come out of her bank account, she thought wryly. She didn't have that much in there.

Rachel set the plate of cat food on the floor for Peter, who gave her a disdainful glare before deigning to eat. "You could survive quite well on dry food," she suggested absently, then reached for the phone as it rang again. "Rain Country Landscaping. Rachel speaking."

"Rachel O'Connor?" the male caller asked. "You were working for Eloise Johnston."

"Yes. That's me."

"I'm Andrew Johnston, Eloise's son." The man cleared his voice. "I . . . got the news about Mother today."

"I'm terribly sorry."

"Yes, well, it wasn't exactly unexpected. Her heart was bad. I didn't know how far Mother had gone in her discussions with you about renovating the property, but I just wanted you to know that things will, of course, have to come to a halt now. I'm sorry."

There was something about his smooth tone that made Rachel bristle. "I don't see that I need to stop," she said briskly. "We signed a contract last night, and Eloise gave me a check to seal it."

"That's no longer valid of course," the man said breezily. "I'm sorry that you lost a job, but I'm sure you understand."

"I don't understand at all, and I think the check *is* valid." Rachel gripped the receiver tightly. "I'll discuss it with my lawyer in the morning."

"Mother was not of sound mind. She was obsessing over that jungle, giving all her property away. She was, perhaps, suffering from the onset of Alzheimer's disease. I mean, come now. It's one thing to give away valuable real estate to a bunch of garden-club fanatics, but it's another to throw away the rest of our inheritance to pay for pulling weeds."

Well, now she knew why that bank account had been frozen. She wondered how he had known about the check. "As I said, I'll take it up with my lawyer," Rachel said in her most polite business voice. This man was bringing out every stubborn molecule in her being.

"We're not going to let it happen." Johnston dropped his pleasant tone. "Don't waste your money fighting it," he said coldly, and hung up.

Rachel replaced the receiver slowly. "I think I don't like Andrew Johnston," she said slowly. Peter looked up from washing his face and purred.

"I'm glad you liked dinner, cat." She sighed. "I think I'm going to go take a long walk along the river. I think I need to cool off for a while."

CHAPTER

6

A long walk along the Columbia put the unpleasant Andrew Johnston in perspective. First thing the next morning, Rachel called her lawyer. Gladys Killingsworth had retired from a large Seattle firm at age forty and opened a small practice in Blossom, of all places. Specializing in business law, with no previous experience with the agricultural industry and a policy of refusing divorce cases, she cheerfully admitted that she wasn't making any money. But she was having a lot more fun with her life, she always added. Rachel frequently saw her out jogging along the county roads in the morning, her short muscular frame clad in baggy sweats, a Walkman clipped to her waistband. She had heard that Gladys had a black belt in aikido, but that might have been a rumor. She certainly spent many afternoons sailboarding with the twentysomethings on the broad, windy Columbia. And she rode a huge Harley-Davidson motorcycle, which had not added to her clientele among the longtime residents of Blossom. Lawyers did not ride motorcycles. Especially not women lawyers.

Gladys answered her own phone when Rachel called, and told her she could see her at one. Restless, with nothing on the schedule for the day, Rachel spent two boring hours vacuuming and dusting the apartment and doing a load of laundry. Then it occurred to her that Beck probably didn't know that Eloise was dead and that the job was on hold.

It was an excuse to escape the housework, Rachel admitted. She eyed the bathroom, swiped at the sink with a damp sponge, and proclaimed it clean enough. It was a lovely day. The damp marine weather had finally given way to high pressure and sun, and the earliest cherries were just beginning to form on Mrs Frey's cranky and fungus-ridden tree. As she drove east, out toward Beck's property, she rolled her window down and enjoyed the rush of warm wind through the window. Perhaps the long, cold spring was finally giving way to more usual weather. In an orchard along the road, young pear saplings stretched toward the sun, their grafts still quite visible. Asian pears, Rachel guessed. They were increasingly popular and beginning to replace the standard European varieties. The weather should help her uncle Jack's temper, anyway. Wet springs like this one sent him into a dark surly mood every time the sky clouded up. Cold damp brought fungus diseases, and spraying cost money.

Rachel turned off the county road onto the graveled lane that led up toward Mount Hood. She left the orchards behind and wound through second-growth forest. The road connected farther on with another county road. In the summer it was a convenient shortcut, and a good place to go parking for the high-school-age crowd. In the winter, some truly amazing potholes made it a hazardous road for anyone without four-wheel drive. On a lonely stretch, Rachel braked and turned onto the narrow track that led to Beck's cabin. She put the truck into four-wheel mode, since the wet spring had left the dirt road muddy and soft even this late. But a dozen yards down the lane, a young alder had fallen across the track, blocking it utterly. The truck slithered to a halt.

The alder hadn't been there when she had picked Beck up for their trip to Portland. Perhaps the storm that had

battered the Johnston garden had brought it down. Rachel
got out of the truck, stepping carefully through the drying
mud, and made her way around the fallen tree.

The trunk had been cut with a chain saw. Rachel stared
at the neat cut, worry curling in her belly. Beck had done
this. To keep people out? She stared toward the cabin, but
the lush undergrowth and dense mix of firs and alders hid
it from view. People in town called Beck strange. And he
was strange—reclusive and reticent, but harmless. She'd
gotten used to his strangeness—it had become predictable
and normal.

This cut-down tree blocking his driveway was not normal, or predicted. Not at all.

Slowly, Rachel hiked along the weedy edge of the rutted
track. A thread of smoke from a dying fire wafted from the
river-stone chimney at the end of the old log cabin that
Beck called home. The doors to his huge metal-sided shop
were closed and locked. She would have assumed that he
wasn't home, only his battered Chevy truck stood in its
usual spot beneath the ancient apple tree at the edge of the
small clearing. A few of Beck's seemingly numberless
black cats stared at her from various perches in the sun,
their tails unanimously twitching with their disapproval.
Something about the still scene raised the hairs on the back
of her neck. Rachel opened her mouth to call him, then
closed it.

Almost tiptoeing, she started back up the track, then
veered off into the underbrush, intercepting a narrow path
a few yards from the drive. He might be working on his
sculpture, she reasoned. It stood back in the woods—an
enormous chunk of old-growth wood. For as long as she
had known him, he had been slowly carving at it. That
clearing was the place he went to think, while he carved a
few more curls of wood from the sculpture. As far as she
knew, Rachel was the only person he had ever invited to
visit this private sanctuary. Quietly, Rachel followed the
path as it wound between firs and cedars.

The path ended at the sculpture clearing. Beck was there,

seated on a fallen log in front of the tarped sculpture, his back to her. April Gerard sat curled at his feet, her head on his thigh, his arm around her in a posture that was so full of comfort and protection that it stilled Rachel utterly.

He had heard her in spite of her stealth. Head turning, he looked directly at her, as if he had expected her to arrive, no hint of surprise visible on his face. April, following his gaze, gasped and leaped to her feet. "Oh, damn," she said.

"It's all right." Beck stretched out a lanky arm and drew her against him without getting up. "Rachel's all right."

"Nobody's all right, Beck." Hands tucked beneath her armpits, April stared at Rachel defiantly. "Now I've got to go."

"April, what's going on here?" Rachel took a step nearer, watched April tense. Her body language reminded Rachel of one of the feral cats. "What happened?"

"They came to arrest me is what. Somebody murdered Eloise, and they're going to pin it on me, and nobody's going to care, so I'll really go to prison this time." She lifted her chin. "Once you're a loser, they don't let you be anything else. Who cares?"

Beck got slowly to his feet and moved around to stand in front of her, looking down at her, so that she had to meet his eyes. "I care." The soft words carried the still weight of the shadows beneath the firs. April opened her mouth, started to speak, then fell silent. She lowered her head.

"You don't know me," she said softly. "You don't know what I did with my life. You don't know who I was, Beck . . ."

"I killed people." The quiet words seemed to silence even the bird and insect noises in the clearing. "I liked it."

Rachel looked away, an outsider, a voyeur to this intensely private moment. All the local hints and rumors about Beck's past, and his time in the military, suddenly made more sense. A lot of things about Beck came back to her. She looked again, found April with her arms at her side, her face against Beck's chest, her shoulders slumped in an attitude of resignation. Beck's arms were around her, and a fierce light glowed in his pale eyes. "They can't have her," he said softly. "I promised her, okay?"

Rachel swallowed, thinking hard and fast. "I won't tell anyone she's here." The rash promise popped out before she could stop herself, and she stifled a sigh, because it was too late now to take it back. Beck's eyes had acknowledged her promise. "I was going to go see Gladys, my lawyer. Let me talk to her. She'll know how to handle this."

"There's no way to handle this." April raised a defiant face. "I just have to go, that's all."

"No." Beck's arms tightened around her. "Not yet."

Rachel expected April to disagree, but to her surprise, she lowered her head and nodded.

"Go talk to your lawyer." Beck nodded shortly. "Right now."

"I'll come back this evening," Rachel promised. "We'll do something, April. You're not on your own. And you didn't kill Eloise. I know that."

"No." April's eyes pierced her, full of moving shadows. "I didn't kill her. Her son killed her. He wants the land. He hates it that she's giving it away." She snorted. "Like he needs money, with his Jag and his cell phone. He was in town." Her eyes blazed. "He called her. I can always tell when he's on the phone."

"Did you tell that to the police?" Rachel asked.

"Why?" April tossed her head defiantly, but her eyes slid away from Rachel. "They don't listen to people like me."

"Not when you don't tell them anything." Rachel looked at Beck. "I'll go talk to Gladys. I'll be back later, okay?"

"She'll be here," Beck promised softly.

Rachel nodded and made her way back to her truck, her earlier unease flowering fully inside her. That light in Beck's eyes worried her. For the first time she understood Sandy's reservations about Beck.

She was—for the first time—a little afraid of him. Or, rather, of what he might do.

•   •   •

Gladys Killingsworth's receptionist-cum-clerk, Nancy Barringer, looked up with a questioning smile as Rachel entered the tiny office in Blossom's small medical-dental plaza. "You're early," she said, and one of her thick dark eyebrows rose slightly. "Something wrong?"

"I hope not." Rachel glanced restlessly at her watch. "Any chance I could sneak in sooner rather than later?"

"Probably." Nancy glanced at the desk calendar in front of her, frowned, and ran a short-fingered hand through her cropped black hair. "She was working on a couple of projects, but you're the only client before three. Let me check." She got to her feet, adjusted the waistband of her tan chinos, and vanished into the interior office. A moment later she reemerged and nodded briskly. "No problem."

"Thanks, Nancy." Rachel went around her desk and into the small cluttered office, where Gladys was hammering at the keyboard of her computer, at a long teak desk piled with manila folders and paper-clipped letters. Corners of blue, pink, and green Post-it notes stuck out from the layers of paper, and a Barbie doll, incongruously dressed in Native American beads and skins, leaned stiffly against the side of the monitor. Gladys was dressed in her usual combination of pleated khaki pants, a severely cut shirt, and a brocaded vest that was never, as far as Rachel knew, buttoned.

"Looks like an archeological dig, doesn't it?" Gladys Killingsworth turned away from her computer screen and waved cheerfully at her desk. She caught the Barbie doll as it toppled, laughed, and sat it down in an indecent spraddle atop a pile of legal forms. "My niece's American History project. I gather she's a Clatsop maiden. Patricia made the bark cloth herself. Not bad for an eighth-grader. I told her she could build me a birch-bark canoe for next year's project, but she has informed me that Hiawatha-type birch don't grow in the Northwest. But she'll make me a cedar-log dugout if I want." Gladys laughed again and leaned back in her antique wooden office chair. "I may say yes. I bet she'll do it. So what's wrong? Nancy said you were upset."

"It shows, huh?" Rachel sat down in the comfortably

upholstered chair across the desk. "I was going to consult about a client contract and a check, but something else came up." She recounted her visit to Beck and April briefly.

Gladys stared at the acoustic tile in the low ceiling, her hands relaxed on the curved oak arms of the chair, her expression unreadable. When Rachel had finished, she sighed and gave her an ironic glance. "And just how many stray dogs, dumped kittens, and orphaned possums did you drag home to take care of when you were a kid, huh?" She gave Rachel a crooked smile that didn't quite match the thoughtful expression in her eyes. "So you're convinced she didn't kill this woman?"

"I know she didn't." Rachel's lips tightened at Gladys's expression. "I mean it, Gladys. She couldn't."

"You sound like me, before I spent a couple of years as a junior, doing the court-appointed lawyer thing. You shed a lot of youthful idealism that way, girl. Okay." She sat forward, elbows on her cluttered desktop. "I'll skip the lecture. What exactly do you want me to do here?"

"April has been hinting that she's been in trouble with the law before," Rachel went on stubbornly. "I'm afraid she'll just take off and I'm afraid . . ." She hesitated, because it was hard to put that particular fear into words. "You've met Beck, right?"

"Your backwoods-hippie type?" Gladys made a face.

"I . . . I've never seen him act like he cared about anything or anyone except his wood. And maybe his cats." She hesitated, trying to read her lawyer's expression, then went on. "I think . . . he cares about her. A lot. I'm afraid . . . what it'll do to him. If she just takes off. Or if somebody . . . tries to arrest her there." And people would find out that a woman was staying with Beck, she thought. Around Blossom, somebody always noticed something. She had a feeling that it wouldn't take Spiros long to find her.

Gladys was frowning, tapping an unsharpened pencil against her lips. "I don't know much about Beck. I've heard a couple of stories." She pinned Rachel with a hard stare. "Is he going to shoot someone over this? Like you, for example? Or me, or a police officer? Is that what you're so delicately trying to tell me?"

Rachel's lips tried to form the words, "No, of course not." But the sound wouldn't come. "I . . . don't know." She looked away, miserable, knowing she'd just blown it. "I would have said he couldn't yesterday, but now . . . I just . . . don't know."

"Huh. There might be hope for you yet, in spite of the possums." Gladys got to her feet and stretched her sturdy shoulders. "If I'm going to do anything—negotiate with the Portland police or the prosecutor's office—I'd better be her lawyer. Let's go see if I can get hired."

"Really?" Rachel looked up, startled. "You'll do this? Gladys . . . thank you."

"Don't sound so grateful, girl. I haven't done anything yet." She pulled a key from her pocket and unlocked a drawer. "Do I need to bring this?"

Rachel looked over her shoulder at the small solid handgun in the felt-lined drawer. She swallowed. "No," she said, looking at Gladys and realizing that she didn't really know this woman at all. "You don't."

"Okay." Gladys closed the drawer and locked it. "If you're sure. Nancy, I'm going recruiting." She stuck her head through the office door. "I should be back in an hour or two."

"Have fun. Don't forget the Kieser appointment at three." If she was curious, she didn't let it show.

"If I'm not back by then, call the cops," Gladys said cheerfully. She ushered Rachel through the back door of the office and out into the parking lot. "I've got an extra helmet, but it's fine with me if we take your car," she said.

Rachel eyed the lawyer's spotlessly maintained Harley-Davidson motorcycle. "It would be fun," she said, "but I'm not sure it would handle Beck's driveway."

"You might be surprised. I'll take you out for a run some nice afternoon."

People in Blossom had finally gotten used to seeing the

lawyer tooling through town on her motorcycle, dressed in black leather. Sort of.

"So tell me why you were coming to see me before you ran into this stray," Gladys said as they pulled out onto Blossom's main street. "Since I'm billing you for the time anyway," she said sweetly.

"I wanted to know if a handwritten contract I have with a client is legal." Rachel halted briefly at Blossom's single traffic light. "It's on the seat there, in that folder. Eloise is . . . She died." She retraced her route to Beck's place, listening to the rustle of the page as Gladys read it over.

"It's a contract." She finally laid it down. "I don't see why it shouldn't be binding."

"I think the family—a son, anyway—is going to claim that she was senile."

"Doesn't read senile to me, but hey, I'm just a lawyer." She spread her hands, then grabbed for the door handle as they hit the bad stretch of the gravel road. "I think it's a good thing we didn't bring the bike," she remarked, as they turned into Beck's driveway. The tree was still there.

"We'll have to walk," Rachel said. She hesitated as the lawyer climbed out of the truck, unwilling to take anyone to Beck's private clearing. "They're probably at the cabin," she said, hoping so—hoping that April hadn't run, and that Beck hadn't agreed to run with her. As they reached the end of the driveway, she held her breath.

A half dozen black cats sunning themselves on the plank porch of the cabin lifted their heads to glower. The door stood open, and more smoke trickled from the chimney. Rachel let her breath out in a sigh of relief as Beck appeared in the doorway.

"I'd heard about the cats," Gladys said in a low voice. "I hadn't quite believed it."

"This is Gladys." Rachel raised her voice, and one of the cats skittered for the woods. "My lawyer. Where's April?"

Beck said nothing, merely stood aside. April came reluctantly to the door of the cabin. She was wearing the same jeans and T-shirt she'd been wearing earlier, but her hair was loose, and a small white daisy nestled in the thick waves, just above her ear. She was wearing a single carved wooden bead on a fine braided string, Rachel saw as they came closer. One of Beck's carved beads.

"Hi." Gladys offered a hand to April as they reached the top of the three split-log steps that led to the porch. "I'm Gladys Killingsworth. Rachel said you could use a lawyer."

"I don't know." April looked at Gladys's palm. "I think mostly I just need to get out of here." But she looked at Beck, then back at Gladys. "So what can you do for me? I mean, they're going to put me in jail for killing Eloise, and how am I going to pay for a lawyer?" She rubbed her arms as if she was cold and looked away. "I mean . . . my only decent job just sort of ended. You don't pay a lawyer flipping burgers."

"You got a dollar?" Gladys had withdrawn her hand without a quiver. "You give it to me, and you've hired me. That's my retainer. We'll talk about money later, but for right now, it means we've got a lawyer-client relationship established," she said briskly. "So I can go talk to the police on your behalf."

"No." April's head jerked up. "No way I turn myself in."

"Do you know for sure that they actually have a warrant?" Hands in her pockets, Gladys leaned against the peeled tree trunk that supported the porch roof. "Or did you just panic and run? Of course, if they were coming to question you, and you took off, they might have talked a judge into a warrant by now. Running makes the best of folk doubt your innocence."

"I . . ." April licked her lips, her eyes on the warped planks of the porch. "I know how they work. I've got a record. I was into drugs when I was young and stupid. Got busted for that, for shoplifting . . . for all the . . . all the things you do to get money for drugs." Her eyes went swiftly to Beck, then shied away. "Once they know you, once they've got you tagged as a loser, they look for you when they need someone. For anything."

"So, are you a loser?" Gladys smiled benignly at the

young woman. "Are you?" she repeated when April didn't speak. "Better make up your mind, girl. It's your choice."

"Is it?" Hot anger leaped in April's eyes. "That's so easy for you to say. You sound like the counselors they sent me to. Lecturing me on my self-esteem all the time."

"I don't give a damn about your self-esteem," Gladys said pleasantly. "But if you don't want to do the run, hide, and get caught loser thing, then you need to hand me a buck, and I need to start making phone calls and find out what's really going on. You should hurry up and decide because Rachel is paying for this time." She glanced at her watch. "Speaking of time, we'd better start back," she said to Rachel. "I've got that appointment Nancy so carefully reminded me of. Good luck to you both." With a nod to April, Gladys turned on her heel and started down the porch steps.

Rachel looked from the glowering April to silent Beck, who was carefully cleaning dirt from his nails with a small pocketknife. She shrugged, suppressing a sigh, turned, and hurried after Gladys. "I'm sorry I brought you all the way out here," she said as she caught up with the older woman. "She's so stubborn."

"Hush, girl." Gladys neither looked at her nor slowed as she followed the dirt track back to the parked truck. "You're premature."

"Wait!" The breathless syllable stopped them as they were clambering over the felled tree. Without any apparent surprise, Gladys sat down on the smooth bark, her hands folded in her lap. April ran up, her worn Nikes spattering mud that spotted the hem of her jeans.

"All right, all right, I need a lawyer, okay?" she panted. "Only I can't pay you, and I don't know when I'll be able to pay you, just so you know. Here." Her hand jerked as she shoved a crumpled five at Gladys. "You're hired, okay?"

"Yes, I am, thank you." Gladys took the bill and tucked it into the pocket of her tailored pants. She pulled out a small notebook, hand-wrote a receipt for the money, signed it, and handed it over. "So now you can talk to me. I hear a woman died, might have been murdered. Rachel says you didn't do it."

"No. Why should I? She paid me—a whole lot better than anyone else is going to do. I didn't have any reason to kill her."

"You could have been stealing from her. Embezzling. She was about to fire you, and you lost your temper." Dryly Gladys ticked the reasons off on her fingers. "You discovered that she left money to you . . ."

"She didn't!"

"She found you using drugs and was going to call your parole officer."

"What are you saying?" Ashen-faced, April clenched her fists. "Give me my five back."

"You said you had no reason to kill this woman." Gladys gave her a gentle smile. "I'm offering you the possible motives that will most certainly occur to both the police and the prosecutor's office."

"But I . . . I . . ." April swallowed and looked away, hands twisting the front of her T-shirt into a strangled wad. "I loved her. Oh, God, no." She covered her mouth with her hand. "I mean, she was nice to me. For no reason. Just because she . . . liked me."

"I'm going to have a talk with the people handling the investigation," Gladys said briskly. "They're going to want you to turn yourself in if there is a warrant out for your arrest."

"No!"

"I'll do the best dealing I can." Gladys put a hand on her arm. "You ran, girl. There's a price for that. The only way to fix it is to tough it out."

Face tight, April turned her back on them.

"Are you going to take off?" Gladys slid to her feet, brushing bits of bark from the back of her slacks. "I hate to look stupid when I deal with Portland's Finest."

"No." April's voice was low and harsh, barely audible. "I promised Beck."

"Good." Gladys nodded briskly. "I'll do my best." She glanced back toward the clearing. "No phone, right?" Sighed at April's silent nod. "I figured. Oh, well." She turned to Rachel. "I'll just send you over here with messages. You've got nothing better to do, right?"

"Yes, ma'am," Rachel said meekly, which earned her a narrow stare.

As Rachel backed the truck slowly out the driveway, Gladys picked up the handwritten contract from the front seat. "Eloise Johnston," she said, enunciating the syllables precisely. "Any relation to the Eloise that this girl is suspected of killing?"

"Yes." Rachel kept her eyes resolutely on the mirror as she backed out onto the gravel county road. She still caught Gladys's rolled eyes and headshake.

"Got yourself into this one up to your neck, didn't you?" She let out an exasperated breath. "I hope I'm not going to have to make bail on you."

"I think my mom would do that," Rachel said in a very quiet voice.

"Probably," Gladys said, and began to laugh. "Oh, kid, you bring home the best strays," she said as they drove back into town. "The very best."

CHAPTER

7

Rachel let Gladys off at her office. "Do you think she's going to do what I tell her to?" the lawyer asked her. "If you're both giving me a straight story—and I wonder about you"—she gave Rachel a severe look—"then I will bet my weekend that there's a warrant out for her. I can bargain, but she'll need to turn herself in. Will she run?"

"I don't know," Rachel said slowly. "I really don't know her at all."

"I think I'm going to take my bike out there after I wrap up today. We need to spend a little more time talking about options. That is, after I've found out if the police really have a warrant out for her, or if she's just being hysterical. If worse comes to worst, a couple of good criminal lawyers owe me favors."

"I thought you were a criminal lawyer once," Rachel said.

"Once." Gladys gave her a lopsided smile. "If you don't keep in practice, it shows."

"Keep me posted."

"Oh, honey, I intend to." Gladys laughed and let herself in through the back door.

Rachel sat behind the wheel for a few moments, debating whether or not to drive back out to Beck's and talk to April some more herself. But she had a feeling that Beck made the better persuader and that she could do more harm than good by meddling. Besides, it was midafternoon, and Sandy's fancy buffet reception for Representative Claymore was in a few hours. So she drove on over to the Bread Box to see if Joylinn needed any help.

"I'm doing okay, girl, I've got it mostly under control," Joylinn called from the kitchen, where she was arranging a tray of canapes. Celia was dealing with the sparse afternoon crowd out front. "This is the last of them—cherry tomatoes filled with salmon mousse and a sprig of fresh dill. Very Northwest, don't you think? We won't tell your uncle that the tomatoes come from Mexico this time of year, okay?"

"As long as they aren't apples or pears, he won't care." Rachel picked up a colander full of washed and halved tomatoes and set it down on the work counter next to Joylinn's elbow. "Want some help?"

"Sure." Joylinn piped another pink rosette of the salmon mousse into a tiny tomato half and placed it carefully on the tray. "You could stick a bit of dill into each of those if you don't mind. Not too much. You know, this whole visit by Mr. Claymore is kind of odd."

"How so?" Rachel washed her hands, scooped a handful of fresh dill from a plastic salad spinner, and began to separate the finely cut sprigs. "Although, yeah, I would have thought he'd do the public-meeting thing in Hood River."

"I'm glad he didn't." Joylinn grinned and scooped more salmon into her pastry bag. "I've already hired a couple of extra people for the day. But, yeah, it is kind of strange that he came here. It's an off year. The legislature is out of session. He's not up for reelection. What's his game? Maybe he's laying the groundwork for a Senate bid. Although Hood River is just about as grass roots as we are, and they have bigger facilities."

"Maybe it's because he lived here." Rachel bit her lip as she tried to tuck the slippery dill sprigs artistically into the pink swirls of chilled mousse. "I didn't know he knew Sandy's dad."

"Me neither. Sandy said her dad used to take him fishing, back when he was living with the Johnstons."

"What?" Rachel paused, bits of dill in each hand. "What about the Johnstons?"

"He lived with them. I didn't know that either until Sandy told me. I guess it was in those memoirs she was working on. Was news to me." She shrugged. "But he was a lot older than us. It wasn't like I knew him or anything. Sandy told me he moved in with them after his parents died in a car accident. I guess it was just for a year or two, and then he went off to college." Joylinn finished the tray and deposited it in one of the big steel-fronted refrigerators that lined the wall of the kitchen. "It's kind of neat that he kept the family orchard, even if he doesn't live there. I guess it's the main reason I vote for him, to be honest. Here, I'll take that." She whisked the salad spinner with its remnants of dill into the big steel pot sink at the far side of the room. "So what are you going to wear?" She winked as she ran steaming water into the sink. "Something to impress Jeff?"

"Oh, Lord, that's right!" Rachel clapped a hand to her forehead. "I'm supposed to be his date! I wonder if he knows that . . ."

"I don't think he's got other plans," Joylinn drawled. "So you haven't bought anything new for this gala event? Girl, where are your mercenary instincts?" She planted dripping fists on her aproned hips. "I mean, this man hobnobs with all the money in this part of the state."

"All the Republican money," Rachel murmured.

"And here's your chance to put a pretty face on Rain Country Landscaping for him to mention when cocktail-party chat shifts around to those yard and garden woes . . ."

"Aw, come on. A politician's gonna advise somebody on landscaping?"

"No, dear, but he's going to enthuse about this lovely and talented woman who has her own business and does such a great job, he hears . . ." Joylinn winked at her and dried her hands on her stained denim apron. "Just go be your charming self in his immediate vicinity. And be sure to talk about how his legislation has helped you, the small-business owner."

"God, I don't know if his legislation has helped me at all." Rachel rolled her eyes.

"So fake it." Joylinn laughed. "You did that kind of thing just fine on those godawful world history essay tests Mr. Wright used to give us."

"Well, that was different . . ." Rachel wrinkled her nose, regretting in spite of herself that she hadn't done a little shopping. It had been a long time since she had bought a new dress . . .

"Here. I brought this in to loan you. I knew you'd be too busy to get anything." Grinning, Joylinn grabbed her arm and hauled her across the kitchen to her cluttered office. She rummaged briefly in a small closet while Rachel studied the piles of invoices and *Gourmet* magazines littering the small desk.

"It'll look stunning with that long flowered dress you wore when we went to that Orchard Association tea over at the Grange Hall." Joylinn emerged with a long pale blue jacket draped in a cleaner's bag. "It's raw silk and elegant, and I know it matches your dress because I was wearing it that day, if you remember. Just be sure to wear heels and stick something glittery in that mop you neglect, okay?" She tugged at Rachel's short, dense curls. "Like this." She offered her a small white paper bag. "I was in Portland last week and I thought of you when I saw this."

"Oh, my gosh." Rachel extracted the beaded hair clip from the folded tissue inside the bag. A butterfly crafted of delicately woven glass beads and wire glittered on her palm, its blue-and-silver wings unfurled, its antennae made of tiny jet beads. "It's lovely!"

"You spend too much time in blue jeans." Joylinn hugged her. "Now beat it, so I can get this stuff over to Herbert's house before the unfashionable early birds start showing up. You do not get to help!" She made shooing motions as she chased the laughing Rachel out of the kitchen. "And you'd better pitch your business, girl, or I just might take that clip back!"

"Don't worry," Rachel called, earning a couple of bemused looks from afternoon loiterers. "I will."

She hurried back to her apartment, smiling, looking forward to the evening. And promising herself that she would do as Joylinn asked and be sure to mention her business to the esteemed member of the Oregon State House of Representatives, Paul Claymore. Promoting her business was not her long suit, she was the first to admit.

The answering machine was blinking when she got back to her apartment. Along with one or two minor business calls, Jeff had indeed left a message proposing to pick her up at six. She glanced at the clock as she left him an answering message and Peter prowled the kitchen hungrily. Plenty of time. She fed the cat, took a shower, then spent a leisurely hour dressing, playing with makeup, and deciding which scarf or necklace would best suit Joylinn's lovely silk jacket.

Well . . . more than an hour. A familiar knock on the door startled her as she held a fine chain studded with freshwater pearls to her throat. Not enough to match the glistening butterfly in her hair. She dropped it into its box and hurried to the door.

"I wondered if you'd remembered." Jeff smiled at her. "I thought you might be knee-deep in someone's yard."

"Not a chance. And I'm all ready." She really didn't have any jewelry to complement the butterfly anyway. "Shall we?"

"I'll bring her back. I promise," Jeff announced solemnly to Peter. The cat leaped to the back of the sofa, gave them both a brief, severe stare, and began to wash himself vigorously. "I guess that's permission," Jeff said with a wink.

"I hope so."

"Have you decided about continuing with the Johnston property?" Jeff asked as they made the brief drive out to Herbert Southern's house on the outskirts of town.

"Oh, I'm not going to change my mind." Unless the heirs managed to permanently block the check Eloise had given her. She ignored Jeff's resigned sigh.

The circular driveway in front of Herbert Southern's small house was clogged with cars—pickups rubbing bumpers with Mercedes and BMWs. Joylinn's new white van was just visible, parked on the grass at the rear of the house, its doors open. "They should have rented the school gym for this," Rachel said, as Jeff maneuvered the Jeep into a narrow space at the end of the driveway. "Maybe the Taxi Sisters could have run a shuttle service."

Guests overflowed the house, crowding the porch, where smokers produced a drift of pale smoke that scented the fading day with tobacco. Rachel and Jeff made their way up the stairs, greeting the people they knew. Her aunt and uncle were there. Rachel waved to them where they stood in one corner of the porch, her uncle in animated conversation with another orchard owner. The crowd was an interesting mix of local people whom she knew at least by sight and well-dressed strangers whom she didn't know at all. Sandy greeted them at the door, flushed and beaming, her eyes sparkling with excitement. "I'm so glad you could make it." She ushered them into the house.

A big dining and living room backed by a spacious kitchen, formed the front of the older house. Coats had been piled on the beds in two bedrooms, and the furniture in the front rooms had been rearranged or removed to yield maximum space. A portable bar occupied the wall space next to the fireplace, where a black-coated young man with a blond ponytail and a smooth professional smile filled glasses from the array of bottles on the small bar top. Yellow rosebuds gleamed in small vases on the mantel and end tables, and a larger arrangement of roses and daisies occupied the center of the dining table, which now served as the buffet. Candles flickered above platters of Joylinn's tomatoes, small sandwiches, and cream-cheese-filled endive leaves topped with caviar. Baskets of breadsticks flanked the platters of food, and dishes of nuts occupied convenient tabletops and bookshelves.

"Sandy, this looks so lovely." Rachel waved at the animated guests. "You did a great job."

"It *is* nice, isn't it?" Sandy beamed. "Dad's pleased. This way." She tugged Rachel determinedly across the room. "Let me introduce you. Paul is such a nice man. He's so interesting!"

Rachel and Jeff managed to follow her darting form through the throng, greeting people as they went. Herbert Southern and Representative Claymore occupied a space at the end of the buffet table, beneath the arch that opened into the hallway that led to bedrooms and bathroom. The crowd around him was thick, but Sandy parted the human sea effortlessly.

"Well, hello. Howdy. Haven't seen you for a while." A glass of bourbon in his hand, Herbert Southern greeted Jeff and Rachel enthusiastically. If his greeting was perhaps a bit too enthusiastic, he wasn't to blame. He had become more than a little involved with a woman who had turned out to be a murderess, and the echo of that episode would probably haunt him for his lifetime in Blossom. "I'd like you to meet our esteemed representative and a defender of agriculture in Salem." He waved a hand at the tall man standing beside him. "Paul Claymore, this is Rachel O'Connor, whose family has one of the best pear orchards in the area. And Jeff Price is our young and very capable chief of police."

"Glad to meet you." Claymore greeted them both, but his eyes lingered on Rachel. "Your friend Sandy sang your praises," he said with a smile. "Congratulations on your landscaping business."

"Thank you." Rachel smiled, a faint blush rising at his intent stare. "Everyone is looking forward to your conference."

"This is a hard time for the working farmer." Claymore's dark eyes flashed but didn't leave her face. "We need to pull together, before we're run completely out of business by environmentalists and urban dwellers who take their food way too much for granted." There was a fervor in his voice and a resonance to his words that elicited scattered applause from the surrounding guests. "They go to the store to buy their apples and bread, and they don't have a clue about what it takes to get that food onto the shelves."

"You bet!" Herbert clapped. So did a number of other guests. Claymore smiled and lifted a hand. "But let's save the politics for tomorrow. This is a party. And a lovely one, Sandy." He turned his attention to her. "I should hire you to run this kind of thing for me in Salem."

"I just might go into business!" She dimpled and turned to Rachel and Jeff. "The bar is there. And we've got juice, too, as well as pop." She leaned close to Rachel. "Paul certainly likes you."

"Paul is married," Rachel whispered back.

"Oh, I know." Sandy made a face. "But isn't it kind of flattering? If you need anything, let me know." Fluttering her fingers in a brief wave, she hurried off to greet more guests.

"She's having fun." Jeff looked after her and laughed. "This is too crowded for me. And did you notice that our mayor doesn't seem to be present?"

"I wondered." Rachel looked around, but sure enough, there was no sign of Phil Ventura. He criticized what he referred to as "Paul Claymore's tunnel vision" openly, which earned him few popularity points with orchardists like Rachel's uncle. "I'm sure they invited him."

"Oh, they did." Jeff's lips twitched. "He told me he thought he'd have urgent business out of town this evening. Just a premonition, you know. What would you like?" he asked, as they reached the busy bar.

"Red wine, please. I think our mayor is finally learning to keep his feet out of his mouth." Rachel smiled. "If he keeps that up, he might actually get reelected next term."

"Maybe." Jeff handed Rachel a glass of Pinot Noir and accepted a bottle of Hood River's ale for himself. "Let's try for the outside and some fresh air." He stiffened suddenly, the bottle of beer halted on its way to his lips. "Well, I'll be . . ."

Rachel turned to find a tall, familiar figure making his way through the throng. "Lieutenant Spiros." Her eyebrows rose. "You're the last person I expected to meet here. Jeff, this is . . ."

"We've met." Jeff's tone was odd, and he offered his hand, his expression wary. "How are you doing, Carey?"

"Is this your turf?" Spiros looked around, his expression enigmatic. "I heard you took off for some hick town. Too bad."

"I like it." A smile lifted the corner of Jeff's mouth, and he relaxed a bit. "Calling Blossom a hick town is not going to win you many friends around here. Not that it would bother you much, I guess. So how's Portland? Quiet after LA?"

"Not as quiet as this place, I bet." Spiros laughed a low, deep chuckle. "You get bored, you give me a call."

"Not likely," Jeff drawled. "I had my fill of city life." In spite of his smile, his expression was thoughtful.

"Rachel." Sandy's excited whisper in her ear failed to jolt Rachel from her fascinated observation of this exchange between the Portland Homicide lieutenant and Jeff, who had originally begun his career with the police down in Los Angeles. Those years were pretty much a mystery, even now. Whatever had happened there, it had not been something he was willing to share much about.

"Rachel! Will you come on! Representative Claymore wants to talk to you about a job!" Sandy's fingers pinched her elbow as she dragged her friend bodily away from the two men.

"All right, I'm coming." Making a show of rubbing her arm, Rachel followed Sandy through the crowd, toward the back of the house. "For heaven's sake, girl, he's not going anywhere."

"He wants to landscape the family home! He's moving back here for his new baby. I told him you were the best!" Sandy rolled her eyes and expelled her breath in a rush of exasperation. "Honestly. Will you at least look excited? This is a *huge* opportunity for you. Think of the publicity! Do you want to get ahead or not? Sometimes I feel as if I have to take you by the hand . . ."

Smiling at her friend's mother-hen clucking, Rachel let herself be propelled over to the patio doors that opened onto a small concrete patio at the side of the house. Claymore was holding court outside, leaning easily against a trellis covered with wisteria, used to shade the small space from afternoon sun. Drink in hand, he was laughing at some joke or other with several of the orchardists, including her uncle Jack.

"There she is." Her uncle Jack waved her out onto the patio to join them. "She doesn't think much of pears, but she plants a fine flower garden." He waved his second bourbon at her, his square face flushed and shining with a fine dew of sweat in the warm evening. "Paul here wants to fix up his place, gal. What do you think?"

"I've been hearing from a lot of people that you're quite a landscaper." Claymore smiled down at her, his blue eyes bright with laughter. "Dare I say that I was contemplating hiring a Portland firm? I admit that I didn't realize we had such local talent!"

"I . . . I'm flattered." Rachel smiled. "What exactly are you looking for?"

"I'm moving back into the family house. It'll be a summer and weekend retreat mostly. But I plan to do a lot of entertaining here." He gave her a shrewd look. "I want to update the landscaping—give it a modern, Northwest look, with space for outdoor entertaining, of course. I want garden rooms, a covered patio, all that stuff. And I expect you can take care of the maintenance, too?"

"I have an assistant who just started his own maintenance business," Rachel said. She wasn't sure if she'd ever been out at the Claymore place, but it would be a good job, publicity-wise, certainly. "I'd be glad to come and take a look at the property. You can tell me what you want, and I'll draw up a design and estimate for you."

"Great." He beamed at her. "How about tomorrow morning? Say, ten?"

"I'd be glad to come by."

"Good. I'll see you then. It's out Springwater Road. Look for the big brick pillars on the left." He turned abruptly away to greet a man in expensive clothes who had just stepped out onto the patio. Feeling a bit dizzy, Rachel made her way back inside.

"Did I overhear Claymore offering you a job?" Jeff joined her just inside the door. "Not a bad evening's work." He grinned and lifted his dewed bottle in a salute. "To prosperity."

"I haven't even looked at the place yet." She made a face and laughed. "He'll probably turn out to be another client who wants a ten-foot-deep koi pond and fountain in the middle of a basalt shelf." But she touched the rim of her wineglass to his beer bottle. "To prosperity," she echoed. "Maybe Uncle Jack will finally admit that landscaping is a real job, like orcharding."

"You know that's never going to happen." In spite of his light tone, Jeff's eyes were sympathetic. "So Carey is handling the Johnston murder," he said thoughtfully. "He's good."

"So it *was* murder?" Lowering her voice, Rachel stepped closer, glancing automatically around for Sandy. But her friend was happily chatting with a small knot of guests near the now-busy buffet table. "What happened?" she whispered.

"Apparently she was poisoned." Jeff touched her elbow, steering her over to an empty corner. "She was taking a digoxin compound for her heart, and somebody apparently gave her an overdose. They probably thought it would look like a heart attack. The forensic report came back this afternoon." He regarded her with a dark expression. "Rachel, this is now a murder. Somebody had reason to kill this old woman, and you don't know what that reason was."

"It didn't have anything to do with me . . ."

"You don't know what it had to do with. I don't want

you to go out there. Don't bristle at me." He matched her glare. "Is the job worth dying for?"

"I'm not going to . . ." She swallowed, counting to ten, struggling as the Irish temper she'd inherited from her father threatened to get the better of her again. "I can't do much of anything anyway," she said in her most reasonable tone, "until the money issue gets straightened out."

"Good." But Jeff's eyes still brooded.

"So how did you know Spiros?" Rachel raised an eyebrow at him, figuring that this was a good time to change the subject. "From Los Angeles, I gather."

"Yes." Jeff took a swallow of his beer. "He left the force about the same time I did. A little later."

"Is that so?" Rachel eyed him for a moment. "You ever going to tell me about that time?"

"Yes." He held her eyes for a moment. "Sometime."

"Okay." She touched his arm lightly. "I guess I'll take that." She turned away as a lanky woman in a flowered dress approached. She was the wife of one of her uncle's friends—another fruit grower. Rachel greeted her, introduced her to Jeff, then was distracted by Sandy, who wanted to introduce her to someone from Portland. She and Jeff drifted apart and back together later at the food.

"Ready to go?" Rachel mouthed as she picked up one of the tomatoes she'd helped Joylinn fill.

Jeff nodded, rolled his eyes, then shot Sandy a look so theatrically guilty that Rachel had to stifle a giggle with the last swallow of her wine. He was not the cocktail-party type, she thought, as they made their farewells to Sandy and her father—who had spent the entire evening talking animatedly with Claymore whenever possible, waxing enthusiastic and insistent on a host of agricultural and political topics. The representative had a somewhat resigned expression on his face, but brightened as Rachel and Jeff approached.

"I'm sorry I didn't get more time to talk with you." He shook Jeff's hand. "I wanted to become a police officer when I was in college." He gave Jeff a warm smile, then turned it on Rachel. "Tomorrow, remember. I'm looking forward to hearing your ideas for the old place. It's pretty much a typical farmhouse yard right now."

"I'll do my best." Rachel smiled and withdrew, a little uncomfortable in the face of another of his intense, almost intimate stares.

Farewells finally made, they escaped into the cool evening. "Whew," Jeff said, shaking his head. "I could never be a politician. I'd blow it at the parties."

"You seemed quite elegant to me." Rachel smiled.

"Elegant?" Jeff snorted. "Try stiff with boredom."

"Jeff, tell me about Eloise." Rachel turned sideways on the car seat, tapping her chin restlessly with one finger. "I still can't believe that somebody poisoned her. I mean . . . nobody was there, except April and . . ." She shook her head. "April didn't do it. I'm sure of it. As sure as I've ever been about anything!"

"Spiros told me they have a pretty good chunk of circumstantial evidence against her. I guess the forensic people found evidence of digitalis and herbal tea in her stomach. And they found dried foxglove on the shelf with the herbal teas in the kitchen—way in the back."

"Why should she have left it there?" Rachel shook her head. "If she did this—gave Eloise the poison—wouldn't she have thrown away the evidence? No." She crossed her arms. "That girl isn't pretending. She cared about Eloise. She didn't do this."

"Spiros asked me if I'd seen her." Jeff gave her a narrow look. "He seemed to think she might have some connection to your crazy carpenter."

"Beck?" Rachel laughed weakly. "Why would he think that?"

"Rachel, you're not a very good liar." Jeff took her hand, his eyes on her face. "You can't hide someone suspected of murder."

"I . . . I'm not." She swallowed. "Jeff—don't take Spiros out to Beck's house. He . . . I think he's harmless, but he could feel. . . . attacked."

"She's there." Jeff wasn't asking.

"I took my lawyer out to talk to her. She's going to convince April to turn herself in."

"Rachel, I can't stand back and pretend you didn't tell me this." He let go of her hand and leaned back in his seat, his eyes closed. "Spiros is on his way out to see Beck right now."

"Oh, no." Rachel buried her face in her hands, thinking fast. "Let me call Gladys. Can you get hold of him? Ask him to wait?"

"I can ask him." Jeff slipped his cell phone from its belt clip. He got out of the car and leaned on the roof, talking briefly and tersely. After a moment, he slid back behind the wheel. "I got to him in time. He'll give us fifteen minutes." He handed Rachel the phone. "Call your lawyer."

Gladys answered on the second ring. "I'm on my way," she told Rachel, when Rachel explained. "Don't do anything without me." She hung up.

Rachel turned off the cell phone. "Let's go," she said, and handed him the phone.

CHAPTER

8

The moon was too low in the sky to be visible, but the summer stars glittered overhead as Rachel and Jeff pulled up alongside a plain white car parked beside the county road where the gravel secondary road that led to Beck's house turned off. Jeff rolled down the window and spoke briefly to Spiros before pulling the Jeep around the parked car and proceeding slowly down the rutted gravel road. Spiros pulled in behind them, following at a respectable distance.

"He used to be a cop out here," Jeff remarked as he searched the wall of hawthorn and Indian plum for Beck's driveway. "Twenty-odd years ago. Before he moved on to the LAPD."

"You're kidding. He never said anything about that. Small world, huh? There's the driveway." She pointed as they reached the narrow mouth of Beck's lane. "I wonder if he knew Eloise back then?"

"It is indeed a small world, isn't it?" Jeff sounded grim as he eased the car down the track, riding the ridges between the deep ruts. "I gather that he got to know Eloise very well. He investigated her daughter's death."

"The tree's gone." Rachel blinked as the headlight beam flooded the narrow track, glinting from the cabin windows in the distant clearing. "He felled a tree to block the road earlier. I guess it was to keep people from coming down and finding April."

"I don't like it that it's gone," Jeff said tightly. "Why move it, unless you plan to leave?"

"April told Gladys that she wouldn't run. Oh, no," Rachel whispered as they reached the end of the lane and entered the clearing.

"What is it?" Jeff tensed.

"Beck's truck. It's always here. It's gone."

"Damn. Stay here." Jeff got out, leaving the headlights on, flooding the shop and cabin with light. "Beck? You there?" he yelled. "It's me. Jeff Price."

Not a single cat showed so much as a whisker. Her heart sinking, Rachel opened the car door. She yelped as a dark figure appeared from nowhere to shove it closed against her.

"Stay in the car." Spiros's voice was cold. "Don't get out." He moved sideways and disappeared into the darkness utterly, as if he'd evaporated. He had a gun in his hand.

"You don't need that," she said, but he was gone. If Beck was here after all . . . She flung the door open and got out, walked quickly across the harshly lighted space to where Jeff stood on the porch, to the left of the door. He held out a hand to stop her, his expression angry.

"Beck, it's me. Rachel," she called. "Jeff and I need to talk to you. It's important." She stepped forward quickly and knocked on the door. "Please come out and . . ." She gasped as Jeff's hand closed like a vise on her arm. He yanked her sideways so hard that she stumbled, then flung her behind him with a wrench that twisted her shoulder.

"Beck? Are you there?" He approached the door from the side and pushed on it lightly. It swung open with a creak of rusty hinges.

"You're careless, and she's worse. He could have shot you from an armchair just now. As for you . . ." Spiros gave

Rachel a cold stare. "If you were my girlfriend, I'd be tempted to slap some common sense into your head."

"She's not your girlfriend," Jeff said very softly. He turned to Rachel. "You should have stayed in the car." His voice was very very gentle. "Don't ever do that again. They're gone." He spoke to Spiros now. "They've been gone a long time." A muttering grumble made Spiros tense and face the drive.

"Gladys." Rachel rubbed her arm, feeling chastised. "That's her bike, I bet."

"The girl's lawyer," Jeff said.

Spiros muttered a curse in a language Rachel didn't recognize, and gently closed the cabin door. A moment later, the big Harley rolled into the clearing. "A lawyer rides that?" he asked in disbelief.

"I told you guys to wait for me." Gladys ripped off her black helmet and threw it on the ground. "I sure hope you cowboys went by the book."

"She's gone." Jeff spoke up. "They're both gone."

Sitting on the bike, Gladys swore, using very unladylike words, pounding one gloved fist against the Harley's gas tank.

"They were gone long before we got here," Jeff said.

"You keep saying that." Spiros sounded pained. "Since you trusted it enough to walk right up and play target, I'd like to know how you knew. ESP? The trees told you?"

"No smoke," Jeff said. "Damp and still as it is tonight, you'd smell it. The stove," he amplified for the perplexed Spiros. "He heats the cabin with wood unless it's ninety degrees out. Takes hours for a fire in a good woodstove to go out."

"I sure hope you're right. I'd hate to think they took off after you told me to wait," Spiros growled.

Jeff looked at him without speaking.

"Yeah. Shit, what am I saying?" Spiros turned away, his tone embarrassed. "Sorry, I was out of line. Not enough sleep." He started as an owl hooted loudly.

"Great horned owl," Jeff said. "They don't bite people."

"You really do belong out here, don't you? Woodstoves, owls . . ." Spiros hunched his shoulders. "Guess I can stop feeling sorry for you. But I always figured you were nuts." He laughed, as if he'd said something funny. "Well, lawyer-biker-lady, your client has beat it." He turned to Gladys as she climbed the steps. "I'd sure like to have 'em come back in on their own. Save us some time and sweat."

"I'd like that, too, dearie." You could almost hear the grinding tooth enamel. "I'm doing my best to believe that you didn't scare 'em off."

"I'm trying to believe the same thing of you," Spiros muttered under his breath. "Keep in touch, okay? I want her." He punched Jeff on the arm with a bit more force than necessary and headed for his car, ignoring Gladys. He had bowed legs, Rachel noticed. She didn't think he had gotten them from riding a horse.

"What's going on here?" Gladys took Rachel by her bruised arm. Not gently. "I told you to let me handle this."

"I think they decided to handle it themselves, Ms. Killingsworth." Jeff stepped closer. "It's not Rachel's fault."

"Down, boy." Gladys raked him up and down with a sharp stare. "Unless one of you knows something new, *I* sure don't know where they went." She looked from one to the other and growled deep in her throat. "Stupid kids."

"Beck's no kid," Jeff said mildly.

"Birthdays don't count, honey." Gladys turned her back on them and marched back to her Harley. "You hear anything, girl, you call me right away!" Swinging astride the bike, she kicked it to life and roared back up the driveway.

"That is some bike she rides." Jeff stared thoughtfully after her. "It suits her."

Rachel looked at him sideways, thinking that this wasn't precisely a compliment. "She's a good lawyer," she said after a moment.

"Very likely," he said dryly. "Any guesses as to where they might be?"

"No," Rachel said, and shivered. The lack of the usual

cats gave the place an abandoned air, as if nobody had lived there for decades, rather than hours.

"I called for a warrant." Spiros emerged from the darkness again. "We'll have it in a couple of minutes."

They waited. No one said anything. The owl called again, and small things rustled in the weeds. Rachel wondered where the cats were. She jumped when Spiros's cell phone rang. He had his warrant.

"Let's take a look," he said to Jeff. The gun was in his hand again. Jeff looked at it, then turned on his heel without saying anything and walked over to the cabin again. Climbing onto the rough planks of the porch, he pushed the door all the way open. It bumped against the wall, the hinges protesting. Spiros came behind him, standing off to the side as Jeff pulled a flash light from his pocket and clicked it on. As the light probed the darkness, framing Jeff in the doorway, Spiros hissed again under his breath.

Nobody fired a shot. No sound came from the cabin. "Looks empty," Jeff said.

Spiros grunted and followed him in, but didn't holster his gun. Rachel rubbed her arm once more and climbed the steps. The yellow flashlight beam revealed a neat, uncluttered space. The bed was made, and dishes had been washed and stacked beside the chipped porcelain sink set into the wood-plank counter along the far wall. An elderly, round-shouldered refrigerator hummed to itself. There was no range—merely the woodstove at the far end of the room, a tidy box of kindling and firewood beside it. An armchair covered with worn and faded red brocade faced the stove, along with a straight chair with carved arms. Beck had made the chair. She recognized his work in the silken finish of the honey-colored wood. A mayonnaise jar of spring wildflowers—Dutchman's-breeches, buttercups, and wild columbine, stood on the small wooden table—another Beck piece—that occupied the space in front of the window. Everywhere, strings of carved wooden beads hung from pegs driven into the walls. Not nails, Rachel noticed. Wooden pegs.

"The dude was really into beads," Spiros muttered.

"That was his accounting system." Rachel smiled at Spiros's skeptical glower.

Jeff ignored them both, examining the small space without speaking, stopping in front of the single wooden dresser that stood beside the door to the tiny added-on bathroom. Spiros looked over his shoulder as he pulled drawers open and closed them without disturbing anything. In the bathroom, he opened the medicine cabinet. Eerie images slid across the mirrored face as he closed the cabinet again. The metal shower stall contained only a bar of soap and a single bottle of cheap shampoo. There was no toilet. Two towels hung over the shower curtain rod. Jeff touched the towels. "Dry," he said tersely.

"I don't see a single damn light switch," Spiros growled.

"There's a lantern on the table," Jeff said. "He doesn't have electricity in here."

"So how come he's got a fridge?" Spiros used a butane lighter to light the lantern.

"Propane." Copper coils in the back of the woodstove heated water for dishes and washing. An outhouse stood behind the cabin. Rachel followed Jeff back out onto the porch. The cabin might be a monk's cell, she thought, except for the flowers and the beautiful furniture. They went around behind the building. The outhouse contained nothing either—just a roll of toilet paper hung from a nail on a bent coat hanger, and a month-old magazine that featured woodworking techniques.

"Nothing," Spiros said in disgust.

"We might as well go." Jeff sighed.

Spiros stalked silently ahead of them. The clearing beyond the small dance of the flashlight beams seemed very dark. Shadows lurked among crowding bushes like Beck's black cats, and it was cold. Rachel began to shiver. She looked back at the cabin one last time. A shape of lesser darkness in blackness, it had the sagging mournful air of an old ruin, long abandoned. She climbed into the front seat of Jeff's car and wrapped her arms around herself, shivering in earnest now. Jeff turned the heater on as they drove back out the driveway. Rachel looked back once to search for the emerald glint of feline eyes. She saw none.

Jeff was quiet on the drive back to town. He didn't turn off toward her house, but instead continued on up along the side of the Gorge, winding high above the spangled cluster of lights that was Blossom. He turned off onto the short graveled drive that led to the house he'd bought—the same house they'd dared each other to enter as kids, because back then it was empty and boarded up—the Haunted House. When they had finally taunted each other through the loose boards on the back window one sunny afternoon, they had found no ghosts, only the leavings of squirrels and racoons, and pellets of mouse fur and tiny bones beneath an owl's daytime perch in the rafters.

Sometimes she could superimpose that dusty twilight memory on the gleaming white walls and carpeted floors of Jeff's rejuvenation of the old house. Time was such an odd thing. At times you could fold it like a piece of cloth, so that yesterday overlay today. Other times a single yesterday seemed to be separated from today by an infinity. Rachel climbed the wide easy steps of the porch he'd rebuilt, and when Jeff unlocked the door, she walked through the large room that formed living room, kitchen, and dining room together, and let herself out onto the deck behind the house. From there you could see the tiny distant lights moving on the interstate, stitching the edge of the vast, dark Columbia with beads of red and gold light. More lights spangled the bulk of the Washington shore on the far side of that darkness.

Behind her, Jeff appeared in the doorway, a wine bottle in one hand, two glasses in the other, and a crocheted afghan folded over his arm. She had found the afghan at a garage sale, folded neatly in mothballs and plastic, stacked with embroidered linen guest towels, and crocheted lace tablecloths. The embroidery had been tiny and detailed, and the afghan was real wool. Rachel had bought the afghan for Jeff and the towels for herself. She sat down beside him

on the edge of the unrailed deck, their feet dangling into
darkness, the wine gurgling with that wine-bottle sound as
he filled their glasses.

"You're angry," she said at last, breaking the long silence.

"Because you got out of the car. If things had gone
wrong, you could have been shot. If I was busy worrying
about you, we could have both ended up shot."

"Beck wouldn't shoot at you," she said in a small voice.
"Or me."

"You don't really know what someone will or won't do
in a tight situation." His tone was cold and matter-of-fact.
"You can only guess. If you guess wrong . . . someone
maybe dies."

Rachel looked away, stung by the hard truth of his re-
buke. What if she had distracted him? What if . . . She
couldn't bring herself to finish that thought, felt the sting
of tears in her eyes.

Jeff's arm went around her, and he pulled her gently
against him. His warmth against her cold skin started her
shivering again, only it wasn't just the cold. "I'm sorry,"
she whispered. "I didn't think. It's just . . . not Beck. Oh,
Jeff, this is going to destroy him."

"We'll try to help him, okay?"

We. Such a powerful word. "Thanks." She gulped and
wiped her eyes on her sleeve. "It was just . . . Spiros had a
gun out, and I feel so *responsible* for Beck."

"I know." He sighed, laughed ruefully, and leaned in to
kiss her. "That's who you are. And it's one of the things I
love about you. But next time—stay in the car, okay? Let
me do my job. It's dangerous sometimes. More dangerous
for you than for me," he said gently. "Because you haven't
been there, and you don't know."

"Okay," she whispered, fighting another rise of tears.
"I'm sorry."

He kissed her gently, the way you'd kiss a child, and
handed her a glass of ruby wine. When she took it, he
touched the rim of his glass to hers, but offered no toast as

the silvery chime of glass kissing glass sounded against the insect song and leaf rustle.

For a time they sipped their wine in silence, watching the light-beaded river. He kept his arm around her and the afghan wrapped across their laps in warm wooly folds. Below, a small boat moved slowly upriver. *Not a tug, a pleasure boat*, Rachel thought. *Bright with lights as if a party was under way*. She wondered suddenly where her mother was. *Home in bed with Joshua*, she told herself.

"Was Spiros part of why you left the Los Angeles Police Department?" she asked finally. Jeff didn't answer for a while.

"Sort of," he said at last. "I backed the wrong horse. But I knew he was the wrong horse when I did it."

"Spiros?"

"Yeah. Politics." He laughed shortly and sipped his wine. "Carey took on the wrong person once too often. He'd never make it as a diplomat."

"Neither would you."

"Not if it meant lying. I guess not." He leaned back on his elbows, looking up at her. "What's been bothering you? It's not just Beck and this girl, is it?"

"You're getting awfully good at reading me." She sighed. "Actually, I was thinking about my mother."

"Your mother?"

"Something's wrong." She didn't speak for a moment, watching the way the yellow light from the house edged his tawny skin with gold and deepened the shadow beneath his jutting cheekbones. You could see his Native American blood clearly in this light. "Josh thinks she wants to leave him."

"That's crazy." Jeff sat up abruptly. "Those two are the most lovestruck pair I've ever seen."

"I know. But I don't know, either." Rachel stared down into her glass, twirling it so that the dark wine formed a miniature whirlpool. "I saw her in Portland, but Josh didn't know she was there. She's avoiding me." Saying it out loud made it sound so trivial. Why should her mother confide in her? They were both grown-ups. She could have been buying Josh a birthday present—although his birthday was in October. "Oh, I'm being silly. And it's none of my business."

"It's your business if something's wrong." Jeff frowned, his fingertip absently circling the rim of his glass, creating an eerie singing note. "But she loves Joshua. That's as clear as daylight. So it's not that."

"What else could it be?"

"Ask her."

"Just like that?" Rachel blinked at him. "I can't."

"Why not?" He tilted his head. "Maybe she doesn't even realize how worried you are."

"I . . ." Rachel closed her mouth because she couldn't come up with a real reason not to ask. Except that she was afraid of the answer. And that made her feel briefly ashamed. She looked away. "All right," she said in a small voice. "I will. Tomorrow."

"Good." Jeff set his glass down and pulled her down beside him. "So now we've dealt with the serious subjects. Look up," he said softly. "The stars are too nice to waste tonight. Did I ever tell you that you look lovely in a dress, by the way?"

"Once or twice. Dresses don't work well when you're wheelbarrowing topsoil."

He chuckled as she settled her head on his shoulder. The wooden planks still held the faintest memory of the afternoon's sun. Warmed by his nearness, she lay still, listening to the slow, steady rasp of his breathing. They lay there beneath the afghan for a long time, picking out the rising summer constellations, pulling the afghan closer as the night grew chilly. Finally they got up, too cold to linger. Jeff took her home, and she tiptoed up the steps to her apartment, past Mrs. Frey's dark windows. Peter showed no such regard for sleepers, yowling indignantly at her late return. She shushed him and let him inside, turning to wave to the invisible Jeff, who had walked with her up from where he had parked on the street, so that the engine noise wouldn't waken Mrs. Frey. Peter headed for the back of the sofa, having decided to spend the night inside tonight.

"I'll race you to bed, cat," she told him. Blessedly her answering machine stared unwinkingly from its table. No callers. No catastrophes. She grabbed her robe from its hook and began to shed clothes. She beat Peter to sleep by a bare half minute.

In the morning Rachel fed Peter and let him out to terrorize Mrs. Frey's beloved chickadees. Sure enough, she heard her landlady's voice raised in the familiar rant as she came down the stairs. "Now don't you go hanging around under that tree, cat! Those babies aren't going to fall out. That chickadee pair has raised three sets of babies, and not one chick ever fell out. So you just scat!"

"How do you know it's the same pair?" Rachel detoured around to the back picket fence and leaned over the spotless white slats. "Don't they all look alike?" She looked around the neat garden with its weedless stone paths, mounded beds of her landlady's beloved roses, and borders bright with early annuals and wakening perennials. "The garden looks so nice! You put so much work into it!"

"It's a labor of love, dear. And even chickadees look unique if you watch them every day." Brushing crumbs of dirt from her blue gardening gloves, she rose from where she had been digging tiny weeds from between the stones of the path, smiling. "You look very spry after such a short night."

Rachel laughed. "I don't know why I try to tiptoe coming in. Don't you ever sleep?"

"I was always a light sleeper." She drew a young rose cane close to her face and peered at it. "Aphids. I knew they'd show up. No, I don't sleep much anymore. Happens when you get old." A dimple showed in her weathered cheek. "I approve of him, you know. Your young man. I hope you're not tiptoeing on that account."

"No." Rachel laughed, blushing in spite of herself. "Well, not really. I'm just trying to keep from waking you up."

"Uh-huh." Mrs. Frey's eyes twinkled.

"It's true," Rachel protested.

"Of course, dear. So where are you off to this bright morning?"

"Actually, I'm off to meet with our esteemed state representative, Mr. Claymore. I guess he wants some work done on his place here. He said something about moving his family back."

"How interesting." Mrs. Frey bent to pluck a brazen young dandelion from among newly planted pansies along the fence. "His wife hated it here. That's why they leased the house along with the orchard. She thought Blossom was utterly boring and Hood River was full of sailboarders. Which I suppose it is, and we are." Dimples still showed in her aged skin when she smiled. "Perhaps she has changed her mind."

"Did you know him when he lived here?" Rachel asked curiously.

"Oh, yes, I remember him as a boy." Mrs. Frey straightened, a distant look in her pale blue eyes. "He was a sharp one. He turned up at everyone's door in late July, selling wild blackberries that he'd picked. He looked so earnest, with his berry-scratched arms, that everybody bought from him, even though we all picked our own berries for jelly." She laughed. "Turned out he was paying other kids to do the picking and was still making a good profit. I always wondered if he scratched himself up on purpose, so we'd all feel sorry for him. I always wondered how he could pick so many berries and not have purple fingers." She smiled. "Oh, yes, he was a sharp one, even back then. It was such a tragedy—his folks' death. Those freeways are the work of the devil, if you ask me." She shook a finger at Rachel. "Better to go slower and live longer. You won't catch me driving on one."

"He lived with the Johnstons after his parents died, didn't he?"

"Moved in for a little over a year. They were good people, and he was actually a distant nephew or removed

cousin or one of those complicated things. He was friends
with their oldest son, so it was a natural thing to do. Oh,
yes, my dear." Mrs. Frey nodded, her eyes bright. "They
were all close in age, the three kids. Eloise had them nine
months apart, bing, bing, bing. Like she meant to get the
job over and done with." She nodded briskly. "Linda was
a gorgeous girl—one of those children who looks like a
model from the day she's born. I don't know if that's a
good thing or not," she said, "but it never seemed to go to
Linda's head. She was a nice girl—not stuck up at all. It
was a shame, her accident."

"She fell, didn't she?"

"From the cliff west of town. She's not the only one to
have died there. They ought to fence that point off, but then
I suppose the kids would simply climb over the fence."
Mrs. Frey shook her head. "They were out there for a picnic—the whole family. It was right about this time of year.
Sometimes you wonder if there's truly order in the universe." She sighed, then brightened. "Randall is coming
home for the weekend," she said. "For my birthday." She
smiled. "He told me he's bringing his friend Benjamin this
time, for sure. I met him in San Francisco, but Benjamin
always seems to have some kind of crisis at his job whenever Randall comes up here. So he never comes." Her smile
took on a sad tinge. "Not that I believe any of it, of course.
Randall is always so *careful* when he talks about Benjamin.
I wish he'd just tell me outright." She shook her head. "It
makes me a little sad sometimes that he thinks I'd be upset."

"Upset by what?" Perplexed, Rachel eyed the older
woman. "I think you lost me."

"Oh, he and Benjamin—a really nice boy, a very talented
musician—are in love. I keep waiting for Randall to tell
me. I mean, does he really think I don't know?"

"Randall?" Rachel blinked at Mrs. Frey, thinking of her
tall, easygoing son who fixed whatever needed fixing on
his occasional visits from San Francisco. In his late thirties,
he was a custom cabinetmaker with a very upscale clientele.

"Are you saying . . . ?" She couldn't quite get the words out.

"Randall is a homosexual. Oh, yes." Mrs. Frey nodded. "They call it being gay now, but that just doesn't sound right to me. Gay means happy, and so many of those people seem to be so unhappy. Not Randall, though." She smiled. "Certainly not since he started mentioning Benjamin in his letters. That was two years ago."

"I didn't know," Rachel said, feeling a little stunned.

"Of course not," Mrs. Frey said briskly. "It's not the kind of thing you mention at the checkout counter. But you don't gossip, dear." She smiled at Rachel and tugged her gloves on more firmly. "That's one of the things I like about you. Maybe this time Randall will tell me."

"Why don't you tell him you know?" Rachel said slowly, remembering Jeff's admonition last night. "Maybe he's been waiting for you to say something. Maybe he thinks you don't want to know, or at least don't want to talk about it."

"Now that's a thought." Kneeling on the path again, Mrs. Frey looked up with a bright, considering expression. "I'd like to think he knew me better than that, but perhaps he doesn't. Sometimes I think we never really know our parents nearly as well as our parents think we do." She shook her head. "But I'm glad he's found someone to love. I think love is worth it, even if it's the proverbial two-edged sword that can wound your heart forever. It's a dangerous thing, love. I worry about him, even though I'm happy for him." She sighed. "Love can leave your heart bleeding. Look at Paul Claymore, for example."

"Paul Claymore?" Her hand on the gate, Rachel paused. "He's happily married, isn't he?"

"Well, as far as the media is concerned, he is. They certainly don't fight in public. But he's not married to the love of his life." Mrs. Frey wagged a gloved finger at her. "Linda Johnston was his real love. Oh, he was head-over-heels for her. And he was never the same, after she died. A light went out in his soul, if you'll pardon my melodrama. He was still sharp and smart about how he did things, but a lot of the *fun* was gone. Sometimes I think that's why he never really lived in Blossom again. I'm not sure it was all his wife's dislike of us. Perhaps there are just too many memories here."

"But he's moving back here now."

"So you tell me." Mrs. Frey went back to her digging, jabbing vigorously at the stubborn green plants that insisted on poking up through the fine gravel between the stones. "That's interesting. That's very interesting."

Rachel said good-bye, thinking that Mrs. Frey read too many romance novels, and left her landlady to her weeding and her feuding with Peter. It was early yet. Plenty of time for a leisurely late breakfast and chat at the Bread Box before her ten o'clock appointment. She wanted to hear how the rest of the party had gone after she had left. She also wanted to drop by Gladys's office and find out if she had heard from April. She had called that morning and had been told that Gladys would be in late. Suddenly she was looking forward with even more enthusiasm to her visit with Claymore, and she wondered if Lieutenant Spiros had visited the politician to ask about Eloise.

CHAPTER

9

The Bread Box was nearly empty, in that late-morning slump between late breakfasts and the early lunch crowd. Rachel took a table near the window, admiring the sparkle of sun on water and the bright skittish dance of the few midweek sailboarders taking advantage of the fresh breeze. It was still cold enough for wet suits out there.

"So where did you and Jeff run off to, my dear?" Joylinn appeared at the table with a coffee carafe, two mugs, and a plate of scones on a tray. "Slipped out for a romantic drive, huh?"

"Well, less than romantic." Rachel reached for a scone. "Jeff went out to Beck's house with the Portland Homicide detective who's investigating Eloise's death. He was looking for April, the girl who worked for Eloise."

"My Lord, sounds like something out of a detective novel. I hope you're not mixed up with all this, but I bet you are." Joylinn rolled her eyes and took a scone for herself. "Well, you missed an interesting party. Did you notice, by the way, that Mr. Claymore's wife wasn't there?"

"I don't even know what she looks like." Rachel made

approving noises as she bit into her scone. "Blueberry. Thank you, darlin'."

"I know what you like." Joylinn grinned. "Well, she wasn't there, and if Claymore wasn't hitting on Sandy after you left, then I don't know what hitting is. Even Bill noticed. He was looking pretty surly by the time they left, let me tell you." She made a face. "I bet that was a pleasant ride home."

"Sandy?" Rachel said through a mouthful of scone. "You're kidding!"

"Well, I've heard he's a bit of a womanizer." Joylinn shrugged. "Don't know if it's true. He hasn't ended up in court yet anyway, and I haven't seen his face on the cover of any tabloids. These days, that probably means he's a saint."

"That's still kind of odd," Rachel said, but she remembered his intense stare and wondered what would have happened if she had reacted to it. "Sandy flirts with everybody, but I never saw Bill pay any attention to it. Everybody knows she's not serious—it's just the way she is. In fact, I think she'd be horrified if you called it flirting." Rachel laughed. "I don't think she's ever looked at any other male since she and Bill got together in seventh grade."

"Well, trust me, Bill was ticked last night." Joylinn shook her head. "Maybe it was just because Claymore's a celebrity. Maybe Bill thought that might really turn her head." She shrugged. "Claymore may have a roving eye, but I have to admit he's a charmer." She pursed her lips thoughtfully. "Cold, though, I think, under that charm."

Rachel thought of what Mrs. Frey had said. "Do you know anything about when he lived with the Johnstons?"

"Just what Sandy told me." Joylinn poured more coffee. "That's right. Wasn't there a death in the family? Something tragic. The daughter, I remember now. Linda. I remember her name because my mom mentioned it when he got elected. I guess she and Linda were best friends in high school. She said she had nightmares about falling for a month. You know," she said thoughtfully, "at the time I thought she almost seemed to blame Claymore for the girl's death. She never votes for him—says she doesn't trust him." She shook her head and finished her scone. "I'll have to tell her about last night when I'm over there for Sunday dinner."

"I'm surprised Mr. Claymore had any time to talk to Sandy at all." Rachel laughed. "I bet he heard a lot about his agricultural policies."

"Oh, you're right on that one." Joylinn brushed crumbs from her lap as she stood. "Everybody had something to say to him." She laughed again. "Your uncle, for one."

"I'll bet he did." It was Rachel's turn to roll her eyes. "Even when he approves of someone—and he thinks Claymore is great—he's still going to tell that person how to do his job better."

"Which is why you're a landscaper and not an orchardist, right?" Joylinn gave her a sly look.

"You bet. Not a chance we'd do anything any way but his if I was working there," she said cheerfully. "Oh, well. I have a lot more fun with my penstemons and ornamental grasses than I've ever had with apples and pears."

"Ha." Joylinn winked. "Bet you'd take over that orchard in a minute if your aunt and uncle decided to move to Florida."

"They won't. She's terrified of alligators, and he'd be bored." Rachel laughed. "So there's no point in playing what if." She looked up as a new customer pushed through the door. It was her mother. Rachel's laughter faded. Deborah looked strained, her face pale and taut, as if the skin had been stretched too tightly over the bones. It made her look years older, in spite of her still-black curls that showed only the first traces of silver.

"I think I'd better go check on that dough I'm proofing." Joylinn followed her gaze. "Find out what's wrong, kid. Something is." With that, she picked up her cup and vanished into the kitchen.

Deborah O'Connor's eyes scanned the tables, flickering when she spotted Rachel. She hesitated, her manner uncharacteristically indecisive. For a moment Rachel had the idea that her mother wanted to turn around and leave, only couldn't quite bring herself to do something that blatant.

"Hi!" Rachel waved.

"Why, hello." She made her way slowly over to the table. "I didn't expect to run into you on a working morning."

Translation: I didn't want to run into you? "I saw you in Portland, yesterday." Rachel said it bluntly. "I thought you had a class with Julio."

"I . . . forgot." Her eyelids twitched. "I guess I'm getting senile." She forced a smile. "So did you enjoy the party last night?"

"I take it Joshua and you weren't on the guest list."

"Well, Joshua is pretty vocal about what he thinks of Claymore." Her mother shrugged. "I don't think we were missed much. I don't care much for the man either."

Right after her father had died, her mother had retreated into a small glass chamber and had closed the door, shutting out her daughter, her relatives, and the seasons. She had smiled and talked and packed lunches. But she had been untouchable, sealed up tight inside that glass shell.

She was like that now. Rachel's heart contracted in her chest. "Something's wrong, Mom. Jeff told me to just ask you. He said you might not know that I was worried, that I knew something wasn't right. He said to ask you, and you'd probably tell me."

"Tell you . . . about what?" Her mother looked around, her movements stiff, then finally, reluctantly, sat down across from Rachel. "Nothing's wrong, dear."

"Sure." Rachel let her breath out in a long sigh as Joylinn approached, depositing a white china cup of frothy cappuccino on the table in front of Deborah.

"On the house," Joylinn said cheerfully. "We're celebrating my catering triumph last night." She gave Rachel a meaningful look and hurried off to greet a pair of new customers. Sailboarders, Rachel thought absently, as she took in their shorts, leather sandals, and bright knit shirts. She wondered what they did for a living that they could buy all those clothes and gear and still play on a weekday morning. With an effort, she turned her attention back on her mother. Deborah was drawing her spoon slowly through the foamy milk piled on her cappuccino, making creamy patterns in the white froth.

"Mom?"

Her mother looked up at her, her dark eyes unreadable. "I'm catching a plane to New York tomorrow." She said the words carefully, as if she was setting out fragile eggs one at a time on the tabletop. "I'll probably stay there for quite a while. I'm staying with Aunt Esther."

"What?" The word didn't quite make it out—it stuck in her throat, came out as a rasp of air. "Why?" She cleared her throat and tried again. "Mom, why are you doing this? What is going on?"

"I . . . explained this all to Joshua. I need a little time with my family. I guess I didn't realize how much I've missed them all these years—missed the family, the Friday night dinners, all the grandkids and the get-togethers. I just . . . need a little time with them." She said the words quickly now, and they had a polished feeling.

Rehearsed. The word popped unbidden into Rachel's head.

"I'm sorry I didn't tell you sooner, but I . . . I just made up my mind." The polished, rapid words went on. "I wasn't sure for a while what was bothering me, but now I am. It'll be fine." She gave Rachel a smile with the same polish. "I'll call you when I get there. And now I'd better go." She glanced quickly at her watch. "I've got packing to do. All kinds of things." She got hurriedly to her feet. "I'll call you before I go, dear."

She hurried away, her heels tapping on the marble tiles, before Rachel could say a word. Rachel started to get up, then sat down again. She looked at her mother's untasted cappuccino.

"So what's up?" Joylinn paused at the table, a tray balanced on her palm. "What's eating her, anyway?"

"I don't know." Rachel got abruptly to her feet. "I have

no idea." She didn't quite run as she left the Bread Box, but she might as well have stayed at the table. There was no sign of her mother or her car. Looking for her would net her nothing, Rachel decided with a sigh. Her mother had a tendency to go driving when she was upset, and Rachel had long ago learned the hard way that trying to play catch was a dangerous game. Her mother could have been a race driver in a past life. Rachel looked at her watch and made a face because she needed to head out to Paul Claymore's place.

As she reached her car, a dusty blue Toyota pulled up beside her. "Ms. O'Connor?" the dark-haired man who leaned through the window looked vaguely familiar. "Can I have a word with you? I'm Randy Balfor with the *Bee*."

The *Blossom Bee* was the town's small weekly paper. "Hello," Rachel said, thinking he was going to solicit an ad. "I think I talked to you last month. I don't really have enough business . . ."

"I just wanted to ask you about the murder of Eloise Johnston." The man hopped out of his car, a small leather-bound notebook in his hand. "I hear that you were there when Mrs. Johnston was murdered and that she shared some very important information with you—information that was supposed to appear in the memoirs that vanished at the same time as the murder took place." He sounded as if he were reading headlines.

"What?" Rachel stared at him. "What are you talking about? Eloise Johnston hired me to rehabilitate her landscaping, that's all."

"Oh, yeah?" He gave her a bright "aha" grin. "Then why did a Portland Homicide dick come all the way out here to ask questions about you?"

"Does anybody really call a policeman a 'dick' anymore?" Rachel raised an eyebrow at him. "I think you've been watching too much TV. As for Lieutenant Spiros, he wasn't out here to ask me any questions." But her heart sank. If this story ended up in the *Bee*, she would be linked to Spiros and the investigation forever around Blossom.

Balfor's grind had widened considerably. "Rumor is that somebody else in Blossom is strongly implicated in the murder. Want to name names?"

"No! There's nobody." Rachel fled the still-grinning Balfor, taking sanctuary in her truck. He didn't follow her as she pulled out of the parking lot, at least, but she didn't feel very triumphant. She had certainly confirmed his suspicions. Rachel ground her teeth, wishing he hadn't caught her off guard, wishing she had managed to act more confused by his accusations.

How long was it going to take people in town to link her to Beck and to April? Not long, she thought sourly. She watched her mirror, but Balfor didn't follow her as she drove through town. She paused briefly in front of the drugstore to buy the weekly paper, which had just come out. Sure enough. She groaned. LOCAL LANDSCAPER INVOLVED WITH PORTLAND MURDER, blared the headline. The story continued on page two, detailing Rachel's involvement with Eloise, but managing to make it sound much more sinister than a simple landscaping contract. It made her sound as if she was the pivotal link in an ongoing police investigation. Which should surprise Spiros, she thought grimly as she tossed the paper onto the backseat. And now she was late.

The Claymore orchard lay in the Hood River valley, back from the confluence of the Columbia and Hood Rivers, near Parkdale. The orchard produced pears—both European and two varieties of the round Asian pears. Rachel took the back roads over to the valley, enjoying the last of the year's apple blossoms. The pears had already lost their petals, and tiny green fruit gleamed from the neatly pruned branches along the roadside. The smudge pots still stood beneath the rows, testifying to the anxious weeks when the blossoms could be damaged by a frost, and you went to bed listening for the fire-hall siren that alerted growers to the threat of unexpected frost. She remembered nights of stumbling down the dark rows, shivering behind her flashlight's dancing beam, as she and her cousins lit the smudge pots beneath the lacy white canopy of blossoms. It hadn't seemed like a lot of fun at the time, as the thick oily smoke began to rise in the still, cold air, stinging their eyes and making them cough. She had finally convinced her uncle to install a wind machine after her cousins had left home. Now that he and Aunt Catherine were alone at the orchard most of the year, she suspected he was glad he had listened to her. Her aunt Catherine certainly was. She had always been vocal about how much she hated lighting pots, and usually managed to stay in the kitchen making hot chocolate and grilled cheese sandwiches for the midnight workers.

Smiling at the memories, a little sad, too, Rachel braked as she watched for the orchard entrance. The trees looked good—the rows neat and clean, the branches well pruned. Whoever leased the trees from Claymore was doing a good job, she decided. The entrance was marked only by a small sign with the name River Flat Orchards painted in black on a silver-gray background. She drove up the freshly graveled drive, pausing as a covy of five quail skittered across in front of her truck. The house came into view as the tree-lined drive bent eastward. The classic white building with its wide porch looked like many other orchard houses—much like the O'Connor house, for that matter.

She pulled into a wide, graveled parking space, but sat for a few minutes after she had turned off the engine, regarding the house. It had been built on a low rise, so that the yard sloped down in front, leveling off for a space of twenty or thirty feet, then dropping again to the level of the surrounding trees. It had originally been maintained in what she had dubbed lawn-mower landscape. In other words, mostly grass and evergreens, easily maintained with a lawn mower. Rhododendron and azalea edged the foundation. A narrow bulb-and-annual border flanked the walk from that led from the porch to parking space. Everything else was grass. Behind the house, the big metal shed that would house the orchard equipment looked neat and well kept, all weeds kept under control with weekly doses of herbicide around the foundation, she guessed.

Someone had recently begun to work on the yard. What had once been a straight path from the porch had been dug out for a curving walk. Sand floored the neat excavation, but no stones or gravel had been laid yet. Foot traffic had begun to crumble the precise edges of the excavation and track lumps of mud onto the sand. Brown lines of turned earth marked irrigation lines for lawn and borders, and when she got out of the truck and crossed the weedless lawn to the porch steps, she noticed ribbon-marked stakes that laid out areas of the terraced ground below the house for some purpose.

"Well, hello." Claymore opened the old-fashioned screen door, dressed in an open-necked work shirt and chino slacks. "I appreciate punctuality, let me tell you. It says a lot about a person. Come in, come in." He waved her up the steps and ushered her into the house.

The inside had obviously been redone recently. The wooden floor in the entry gleamed, and the rooms had been freshly painted. Wide stairs rose to the second floor, covered with a white fall of carpet. Elegant dark cherry furniture filled the living room in tasteful groupings, lightened by the white carpet, and white brocade upholstery of the matching chairs and sofa. Paintings hung on the walls, and Rachel recognized what she was pretty sure was a Wyeth. Well, his wife had money, according to what she'd heard. She was the daughter of a wealthy meatpacking family whom Claymore had met at a summer-camp program, the year before he went to college.

Rachel wondered how the bride white room was going to look after a nice smudgy spring. Soot from the burners seeped through crevices and tracked in on shoes.

"Claire—my wife—has been doing the decorating." Claymore followed her gaze. "She's very talented at it."

"It's lovely." Rachel bent down to unlace her boots. One step on that carpet, and they'd probably throw her out on the spot.

"You don't need to do that." He clucked his tongue. "We have a full-time housekeeper. She does the cooking, too.

Lovely woman, although the language is a problem." He shrugged. "She and Claire seem able to communicate, at least. She's from Guatemala. My wife found her in Portland. She'll help with the baby when it comes."

"Congratulations." Rachel glanced up at him. "I heard you were expecting."

"We're delighted." The state representative beamed at her as she straightened. "We just found out. That's why Claire wanted to move out here. She feels it's a much healthier environment for a child than the Salem area. We tried for a long time to have a child, you know." He beamed at her. "This is quite the gift to us."

"That's wonderful." Rachel nodded and smiled. "So what are you thinking of, in terms of landscaping?"

"Oh, I've had a lot of ideas. Come sit down in the study, and I'll have Anita bring some coffee." He ushered her across the entry and through a pair of glass-paned doors that looked new, into a large square room with a pair of French doors that opened onto a small side deck. A new computer stood on a teak desk, with pens and a few files aligned neatly beside it. A leather armchair beneath a brass-and-green reading lamp and floor-to-ceiling bookshelves that lined two walls gave the room the weighty air of a library, or perhaps the dean's office in a prestigious college, Rachel decided.

"You can see the whole yard from this window." Claymore waved her over to the large front window. "Triple-pane glass." He tapped it with a forefinger. "I replaced all the old windows and had insulation blown in. There was none, can you believe it? I'd forgotten how cold we used to get in this place."

"The Johnstons' house, too?" Rachel asked.

"I . . . don't remember their house being cold." His eyes rested on her for a moment. "They lived outside of town in a big stone house at the time. I wasn't there long." He regarded her without speaking for a moment. "I saw in the paper that you're helping the police with their investigation of Eloise's death," he said at last. "I was devastated by the news. Simply devastated. She was like a second mother to me."

"The paper exaggerated," Rachel said, thinking that Eloise had assumed mother status pretty quickly, if the accounts she'd heard of the brief duration of his stay with the Johnstons were accurate. "I'm not really involved much at all."

"I see." Another awkward pause ensued.

"So you've had some work done here already?" she said at last. Brightly. This interview was going wrong, and she wasn't sure just why. "I noticed the digging."

"Oh, Claire hired this Portland firm." He waved his hand dismissively. "They weren't satisfactory. I let them go."

"Oh." A tiny warning bell sounded in Rachel's head. Clients who were dissatisfied with one landscaper were frequently dissatisfied with any landscaper they hired. Like plastic surgery, a client's vision of the finished project did not always match an achievable reality. "What weren't you satisfied with?" She smiled politely as he frowned.

"They were sloppy," he said at last. "And they were scamming me. Every time I turned around, Claire was telling me how it was going to cost a little more here, a little more there. It was going to end up costing me twice what they'd estimated by the time we were through here. She's still annoyed that I fired them," he said thoughtfully. Then he smiled. "But I'm sure she'll be delighted with your work. You come highly recommended."

Uh-oh. Rachel kept her smile on her face, but it required an effort. This sounded as if she was about to step into the middle of a family dispute. Not a good place to be. "Well, we'll find out what the two of you want today," she said smoothly, "then I'll write up an estimate and give it to you. You'll get other estimates, too, of course." She should probably bid this one high, she thought. It sounded as if it could become more of a headache than she wanted to take on. "Is your wife home?"

"Oh, no, she's in Portland this week. Shopping for the baby." He frowned and reached under the edge of his desk.

"Where is that girl? I buzzed her ten minutes ago."

A young woman appeared in the doorway, a tray in her hands. She was small and stocky, with dark hair and eyes, skin a shade darker than Julio's bronze, and a dramatic profile. She eyed Claymore with a worried expression.

"That's fine, Anita." He raised his voice slightly, as if she was hard of hearing. "Put it on the table. There. No, there!" He pointed at the gate-legged table beneath the front window when the girl hesitated. She bent her head, hurried over, and began to set out a thermal coffee carafe, cups, cream, sugar, and a plate of dark cookies.

"Her name isn't really Anita," Claymore confided to Rachel. "We're being very non-PC, but she's Mayan, or something like that. Her name is impossible to pronounce. Actually we don't even know that she's Mayan. It was Claire who decided that she must be. Claire never lets reality get in the way of things." He laughed conspiratorially and intimately, as if he and Rachel were sharing a private joke. His smile faded quickly when Rachel didn't join in. "You can go," he told the waiting girl. "Go," he said sharply when she didn't move. "Kitchen."

She nodded finally and turned toward the door.

"Gracias," Rachel said and received a brief, shy smile in return.

"She doesn't speak much Spanish, either." Claymore shook his head and sighed. "That's Claire for you—act first, think later. She hired the girl sight-unseen through one of those refugee-placement organizations. So now I guess we're responsible for her. Last thing in the world we need right now—a maid who doesn't speak a word of English. If she spoke Spanish, at least our gardener could translate," he complained.

"My assistant is Guatemalan." Rachel looked thoughtfully after the girl. "I know he speaks something besides Spanish at home. Maybe he could translate."

"Oh, please, send him over. It would be a big help, but I'll bet the language is different in every little village. Shall we take our coffee outside?" He glanced at his watch. "I've got a couple of appointments this afternoon."

"Of course." Rachel picked up her notebook and a mug of coffee and followed him. At the entry again, a pile of mail and opened bills on a small teak table caught her eye. One of the bills was from a big landscaping company in Portland. She nodded, recognizing their handiwork now. They did a lot of work in the greater Portland area. She had talked to the owner at various garden shows and trade shows. Once he had asked her to work for them. He wanted to start a branch in Hood River.

"I want garden rooms." Claymore was nodding at the staked lawn in front of the house. "I want to look into a different one from each front window. And down below, I want water and an entertainment space—a patio, a gazebo. Something like that. How about a brick barbecue? With a built-in propane grill, for when I want to take things easy. I want flagstone—none of these tacky pavers. And I want one nice area with an Asian feel. I entertain a lot of Chinese and Japanese guests these days. Heck, most of our agricultural products are going to Pacific Rim countries, and the Chinese grain market is a gold mine waiting to happen." He nodded. "Maybe give the gazebo more of a teahouse feel than the classic sort of thing."

"Okay." Rachel scribbled furiously. There seemed to be a lot of maybes here. She eyed the dug irrigation lines and the staked layout of beds. The last company had probably intended to enclose the desired rooms with walls of hedge or tall plantings rather than hardscape, such as a wall. She walked over and scooped up a handful of soil from one of the prepared beds. She squeezed it and released it, guessing mushroom compost and a little sand in the mix. Whoever had done the work had done a lot before they were let go. "What about a bamboo hedge for one of your walls," she suggested thoughtfully. She was feeling less and less certain about this job. "Bamboo will give you your Asian theme, and the grassy cultivars form a solid screen very quickly. We can contain it with a deep plastic edging so that it doesn't spread."

"That sounds good. I like it. You're innovative. I like that." He smiled widely. "So you were working on Eloise's garden?" He took her elbow very casually as they strolled down to the terrace level. "You know, I used to drop in and visit her when I was in Portland." He looked down at her, his face mournful. "She was very special to me, you know. She really tried to be a mother to me after my folks died." He smiled at her, his eyes holding hers. "I'm looking forward to her memoir. I just hope . . . I mean, some of her memories of Blossom must have been pretty bitter. She blamed a lot of people for Linda's death."

"Oh?" That was news to her. "Actually, I'm looking forward to reading her memoirs, too." Rachel made a few notes. The slope was north-facing, so she could use some plants that couldn't handle a south slope in the hot summer. If she decided to do this job. "Maybe the book was her way to finally talk about her daughter." She looked up at him and smiled. "I heard that she never spoke of it afterward."

"Well, she made some accusations. People have probably forgotten about them," he said hastily. "I think she was suffering from parental guilt. Wouldn't you, if you took your daughter on a picnic, and she died when you weren't supervising her?"

"Linda was seventeen, wasn't she? Not really in need of constant supervision."

"I guess she was." His expression annoyed, Claymore glanced openly at his watch. "It was a terrible thing. And it happened almost in front of us. Well, not quite. We were all together building the fire and setting out the picnic stuff, and she went for a walk. None of us thought . . ." He paused to look away and clear his throat. "We never went on another family picnic together. I left for college that fall."

"I'm sorry," Rachel said. "I'd heard you were close to her."

"We were all close," he snapped. "It was a close and intimate family. I'm sorry." He glanced down at his watch again. "You know, I'm not so good at time management when I'm not in the office. I have to be off. Why don't you draw a general plan for me, and we'll fine-tune it together when I'm free."

Which would probably mean that she'd have to redo the whole plan and spend twice as much time on it as she would have if he'd given her another half hour. "All right," she said, reviewing her misgivings one more time. "When would you like to get together?"

"Hmmm." He frowned. "Can you get it done in two days? I've got to go out of town after that, and I don't know when I'll be back."

"I'll do my best." She stifled a sigh. "I'll call you when I have it ready."

"Do that. Here. I'll take your mug." He started for the house, then turned back. "And don't forget to send your man over here. It would help poor Claire a lot to have a translator on hand."

"I'll ask Julio to drop by." Rachel nodded and headed for her truck, feeling dismissed. As of this moment, she thought, she could think of three good reasons not to take this job. He hadn't included his wife in the planning, and she was willing to bet that his wife had her own ideas of what she wanted. He had already fired another firm for unspecified reasons. He could fire her in the same way, and very likely would, she thought grimly. First time she told him politely that some pet planting he wanted wouldn't work. Third reason to ditch this was that he was going to be darned hard to get hold of with questions if he was in Salem all the time.

Common sense warred with the thought that a politician knew a lot of people who might need landscaping jobs. He'd look good on the résumé, which was a bit sparse at this stage of the game.

"Later," Rachel growled out loud as she drove back to Blossom. "I'll decide later." By midnight tonight, she promised herself as she made her way home. That would be her own deadline. It wasn't fair to keep him dangling if she wasn't going to do the job.

Back home, she hurried upstairs, surprising Peter, who was sunning himself on the railing of the landing. "You're going to fall off and splatter into cat butter," she admonished him as she unlocked the door. A car pulled into the driveway, and she paused, looking down to see who might be visiting. She smiled as the black-and-white Blossom Police car pulled to a stop beside her truck. As Jeff got out, Mrs. Frey emerged from the wilderness of rhododendrons in the front yard and took him by the arm, today's garden hat—a broad-brimmed construction of straw, trimmed with blue and pink silk poppies twined with ivy and fluttering satin ribbons—turned up as if she engaged him in earnest conversation. Head bent politely to her, he let her lead him around to the rose garden in back, nodding now and then at what she was saying.

Still smiling, shaking her head, Rachel went on inside, leaving Peter to his sun and contemplation of chickadee cutlets. No wonder Mrs. Frey approved of Jeff, she thought as she tossed her notebook onto the table. Glancing through the rear bedroom window, she saw them still together, her gesturing dramatically with one hand, the other firmly gripping his uniform sleeve. He was nodding gravely, adding a comment now and then.

"You could be a politician," she murmured. She laughed and withdrew. On a whim, she detoured into the kitchen and flipped open her notebook, reaching for the phone. She called information and got the number for the landscape company that had worked on the Claymore job. Jim. She remembered the owner's name. Jim Crosby. He wasn't much older than she.

When a woman answered, she introduced herself and asked for him. The woman told her cheerfully that she thought he was out on a job, but that she'd check. Which meant he was there, but would only talk to her if he wanted to. Rachel waited, listening for Jeff's step on the stairs.

"Jim here." His voice came over the phone. "Hi, Rachel. You decided to throw in with me after all?"

"Sorry, I'm having too much fun on my own." She smiled, because she had always liked his bluff and easy-going manner. Beneath it, he was a tenacious and meticulous businessman. Employees who misread that easy manner and thought they could take advantage didn't last long. He was a demanding boss. "Besides, you work too hard."

"You got to work hard if you want to make it in this business. I took a look at one of your jobs the other day. Out in that hick town you live in. Right off Main Street—such as it is. I saw your sign."

"Oh, yeah, that one." She smiled, because he was talking about Gladys's little craftsman bungalow. "She's my lawyer. It's trade."

"Don't do trade. It doesn't pay. Nice job, by the way. Nice use of color in the foliage. I like that variegated hydrangea you put in in front. Goes nicely with that yellow carex and the miscanthus. Where'd you find those variegated aquilegia, by the way? First I've seen them."

"I got them from our local nursery. You should check out the Rhinehoffers' stock sometime." The columbine had plain blue and white flowers, but the leaves were a stunning shade of chartreuse. Planted against the dark green fountain of the miscanthus grass, they glowed like neon. "Iko said they're brand-new. I got a great purple heuchera from them, too. They're specializing in colored foliage plants. And thank you for the praise." She smiled. "That job was a challenge. My lawyer hates flowers and likes color." Actually, she was impressed. Jim didn't praise the competition lightly.

"Well, it just proves my point. You ought to come in out of the boonies, where you'll get some decent projects."

"I like the boonies." She smiled, hearing Jeff's tread on the steps. "I wanted to ask you about a job. For Paul Claymore?"

"Our esteemed representative?" Jim snorted. "Too bad I

can't vote against him. What a runaround. For once, I'm glad the client kicked us off the job. Saved me dumping him."

"That bad, huh?" She waved at Jeff as he peeked in the door. "It sure looked like a good start to me."

"Oh, we did a good job. It's just that the job kept changing every time he talked to his wife. She was the one we'd done the original consultation with. He'd show up and tell us he wanted this or that changed. Then she'd have us change it back. It was all down on paper. I'm a stickler for getting everything in writing. But it turned into a family fight—and we got caught in the middle."

"That's what I thought." Rachel sighed. "I think I'll pass on it. She wasn't even there when we did the consultation. I bet I'm not her favorite person at the moment."

"Well, it's a big-money job. Maybe you'll get along with them better than we did. You're local."

"I don't think that will make one bit of difference. I wondered, to be honest. The job felt wrong to me." She rolled her eyes at Jeff's curiosity. "Thanks for letting me know. I appreciate it."

"Remember, anytime you get tired of doing the whole show yourself . . ." His grin sounded over the line. "We could negotiate just about anything. I want you, sweetheart. We could make it work."

"I'll keep it in mind. Take it easy." She hung up. "I was just getting confirmation on my decision to say no to our esteemed representative's request that I landscape his property," she told Jeff. "Seems he just fired a good Portland company. For no good reason."

"Claymore?" Jeff sprawled on the sofa, his face thoughtful. "So you're turning it down? I'm glad."

"Me, too." Rachel sat down beside him and leaned back against his shoulder. "What is this? Your lunch break?"

"Belated one, yes." But his smile didn't reach his eyes. "I wanted to stop by and share a little bit of info with you. Carey and I had a late breakfast together. They still don't have any kind of lead on Beck and April, by the way."

"Beck knows the Mount Hood National Forest like his backyard," Rachel said slowly. "He disappears for days. Sometimes for weeks."

Jeff grunted. "I told Carey he wouldn't show up here, but he's still hoping. You really are turning down the Claymore job?"

"Yes." She nodded decisively. "I don't like it. It feels like trouble."

"It might be," he said soberly. "Did Carey tell you that he was on the force here, back when Claymore lived with the Johnstons?"

"No, but I heard the rumor. Did he grow up here?"

"Portland. He had some cousins in Hood River and got a job in Blossom because he was in love with one of them, or something like that. He was the one who got the call about the Johnston girl." Jeff paused to stroke Peter, who stalked in and leaped up to the arm of the sofa. "He was convinced that Paul Claymore pushed her off that cliff. Maybe because she was pregnant by him."

Rachel thought of what Mrs. Frey had told her. "I heard something about that," she said slowly. "That he loved her."

"I guess it got noticed." Jeff sighed. "Spiros really wanted to pursue it, but the family didn't, and they were close with the chief of police and the mayor at the time. Spiros got told in words of one syllable to knock it off. He didn't and ended up getting canned. I guess he's been nursing this vendetta ever since. He's bound and determined to bust Claymore, if it takes the rest of his life."

"That's why he showed up at the garden," Rachel said softly.

"He heard it reported over the radio—accidental death. Turns out he'd been visiting her recently. I suspect he was pushing her to make a public statement about her daughter's death. He was convinced she shared his suspicions, although her husband was convinced of Claymore's innocence." He paused, his eyes dark with worry. "According to Carey, she told him that she was full of doubt and wanted to sleep on it. She called his home later and left a message that she wanted to see him the next day."

"The next day?" Rachel said softly.

"Right," Jeff said soberly. "Only that night she was killed. When Carey heard the report on the scanner, he went over there and took over. If he hadn't gotten involved, her death might have been attributed to her heart condition. It happens."

"Chance," Rachel said slowly.

"I'm not sure chance operates with Carey." Jeff shook his head. "He is certain that Claymore is involved. He thinks she was going to publish something in her memoirs, and Claymore didn't want it published."

"Well, someone destroyed the computer files." Rachel nodded.

"I guess a couple of witnesses put him there two days before the murder."

"He told me he went to visit her regularly."

"Smart man." Jeff didn't look happy. "So you be careful, please. I'm glad you're not going to be working for him." He stood and looked down at her. "I worry about you," he said soberly. "You're too darned independent. I guess that's partly why I love you, but you still worry me."

Why I love you . . . The words hung there, freezing Rachel briefly to stone. He had never said that out loud before, and she looked away, a sudden turmoil tumbling in her chest. *How do I feel about this?* she asked herself. *What do I say?* Every time she tried to look at that slippery thing—love—it twisted into a knot that she couldn't unravel, couldn't get hold of, couldn't grasp or examine at all.

"Anyway, I just wanted you to know what Carey told me."

"What did the name Carey come from?" she asked, letting that pesky word "love" slide downstream unrescued.

"Icarus." Jeff's eyes smiled, above his solemn expression. "He told me once that Icarus was a stupid twit who blew a great afternoon."

"His brother isn't named Daedelus is he?"

"Aristotle."

Rachel groaned, then laughed. "Ari and Carey?"

"Robert and Carey. His brother changed his name."

Rachel laughed again. Slipping her arm through Jeff's, she escorted him to the door. "I'll be careful," she said. "I'm not sure I trusted Mr. Claymore much anyway. And I'm definitely turning down the job."

"Good." He kissed her lightly and reached over to stroke Peter, who had resumed his perch on the railing. "I'm off tomorrow. How about if we go do something?"

"Sounds great. I'm not busy." She leaned over the railing as he started down the stairs. "What did Mrs. Frey want to tell you, anyway?"

He winked. "She was lecturing me on life, liberty, and the pursuit of happiness." He waved, climbed into his car, and backed down the driveway.

She would have loved to have listened to that lecture. Smiling to herself, Rachel went back inside to type up a nice polite letter to Mr. Claymore declining his business.

CHAPTER

10

In the bright morning—too early yet to call Jeff—Rachel drove over to the trailer home Julio shared with his sister and brother-in-law, above the main part of town. His brother-in-law was home, working on a blue Honda motorcycle in the neat front yard. He cooked for one of the restaurants in Hood River and planned to open his own restaurant one day. Julio's sister worked for one of the new motels that had moved into the area to cater to the tourists and windsurfers. When Rachel arrived, Julio was sitting cross-legged in the sun on the small front porch they had added on to the trailer, frowning down at a book spread open on his lap.

It was an advanced biology text. Rachel looked over his down-curving shoulders, her shadow falling across the page. He was reading about the Krebs Cycle in plants. Photosynthesis. He wanted to learn botany, he had told her once, because he would have his own landscaping business one day, and botany would make him better at it. She had a feeling he was going to do just that. He looked up, startled, smiling, getting quickly to his feet. "I did not hear you."

"I didn't know you were taking so much science this semester." She nodded at the book. "You were studying chemistry on your lunch break the other day."

"The chemistry is most hard." He smiled, his eyes sparkling. "I bought a special dictionary. Final tests are next week. I will get an A."

"I believe you." Rachel matched his smile. He worked incredibly hard at the community college, taking a few classes each quarter so that he could work, too. When he had first started taking classes there, when his English had been marginal at best, he had taped some of his lectures. When they took their breaks, he had shyly asked her to explain some words to him. He no longer needed any help from her.

"I met a young woman who works for a family over in Hood River," Rachel went on slowly. "She comes from Guatemala and doesn't speak English or even much Spanish. The family can't really talk to her." She lifted her palms and shrugged. "Would you be willing to go see her? Maybe you can understand her."

"I could try." Julio looked doubtful. "Did you ask her the name of her village? There are many languages in Guatemala," he said when Rachel shook her head. "I will go see her."

"Thanks for going." She took her little notebook from her pocket and jotted down the directions. "They're expecting you to come by. Poor woman." Rachel shook her head. "She must be lonely. I hope you speak the same language."

"It may be." Politely he accepted the address. "Would you like some water? Or some pop? We have Coke. My sister is at work," he explained as he closed his book.

"Thank you. I've got errands to do, and I don't want to keep you from your studying. Will you have time to help me in Portland?" she asked as he ushered her back to her truck. "I'm going to be working on that garden I told you about."

"The one where the senora died?" Julio's eyes widened

slightly. "I can do it." He hesitated. "Maybe after finals? They are only next week. If I did not have the chemistry and biology, I would say right now is good. But . . ."

"After finals is fine, Julio. Really." She shook her head at his worried expression. "Will you talk to your friend Eduardo for me? Find out if he can come with a crew of two more? He doesn't know as much as you do, but he's a good worker."

"I know because I listen to you. And I remember what you say." He grinned at her. "I will tell Eduardo you need him. He may not be busy. See you later, *Senorita* Boss." He waved cheerfully as she left, was bent over his book before she had even backed the truck out of his driveway. His brother-in-law looked up from his cycle and waved a greasy hand.

At the intersection where Julio's street joined the county road, she hesitated, then turned right, up the side of the Gorge, taking the winding road that led to Beck's cabin. Turning onto his rutted lane, she drove into the clearing and parked. Birds chirped and sang in the early-afternoon sun, and not a cat showed a whisker anywhere. The cabin looked utterly desolate and abandoned. Yellow dandelions bloomed along the edge of the steps, and a big pileated woodpecker, large as a crow, flew from the cabin roof to the woods, red feathers flashing bright on his black-and-white plumage. Beck might well come home to fist-sized holes in his roof, if the pileated was working up there, Rachel thought. Although she closed the truck door gently, even that much noise silenced the birds and insects briefly.

Her footsteps crunched on gravel as she crossed the yard, and the silence raised gooseflesh on her arms. She crossed the driveway and took the faint, unmarked path through the red huckleberry and wild Indian plum, wading through drifts of duck's-foot and vanilla leaf in the moist shade. The path led to Beck's private clearing. She wasn't really sure why she had come here. Perhaps, she thought, because she could see him abandoning his cabin and even his shop—but not the clearing. That slowly evolving sculpture meant something to him. She paused as the path emptied into the small space. Emerald light filtered through the boughs of cedar and alder, spangling the mossy logs and needled ground with a shifting luminescence that gave the clearing an underwater feel.

More of the face had emerged from the huge old-growth stump. It was clearly Beck's own face. She nodded, certain of it now. His cheek, brows, one eye and part of the other, and the corner of his mouth were recognizably him. She peered at the polished curve of his cheek and upper lip, wondering what his expression was. You couldn't tell yet. She took a step out into the clearing and bent to look more closely.

An unseen force yanked her backward, so that she lost her balance, arms flailing. A hard forearm, smelling of sweat and woodsmoke pressed against her throat lightly. Rachel smelled musky human scent, sharp sweat, and cried out, utterly powerless in the grasp of her attacker.

Abruptly the iron grip relaxed.

"Don't ever do that again." Beck turned her around gently to face him. "You move too quietly," he said tenderly. "Just say my name when you come here. So I know it's you."

Rachel swallowed, her knees wobbly, her heart thudding, because in that instant of light pressure against her throat she had felt death breathing in her ear. It would have taken Beck an instant to break her neck if he hadn't recognized her. "Beck?" She shuddered all over in one convulsive spasm. "Don't hurt anyone. Please?"

"It's all right." He hugged her, his arms as gentle around her as if he were her big brother helping her up after a fall from her bike. "Don't worry about me."

"Beck, Beck." A low voice and the rustle of brush broke the quiet. "There's a truck . . ." April burst into the clearing and halted, falling instantly silent. "Oh," she said in a small voice.

"Hi, April," Rachel said. They had been up in the woods as she had guessed. They had been camping out in some remote and isolated spot while Jeff and Spiros sent out APBs and alerted the state police. Beck vanished now and again, and she had always suspected that he simply went on his own private walkabouts through the huge national forest that surrounded Mount Hood. That's where the cats had gone, she thought. They had been camping out, too.

"Now I don't have to sneak down to a phone." April faced her, legs spread, shoulders back beneath her defiant face. "You can give me a ride to the lawyer's office. Right now."

"What?" Rachel gaped at her.

"You know. To the lawyer? So she can make a deal with the cops?" April tossed her tangled hair impatiently back, clawed her fingers through it, and made a face. "God, I need a shower. But I'm ready, okay? And I know I was stupid, and I'm going to pay for it, so now we've said it and nobody else needs to, okay?"

Rachel stared at her, barely noticing the girl's belligerent tone. "My cell phone's in the truck," she said finally. "Maybe we should call Gladys and warn her."

"Yeah. I guess so." April's shoulders slumped, and some of her defiance leaked away. Beck went over to put an arm around her. She looked quickly up at him, smiled, touched his hand. "Okay," she said. "Let's go."

They walked together back along the narrow path, single file, Rachel first, Beck last. April walked, head down, between them, as if watching for roots on the trail. Her hair tumbled forward around her face, hiding her expression. But when they reached the truck, and Rachel retrieved her cell phone from the front seat, she noticed the gleam of moisture on April's cheeks. Stifling a sigh, she called Gladys.

"Damn," Gladys said. She grunted. "Put her in your truck and bring her here right now. Just don't run into that boyfriend of yours on the way over. We don't need any complications, thank you." She banged the receiver down.

"You'll stay here? Please?" April spoke to Beck, as if they were alone together in the clearing. "I need to do this by myself. I need to know you're here safe, working in your shop. I want to be able to close my eyes and be in the cabin, and watch you sitting in your chair, carving. Please do that for me? I don't think I can go through with this if I can't see you here and know it's for real."

Beck leaned down slowly, and gently, without haste, kissed her on the lips. April's eyes closed, and when she finally stepped back, her face was pale, except for twin spots of bright color on each cheek. "I'll be back," she told him. "I promised you, remember? That I'll come back here."

He nodded, stepped back, and watched silently as April climbed into the truck. He didn't move as Rachel backed the truck around and started down the driveway. As they rounded the curve that would block him from their sight, Rachel glanced in the rearview mirror. He hadn't moved, didn't lift his hand, didn't even twitch. He might have been one of his own carvings.

April leaned her forehead against the window and began to cry silently as they drove quickly down toward town and Gladys's office. "You know why I'm doing this?" she asked bitterly as they reached the main road. "You know why I'm jumping into this, when I know the deck is stacked against me? Because of Beck." She stared through the window, her eyes on the asphalt sliding beneath the truck's front bumper. "He's willing to give up everything for me. Everything." She shook her head, her laugh fragile and uncertain. "Nobody's really like that," she said. "Nobody loves like that." She looked at Rachel, her eyes like depthless pools, filled with shadow. "But he does," she said softly. "And he loves me. I . . . I can't mess that up."

For some reason—no reason whatsoever—Rachel thought of her mother. Swallowing hard, she turned into the parking lot of Gladys's building and drove around to the rear door.

"Good girl." Gladys swung it open instantly, as if she'd been standing there waiting for them. "Come on in, and let's do some calling. This is going to make them like you a little more downtown," she said as she ushered the pale and taut April into her office. Gladys glanced back at Rachel, mouthed "Good work. I'll call you," and closed the door in her face.

Rachel let her breath out in a long sigh, turned back to her truck, but didn't get in. She locked it instead and walked slowly toward the center of town, her throat still painful. She could summon up the smell of Beck as he choked her: male body scent and sweat. She touched her throat as she reached the corner of Maine and Cedar, and the Memorial Park that she and Julio and a young delinquent on work release from the Youth Farm had renovated last spring. She thought of the last letter she'd received from the teenager, Spider, and smiled. He would graduate from high school in a few weeks. He had invited her and Julio to attend, and he had shyly mentioned that he had made the honor roll this year. Joshua Meier had set up a trust to pay his tuition at college in the fall—although Spider didn't know who was behind it. Joshua had named it the Deborah Fund. Rachel smiled as she turned the corner past the park, making a note to herself that the bed in front of the memorial stone commemorating all Blossom's war dead needed to be weeded and planted with heat-tolerant summer annuals.

A car was parked crookedly against the curb. Rachel recognized her mother's MG, and sudden anger rose up inside her. For a moment the strength of her own emotion startled her. She wasn't really sure why she was angry. Love had always frightened her—that it could be shattered, as her mother's had been, at her father's death. Maybe, Rachel thought, she was angry because what her mother had seemed to share with Joshua reassured her that even if it was smashed once, it could grow again.

Only now . . . her mother was denying it. Leaving her afraid, all over again.

She looked into the tiny park, with its young shade trees. There in the corner, sitting on a stone bench, in the lacy shadow cast by the new spring leaves, sat her mother.

Shoulders bowed, she stared down at her hands, clasped on her knees, oblivious to Rachel's stare. Rachel set her jaw and prepared to march on by. As she passed the MG, her mother's cell phone chimed from the front seat.

Rachel halted again, annoyed, because even in Blossom it was stupid to leave a cell phone on the front seat of an open convertible. She hesitated, then picked up the phone. Answered it.

"Deborah?" A man's voice came over the line, tinted with a faint foreign accent. "I'm glad I caught you, since you asked me not to leave messages on your answering machine."

So. Rachel stood frozen in silence, heat and cold rippling in waves down her spine.

"I spoke to Dr. Schwartz at Beth Israel Hospital in New York. He's the surgeon we discussed yesterday morning," he went on. "He'll be able to schedule you for surgery as soon as you arrive. We'll make our decisions about the extent of chemotherapy and radiation after we've taken a look at what we've got."

"I . . . I'm sorry." Rachel's voice trembled, harsh in her raw throat. "This is Deborah's daughter, Rachel."

"Oh." The man's silence beat on the line for a few seconds. "I apologize. You sound just like your mother. This is Dr. Li," he went on more cautiously. "Is your mother there?"

"Uh . . . not at the moment," Rachel stammered.

"Well, please have her call me as soon as possible. I need to speak with her before her plane leaves for New York. I'm only going to be here in the office until three."

"I . . . I'll have her call you. Right away. Good-bye." Reeling, as unsteady as if Blossom was suffering an earthquake, she slowly pocketed the phone.

Turning stiffly, she retraced her steps to the entrance of the park, feeling as if she was walking in a dream, feeling as if the air had turned to molasses, holding her back, parting heavily at the slow thrust of her body, so that she had to lean into the thick air, struggling through it. Her mother

looked up as she approached and fixed her face into a smile.
It was like watching someone pull on a mask.

"Joshua thinks you have a lover." Her lips moved
numbly. "He thinks he's too old. He thinks you changed
your mind." Blunt words, like heavy stones. She dropped
them wearily.

Her mother looked away, withdrawing, closing up.
"Haven't we been over all this?"

"Oh . . . Mom." She lost it then, dropped to her knees, a
kid once more—that kid who had tried so hard to understand why her father had to die. She had never quite suc-
ceeded. "You didn't tell me," she said. "Why didn't you
tell me?" And she began to cry.

The sobs racked her, deep and rending, and Beck was
part of it, and April, and Jeff, who wouldn't say what he
wanted to say, because she had told him she was afraid.
And mostly she cried for her mother, in the way she had
never let herself cry for her father.

Finally, the storm ebbed, and she realized her mother was
stroking the back of her neck and her shoulders, the way
she stroked Rachel when she was sick as a child. Rachel
raised her head, blinking swollen eyes.

"I'm wet," her mother said, looking down at her tear-
soaked jeans with a fragile smile. "How did you find out?"

"I just answered your phone. Dr. Li thought I was you.
You're supposed to call him before three. Cancer?" She
forced the terrible word out, bit her lip as her mother closed
her eyes and nodded.

"I found a lump," she said. "In my right breast. It was
so tiny." She opened her eyes. "I check every month. And
there it was."

"Why didn't you tell Joshua?"

"His wife died of cancer." Her mother's eyes opened,
huge and dark in her fine-boned face. "It was terrible. He
told me once that the worst part was realizing toward the
end, when things were very bad, that he was beginning to
hope she would die soon. It tore him apart, Rachel. I can't
do that to him. Not again."

"You're doing it to him now. You're doing worse than that to him." Rachel scrambled to her feet. "Mom! Think about it! He loves you. It's too late to change that. Don't hurt him like this to save him a different hurt. Are you so sure this is easier for him? To think that he isn't good enough for you?"

"Not good enough . . . Oh, dear God." Deborah buried her face in her hands.

"Mom, please?" Rachel put her arms around her mother, struggling for words that flew away like birds. "Don't leave. Don't go to New York for this."

"I . . . I've made all the arrangements." Deborah's eyes darted around the small, green park, as if she felt walls closing in around her. "Your uncle Jon is picking me up at the airport. I'm staying with him and Sheila. They're so worried about me."

"Mom! *I'm* worried about you!"

"You wouldn't have been if you hadn't answered my phone," her mother said sharply.

"You're wrong. I've been worried about you for a while now." Rachel swallowed. "Please . . . stay?" she whispered.

"I . . . I need to go think about this. I'll call you." Her mother turned and nearly ran from the park, climbing into the sports car and driving away before Rachel could think of a way to call her back.

Numbly, she stood on the sidewalk, staring after her mother. Then she walked on down the street, past the Homestyle Cafe, which exhaled the scent of lunchtime burgers and fries into the bright noon air. She walked beneath the highway overpass, barely aware of the rumble of wheels above her head. She smelled the river before she reached the renovated dock and the upscale new shops that had been built there. Bright beach towels and wet suits decorated the balcony railings of the blue-and-white condos that ran along the riverbank, west of the shops. Rachel walked slowly up the ramp that led to the boardwalk and pushed open the Bread Box's twin glass-paned doors.

Joylinn was carrying a tray of rolls from the kitchen to

the front display cases. When she saw Rachel, she hesitated, then put the tray down on the counter, called back into the kitchen for Celia, her assistant, to mind the register, and hurried over to take Rachel by the arm. "You look bad, girl." She led her toward a secluded table in the far corner of the room. "Whatever happened?" She sat Rachel down on one of the small chairs. "Stay," she said sternly. "I'll be back with coffee and sustenance." As she hurried away, Rachel looked around the small space. Outside on the wooden deck, a few couples sipped coffee, or bottled beer, or mineral water. Her aunt and uncle sat at one of the riverside tables. Rachel looked hastily away, grateful that they hadn't seen her. They would read it on her face, she thought. Her aunt would ask about her mother, and she'd burst into tears.

"Here." Joylinn returned and plunked a frothy latte down in front of Rachel. "Mocha," she said sternly. "Lots of chocolate, lots of sugar and whipped cream. Drink it and don't whine about calories. You look like you saw a ghost."

"I hope not," Rachel whispered. Her throat was barely working. What a day, she thought, giggled, winced at the hysterical sound, and lifted the mug. Joylinn had also set a plate of her famous gingersnaps on the table, too. Rachel sipped at the mocha. The sweet, hot liquid seemed to soak instantly into her stomach, lightening her mood. She drew a deep breath and drank some more of the mocha.

"And what happened to your voice?" Joylinn asked with concern. "Are you getting a cold?"

"Not really." Rachel drew a slow breath. "Joylinn, Mom isn't having an affair in Portland. She has breast cancer. She's been seeing a doctor."

"What?" Joylinn whispered the syllable. "Oh, girl." She reached for Rachel's hand. "When did you find out?"

"Just now. I answered her cell phone." Rachel gulped more coffee. "She . . . doesn't want Joshua to know."

"That's crazy. What is she thinking?"

"I know." Rachel sighed and looked down at the tabletop. "What do I do? She's planning to go to New York for the surgery and chemotherapy."

"Why?"

"Because Joshua's first wife died of cancer." Rachel looked at Joylinn. "She's doing this because she loves him. That's so crazy." She clenched her fist. "I should just go tell Joshua right now."

"Sweetheart." Joylinn took her hand, her eyes dark with sympathy. "This is between her and Joshua. Right or wrong. She has to decide what to do."

"I hope she changes her mind. I want her to tell him." Rachel pushed her empty cup away and looked at Joylinn. "And I won't be able to be there," she said softly. "I'll be here."

"Did you tell her that?" Joylinn asked gravely.

"I think so. I tried." Rachel sighed. "How can she be sick? She never gets anything, not even a cold."

Joylinn shook her head, looked past her. "Your aunt and uncle are about to leave," she remarked conversationally. "If you need to make a quick exit, you can go through the kitchen."

"Bless you," Rachel mumbled, and got to her feet. "Thanks for listening." She squeezed Joylinn's shoulder and slipped behind the counter and into the kitchen that smelled of rising bread. Her aunt would take one look at her and ask what was wrong. Right now, that's about all it would take to make her dissolve again.

Joylinn was right—it was her mother's decision to tell Joshua or not, no matter how much Rachel knew this silence was wrong.

She exited through the rear door, past the Dumpster that served the block of shops, and across the lot to Cedar Street. She reached the park, looking automatically to see if her mother might have returned. An old man sat on one of the shaded benches, talking to himself, his eyes on the memorial stone. She recognized him. He had started a pear orchard out near Parkdale, upstream from Hood River, and had moved into a small house in town when his son took over the orchard. She didn't know if he had served in any war. She didn't know if he had ever lost anyone.

Rachel drove home and parked in her space, relieved that Mrs. Frey was indoors, probably cooking dinner. Still feeling numb, her throat as sore as if she had the cold Joylinn had suggested, she climbed the stairs to her apartment. Peter was waiting on the landing for her. He yowled at her and arched hard and warm against her ankles, letting her know that she was late, as far as he was concerned. For once, she couldn't muster enough energy to laugh at him. She let herself in. Her machine was flashing, and she hurried over to punch the button. A man's voice told her that he was interested in talking to her about landscaping his Hood River yard, and would she call him, please. She made a note of his number and stuck it on her desk where she would see it in the morning.

She fed Peter, her thoughts circling like Mrs. Frey's chickadees, fluttering and refusing to alight. Not hungry, she made herself a cup of milky tea and decided to catch up on her various magazines and nursery catalogues.

Someone knocked at the door. "You there?" Jeff's voice sounded.

"Hi." She pulled it open. "You're off? It's early."

"I had the day off, remember?"

"We were going to do something. Jeff, I'm so sorry." Rachel closed her eyes. "I . . . forgot."

"I know." His arms went around her. "Joylinn called me," he said gently.

"Oh." She swallowed and leaned against him, empty of words and actions.

"Sandy and Bill have decided that this is a good night for a picnic down at the river—at the park. They have a ton of leftovers from the reception, and it's spring."

"A picnic? It's cold at night." She tried to smile. "And I heard the weatherman predicting showers tonight. Are they crazy?"

"Everybody can bring a sweater. If it rains, there's always the picnic shelter. Hey, I helped roof that thing last spring. We might as well appreciate all those nice cedar shakes I nailed up there." He caught her around the waist and swung her around. "Come on, girl. Life is full enough of grief. You won't make it better moping in here. Let's go celebrate a starry, cold, maybe-raining spring night with Bill and Sandy."

"We'll, they're Joylinn's leftovers." This time the smile came a little easier. "They'll be good."

"They're calling Joylinn, too." He glanced at his watch. "Let's go. I've got the firewood."

"You guys really are crazy," she said and touched his face lightly. "I think this is just what I need right now."

"Me, too." He bent and kissed her on the forehead. "Now go get a sweater."

CHAPTER

11

Riverside Park had belonged to the Parker orchard originally. When the interstate came through, it divided the small spit of riverbank from the rest of the property. Part of the original homestead planting, the old apple trees on the river side of the property no longer bore well. Rather than cut them down and plant pears, as he had done with the rest of his acreage, old Clement Parker donated the plot to the city of Blossom as a public park. Potluck suppers and community rummage sales had funded the building of a rustic log shelter, a swimming dock on the riverbank, and a ball field. The dock had been destroyed by winter floods more than once, but the community seemed eternally willing to gather on the grassy slope to rebuild it, plant new shrubs, or groom the baseball diamond.

This early in the year it wasn't used much, so Rachel was surprised to find five or six cars parked in the graveled lot close to the freeway. A path led from the lot, through the tall spring grass to the octagonal shelter set amongst picnic tables and brick fire pits. A small knot of people turned to look as they parked, waving and calling. Sandy and Bill were there, as well as some other friends. With some surprise, Rachel recognized Mayor Ventura. Joylinn was arranging food and utensils on the covered table, while her elderly Quebecoise grandmother, Madame DeRochers, sat primly upright on the bench beside her, hands clasped neatly on her black-clad lap, obviously directing the arranging process.

"What is this? A community party?" Rachel rolled her eyes at Sandy as she returned greetings and looked around.

"Well, I called Chuck and Candy, and they called somebody who called somebody." Sandy grinned. "I guess you could call it a chain-letter party. At least they're all bringing food. I thought you'd never get here with that wood." She turned to scold Jeff. "Everything down here is either green or too wet to burn. Let's get it started, or we'll be cooking hot dogs at midnight."

"This is some chain letter." Rachel eyed the bags of chips and cardboard deli containers of potato and macaroni salad, packages of cookies and hot dog buns, a plastic-wrapped plate of brownies, and a whole watermelon. "Where did you get a watermelon this time of year?"

"From Safeway." Jenny, a high-school friend of theirs spoke up. "It was probably grown in South America and won't be ripe, but, hey, it fit the mood."

"So how did you end up here?" Rachel went over to help the mayor stick cans of pop and bottles of beer into a cooler full of ice. "Did someone drive through town with a loudspeaker?"

"Almost." Ventura grinned and opened a bottle of ale. "Here, Jeff." He opened a second and handed it to him. "All city officials are required to drink beer tonight. Mayoral edict. One for you, Rachel? Actually, I was walking home from from City Hall when Sandy and Bill pulled over. They told me there was a party, and I should come."

"Chain letter, ha!" Rachel laughed and took the beer he handed her. "I bet Sandy called everyone. Catering Claymore's party has gone to her head."

"I hear she did a nice job." Ventura stuck the last cans of Coke into the ice and took a swallow of his own beer. "You should have come to the town meeting Claymore held here. Talk about a free-for-all! Whew!" He shook his head. "I thought the high school roof might come off. We've had basketball games with Hood River High that were quieter!"

Which was hard to believe, because Hood River was their biggest rival. "I think I'm glad I wasn't there." Rachel shook her head. "How's your hearing?"

"Impaired." Ventura grimaced. "Actually, the tough part was trying to keep a low profile. I have enough trouble with some of our upstanding citizens without putting my foot publicly in my mouth yet again."

"You're not capable of keeping a low profile." Jeff laughed. "As I recall, you had a few things to say about our changing times."

"Well, I guess I haven't really learned how to keep my mouth shut yet." Ventura looked abashed. "Looks like they got the fire started. I brought some sausage—some of that hot Polish sausage Bill Schmidt makes out at his place."

Bill Schmidt ran a meat-cutting and wrapping operation, catering mostly to hunters processing deer, but also handling a few locally grown steers, pigs, and lambs. His family had been sausage makers for generations, and the sausages he sold were legend. "I hope you brought something us mere mortals can eat," Rachel said. "He's as heavy with the hot pepper as Bill."

"Oh, I brought some of the garlic stuff, too." Ventura laughed. "You won't come down with a cold for a while. Come on, Jeff. Let's go cut some sticks for the hot dogs and sausages. I'm starving."

As the two men headed for the willow thickets at the edge of the park, Rachel went over to the table, to sit down beside Madame DeRochers. "It's nice to see you," Rachel said to the eighty-year-old woman. "I'm sorry I haven't been out to visit you for a while."

"Ah, my child, you attend more than many of my grandchildren." She smiled, her oval face still handsome, hinting at the beauty she had been when she was young. "Monsieur Harris, *mon cher ami*, is a bit in love with you, I think.

Although he tells me that you are too young for him."

"He is not." Rachel took the woman's long-fingered hand. "He's madly in love with you and has been since I first met him. So where is he tonight? What's his excuse?"

"Ah, I am too old for him." But she smiled, her blue eyes twinkling. "He is having dinner with his daughter and her utterly boring husband. I told him that not even for him would I sit through an evening listening to that man talk on and on forever about his stock-market investments. He has no conversation!"

No conversation was Madame DeRochers's greatest criticism.

"But, look." She offered her right hand. "See what Monsieur Harris gave me for my birthday." A blue sapphire set in silver glimmered on her finger. Tiny diamonds sparkled on the band.

"It's lovely! It matches your eyes." Rachel admired the ring, then gave Madame DeRochers a sly look. "But it's on the wrong hand, isn't it?"

"Ah, my dear, you are so young." Madame DeRochers waggled a finger at her. "Marriage I have done, and done well, if I may say so. I will not do that again. Why should I? I will raise no more children. I will not share another orchard and the work." Her eyes crinkled with her smile. "For me there is only love, and love has never required marriage."

"Such a thing to hear from someone your age." Rachel pretended shock.

"As I said." Madame DeRochers peered at her with mock severity. "You are very young. And I hear that our esteemed politician wishes you to work on his landscaping, *chérie*." She was no longer smiling. "Will you take the project?"

"I . . . don't think so." Rachel looked down at the bench beneath them. "It . . . doesn't feel like something I will do well."

"Very carefully said, child." Madame's chiming laugh might have belonged to a younger woman. "You say no more than is needed. That is a precious thing in our world today, where idiots babble nonsense without thought." She gave Rachel a narrow, approving look. "I think you would not do that project well myself. I congratulate you on your perception."

Rachel blushed, pleased at the praise, because Joylinn's grandmother did not praise lightly. "Did you know him when he lived in Blossom?" she asked on a whim. "That was quite some time ago."

"My dear, I know *everyone*." Madame gave her an arch look. "Oh, yes, I remember that boy. He was, even then, attractive, and very aware of it. Oh, the Johnston girl loved him, *pauvre petite*. I felt so bad for her, but what can one say?" She shrugged elegantly. "Even then I was an old woman to her. How many young ones listen to the old, when their heart speaks to them? Ha."

"I heard that he was in love with her. That he was devastated when she died."

"Oh, he was distraught, *oui*." She sniffed. "What would people say if he was not? He enjoyed her attention, certainly. She was a lovely child. But, no, even as a very young man, he was never one to give his heart where there was no benefit to him, if you understand me. And what could the Johnstons offer him? They were not rich. They dug in the hills for plants. They had no connections to anyone who could be of use to an orphaned young man with ambition."

"That's cold," Rachel said.

"The truth is often cold, my child." Madame DeRochers shrugged. "That does not make it less the truth. No, the poor innocent looked after him with eyes that dreamed. And then she died." Madame DeRochers stared off across the sunset river. "When I heard of her death . . . I wondered. The young are so full of tragedy. They have not yet learned how precious life can be."

"You think she killed herself?" Rachel said softly.

"I think many things." Madame DeRochers turned to her finally, her face as cool and still as a marble bust. "I know

little. But I do know that it was only a few months later
that our young Claymore appeared in Blossom with a new
girlfriend—the daughter of very wealthy parents. I heard
the story that he had met her while he was working at a
resort, that summer before. It was the summer before *la
petite* fell from the cliff and died." She pressed her lips
together. "As I said. I know nothing."

Rachel crossed her arms, suddenly chilly in the gentle
evening breeze.

"The fire's ready for roasting hot dogs." Sandy tripped
over. "How are you, Madame?" She smiled down at the
elderly woman. "It's so nice to see you."

"It is very pleasant to be here, listening to the chatter of
youth." The elderly woman inclined her head with a smile.
"I am pleased to be included."

"I'm pleased that you were willing to put up with us."
Sandy's dimples showed as she smiled. "Shall I make you
a sausage? I bought some chicken and rosemary ones over
in Hood River."

"I would like a plain hot dog." Madame DeRochers
smiled up at her. "The taste of a hot dog roasted over a
picnic fire has its own special flavor. Thank you, my dear."

"Come on, Rachel. I've got good sticks for us." Sandy
brandished two willow whips, her face flushed with laughter. "Just watch out for those hot sausages our mayor
brought. Even Bill said they're peppery."

"If Bill thinks they're hot, I'm not touching them." Rachel laughed. Bill, Sandy's husband, was famous for his
incendiary salsas. She took one of the willow sticks. "I'll
bring you a hot dog," she told Madame DeRochers, and
followed Sandy over to the fire. The hot dogs and sausages
had been piled on paper plates at the end of the table. A
half dozen already sizzled on sticks held by heat-flushed
picnickers gathered around the mound of glowing coals. As
Rachel selected hot dogs for her stick, another car arrived
in the parking area, its headlights bright in the gathering
dusk.

"Oh, good." Sandy clapped her hands. "Its the Taxi Sis-

ters. I saw Earlene in town and told her to come on down.
She said she'd close up the station early."

"Good thing they carry pagers," Jeff drawled as he
scooped coleslaw onto his plate. "I'd hate to be sitting out
in the middle of nowhere with a broken axle, waiting for
Earlene to finish partying."

One of Blossom's two identical taxis—a gray Jeep Eagle
with *Independently Owned and Operated since 1977, Cash
Only* hand-lettered on the side—parked next to Jeff's truck
in the graveled lot. Operated by Roberta and Earlene Guar-
nieri, who also ran the town's only gas station and owned
the only tow truck, the taxi's strict cash only policy rou-
tinely irritated credit-card carrying tourists and out-of-
towners. Earlene and Roberta got out of the car and waved.
Roberta, tall and lanky, was the exact opposite of the squat
muscular Earlene. Earlene's perennial unlit cigar jutted at
a jaunty angle from her mouth as she waved at the crowd.

"I think they kidnapped a fare," Jeff said, as two more
people emerged from the Jeep's back seat.

"Mom," Rachel said faintly. She had managed to put the
afternoon aside for the past hour by focusing on the im-
promptu party and her friends. Now the full weight of her
mother's revelation returned with undiminished force. Jeff
took her hand and squeezed it.

Her mother and Joshua had reached the fringes of the
party. Phil Ventura was greeting them, waving two fresh
beers aloft. The party reshaped itself, engulfing them, re-
locating around the fire where hot dogs and sausages already spat and sizzled on sticks stuck into the soft ground.
Madame DeRochers lifted herself from the bench and went
over to greet the newcomers, her spine as straight at eigh-
tysomething as it had been at twenty. Perhaps more so.

"I wonder . . ." A sudden suspicion seized her, and she
marched over to where Sandy was opening the gigantic
bags of tortilla chips and plastic tubs of salsa that consti-
tuted Roberta and Earlene's offering. "So what is really
going on here?" she demanded of her friend.

"A party." Sandy gave her a wide-eyed, innocent look. "What did you think was going on here?"

"A party." Rachel smiled, feeling suddenly better than she had since she had first begun to worry about her mother. "A rather wonderful party."

"So go cook those sausages you were skewering." Sandy rolled her eyes. "Jeff's being polite and waiting for you, and Madame is expecting you to feed her."

"Yes, ma'am," Rachel said meekly, and went back to the table for the willow stick she had set down.

She joined the crowd around the glowing fire, roasting her cheeks as well as the hot dogs on her stick, leaning back against Jeff, the heat from the fire beating on her face and body, welcome as the night cooled and the breeze picked up. Across from her, Deborah O'Connor smiled at jokes and chatted as she and Joshua shared sausage and chips. But in spite of her laughter, her face looked tight and tired, and her eyes had a too-bright glitter, as of tears too long suppressed.

Bill came over to tell Jeff about his recent fishing trip and the spring Chinook salmon he'd landed. Pretty soon they were planning the next trip, and Rachel was talking to Joylinn about her plans to enclose part of the Bread Box's deck and turn it into greenhouse seating for the winter months, with sliding walls that could telescope open for the summer weather. "So how about if you do the indoor landscaping?" she asked Rachel. "I'd love to do tropicals— passion fruit vines, banana trees, dwarf pomegranates—that kind of thing. I want flowers, too. And water. Maybe a little fountain, or something in bamboo—sort of teahouse style."

"I'm not sure that a teahouse goes with your tropical jungle motif." Rachel laughed. "How about something in old stone? The effect of ancient ruins, just glimpsed through the leaves—a basin, trickling water. How does that sound?"

"Oh, cool. I like that." Joylinn decanted a second hot dog into a bun, and squirted brown mustard from a plastic squeeze bottle onto it in a wavy line.

"You're such a gourmet cook," Rachel said watching her. "How can you stand to eat basic supermarket hot dogs on a squishy white bun?"

"Oh, come on." Joylinn laughed as she scooped sauerkraut on top of the mustard. "Picnic-roasted hot dogs are something you just can't reproduce in the kitchen, no matter how much you spend on your stove and utensils." She took a huge bite and rolled her eyes appreciatively. "Mmm. Perfect. You couldn't get this at the best restaurant in San Francisco."

"I guess you're right." Rachel banished all guilt about calories for the occasion and accepted the gooey, stringy s'more that Jeff was holding out. "You couldn't do these in the kitchen, either." She bit into the crunchy sandwich of graham cracker, melting chocolate bar, and toasted marshmallow, fresh from the fire. "Must be the woods-smoke."

"Or the fact that everybody is starving by the time the fire is finally ready," Jeff murmured.

"That doesn't hurt." Joylinn laughed. "My esteemed grandmother is charming the socks off our mayor." She nodded toward the far side of the fire where Madame DeRochers and Ventura stood in deep conversation. The older woman's silvery laugh chimed above the murmur of voices. "I swear, she'll still be sexy at ninety-five."

Phil Ventura did indeed look mesmerized, laughing appreciatively as she tilted her head confidentially to him, the long line of her throat highlighted by the fire's glow. "Maybe you should tell him that she's got a boyfriend," Rachel suggested. "She told me something interesting tonight." She turned to Jeff. "She said that the Johnston girl—the one who died—was in love with Paul Claymore. She kind of hinted that her death might have been suicide. At least I think she was hinting that."

"Well, there was probably a lot of rumor flying around." Jeff shrugged. "But there wasn't any evidence to suggest anything but an accident. I get the feeling that Carey tried awfully hard to find some."

"Carey?" Joylinn looked puzzled.

"As in Icarus Spiros, who is now a Homicide detective with the Portland Police, but was on the force here, back then. Just out of the academy, I think." He shrugged. "He and Claymore do not get along."

"I should ask my Mom if she knew this Carey person." She finished her hot dog and licked the last bit of mustard from her fingertips. "I know she had a crush on some young police officer back then. Maybe it was him." She looked around. "I think our beach party is starting to fade."

She was right. People were leaving, picking up food containers and trash, calling out farewells as they trudged back up the path to their parked cars. Moonlight flashed on metal, and Rachel smiled as a wheelchair maneuvered briskly down the path. It was Harris, Madame DeRocher's lover. "I don't think you'll have to give Madame a ride home," Rachel remarked. "I guess the family dinner is over."

"I had a feeling he'd end that evening early." Joylinn laughed softly. "His son-in-law really is a jerk. And his daughter seems so nice. I guess she sees something in him that no one else does." Her smile grew as he reached Madame DeRochers, nodded a brief greeting to the mayor, then bent from the waist in a courtly bow over Madame's hand. She said something to the mayor, fluttered her fingers at him, then went off, walking gracefully beside Harris's chair, one hand resting lightly on his shoulder.

"They are quite the couple." Jeff smiled. "When are they getting married, Joylinn?"

"Oh, never, I'm sure." She laughed and rolled her eyes. "But they're scandalizing the administrator at the residence. She asked me into her office once when I was down there visiting—on the pretext of telling me how nicely my grandmother was adjusting to life there. What she really wanted to do was let me know that the two of them were acting like teenagers." Joylinn giggled. "Let's see. How did she put it? Acting in a manner not really in keeping with the age and decorum of the other residents here. I'm afraid I wasn't very sympathetic." Joylinn managed an almost penitent expression. "I mean, they are so in love." She smiled, but there was a thoughtful look in her eyes. "You know, love is kind of a two-edged sword. It has its bright side— like Madame and Harris. And then it has its dark side. Like Madame thinking the Johnston girl might have killed herself for it."

"Yin and yang," Jeff said.

Sobered by this turn in the conversation, Rachel looked around for her mother and Joshua. They had vanished. Frowning, she shaded her eyes against the glow of the dying embers, searching for them among the picnic tables. "They must have gone for a walk along the riverbank," she said. "Unless they left." But Earlene and Roberta still lingered, sitting side by side on a driftwood log that they had hauled over to the fire pit, toasting the last of the marshmallows over the coals.

"Are you looking for your mom?" Joylinn paused as she gathered unused paper plates and plastic utensils. "That's them, isn't it? Way down there?" She pointed downstream.

Two shadowy figures strolled toward them, not hurrying, still quite some distance away. Rachel recognized her mother's silhouette as the moonlight gleamed on her dark hair. Rachel watched them pause and turn toward each other, her hands full of leftover hot dogs.

"Voyeur!" Joylinn whispered in her ear. "Wrap those up and stop staring. They might like a little privacy."

"Yes, ma'am." She took the plastic bag Joylinn handed her and dumped the leftover hot dogs into it. The picnic leavings and most of the trash had disappeared with the departing partygoers. Rachel and Jeff drained the water from the ice chest that had cooled the beverages, then carried it up to Sandy and Bill's car.

"Have you heard any more about Eloise and the garden?" Sandy asked, as Bill stowed the ice chest in the trunk. "Are you going to be working there?"

"I hope so." Rachel stuffed bags of chips into the backseat.

"No fair!" Laughing, Sandy hauled one of them back out and thrust it at Rachel. "You get to share the leftover calories, girl. Well, if you get back there, will you keep an eye out for any microcassette tapes you might find lying around? I'd really like to hear what Eloise saved until last. I'm sure it had to do with her daughter's death." Her expression faltered. "What if . . . someone killed her because of it?" She spoke slowly, her brows furrowed. "I mean . . . someone erased the hard drive. What if they think I have another tape? Or something?" Fear glimmered in her pale eyes. "Jeff, what should I do?"

"Actually, Carey and I talked about that." Jeff nodded. "The Blossom Police have been keeping a pretty close eye on your house."

"You're kidding!" Her eyes widened. "And you told me I was being silly, Bill Daris!" She turned to her husband. "Thanks a lot."

"Well, it doesn't seem to be something to worry much about. At least we haven't seen anything unusual." Jeff seemed to be trying to suppress a smile. "Have you seen or heard anything suspicious?"

"No." She gave Bill another look. "But I'll call you if I do." She stressed the "you" slightly.

"Come on." Bill rolled his eyes. "Whoever stole the tape recorder and wiped the hard drive got what they wanted. Why do more?"

"They killed Eloise." She glared at him. "They're evil. They could do anything. And Jeff is taking it seriously."

"I have a feeling I'm going to wish you hadn't told her all this," Bill told Jeff wryly. "Just when the excitement of the big party was over, and I thought we could go back to a nice normal life." He heaved a deep sigh.

"Oh, come off it." Sandy elbowed him in the ribs. "Let's get out of here." She glanced toward the beach. "I think we're intruding."

Joshua and Rachel's mother were strolling up from the riverbank, arms around each other. "See you," Sandy said to Rachel. "Talk to you soon." She hopped into the car, and they pulled away just as Rachel's mother and her husband reached the parking space.

"Were you waiting for us?" Rachel's mother smiled at her. "I'm sorry. We lost track of time. I think we owe Roberta and Earlene an apology." Her face glowed in the moonlight. The lines of tension that had tightened her features for the last few days had vanished. She still looked tired, but she no longer looked so strained. "I wonder where they went?" she said, looking around.

Rachel cleared her throat, trying to get rid of the sudden lump there. "They were down by the fire a minute ago. Oh." She pointed. "There they are—on their way up the path. I guess they were putting the fire out."

"I'm so glad we came tonight." Deborah O'Connor smiled gently at her daughter. "Can we have lunch tomorrow? I think I owe you a good one."

"I'd love to," Rachel said huskily. Earlene and Roberta arrived at that moment, and they all piled into their respective cars. Beyond the lot, the tiny park stood deserted beneath the moon, its ground as clean as if the party had never occurred. "This was for her, wasn't it?" Rachel murmured, as Jeff started the car.

"I think it was for you, too." Jeff followed the taxi's taillights as they made their way back to the main road. "I think it was for all three of you."

"Whose idea was it?"

"You know, I don't think any one person thought of it." Jeff smiled and shook his head. "It just sort of started happening. I think we all did good." He reached for Rachel's hand.

"Me, too. She told Joshua. I'm sure of it." Rachel sighed and leaned her head back against the seat. "I'm still worried about her—but in a different way than I was. Easier to take," she murmured. "I think."

Jeff didn't answer, but when they reached Mrs. Frey's house, he climbed the steps to the apartment behind her. This time neither of them tiptoed. Peter wasn't on the landing. Apparently he had given up on them and gone out hunting. Rachel unlocked the door, and Jeff followed her inside without a word. She turned around and stepped into his arms, and nothing needed to be said. Not right then. Not for a while.

After a few minutes, they moved slightly apart. The yellow glow from the kitchen light she'd left on burnished Jeff's tawny skin and made his hair look black as night. Rachel drew a deep breath, her heart beating as if she'd been running. "Would you like to stay here tonight?" she asked softly.

He hesitated. For some time now, there had been the sense of boundaries between them. We will go this far, and no farther. *My doing,* Rachel thought. *My fear.*

"Are you sure?" He touched the edge of her jaw with one fingertip, tracing its line to her chin.

"Yes," she whispered. She locked the front door and took his hand to lead him into the bedroom.

The light on her answering machine was blinking. "No," she said out loud.

"Yes," he said. "It might be important."

She sighed and hit the replay button.

"This is Paul Claymore," his booming voice emerged from the speaker. *"I'm going to be in town for the next two days. Perhaps we can get together and look over your ideas."*

"He already told me this," Rachel said impatiently.

"Maybe he thought you'd forget."

"This is Roger Tourelle from the Garden Conservancy." His urgent words made her reach for the volume control. *"Somebody vandalized the garden today. Oh, my God, we've already got the advertising out for the open house in two weeks. Please call me. We need help getting things fixed, right away."*

"Oh, Lord." Rachel closed her eyes. "This can't have anything to do with Eloise's death. It can't."

"If you go down there tomorrow, I'm going with you," Jeff said grimly. "You have just acquired a new assistant. Tell Julio not to be jealous. I'm not after his job."

"I doubt he'll mind," Rachel said faintly. "He has finals."

Jeff moved toward the door and hesitated. "I guess you need your sleep. You'll want to start early tomorrow, huh?"

"Yes," she said, and reached out to catch his hand. "Where do you think you're going?"

He looked down at her. Smiled slowly. "Nowhere."

"Darn right," she said.

Rachel woke with the first hint of sunrise, curled against Jeff's back. She sat up slowly and stretched, trying not to waken him, watching his rib cage rise and fall with the deep, even breathing of his slumber. He lay on his side, his face drowned in sleep. Rachel smiled, seized by memory of the infamous summer night when she had slipped out to watch the stars with Jeff, and they had fallen asleep on a blanket out in a mowed hayfield up above the Gorge and the sparse lights of Blossom. They had wakened, soaked with dew in the gray hour before dawn. Rachel had tiptoed through the sleeping house when Jeff brought her home, holding her breath in terror that she'd wake someone. She had made it safely to her room. Jeff's mother had been gone for the weekend, so they had both escaped retribution.

Outside, the birds trilled their morning songs, and the first yellow glow of sunrise lighted Mrs. Frey's garden. Still smiling, Rachel slid carefully from beneath the quilt. Peter crouched outside, glaring from the windowsill. She touched her finger to her lips, grabbed her cotton robe from the closet door, and slipped out of the bedroom.

This was the first time Jeff had spent the night there.

The linoleum chilled her feet as she went into the kitchen to start a pot of coffee. The room looked slightly out of proportion, as if it had changed during the night. The first dark trickle spattered into the glass urn, and she went to let Peter in. The scent of brewing coffee banished her brief sense of strangeness. Peter stalked past her, tail in the air, leaped onto the back of the sofa, and began to groom himself aggressively.

"I'll feed you in a minute, cat." She patted him, which made him flatten his ears, and went back into the kitchen to get the cat food, and to see what kind of breakfast she could produce. Can opener in hand, she stared distractedly at the refrigerator, filled with dismay at the evidence of a much-postponed shopping trip. *Apples*, she thought grimly. *And one egg each. And a stale bagel to share if we're really desperate.*

An explosive grunt followed by a single four-letter word erupted from the bedroom.

"Peter!" As she burst into the hall, Peter stalked from the bedroom, his tail straight up in the air, and a decidedly smug expression on his face.

"Your cat needs to go on a diet." Jeff appeared in the doorway, wearing only his undershorts. "When he launches himself from your dresser, he gains quite a bit of momentum by the time he hits the bed. He's a good aim, too." He rubbed his flat belly and winced. "I think I'm going to have black-and-blue cat prints there tomorrow."

"Been there, done that." Rachel stifled a giggle. "He likes to make his presence felt."

"Oh, his presence got felt all right." Jeff stretched. "You might say he made an impact." He ignored Rachel's groan. "Is that can opener intended for people food or cat chow?"

"Well, I can offer you good coffee. And cat food." Rachel made a face. "Shall we stop for breakfast on the way to Portland?" She glanced at the small clock on the bookshelf in the main room. "And I'd better call Roger. The poor man probably decided that I dumped him and the garden." She reached for the phone. "Could you open a can

of cat food for the Flying Feline? I left it on the counter.
Feel free to check out the kitchen resources while you're
there." She made a face. "Maybe you can think of a way
to feed us from what's on hand. Roger?" She turned her
attention to the phone. "This is Rachel O'Connor." She
nodded and settled herself into the corner of the sofa as he
launched into a frenzy of angry description.

The garden had been vandalized with the intention to
harm the plantings. She listened with growing dismay as
he described tender plants trampled or hacked from the
earth, branches broken, and bark gouged from tree trunks.
This didn't sound like drunken teenagers. It sounded more
like someone with a grudge.

"Did you call the police?" she asked him, accepting the
mug of coffee Jeff handed her. "Did they send someone
out?"

"They think it was kids. It wasn't kids," Tourelle sput-
tered. "It wasn't. Whoever did this picked out Eloise's favorite plants and her taxonomic collections to destroy. But
try to explain how you know that to some cop who doesn't
know a daisy from an orchid and figures nobody else does
either. If we have to cancel this event, God knows if all
our donors will be willing to help us out again. This was
going to be so great! And it's still a good season for plant
sales. We had a lot of nurseries willing to come along and
give us a percentage. It would have been just what we
needed to get us off the ground."

"Don't cancel it yet." Rachel took a swallow of the hot
coffee. "I'll be down there this morning, and I'll give you
an estimate on how long it'll take to clean things up. I can't
believe some one person destroyed that garden in a single
night. Not without a back hoe."

"You haven't seen it yet." Roger sounded utterly depressed. "You have my cell-phone number, but I'm catching a ten o'clock plane to the Bay Area. I won't be back
until late tonight." He hung up.

"Sounds ugly." Rachel looked up at Jeff, who had
perched himself on the arm of the sofa. "It sounds as if

someone had a grudge against Eloise—if he's right about her favorite plants being destroyed. Why wouldn't the police look into it?" She frowned. "Maybe the vandal left fingerprints on a shovel or something?"

"I'm a little surprised that Carey didn't prick up his ears, if you want to know." Jeff stared thoughtfully into his coffee mug. "I wonder if your excitable friend is telling you everything."

"Me, too. He is a bit hyper at times. I can't wait to meet him in person and see if he matches his telephone persona." Rachel sighed and got to her feet. "You want the shower first?"

"I'd suggest both at the same time." Jeff leaned down to brush his lips across the top of her head. "But then we might not make it down to Portland. At least not soon."

"So go. And don't use all the hot water." She gave him a shove.

"I'm going. And breakfast is my treat. I couldn't come up with any breakfast ideas, either." He laughed and headed for the bathroom.

While he showered, she poured another cup of coffee and called her mother. She got their voice mail after the first ring. Which was a good sign, since they didn't turn the phone back on until they got out of bed in the morning. And they usually got up with the sun. Smiling, she replaced the receiver and looked down at the untouched mound of cat food on Peter's plate. "Is this a boycott, cat?" She looked through the archway to where he sat washing himself on the back of the sofa. "I really don't think you're in danger of starving to death."

Peter ignored her.

"Your turn." Jeff emerged from the bathroom, his hair wet, haloed by steam. "There's plenty of hot water left. If you're quick." With a grin, he vanished into the bedroom.

She was quick. To be honest, the thought of Eloise's beloved garden having been seriously damaged filled her with anger. Who? And why? And why hadn't Spiros investigated? She kept running those questions through her mind over and over as she showered. While she dressed, she called Julio from the bedroom. She told him she would need Eduardo and his crew right away. She would need them for at least three days and perhaps more. She would know when she'd been to the site. Julio told her he would talk to Eduardo, then hesitated, and finally told her that he had gone to see the Claymore's maid yesterday evening.

"She is not from our village, but she lived in the village on the other side of the river. She is a cousin of a cousin on my mother's side," he said happily. "We know some people, you know? She will eat dinner with us after mass today. She is so happy to have someone to speak with."

"That's great," Rachel said, pleased that he sounded so pleased. "Have a wonderful day."

"I told her my uncle would come there. To check on the house, you know? She is alone there many times when *Senor* and *Senora* are not home. She is frightened."

"I'm so glad this worked out." Rachel buckled the belt of her jeans. "I'll call you tonight when you've talked to Eduardo. I'm willing to pay extra for the travel. Be sure to tell him."

"I will," he said gravely. "I will wait for your call."

Jeff had let Peter out and was waiting by the door for her. Rachel smiled as she passed the kitchen. Peter's plate had been polished clean. He wasn't as upset as he pretended.

Mrs. Frey was, of course, in her garden as they descended the stairs, kneeling at the feet of her prize roses, weeding. This morning she was wearing an enormous palm-leaf hat, decorated with scarlet and orange poppies that had been plaited out of straw. A small green-plastic chameleon crouched realistically on the brim.

"Good morning, Rachel. Good morning, Jeff." Mrs. Frey looked up, her trowel dripping crumbs of black dirt onto her blue jeans. "I think we've finally seen the last of our Portland weather." Her eyes twinkled in spite of her casual tone. "Did you hear the chickadees this morning? They had quite the fight in the feeder, from the sound of it."

"I guess we slept through it," Jeff said gravely. "That's a very nice hat."

"My son sent it to me from Mexico." Her face folded into a thousand lines as she smiled. "He sends me the most wonderful hats. Have a nice day." She waved a gloved hand as they headed for Rachel's truck.

"I don't think my landlady was surprised to see you." Rachel climbed behind the wheel.

"I think she's been feeling a bit impatient," Jeff said.

"Was that what she was giving you advice about the other day?"

"It was just advice." His eyes twinkled.

They stopped briefly at the Bread Box for oversize cups of coffee and a bag of assorted rolls and pastries. Fortified against starvation, Rachel drove back through town and took the ramp onto the freeway. It was a beautiful morning, sunny and clear. This had been a cold, wet spring, and Rachel enjoyed the warm kiss of the sun on her face as she negotiated the light, midmorning traffic on the interstate.

"I guess I ought to tell you why I left LAPD," Jeff said.

Rachel nearly swerved onto the center line. "I'd like that," she said with rather impressive calm. "I've wondered."

"I know you have." He stared out the window at the expanse of the Columbia. Beneath the cloudless sky, the water looked nearly blue, sprinkled with white wave crests that meant wind. "It was just . . . I was stupid, I guess." He looked at her, a brooding expression on his face. "But I wouldn't do it any differently now, so I guess I'm still stupid."

"Stupid how?" Rachel eased past a tractor pulling a double-trailer rig.

"I didn't pay attention to politics." He smiled dryly. "I decided I was above politics."

"It had to do with Spiros."

He nodded. "Carey doesn't play politics, either. But he was good—he *is* good. So he got away with stepping on the wrong toes. Until he stepped once too often, and somebody didn't care anymore whether he was good or not."

"So he got in trouble, and you backed him."

"That's the short version." Jeff nodded. Sighed. "I said the wrong things to the wrong people, and it got around. There was a situation." He cleared his throat, his eyes on the river again. "I didn't handle it well. But a lot of guys would have handled it worse. I had the choice of quitting. Or . . ." He shrugged.

What kind of situation? she wanted to ask him. She touched his knee lightly with her fingertips instead.

"I got rough with a dealer," he said abruptly. "I was carrying a lot of anger right then and I . . . sort of took it out on him. It happens," he said. "Doesn't excuse it. This time—it got singled out. I was going to be an example for the media."

"If you didn't quit first," Rachel said softly.

Jeff had never once backed down from a confrontation in all the years she'd known him. He had backed down this time, she felt. Or he thought he had.

"An example for the media of what?" she asked when he didn't say anything. "Spiros's bad judgment in hiring? His bad leadership?"

Jeff didn't say anything for a few moments. "Something like that," he said at last. Reluctantly. "Maybe."

Yeah, maybe. Rachel sighed and touched him again.

"I put that guy in the hospital. He deserved it, but not from me." His voice was harsh. "Just so you know."

I killed people, Beck had said. *I liked it.*

How many people walked around with a splinter of darkness inside them? Rachel wondered. How often did it fester, like an abscess, invisible from outside? "So I know." Unexpected anger colored her tone. "So you did something that I bet a whole lot of people do every day. Once, Jeff. Wow. I guess that makes you a villain, huh? Should I run screaming?"

"Okay, so I guess I'm just a puny villain." He smiled. It was a crooked smile, but it was a smile.

"Thanks for telling me," she said, and cleared a sudden thickness from her throat. "I wondered."

"Yeah, you did." He took her hand, kissed it gently on the palm, and placed it firmly on the wheel. "No more revelations while you're driving. I promise."

"Well, it's better than listening to the radio." She matched his light tone, braking as she reached their exit.

They followed a main street through the eastside suburban neighborhoods of Portland, passing fast-food stands, gas stations, and car lots. The busy retail atmosphere petered out abruptly, and they passed small homes and lawns, backyard apple trees still in late bloom this cold spring. To the west, a low wall of gray clouds loomed, sending out veils of thin clouds that dimmed the bright sunlight.

"So much for our lovely day," Rachel murmured, as the street narrowed at an intersection from a major residential artery to a curving two-lane road that dipped down to the rushing creek. "I'd grow moss if I lived here."

"I don't know how Carey stands the winters. The weather report said there was a big low heading this way. Lots of rain tonight—straight from Hawaii." Jeff peered through the windshield. "Let's hope it holds off, or we may all be swimming if the snowpack melts. Is that it?" he asked as they switch-backed down into the narrow canyon formed by the creek. "Those big iron gates?"

"That's it." She let her breath out slowly as they turned off the street and passed between the stone gateposts. For a moment Rachel imagined that she could feel Eloise's presence in the tangle of greenery that fenced the parking area and crowded the house. She parked her truck in front of the thick stand of black bamboo in the courtyard, and they got out.

The sun had vanished behind the increasing clouds, and the dim light filtering through cedar boughs and bamboo fronds gave the light an almost tropical quality, as if they stood in an Amazon jungle. A breeze gusted suddenly, eerily warm and tropical, heavy with moisture, increasing the jungle feel.

"At least we won't get too cold, if it starts raining," Rachel said, peering up at the slope above the house. Even from here, she could see broken stems and the pale flutter of bruised and wilting leaves. "Roger wasn't exaggerating the damage," she said grimly. "I'll get us some gloves and pruning shears, and we'll go take a look."

A sudden motion and scuff of feet startled her as she unlocked her truck box. She turned, just in time to see Jeff vault over the low stone wall that edged the entry terrace, and vanish down the bank below the house with a crash of disturbed foliage. Rachel ran to the wall. Below, Jeff launched a flying tackle at a bulky shape disappearing into the ferns and weeds that grew lush and high in the low boggy ground between the creek and the high bank. He connected, and the fleeing man fell with a grunt and a cry. They vanished into the weeds beneath an alder. Leaves and branches shook, and she heard the sound of a scuffle. Someone grunted again, a hoarse, hard coughing sound, and then she heard voices, one sharp and shrill with anger or fear. Jeff rose to his feet, dragging a shorter, stocky man erect with a hand in his collar.

"My face is on fire," he yelped, rubbing at his cheeks. "I'm going to charge you with assault for this. We landed in the damn nettles."

"You can talk to the replying officer about assault," Jeff said between his teeth as he hauled the man back along the path. "How do we get up there?" He looked up at Rachel, nettle welts rising on his face and neck, also. "And do you know any antidote for nettles?"

"Rub leaves on the welts," Rachel instructed. "Anything juicy will work."

"The steps are over there." The man in Jeff's grasp pointed a stubby finger to the right of the house. A diamond glittered in a thick ring. "I'll have you know I'm Eloise Johnstons's son Alan, and I have every right to be here. Let go of me, damn it."

"You sure acted odd for a man with the right to be here,"

Jeff drawled. "Were you out picking a few flowers, per-haps?"

"I don't know what the hell you're talking about." The pudgy man snatched a handful of ferns from a clump and began to gingerly rub at his face. "This isn't helping."

"It will." Rachel crossed the terrace to meet them as they climbed the narrow rock stairway that led up to the house level. The downstairs office door opened onto the landing. It stood open. "You really have to smash the leaves. Here." She plucked several leaves of curly dock that had sprouted along the edge of the stone patio. "Use these."

The lawyer snatched the leaves from her as he reached the patio and gave her a dark glare. "And just who are you, anyway?" He turned the glare on Jeff. "What are you two doing here?"

"Do you always run when you hear someone drive up?" Jeff asked casually. He flipped open his wallet and offered his badge—which made Mr. Alan Johnston's mouth tighten. "Most people who are at home tend to greet visitors. We're investigating a report of vandalism here."

"I didn't do anything." But Johnston paled slightly. "Look, I didn't know who you were. I was just . . . looking over my mother's things. You startled me. I thought you were burglars." He flung the handful of crushed leaves down and looked with disgust at his hands. "I need to wash up."

"Let's go downstairs," Jeff said pleasantly. "Since the door's open." He smiled as the heavyset man hesitated.

"All right, all right." Turning his back on them, he stomped down the stone stairs and into the office.

Jeff and Rachel followed him down. His suit had the elegance of an expensive custom garment, although it was a mess now, and he wore a Rolex watch on his left wrist. He certainly seemed to be doing well for himself, Rachel thought. That's what April had told her—that the sons weren't in need financially. As they entered the office, she halted. Papers littered the floor and piled like snowdrifts around the file cabinet. The desk had been swept clean.

Pens and pencils, a stapler, and a litter of colored paper
clips strewed the floor.

"Looks like we had a bit of wind in here." Jeff kept his
eyes on Johnston. "Any idea what caused this little mess?"

"No." A slow flush crept up the lawyer's face. "I . . . It
was like this when I got here. I . . . don't know anything
about it. And I have every right to be here. This is my
mother's house."

"Your mother was murdered."

"I . . . Oh, my God." Johnston puffed with outrage. "You
can't seriously . . . I don't even live in the state. I live in
San Antonio. I came up here to settle my mother's affairs.
How dare you even suggest—"

"I'm not suggesting anything at all." Jeff leaned against
the opened and empty file cabinet, his arms crossed, his
expression almost lazy. "Me, I'm simply wondering why
you went through the office like this. Temper?" He tilted
his head. "Are you angry that she's giving away this nice
piece of real estate?"

"Of course I'm angry about that," he said mechanically.
"No one ever has enough money. Just ask my wife." But
his brief bravado had fizzled. He looked down at his rumpled suit, wiping ineffectually at the mud stains on his trou-
sers. He looked almost pathetic with his welted face,
smeared with green streaks of leaf pulp. He sighed, slump-
ing like a deflating baloon. "Yes, I threw things around in
here." He pulled up the leather upholstered chair, grimaced
at his filthy clothes, then sat down. "I was looking for . . .
something that belonged to me. I didn't find it." His eyes
strayed to the computer. "It isn't working."

"Somebody messed up the hard drive to destroy the
memoirs." Rachel spoke up and felt both men's eyes fix on
her. "The manuscript is missing, too. That's what you were
looking for, isn't it?"

It was a guess, but she wasn't prepared for the sudden
pallor on Johnston's face. He gasped, the nettle stings
standing out vividly against his waxy skin. Jeff straightened, his expression suddenly concerned, and Rachel won-

dered if the man was having a heart attack. He slumped back in the chair, his body flaccid and fleshy. "Someone took it?" he whispered. "The memoirs?"

"I really want to read this," Jeff said.

Johnston ignored him, turning an urgent look on Rachel. "You must be the woman who's been working on it for her. So you read it, right?"

"Not me." Rachel shook her head. "I've never read a word of it."

"But now someone has it," Johnston said dully. "How wonderful."

"So what's in it?" Jeff moved to stand in front of Johnston, staring down until the lawyer slowly raised his head. "Something bad enough that someone might kill to keep it from being published?"

"You're asking me if I killed my mother," Johnston said dully. His laugh sounded more like a cough. "No, I didn't kill her. Nothing could make me do that—not even her damn collected family confessions. And, no, I don't think anyone else killed her for that manuscript either." He made his coughing laugh again. "Our sins were pretty pedestrian. It's just that I decided to try politics. And . . . I went through your basic adolescent rebellion period. Not something I'm awfully proud of now." He made a face. "But nothing earthshaking. Unless you're planning on putting yourself under our current political microscope. No point in giving the media scandal-mongers a head start in the dirt-digging race. If she even mentioned me."

"So you didn't do the damage in the garden?" Jeff drawled.

"What damage?" Johnston blinked at him. "Who damaged the garden?"

"I was thinking you might have done it." Jeff looked around the paper-strewn office.

"Not me. I'd get too dirty." Johnston looked ruefully down at his ruined suit. "I never knew one plant from another. I was our mother's great disappointment on that score." He looked up, his eyes narrowing. "And for your

information, on the day—and night—my mother died, I
was in San Antonio working on an interminable contract
negotiation for a a real-estate group that wants to develop
a new retail center near the downtown. Believe me," he
said ruefully, "I wish I *had* been somewhere else. But I
wasn't, and lots of people can testify to that. The police
have already checked." He stood up. "I don't think you can
charge me with anything, since I let myself in here with
my own key. I'll be happy to give you my name and ad-
ress—I'll be staying at the Portland Marriott until tomorrow." He looked at his pants again and sighed. "I need to
call a cab. If I can go."

"You can go." Jeff nodded toward the phone on the desk.
"I may call you later."

The lawyer got to his feet, limping a little as he stepped
over to the phone. He made his call for a cab and looked
once more at Jeff. "I'm going to wait upstairs in the hall if
you don't mind."

"Go ahead." Jeff nodded. "We'll wait with you."

Johnston sighed and trudged up the stairs, leaving bits
of dirt and leaves on the stairs. He looked uneasily around
the house as he settled himself in a straight-backed chair
with a leather seat in the wood-paneled entryway. Jeff
looked at Rachel and raised an eyebrow.

"Why don't you go on and take a look around," he said.
"I'm going to make a call."

To Spiros, Rachel guessed. Jeff was angry. She wasn't
quite sure why.

She nodded and went out through the door that led into
the breezeway. It wasn't raining yet, but the heavy sky
threatened as she went around behind the house and looked
up at the rock garden. It was still almost tropically warm.
Chinook wind, she thought as she peered at the tiny plants
clinging to the dirt-filled crevices between the stones. Pineapple Express, they called it around here—a warm, wet
wind that seemed to blow straight from Hawaii's tropical
shores. Uneasily, Rachel thought of the above-normal
snowpack still coating the mountains and hoped that this

Chinook didn't last long. Below the house, the creek was already rising.

From inside, she heard Jeff's voice raised in anger. "Don't give me that teenage vandalism crap," he was saying. "Somebody wrecked the property where a woman was murdered, and you say it's coincidence? Come on, Carey, what is this? You've made up your mind it's the girl? Is that it?"

Feeling guilty for eavesdropping, but even more worried about April now, Rachel climbed up into the rock garden. It seemed to be intact, except for a couple of boulders that had been rolled down onto the patio below. She clenched her teeth at Spiros's obstinance as she examined the damage. A few early-blooming penstemons and some Lewisias had been trampled, but other than that, little had been harmed. A rare and endangered *Penstemon barretti* was undamaged. Another rare plant, the *Kalmiopsis leachiana* was also intact. Mostly the early-blooming shrubs had been damaged. Branches had been ripped from witch hazels, rhododendrons, camellia, and mahonias. It looked as if someone had used an ax or a scythe.

With growing anger, Rachel followed the swath of destruction up the hillside. The viburnums had been hacked, obviously by an ax. A bed of trillium and hellebores had been trampled. Rachel straightened a bruised and broken stem of trillium, the anger in her chest congealing to a hot, hard lump. Trillium had only its three leaves. Cut the stem, trample it, and the plant got no nourishment. With luck, they'd come back next year, smaller and less vigorous. With luck. The hellebore, just past bloom, was more resilient. She propped bruised plants upright with twigs picked up from the ground, pulling competing weeds from the ground around them, to give them the best chance of recovery. The foamy spikes of blooming vanilla leaf had been trampled along with the tender leaves and stems of the duck's-foot. Those plants would recover. Rachel bent to pull a clump of a weedy wild geranium from where it had invaded a clump of hellebore. She straightened as Jeff caught up with her.

"No help from Lieutenant Spiros," Jeff said tightly. "And he says Mr. Alan Johnston has every right to be in the house." He shook his head, frustration evident on his face. "Carey's playing this wrong, and I don't get it. He's too good a cop to be this sloppy. I'm still betting that our muddy Alan did this." He looked around grimly. "He sure did a job, didn't he?"

"Not as bad as it looks." Rachel tossed her handful of weeds onto the ground. "Our prowler really didn't know much about plants, let alone the plants here. There's a lot of ugly damage, but our vandal either didn't know how to kill plants or wasn't really trying to. And he missed the really rare plants entirely. He just went for the blooming stuff." She shook her head. "I don't think it was either of the sons. Or was Mr. Alan already muddy when you dumped him?"

"Sweetheart, I didn't notice." Jeff gave her wolfish grin. "I was too busy trying to catch up to him. He ran. That sure makes me think he's guilty of something."

"Maybe." Rachel shrugged. "But if he was really mad at his mother, why not do some real damage?"

"Because he didn't know which plants were rare," Jeff said slowly. "Alan even said he didn't know plants."

"I think they'd have heard about the rare plants enough to go for them first," Rachel said. "I remember once when my cousin Eric was really having a bad time with my aunt and uncle, he went out one night and trashed a few young trees. He just happened to get every one of the new cultivar Uncle Jack had finally decided to try and was certain would turn the orchard around." Rachel wrinkled her nose, remembering the family storm that had resulted. "He swore he didn't know that this row was more important than any other—but Uncle Jack had been boasting about those trees for weeks before Eric took the ax to them." She shrugged. "I bet he knew they were important, even if unconsciously."

"You getting a degree in psychology next?" But Jeff

looked thoughtful. "Actually, I think you've got a serious point. So if it wasn't one of the disgruntled heirs, who was it?"

"Good question." Rachel dropped her handful of weeds onto the path. "One we can contemplate when you're a cop again, but right now you're a day laborer, and we need to get to work. If you're finished with our muddy burglar?"

"I'm finished. Can you save anything?" Jeff nodded downslope toward the wreckage of wilting branches and herbaceous plants. "It looks like a mess to me."

"Oh, most of it will recover fine. Not the trilliums maybe, but a lot of the other species." She nodded as she headed purposefully down to her truck. "The big task is going to be cleaning up the mess so that the place looks decent for that open house. And weeding." She sighed. "This is a good spring for weeds. I'd like to get these beds cleaned up a bit."

"Weeding?" Jeff groaned theatrically. "I was all set to slash and haul, but weeding . . . I don't know."

"It's a long walk back to Blossom." Rachel laughed as he swiped at her backside, dodged, and ran down the path to the truck. When he came charging after her, she shoved a pair of gloves and a long-handled lopper into his hands. "Time to work."

"I'm set." But he was no longer laughing. "Promise me, though, that you won't go wandering off without me." He looked uneasily at the trees and the riotous undergrowth beneath them. "We don't really know what's going on here. Whoever used that ax on the plants might still be around. A camellia is one thing—you are another."

"We'll be working together," Rachel said lightly. But the gloomy weather and the wanton damage left her sharing his unease. The gathering clouds and the unexpectedly warm temperature added an urgency to their actions as they began to remove damaged herbaceous shrubs and pull the rampant weeds along the paths above the rock garden. Above them, the empty stone house on the crest of the slope loomed, full of shadow. The windows were glassless, and drifts of rotting needles covered the shingled roof. Rachel found herself looking over her shoulder every few minutes as she trimmed broken stems of duck's-foot and vanilla leaf and pulled up handfuls of invasive wild geranium. Abruptly she straightened, tossing down her grub hoe. "I swear someone's watching us."

"Did you see something?" Jeff set down the wheelbarrow full of camellia prunings he was pushing up to the compost pile they'd established above the garden.

"No. It's just a feeling." Rachel pulled off her gloves and tossed them down. "Want to go take a look?" But Jeff was already heading up the slope, circling cautiously around the broken remnants of a fence that had once separated the house and the meadow out front from the main part of the property.

The house belonged to the Johnstons, but it had obviously not been lived in for a long time. The door had no knob. A rusty chain had been run through the hole where a door handle had once existed, and had been padlocked to a heavy staple nailed into the frame of the door. The windows on the near side of the house had been covered with weathered plywood, streaked with water stains from the needle-clogged gutters. Jeff rattled the chain thoughtfully. Then he frowned and began to work at the thick staple. To Rachel's surprise, it pulled out of the rotted wood of the doorframe with only minor resistance.

Jeff looked at her and gestured for her to stand back. With a thrust of his shoulder, he flung the door open and stepped quickly to the side. The door crashed back against the wall, and a startled barn swallow darted out, zigzagging away through the trees with a shrill, frightened peep. Light streamed in, illuminating a broken table, a few rotting cardboard boxes, and an ancient refrigerator without a door. Slowly Jeff stepped into the house, looking around carefully as he moved cautiously out of sight. "Nobody home," he called out a moment later.

Rachel followed him inside. A small porcelain sink was set into a plywood counter. A rust stain marked a longtime drip, but when she turned the antique porcelain faucet handles, nothing happened. From the cloudy kitchen windows, draped with cobwebs and dead flies, she could see the garden above the parking area. She turned away from the counter and followed Jeff down the narrow hallway. A closet and a bathroom opened from the hall. Two bedrooms occupied the eastern end of the house. One looked out over the overgrown meadow in front of the house. Its windows had been boarded up, filling the space with near darkness. She made out a broken bed frame and a closet wtih a few empty wire hangers inside.

The other bedroom offered a clear view of the garden above the rock garden. She came up beside Jeff, who was staring through the smeared glass. The wheelbarrow was clearly visible. "Well, if somebody was here, he had a good view." Rachel spoke lightly, but the hairs on the back of her neck stirred. On the floor at their feet lay a crumpled candy wrapper. A Baby Ruth. The dust that lay so thickly on most surfaces in the house, had been smeared and disturbed on the floor, she realized. Looking back down the hall, she could see a clear trail that led down the hall and toward the front door in the main room. "Somebody has been in here," she said softly.

"More than once, I think." Jeff turned to her, his expression serious. "I don't want you coming here by yourself."

"Me, neither!" Rachel laughed faintly. "But don't worry. Considering the work that needs to be done, I'll have Eduardo and at least two of his friends down here with me. What I really need is a full crew. I'll be perfectly safe." She smiled. "Eduardo is almost as protective as Julio. I might as well have a bodyguard with me."

"You might need a bodyguard," Jeff said grimly. He nodded toward the corner of the window. Several dark spots marked the floor. When Rachel bent down, she realized that someone has spilled liquid there. Coffee, perhaps. The tiny puddles were still wet. She looked up at Jeff, her eyes widening.

"I wish we'd found the ax here." He looked around the

house, his expression still serious. "Let's get back to work. I don't think our watcher is going to come back, but we can keep an eye out anyway."

Goose bumps prickling her skin—not from chill on this tropical-warm day—Rachel followed him back to their work site. They spent the rest of the day working hard to remove the damaged plants, leaving most of the weeding for the crew she would bring down. They shared a late lunch and walked along the creek, where she pointed out the dozens of ferns—some native and some not—that grew thickly along the low ground. As they joined the path that led to the footbridge and the steps to the parking area, Rachel hesitated. This was where they had found Eloise. The dense sky seemed to press down on them, and her skin prickled with unease. "Let's go back this way," she said abruptly. Turning around, she led the way back through the ferns and up the steps that led to the terrace.

The first drops of rain began to fall as they stowed their tools at the end of the day. "Anytime you want a job," Rachel said wearily as Jeff heaved the wheelbarrow onto the truck, "just ask. You work as hard as Julio, and I didn't think anybody could equal him."

"I think I'll stick with police work." Jeff chuckled. "I'm glad I was some help, anyway." He put his hand on her shoulder lightly, his expression serious again. "I'm going to worry about you while you're here."

"I'll be careful, and I won't be alone." She leaned against him, warmed by the pressure of his arm. "It scared me today to think that somebody was watching us."

"It *should* scare you," he said, and bent to kiss her. "Be careful."

"I promise." Then they separated as the warm, tropical rain began to fall a in earnest, ducking into the cab of the truck in the thickening dusk.

As they turned onto the main road, Rachel looked back at the house, half-hidden by trees and shrubs. Nothing moved, but she shivered anyway, glad that she would have company down here for the next few days.

CHAPTER

13

They stopped for sandwich makings on the way back to Blossom, since they unanimously decided that they were too grubby for any civilized restaurant, and neither of them was a fan of fast food. They had intended to picnic along the river in Cascade Locks, but the rain had preceded them. It fell in gray curtains, steady and warm, running across the freeway in sheets. Big trucks raised misty clouds of spray that seemed to hang in the thick warm air. Even with her truck's defroster going full blast, the windshield kept fogging up.

They ended up parking along the riverbank and sitting with the windows down a bare inch, watching the rain fall on the gray water of the river. A lone sailboat, its sails furled, churned doggedly upriver, looking lonely and bedraggled in the watery light. It was starting to get dark by the time they reached Blossom, twilight falling early because of the thick cloud cover Rachel yawned as they drove through town, depressed by the weather, wanting a nice hot shower and maybe some hot soup for dinner.

"I hope this doesn't keep up." Jeff peered at the lowering sky. "A couple of days of Chinook weather like this, and we'll lose twelve feet of snowpack off Hood." He was frowning. "We could see some flooding."

"Maybe the weather will change tonight," Rachel said.

"Maybe." Jeff didn't sound hopeful. He made a face. "I thought I was in better shape. I'm going to have some sore muscles in the morning."

"Well, you pushed that wheelbarrow uphill how many times?"

"About three thousand, I think. Feels like it anyway." He grimaced. "Did anyone ever tell you that it makes a lot more sense to put the trash pile downhill from where you're working?"

"I never thought of that," Rachel said with a straight face. She checked her watch as they turned onto her street. "I'll call Julio. Hopefully Eduardo has a crew for me." She sighed. "If this rain keeps up, it's going to be a muddy day tomorrow. I wish we weren't so pressed for time."

"Don't go there by yourself." Jeff's tone was serious. "You promised that, remember?"

"I'm not about to," she said fervently. "Today impressed me."

"Good." Jeff still wasn't smiling. "I hope it did."

Mrs. Frey's lights were on, glowing through the steady rain. They ran from the truck to the relatively dry ground beneath the eaves. "Need any help unloading anything?" Jeff put his hands lightly on her shoulders, his eyes full of the evening's soft light. Raindrops glittered on his raven hair, and he shook his head, laughing. "I'm wet."

"Me, too, and, no, everything can stay in the truck, thanks. It's all cleaned up." She lifted her face and kissed him softly on the mouth, tasting raindrops on his lips. "Thank you for the help," she said. "Sorry I couldn't provide better weather."

"Any time you want help." He brushed his lips gently across her forehead. "Keep it in mind, okay?"

"I will." She stepped back as he went to his car, waving as he climbed in. Up on the landing, Peter yowled piteously, obviously suffering in the barbaric weather. "I'll talk to you tomorrow," she said, as Jeff backed past her, down the driveway.

"I'll call you." He rolled the window up, and his headlights dazzled her eyes briefly as he backed out onto the street.

She climbed the stairs slowly, smiling because she could just see her landlady's silhouette behind the sheer curtains in the downstairs window. She let Peter in and went to check her machine. One message. She sighed, but decided she'd better call Julio before she listened to it, since he might go to bed early. He answered the phone on the first ring, as if he was waiting for a call.

"Eduardo says he can come with two others," he told her, sounding uncharacteristically disappointed at her voice on the line.

"You sound tired," Rachel said. "I bet you've been studying all day."

"Mostly." A smile warmed his voice. "I went to the house of Senor Claymore today. Chankina made lunch. *El Señor* was not at home, or his wife, so we ate at the table outside. They never eat there, Chankina says. But it cost much money, and she has to clean it every day." He sounded disapproving.

"Chankina? Is that Anita's real name?"

"Yes. I am teaching her to speak English," he said smugly. "I told her English is better than Spanish. People respect her more for English."

"So is your name the one you were given?" Rachel asked, curious. "Or were you named something else?"

"Julio is my name," he said. "Many people in the village where I was born had Spanish names. Our mother's name was Maria Bonita. My father's name was Bol."

It was the first time he had mentioned his parents' names. He rarely talked about his family or the village where he had been born in northern Guatemala. She knew his parents were dead, had been dead before he walked north into Mexico. His sister and brother-in-law had finally managed to get him permission to come legally to the United States as a refugee, with the help of their parish priest. That was about all she knew. "I'm glad you and Chankina found each other," she said.

"I also." He sounded suddenly shy. "She is very nice."

Smiling, she said good-bye, wondering if romance had finally caught up with her young assistant. She needed to call Eduardo and Roger Tourelle, but first she checked her machine. The message was from Joshua.

"Rachel, I guess you know what's going on." His voice emerged from the machine. "Deborah and I had a long, long talk last night and . . . Well, I'll fill you in in person. Right now we're leaving for Portland. Your mom is going to stay overnight, and Dr. Li is going to do surgery first thing in the morning. I'll call you from town later, or call me on my cell phone any time."

For a moment, Rachel simply stared at the machine, a knot of dread gathering in her belly. It had seemed like such a triumph last night—her mother and Joshua walking up the riverbank hand in hand. But the cancer was still there. Taking a deep breath, Rachel dialed Joshua's cell phone.

"Rachel?" He answered almost immediately. "I thought it was you." He spoke cheerfully. "We just got back from discovering new bookstores. Your mom's right here."

"Hi, sweetheart." Her mother's voice came over the line, more relaxed than Rachel had heard her in days now. "We talked, Joshua and I. I was an idiot, but you know all that." Warmth colored her tone. "I'm through being an idiot, and Dr. Li is much happier, and just to make sure that I don't get crazy and try to run off again, he's going to do the surgery first thing in the morning. So we came down here for a night out. Since I've got to be at Providence Hospital at the crack of dawn."

"Oh, Mom." Rachel cleared her throat. "I'm so glad that you're staying here."

"Me too," her mother said quietly. "Here. Joshua will fill you in on the details."

"She should be out of recovery by eleven." Joshua's

voice came back on the line. "Dr. Li will be able to tell us more by then."

"We're at the Riverplace Hotel on the Willamette." It sounded as if her mother was sharing the phone with him. "If you need us. But if it's not an emergency, don't bother us. This is a lovely hotel, with a marvelous little bistro right on the water. This is our night. I'll see you tomorrow. And don't worry about me, because I'm not," her mother said serenely. "There's no point."

"I'll see you tomorrow," Rachel said, her voice husky. "I love you."

"I love you, dear. Bye-bye." And they hung up.

For several moments, Rachel sat in the deepening dusk, her eyes fixed unseeing on the window. Finally, Peter leaped onto her lap, startling her, arching his back to rub against her in an uncharacteristic show of affection.

"What is this, cat? Comfort?" She rubbed his tattered ears. "Or is this just a new way of letting me know you're starving?"

Peter meowed and hopped to the floor, heading for the kitchen, tail in the air.

"Okay, okay, I'm coming." Rachel drew a deep breath. "Let me finish up being a businesswoman, first." She swallowed the last of the lump lingering in her throat and dialed Eduardo's number.

He was at home, in the apartment he shared with a relative's family. She told him about the Portland job, promising to pay him and the crew for the extra drive. "I will meet you there in the morning," she told him in her orchard Spanish. "I will have to leave for a time, but I will be back." She arranged to meet them at the Guarnieris' gas station, so that they could follow her to Portland. Eduardo was a good crew boss. She could leave the men working on the overgrown garden and get to the hospital at eleven. No problem. Although she'd have to take a change of clothes if it was still raining. She looked through the window, making a face at the steady fall of rain that glinted in the glow of the outside floodlights mounted on the house.

She fed Peter and began to heat a can of minestrone on the stove. She wasn't really hungry, but soup had been her comfort food since she was a sick grade-school kid tucked into bed with a bowl of homemade chicken-and-rice soup on a tray in her lap. She left a message on Roger Tourelle's machine that the garden was under control, that he could go ahead with the open house, and that she'd call him tomorrow. Telling herself she was not going to answer the phone if he did call back tonight, she headed for the bedroom to undress and finally take her shower.

Someone knocked timidly at the door. For an instant Rachel stood still, her neck prickling with the memory of those fresh drops of coffee in the stone house. Her visitor knocked again, even more softly this time. Taking a deep breath, Rachel went over to the door. "Who is it?" she called, not yet unlocking the door.

"It's April," came the faint reply. "I'm sorry if it's too late."

"April!" Rachel opened the door instantly. "Come in. I'm so glad to see you! They let you go!"

"Yes, they did." April stepped across the threshold and threw her arms around Rachel. "Thank you so much for getting involved. Thank you for getting the cool lawyer to help me. Otherwise, I'd be on the run somewhere, and everything I've tried to do to fix my life would be wrecked."

"So what happened? Did they let you out on bail? Or did they just let you go?"

"Oh, they let me out on bail." She made a face. "But they didn't ask for a lot. Mrs. Killingsworth told me that they'd ask a huge amount so that I couldn't skip again, but they didn't. They didn't charge me with murder or anything like that—just being a witness, or something like that. Gladys says they must have someone else in mind, and she thinks they'll leave me alone if I behave myself. I'm going to behave." She beamed, her blue eyes sparking. "It's just . . . I just can't believe that people are helping me like this."

Rachel smelled soup. "Have you eaten? Have some soup with me," she said when the girl shook her head.

"Beck's waiting for me." April's smile turned suddenly shy. "He's the one who paid the bail. I mean, he just did. I could have left by a back door and taken off. He didn't know I wouldn't do that." Her smile faded. "You know, there was a time in my life when I might have done just that. I'd have never been able to believe in him. I think . . . I'll always owe Eloise for that. For teaching me that people really could be good."

"Go get Beck." Rachel smiled and pushed April gently toward the door. "I'll feed both of you. I'm so glad they let you go."

"I am, too." Gladys Killingsworth stuck her head through the door. "Although it surprised the heck out of me, let me tell you. Obviously the cops have somebody else dead center in their sights. Hi, April." She nodded at the girl. "I had a feeling you'd stop by here when I left you behind on the freeway. Beck is sure one for obeying the speed limit, isn't he?" She chuckled. "Never mind feeding our wayward children here." She nodded at April. "We can go over to Fong's for a late supper. I bet your carpenter friend down there staring at me hasn't eaten since this whole mess started. *I* sure couldn't talk him into eating anything."

"He probably hasn't," April said guiltily.

"Don't hang your head about it. Take it as a major compliment. And it's my treat." Gladys waved away her protest. "This has been an interesting day at least. Are you coming, too?" she asked Rachel. "Or are you through for the day?"

"Oh, I'll come along," Rachel said. She wasn't sure she'd sleep tonight anyway. "I'll meet you there. Let me give Jeff a call and give him the good news."

"Don't be too long." Gladys put an arm around April. "I'm ordering one of their appetizer platters and I have no compunction about eating all the egg rolls if you're slow."

"I won't be slow," Rachel said, and closed the door on the two women as they descended the steps together. Smiling, shaking her head because she never would have predicted this outcome, she called Jeff.

He, too, was surprised. "I agree with your chopper-riding lawyer," he said thoughtfully. "Carey has somebody else in mind here. I'm glad he let her go. She seems like a good kid, in spite of her past."

"I'm so happy for Beck, too."

"She may turn him into a functional human being yet," Jeff said dryly. "More or less. Well, let me know if you hear anything more. Next time I talk to Carey, I'll find out what went on."

"That's not the only thing that happened today." Rachel drew a long breath and told him about her mother.

"I'm glad they're taking care of it now," he said, "instead of waiting any longer. If you want to stay in Portland for a few days," he told her, "I can drop by and feed Peter."

"I might do that," she told him gratefully. "Thanks."

"And if you need company any time of the day or night, let me know. It's not much more than an hour's drive to the hospital."

"Thanks," Rachel said softly. "I'll call you if I need you."

"Do that," he said.

Outside, the rain fell. Rachel put on a clean shirt and pair of jeans and got her good rain jacket from the closet. She would go down to Fong's and eat egg rolls and drink their jasmine tea and celebrate April's release. By tomorrow noon, everybody in Blossom would know that the police didn't think April had murdered Eloise Johnston. And she wondered if that wasn't why Gladys had suggested their celebration supper in the first place. Locking the door behind her, Rachel hurried down the steps through the silvery veil of warm rain, thinking about April's gratitude to Eloise, and about her son, who had expressed not one moment of genuine sorrow for his mother's death, while worrying about what she had recalled in her vanished memoirs.

Maybe he was the person Spiros suspected. As she drove through the rain-wet streets of the deserted downtown, wa-

ter hissed from beneath her tires. She wondered if Alan
Johnston had gotten out of the taxi at the convenience store
down the street that morning. Had he bought a cup of coffee and crept back through the woods to the stone house to
spy on them through the window? Had it been him?

It didn't fit. But that didn't mean that it hadn't happened.
Ahead, Fong's pagoda-and-dragon sign splashed red, gold,
and green neon light across the water filling the street. In
spite of the weather, quite a few cars filled the spaces in
Fong's parking lot. This was the place to gather for news
and rumor late at night if you didn't want to go to the
tavern. Inside, weathered farmers and elderly couples sat
with coffee and egg rolls or cups of hot-and-sour soup, or
plates of sweet-and-sour pork, and talked about past floods
and what Hood River and Apple Blossom Creek were doing.

"Those pears down in the lower orchard are six inches
deep already," one man was saying. "Gonna be worse than
'64 at this rate. Got the sandbags ready for that new equipment shed o' yours, Hal?" He waved his thick white mug
of coffee at another farmer sitting nearby. "I told you that
was a bad place to put the darn thing."

"Heck, I got six feet to go 'fore the water even gets
close." Hal laughed and picked up one of the fried wonton
the waitress had just placed in front of him. "If the water
gets that high, we'd better have the darned ark ready."

"Yeah, sure, you're lower than my pipe shed, and it's
gonna be wet by morning."

"Bet you ten bucks I don't have even a wet tire in there."

"You're on."

"Over here." Gladys waved gaily from the big family
table in the center of the restaurant. Round and large
enough to seat ten, it had a built-in lazy Susan in the center
so that dishes could be easily circulated. It served as center
stage at Fong's. Platters of food steamed fragrantly on the
turntable, along with two pots of tea. "We're waiting for
you," Gladys said. Eyes swiveled toward this table from

nearly every other one. "Let the celebration begin." She beamed at Rachel and winked.

Rachel sat down next to Beck as Gladys began to turn the lazy Susan. He took food from the platters as they paused in front of him, but his attention was fixed on April beside him. Rachel took one of the crispy egg rolls and two crab puffs. She spooned savory hot-and-sour soup into the small white bowl shaped like a lotus flower that had been placed in front of her.

"Rachel, how are you doing?" Mrs. Greening, who worked at the Growers' Co-op, paused at the table. "I ran into Herbert Southern yesterday, and he said you had all kinds of trouble with a job you took in Portland—that someone was killed." Her eyebrows arched in horrified anticipation.

"The woman I was working for died," Rachel told her. "I guess the police are investigaing it."

"Oh, it's obvious that the lieutenant doesn't consider you a suspect at all," Gladys was telling April. "You certainly don't need to lose any sleep over it. He's got a suspect all lined up, or you'd be in jail right now. You're innocent, honey, and he knows it."

Mrs. Greening's ears pricked. "I'm so glad that you're all right." She patted her tightly waved gray hair. "There's so much crime in the big city. I don't know why you'd want to work there."

"Oh, it's not so bad," Rachel murmured, hiding a smile. Gladys's timing was superb, she thought. Lana Greening was a vital link in Blossom's back-fence information network. Certainly news of April's status of exonerated suspect would be all over town in short order. "I wouldn't have taken the job, except that Mrs. Johnston willed the garden to the public. It will be a beautiful park and botanical garden."

"How sweet." Mrs. Greening turned to the other guests. "Mrs. Killingsworth, how are you? I really should drop in and update my will one of these days. The mention of death always makes me think of these things." She shuddered delicately. "And how are you?" she asked Beck enthusiastically. "I haven't seen you for . . . Oh, heavens, it's been ages."

Beck gave her a polite, if slightly wary, smile.

"My dear, my name is Lana. Lana Greening." She offered April a hand and a sunny smile. "How nice to meet you."

"Nice to meet you," April murmured.

"Well, I'm off. Clyde is rolling his eyes. Honestly, that man has no patience! Tell your aunt that I'll get her springform pan back to her as soon as I do that cake for the church supper." With a flutter of her fingers, she scurried away to where her stolid, jeans-clad husband waited patiently by the door, chewing on a mint-flavored toothpick.

"Clyde doesn't seem to be rolling his eyes at all," Gladys observed. "So what do you plan to do now, my girl? Here. Try this. I told Fong to take it easy on the pepper in the kung-pao shrimp tonight." Deftly she scooped shrimp and vegetables onto the girl's plate. "Are you going to look for a job around here?"

"I . . . thought I would." April looked quickly at Beck, then forked up a bite of the spicy shrimp. "I don't know what I can find, though. I mean . . . I don't have a lot of skills. I could wait tables, I guess. Or do basic secretary type stuff. I took courses in office management in the . . . in the program I was in." She blushed faintly.

"Well, my assistant has been threatening to quit if I don't get her some part-time office help." Gladys tapped her front teeth thoughtfully with her chopstick. "Come talk to me when you're feeling settled. If we can all stand each other, it'll be something to tide you over."

"That would be great. I . . . Thank you." April's eyes shone. "I'll call you."

"Just come by." Gladys plucked another egg roll deftly from the platter. "If the bike's there, I'm there."

The party lasted for quite some time. Beck even spoke up occasionally. Rachel told him that he'd have to wait on the Johnston project until she was sure that there would be money. He didn't seem concerned by the delay. Rachel guessed that he had more requests for jobs than he had time to do. You saw Beck's finely crafted decks and wooden furniture all over the county. He certainly didn't need to take out an advertisement to bring in clients.

They were nearly the last patrons out of the restaurant. It was late. She wasn't going to get enough sleep, Rachel thought with a twinge of guilt, but she was glad that she had come along. It would have been too easy to sit in her apartment and worry about her mother. The rain had abated for the moment, but the gutters ran with muddy floods, and water sluiced from every drainpipe that she passed. As she parked beside the house, she looked toward the invisible bulk of Mount Hood to the southwest, and wondered just how much flooding she'd see tomorrow.

One message waited on her machine. "Don't forget to call me," Jeff's voice came softly from the machine. "If you need to. Good night."

"I will," she promised as she climbed into bed. "Good night, Jeff." And she realized, as she drifted off to sleep, that she really would call him. If she needed to. And that was as new as his presence in her bed last night.

It was still raining when Rachel woke in the morning, although the downpour had eased to a steady drizzle. Yawning, she tumbled out of bed, feeling the effects of her late night. Eduardo was prompt. She hurried to dress, and as she packed a lunch, the state emergency broadcast system twice interrupted the morning newscast with its raucous squawk. Both times it offered flood warnings for various Willamette Valley rivers in its tinny electronic voice. Her mother had once told her that growing up in the Cold War years, the interruption of the emergency broadcast system—originally intended to announce a nuclear attack—still gave her a chill. She looked at the clock, imagining her mother on a steel surgery table, beneath hot yellow lights. The picture filled her with disquiet.

Outside, water dripped from the eaves and ran down the driveway, joining into brown streams that tumbled down the streets through town, hurrying on their way to the swollen and ugly Columbia. As she drove down to the Taxi Sisters' gas station to meet Eduardo, she was shocked at how much the river had risen overnight. She knew the power of the Pineapple Express to flood the western half

of the state in a matter of hours as it melted a heavy snowpack like the breath of an invisible dragon, but this was the
first time she had seen it happen. She detoured down to the
old dock to check on the Bread Box. Joylinn hadn't opened
yet, but the shops that had been built on the old pilings
stood reassuringly high above the brown surge. Rachel felt
relieved. But the river was still unsettling. Snags—twisted
masses of roots and limbs—floated down the muddy torrent, moving with the mass of semi-trucks. A big one could
seriously damage the boardwalk if it struck it full on. A
tree trunk hurried past, and Rachel spotted a small bedraggled brown creature hunched on the trunk. A nutria, she
guessed. Swept with its haven from a riverbank, it was
waiting a chance to leap safely for shore.

Eduardo and his crew of two were waiting in his battered
yellow Ford Escort, listening to music on the radio behind
fogged windows. Rachel explained where they were going
and then pulled out of the lot and down onto the freeway.
She wasn't worried about Eduardo keeping up with her.
Julio told stories of his driving with a tinge of awe in his
voice. He would have to seriously restrain himself, she
thought with a smile.

Was the surgery over yet? Rachel forced herself not to
look at her watch, turning on the radio instead. The morning news was full of flood warnings, with predictions as to
when various rivers would crest. At least the rain seemed
to be slackening, although the weather forecaster didn't
seem to think the situation would improve much before
nightfall. The creekbank was going to be a muddy mess for
Roger's open house at the garden, she thought glumly. But
there wasn't anything she could do about that. At least her
family's orchard was situated well up on a slope, far above
the danger of flooding.

The rain had increased again by the time they reached
the garden. Rachel and the three men donned their rain gear
and began to unload the tools. It was not going to be a
pleasant day. Rachel led the way along the upper trails,
pointing out the rock garden and the various upper areas

they would be concentrating on. At each stop, she pulled up the weed species that infested the area most thickly: invasive wild geranium, a European escapee that was a constant headache, morning glory vines, quack grass, and polygonum—knotweed—in the sunnier zones. She laid the weeds out on the path, where they could serve as a reference, since her crew wasn't familiar with many of the plants growing there. The men would pull these species only, leaving the other plants untouched. She took them up to the top of the slope to show them where to dump the weeds. The stone house stood stolidly beneath its huge fir tree, rain dripping from its mossy eaves.

Rachel hesitated, then gestured Eduardo to come with her. As she pushed the door open, her heart pounding, she was aware of his curious expression. "Someone was here," she told him in her orchard Spanish as they entered the dark interior. "Yesterday. Watching me. A bad person."

He nodded sharply, then moved past her, head swiveling, his posture taut and ready, like a bristling dog ready for a fight. She followed him as he stalked down the hall and into the small bedroom that overlooked the garden slope. Nothing had changed. No new trash littered the floor. With a sigh of relief, feeling a little foolish, Rachel thanked him, and they went back to join the others. They worked together through the morning, pulling weeds, piling them in the wheelbarrow, and hauling them up to the compost piles. Some of the deep-rooted grasses required grub hoes, and the tool blades were soon heavy with mud.

Rachel followed her crew, pulling the weeds she hadn't designated to them, pruning some remaining damage from the earlier vandalism, and shaping the more overgrown shrubs a bit. It was slow going. She looked at her watch after what seemed a short time, and was shocked to discover that it was after ten. She went to find Eduardo, who was painstakingly weeding a patch of mayapple. The tender green umbrellas were a native of the East Coast, but they seemed to thrive in the moist shade they inhabited. Eduardo, squatting on his heels with an easy comfort that always made her envious, was meticulously removing grass roots and morning glory from the clump.

"I have to leave," she told him when he looked up. "Go buy lunch when it's time." She handed him a twenty. The men had brought their lunches, but this would buy soda and treats.

"Gracias." Eduardo stood respectfully, grinning, pocketing the money. "We will have done much when you return," he told her.

"I know." She nodded, once again thanking Julio for his connections that provided her with the dependable Eduardo and his crew whenever she needed him. "See you later."

"Later." Eduardo nodded and went back to his limber squat, grimy delicate fingers probing for the offending weeds.

Rachel went back to the truck. The rain had changed to showers, and the air felt cooler, as if the Chinook was finally being displaced by a cooler and more normal flow of air from the Gulf of Alaska. She looked through the wet, heavy stems of the black bamboo, shaking her head at the churning torrent that had just yesterday been a sleepy creek. The footbridge to the other side of the creek, raised to its peak on the metal frame, cleared the foamy crest of the flood by only a few feet. The riparian ramble along the stream lay beneath the chocolate-colored torrent. The ferns and salmonberry would be fine, she reminded herself. They were adapted to this kind of deluge, would poke new growth above the silt, once the water had gone down. The new layer of silt would fertilize them. She would clean up the trash and debris. But the power of flooding streams— so gentle one day, so deadly the next—had always frightened her. She had waded into an angry spring Columbia once, when she was very young. She had a vivid memory of a huge invisible hand grabbing her, closing around her with the casual brute strength of a giant, of gasping a last, damp gulp of air before her head went under, and a cold ravening darkness seized her. Her father had dragged her from the water, hugging her to him, as she coughed and gagged, chiding her at the same time for going in. Rachel shivered and turned away from the water.

She stripped off her rain gear, hanging it on some empty hooks in the covered breezeway beside the house where they could drip onto the concrete walk. Goose bumps rising on her skin, she carried her clean clothes into the house. It was dark inside and cold. When she flipped the light switch, nothing happened. The light in the bathroom didn't work, either. Apparently someone had had the power turned off. She sighed, chilly in the still, unheated air. Water dripped in the kitchen. At least that was still functional, she thought grimly. At least they could clean up the tools this afternoon. The basement office, where Eloise's son had flung papers around in a fit of rage, was a well of darkness at the foot of the stairs. Rachel closed the door on its yawning silence and went into the small dining room that overlooked the terrace to change in the light from the windows. She changed quickly, putting on a pair of slacks, a blouse, and a blue jacket. Hanging her damp clothes on a couple of chair backs to dry a bit, she went on into the kitchen.

The clock on the electric stove read 10:00. Rachel frowned and turned on a burner, holding her hand above the element. It stayed cold, as she had expected. The power had either gone off within the hour, or it might have been off since ten o'clock last night. Hopefully it was a local problem, and electricity would come back on shortly. She sighed and made a mental note to call Tourelle and tell him if the power was still off at the end of the day. A pile of letters on the counter caught her eye as she washed her hands at the sink. Eloise's mail. One name leaped out at her: Dr. Li. Her mother's oncologist. Drying her hands, Rachel picked up the envelope. It looked like a bill. She laid it down thoughtfully.

A brief intense shower pounded the windshield as she drove up the hill from the muddy creek. She searched the Portland airwaves for an offering of news and weather and finally got a brief list of flood warnings and flooding. Johnson Creek was on the list, of course. At least the house was

high enough that it should be safe. An awful lot of snowpack was melting off the mountain in a very short period
of time. Rachel drove slowly through the wet streets, slow-
ing to a crawl where storm sewers had blocked, flooding
the roadway inches deep in brown runoff. A half dozen
town houses under construction looked forlorn in the rain,
bits of plastic sheeting flapping in the gusty winds. Water
the color of chocolate milk poured across the site in spite
of the black silt-screens that had been erected across the
bare, churned earth. More silt to block the creeks, Rachel
thought. More flooding.

She made her way without much trouble to the Providence Hospital, although traffic had slowed to a crawl in
several places where blocked drains had flooded intersec-
tions. She parked in one of the big parking structures next
to the hospital and found her way to the main lobby, glad
for the covered walkways that connected many buildings
in the complex.

In the large lobby, furnished with tasteful clusters of
chairs and small sofas, a handful of people waited, leafing
through dog-eared *Sunset* and *Fishing and Hunting* magazines, or simply staring at the glass entry. Waiting for cabs?
Waiting for friends or relatives to be wheeled out to the
lobby so that they could go home? Rachel went over to the
reception desk and offered her mother's name. She realized
she was holding her breath and made herself breathe.

"She's still in Recovery." The auburn-haired woman behind the desk smiled kindly at her. "There's a waiting room
down that hall." She pointed. "Go through those swinging
doors, clear to the end. They should be moving her to a
room shortly."

Rachel mumbled thanks and started across the lobby. It
seemed larger, as if she was suddenly shrinking. The last
time she had been in a hospital, she had been waiting to
find out if Jeff had a brain injury from an assault. A middle-
aged woman in green surgical scrubs strode briskly past
Rachel, a stethoscope swinging around her neck. A young
orderly steered a steel cart loaded with folded sheets across

her path. *Hospitals all smell alike*, Rachel thought distractedly. It was a mix of disinfectant, cleaners, and something less identifiable. Fear, perhaps. The swinging doors opened, and Joshua looked out, his gaze sweeping the hall.

"Rachel!" He held out a hand to her. "I was afraid you might have trouble finding us."

She caught his hand, squeezing it hard, the question she needed to ask sticking solidly in her throat.

"She's doing fine," he answered it anyway, both his hands clasped tightly around hers. "They'll be taking her up to her room pretty soon." He led Rachel through the doors and into a small space off the hall furnished with chrome and vinyl-cushioned chairs, a fake-wood end table, and frayed and battered magazines. Another set of swinging doors blocked the far end of the hallway. "There's a coffee machine just downstairs," he told her. "Can I get you something?"

"No. Thanks." Rachel paced the small space once, then sat down in one of the chairs. "Have you talked to Dr. Li yet?"

"Just briefly." Joshua nodded. "He'll be back shortly. He said that it looked good—that it didn't look as if the cancer had spread to the lymph system. But he wanted to make a more thorough examination. Aha." Joshua looked up as someone pushed through the inner set of doors. "David." He turned to the small square-faced man dressed in surgical greens. The surgeon's mask dangled around his neck, and a fringe of black hair showed beneath his rumpled green cap. "What did you find out?"

With those few terse words, Rachel saw for an instant just how worried Joshua was, how hard this was for him. She reached over without speaking and took his hand again. This time it was she who gave the comfort. He squeezed briefly, gratefully, in return, but his eyes never left the oncologist's face.

"It looks very good, Joshua." Dr. Li beamed. "The nodes are clean. I think her chances are excellent, after chemo and radiation." He put a hand on Joshua's shoulder as he bent his head. "It will be okay, my friend."

Joshua nodded but didn't speak for a moment. Finally, he looked up. "Is she awake?"

"Oh, yes. I just spoke with her." The surgeon smiled at Rachel. "She'll be out in a minute. They're taking her up to three. I'll drop by later today, when she's a little more awake, and we can talk more about what comes next."

"Thanks," Joshua said, his voice hoarse.

Dr. Li squeezed his shoulder hard and turned to Rachel. "You must be Deborah's daughter," he said. "You look very much like her. Your mother will be fine. We caught this at a very early stage. She is a strong and healthy woman."

"She is. Good." The words emerged as a whisper, awash in a flood of relief.

He took her hand, his dark eyes full of sympathy. "If you have any questions at any time, feel free to call my office. I'll be most happy to speak with you at any time."

"I'll do that, Doctor." Rachel swallowed. "Thank you. Oh, by the way," she went on, "it's a small world. One of my landscaping clients was your patient. Eloise Johnston."

"Ah, Eloise." The doctor shook his head. "She did not show up for our last appointment. I have not heard from her," he said slowly. "I am worried."

"She's dead."

"I . . . am sorry." The oncologist stared down the hall, his expression unreadable. "I did not know."

"She was murdered," Rachel said after a moment.

"Murdered? How can that be?" The doctor stepped backward, shocked. "How terrible," he said, shaking his head. "How awful. It . . . shocks me. I see death every day, I suppose, but I see it coming. I work to stop it. Sometimes I succeed, sometimes I fail." He shook his head again. "Random violence seems so . . . horribly out of control. You cannot fight it. There is no surgery to cure it—no drugs." He looked past them, the frown still on his face. "Did they catch the murderer?"

"Not yet," Joshua said. "But they will, I'm sure. It was a terrible thing."

"Yes." The doctor sighed. "Isn't it always. Eloise seemed to be a woman who lived life thoroughly. I did not know her long, but she seemed to enjoy life very much." He turned back to Rachel. "Your mother is doing very well. And her condition is not at all related to that of Eloise Johnston. Do not worry." Squeezing her hand once more, the doctor left the waiting room, striding quickly down the hall, on his way somewhere in a hurry.

As he turned the corner, the inner doors opened again, and an orderly trundled a gurney through. Rachel's mother lay beneath the white sheet, an IV bag dangling from a pole above her. Her face looked pale as ivory amidst the tangle of her black hair, small and almost childlike on the pillow. But she smiled when she saw Rachel and Joshua and held out her hand.

"What a place to spend the day," she said. "But I'm so glad to see both of you."

Joshua took his wife's free hand and kissed it, and Rachel touched her cheek.

"The doctor says it looks good," Rachel said, squeezed by the need to cry and laugh at the same instant.

"Darn right," her mother said. "I need plenty of time to break in that car of mine."

"You'll be terrorizing the countryside in no time." Joshua kissed her hand gently.

"Soon enough." Smiling, Deborah held her husband's hand as they proceeded on down the hall. "For the next few days, I can catch up on my reading. We discovered a great new bookstore just around the corner," she told Rachel. "Wrigley-Cross Books. You should stop by there. No coffee." She smiled. "But they know their books."

"We'll need another bookcase, for sure." Joshua groaned, then stood back, grinning, as the young man pushing the bed efficiently maneuvered it into the oversize elevator. "I made a tactical error letting you check into a hospital close to a bookstore."

"We had a wonderful time there yesterday," Deborah went on complacently. "I left a list with them."

"You didn't tell me that." Joshua sighed in resignation.

"They'll have everything ready to pick up this afternoon. They were very helpful."

"Do I need to rent a van?" her husband asked plaintively.

"Oh, a small pickup should do." Deborah smiled as her husband groaned again.

Without speaking, Rachel reached across the gurney to take her mother's hand and Joshua's, too. For a few seconds, the three of them remained still and silent. Then the elevator halted, the doors slid open, and the gently smiling orderly pushed the gurney out into the hallway.

A nurse bustled up and took charge of settling Deborah into a room. The second bed was empty, but the nurse drew the curtains around the bed anyway as she and another nurse shifted Deborah into bed, got her settled, checked the IV drip attached to her hand, and hung the bag from a stand beside the bed. Then they withdrew, promising to return with juice for Deborah and coffee for Joshua and Rachel. A television set on an adjustable arm was mounted on the wall, so that it was in easy viewing range from the bed. The window in the far wall offered a view of a couple of young maple trees and the brick facade of the medical building across the street. People strolled by on the street, intent on their errands. It seemed to be clearing up a bit. Rachel blinked at the afternoon light outside, realizing that she had entirely lost track of the time.

"I can't stay all day. I wish I could." Rachel held her mother's hand, tracing the S-curve of tubing taped to the back of it. "I'll come by here on my way home, after I finish at the garden."

"Did you get some lunch?" her mother asked.

"You sound like a mother."

"No kidding." Deborah smiled at her daughter. "So did you?"

"I brought one. It's in the truck." Rachel smiled down at

her mother, swallowing a sudden rush of tears that almost caught her off guard. "I'll eat it. I promise."

"I have a better idea," Joshua said. "I'll take her down to the rather nice cafeteria they have here and feed her. That way you can catch a bit of rest before I bother you again, and you'll know that she's eaten." He took Rachel by the elbow with mock severity. "No arguing, young lady."

"Yes, sir," Rachel said meekly. She leaned down to kiss her mother's forehead, remembering with a giddy sense of déjà vu how her mother had kissed her just like this as she lay in bed with the flu as a child. "I'll be back this evening," she murmured.

"Don't wear yourself out, sweetheart," her mother murmured. "If you're too tired, just go on home. Joshua's here. I'll be fine."

She closed her eyes and seemed to be drifting off to sleep as Rachel and Joshua made their way out of the room. The nurse appeared as they were leaving, carrying a tray with a small can of apple juice on it, and two cups of coffee.

"She's asleep," Joshua said. "We're going to the cafeteria. We'll be back shortly."

"She'll be sleepy for a while, so take your time," the nurse said. "Try the minestrone. It's the soup special today, and it's great."

"Thanks," Joshua said and led the way down the hall to the elevator.

Rachel was glad that Joshua knew where he was going as he strode briskly through the halls, turning right, then left, taking her down a flight of stairs, then through another maze of corridors. They emerged into yet another carpeted hospital corridor, but this time Rachel smelled food—grilling burgers and pizza. Her stomach growled loudly, protesting the lateness of the hour and her spare breakfast so many hours ago.

Small groups of nurses, doctors, and aides strolled past, heading back to their jobs from their lunch break. Rachel heard a comment about someone's kidney and a bet on an

upcoming basketball game. They reached double glass
doors and the cafeteria itself. A long counter offered burger
and fry choices, along with hot roast beef and customary
side dishes. Rachel got a tray and ladled the recommended
soup into a deep bowl. She found fresh rolls and various
salads farther down the line. Passing up the desserts, she
carried her tray over to a beverage bar, filling a large cup
with orange juice from a dispenser. Joshua paid for her
lunch inspite of her protest, and they claimed a table in a
deserted corner.

"I saw umbrellas on the street this morning. It really has
to rain to get Portlanders to use umbrellas," Joshua remarked as he set out his chicken Caesar salad and the rye
rolls he'd chosen. "Save room for ice cream," he told her
with a smile. "They have a bin full of fancy ice-cream bars
on the far side of the checkout stands. In case you didn't
notice."

"I did." She studied him surreptitiously as she broke her
roll in half and tasted her soup. The nurse had been right.
It was wonderful, full of tomato and vegetables, basil and
rich flavor. "You look tired," she said to Joshua. "This has
to be extra tough for you."

"Because of my first wife dying of cancer, you mean."
Joshua speared a piece of chicken breast, but didn't eat it
right away. "Part of me is hurt—that she thought I wouldn't
want to deal with this, or be able to deal with this. I meant
it when I said I do to that bit about sickness or health. In
fact, I was thinking about cancer when I said those words
in that Las Vegas chapel." He gave her a weary smile. "The
other part of me realizes how much she loves me and
wanted to spare me. But . . ." He paused, looking at the
chicken on his fork as if he couldn't quite remember how
it got there. "I think she understands now," he said slowly,
"that we're in this together. No matter what happens to
either of us. I don't think we'll need to keep any secrets
from each other after this." He gave her a wry smile. "That
works both ways. It has occurred to me that the shoe could
be on the other foot here—that I might have tried to spare

her somehow, if it was me who was sick. I think we both learned something. Hard way to learn." He laughed a dry note and began to eat his salad.

"So . . . what is going to happen?" Rachel asked hesitantly. "She's going to be sick during the chemotherapy and radiation, right? And she'll lose her hair from the radiation?"

"From the chemotherapy actually. She'll be tired while it's going on, and she'll feel pretty bad. But then . . . she has a good chance to live the rest of her life without a reoccurrence."

"They took . . . They didn't just take the lump, did they?"

"No." Joshua looked directly at her. "Dr. Li advised against a lumpectomy. After she's healed, she can get a prosthesis. She'll look fine. She looks fine to me right now."

Rachel looked down at her half-finished soup, her hunger gone. Beneath her cotton shirt, her chest ached.

"It's not going to change one bit how beautiful she is," Joshua said softly. "If she can't see it right away, I think I can help her realize it." He reached over to cover her hand with his. "It'll be okay, Rachel."

Not fine. Not great, but *okay*. She could believe in *okay*. Rachel squeezed Joshua's hand gratefully. "I think I'd better get back to my crew." She managed a smile. "They'll think I've fallen into the Willamette."

"Don't do that. The water's pretty high." Joshua finished the last of his salad, eating with the attention of someone who was very hungry. Rachel felt a moment of guilt, guessing that he hadn't eaten since last night.

"Don't hurry," she said. "I can certainly wait for you to finish your lunch."

"I want to get back, too." He piled the dishes onto the stacked trays and took them to the small window where a couple of kitchen employees took them. "A little later I'll sneak her an ice-cream bar," he said when Rachel turned down his offer of one. "I don't think they'll give her much solid food before tomorrow."

"I'll be back before six," Rachel said. "It's such a crummy day that we'll probably quit a little early. That way the men can miss the worst of the rush-hour traffic in Portland."

"Good idea." Joshua nodded. "With this much rain, there will probably be accidents all over the roads."

"Joshua?" Rachel hesitated, searching for just the right words. "I think . . . you're the best thing that could have happened to my mom."

"Thank you." Joshua took her hand in both of his, his eyes full of warmth. "I know it was hard for you at first. But Deborah is the best thing that could have happened to me, too. I'm glad it's okay for you."

"It's more than okay." Rachel stood on tiptoe to kiss him lightly. "See you tonight," she said. "Or sooner, if I can't find my truck."

"If you go down this hallway, it will take you to an elevator that will bring you up to a walkway that leads you to the main parking structure." He pointed her toward a corridor near the elevator.

"Wish me luck. I think I need a ball of twine." Rachel gave him a final hug, then headed down the corridor. When her mother and Joshua had fallen precipitously in love and had run off to get married a few days later, she had been ambivalent about the relationship, if not downright hostile, she admitted to herself. It had been hard at first to think of another man replacing her father. But in the end Joshua had been right. He had told her at the beginning that he could never replace her father, any more than Deborah could replace his dead wife. He had told her that what they shared was its own thing.

It was. A wonderful thing, too. Smiling, Rachel walked briskly across the oil-stained concrete of the parking structure, trying to remember which level she'd parked on. Fourth, she thought as she followed the ramp upward. A gray BMW roared downward, past her, and she coughed at the reek of its exhaust. Her footsteps echoed, and a car door slammed loudly, all sounds magnified by the concrete beams. Her truck was indeed on the fourth level. She backed out of the narrow space and made her way down the spiral ramp, exiting carefully onto the narrow street.

Even though it was early afternoon—not rush hour yet—the streets were crowded with cars. She had taken Glisan east to 122nd Avenue, she remembered, hoping that she wouldn't get lost on the way back. The wind had increased, and signal lights swung and danced above the slow-moving traffic. Exasperated, Rachel leaned back in her seat, eyeing her watch. At this rate, it would be nearly three o'clock by the time she made it back to the garden. As she inched along the surface streets, the cause of the slowdown became apparent. The lights were out at a major intersection, and a yellow-slickered policeman was directing traffic, his whistle blasting as he motioned cautious drivers to cross or palmed the impatient to a reluctant halt. Once she reached 122nd Avenue, traffic increased speed to near normal. Rachel breathed a sigh of relief as she neared the garden.

Still, it was nearly three o'clock by the time she reached the gates. She pulled into the parking area, thinking that something didn't look right. The clouds had thickened again, and the heavy gray sky made it seem like dusk instead of midafternoon. Rachel got out, her hair whipped by the warm, gusty wind. A few drops spattered her, and as she hurried to the house, she realized what looked wrong. Eduardo's car was missing.

Somebody went to the store for pop, she told herself. That was all. Eduardo and his crew wouldn't leave a job. They knew she was coming back. Not particularly worried, she went into the kitchen. Her work clothes were hanging where she had left them—a little drier, but not much. She changed once more and went out into the breezeway to put on her muddy boots and go find the men.

All the tools were there, stacked neatly under cover, cleaned of mud and ready to load. Rachel stared at them in shock. If some kind of emergency had occurred, Eduardo would have called her on her cell phone. He would have at least left her a note. As worry competed with annoyance,

she went back into the house to look around for the note
that had to be there. They hadn't even locked the door—
not that they could have, since it closed only with a dead
bolt. But still—this wasn't like Eduardo. He had worked
for her many times and had always been dependable.

She searched the kitchen counters, the dining room, and
the main room. No note. No fallen scrap of paper beneath
a chest or a chair. Angry now, she returned to the breezeway. It was almost four. She hesitated, thinking that she
should just call it a day and go back to the hospital.

But they would need every hour they had to get the place
cleaned up before the day of the open house. Rachel set
her jaw. If Eduardo and the crew had walked off the job,
she would have to scramble to find a new crew. That would
take time. Stubbornly, she decided to get a little more work
done before she quit. She'd phone Joshua and tell him she'd
be a bit later than she had planned getting to the hospital.
She returned to the truck and called Jeff's number on her
cell phone. "Hi," she said to his machine. "I think I'm going to stay in Portland tonight after all. Mom is doing fine,
but I'm behind on this job. This will give me a few more
hours. I'll call you later. Thanks a lot for feeding Peter for
me. Don't let him tell you he gets two cans of food. He
doesn't." It was starting to rain again. Rachel hung up
quickly and locked up the truck. Well, she thought grimly,
rain or not, she had over three hours until full dark. She
was doing to get a lot done in those three hours.

She found where the men had been working. They had
accomplished quite a bit before they'd departed, at least.
She started working where they had left off, pulling weeds
from the wet soil, shaking off as much of the sticky clay
as she could, then tossing plants into the wheelbarrow. The
sky spat rain, but there was none of the steady downpour
of the morning, at least. Squatting, she fell into the rhythm
of pull, shake, toss, her mind settling into a state that was
almost trancelike, thinking of her mother, of Jeff, of April
and Beck, her thoughts darting like butterflies as her hands
reached, pulled, tossed. Every so often, she trundled the

wheelbarrow up the muddy path to where they had been dumping.

A distant sound—a dull metallic impact—caught her ear over the rush of wind through the needled branches over her head. The sound seemed to have come from the distant road, although it was very hard to tell direction because of the trees. A car crash? She stood, stretching her tired back and shoulders. Looking at her watch, she was shocked to discover that it was after five. Time to call Joshua, she thought, stripping off her wet muddy gloves and rubbing her cold hands together. She'd clean up a few damaged shrubs that she had marked with tape and call it quits after that. She emptied the wheelbarrow a final time, piled the muddy tools in it, and started down the slope. She could get her loppers when she called Joshua. She had missed several native rhododendrons that had been badly broken.

She pushed the wheelbarrow down the steep path west of the rock garden, washing it out at the edge of the driveway with the cracked and ancient hose attached to the spigot on the side of the house. Once the tools were clean, she wheeled it into the breezeway, thinking that she'd leave the tools there, rather than park them outside a motel for the night where they might be stolen. She could put them into the little storage building at the far side of the terrace, she thought. She had noticed a hasp on the door, and she carried a couple of padlocks in her truck box. They'd be safe there. She went to the truck and found the locks. The heavy clouds made it seem much later than it was, and she slammed the box lid, deciding to put her tools away before she called Joshua. Any second now, it would start pouring again. Hurrying to the breezeway, she trundled the wheelbarrow around behind the house, past the trickling fountain on its stone-flagged patio, out to the terrace and the storage shed.

The building smelled of mice and musty old things as she pushed the warped door open. A bird fluttered out through a broken windowpane, and she jumped. Somewhere a litter of baby mice squeaked in high-pitched baby-mouse voices. The hairs stirred on the back of her neck. In the dim light that seeped through the grimy windows, cobwebbed tools and stacks of boxes loomed like the half-remembered monsters of childhood. Rachel forced a laugh at her own creepy unease. A couple of cheap blue-plastic tarps, roughly folded, blocked the door, as if they had been hastily tossed through the door. She picked them up, sneezing at the cloud of dust they released, and piled them on top of a dusty and unused power mower. Its grass-catcher had been shredded to strings—probably by the mice, who had most likely lined their nest with the soft, chewed fibers. She moved a couple of rusty five-gallon gas cans—empty— to the side, and rolled her wheelbarrow through the door and into the mousy dusk.

Outside, the rain began to fall in heavy angry drops that splatted on the flagstones and promised a downpour in moments. Rachel pushed the door closed and worked the padlock into the hasp, snapping it closed just as the sky opened up.

Rain fell in heavy warm curtains as Rachel ran back across the terrace, around behind the house, and past the fountain and the rock garden. She paused in the breezeway, seriously damp, but not quite soaked, reaching for her cell phone to call Joshua. It wasn't on her belt, and she belatedly realized she'd left it in the truck. Calling herself stupid in both English and Spanish, she ran for the truck. Someone upended a bucket over the garden. The water fell straight down, beating harder and harder, a mist rising from the concrete walk and the driveway. Gasping, her hair plastered to her scalp, Rachel yanked the truck door open and flung herself inside, soaked during that short dash, annoyed with herself that she hadn't paused in the breezeway just a few moments more.

A chilly breeze touched her neck, making her shiver. A tiny alarm went off in her head, and she frowned, looking around for the source of the unfamiliar draft. The side window of the extended cab had been neatly broken out. Shards of glass glinted on the carpet covering the floor of the ex-

ended cab, behind the seat. The hairs rose on the back of
her neck again, and she looked around, inventorying automatically. Tape player and radio were still intact. There had
been nothing . . . She cursed her stupidity under her breath.
Her cell phone. She smacked her forehead with the heel of
her hand. *Stupid-idiot-child*, she chided herself. *Leave your
cell phone in the car and wander off into the woods to
weed.* What an invitation! Sure enough, it was gone. She
checked under the seat, behind the seat, and in the glove
box, just in case.

"Serves you right," she muttered under her breath. Jeff
had urged her many times to keep her cell phone with her,
for her own safety, although it certainly would have pre-
vented the theft. She was beginning to shiver now. The air
seeping in through the broken window felt cold, no longer
tropical at all. She turned the key and started the engine.
Putting the truck into reverse, she backed around in the
parking space, flipping on her headlights against the gathering dusk.

Her headlights splashed across the dense growth along
the parking area—and washed across the metal bars of the
closed gate. Rachel stared at the unexpected sight.

The truck engine stalled and died.

For several seconds, Rachel sat still, her hands on the
steering wheel, unmoving. The hair stirred again on the
back of her neck, colder this time, as if someone had
dripped ice water down her spine.

Someone had stolen her cell phone. Someone had closed
the gates. She reached for the key but didn't turn it. There
was no other way out. Not by car. She took her hand away
from the key, her muscles stiff, her movements jerky. She
stared at the gathering shadows beneath the trees from the
corners of her eyes, suddenly afraid to move, as if she was
a rabbit crouched in an open field, hoping the hawk would
miss her.

He was out there. He had taken her cell phone. Closed
the gates. Eloise's murderer.

She could open the gates. They couldn't be that heavy.

Run through and up the winding road—it wasn't that far to the main street, gas stations, and the convenience market where Eduardo had bought soda for his crew.

Eduardo. Someone had found a way to send the crew home. Fear coated her mouth with the taste of old metal. Someone wanted her here, tonight, alone. She closed her eyes, seeing that empty bedroom in the stone house, those fresh coffee drips on the floor. He was out there right now. Watching her. Smiling, perhaps. With a convulsive thrust of her arms, Rachel flung the door open and tumbled out. She burst into a terrified dash for the gate, her boots slipping on the wet asphalt, scrambling, nearly falling. Her running footsteps slapped loudly, filling the windy rush of wet evening with her own private thunder. After a small forever, her outstretched hands slapped the rusty metal bars, the sting of metal impacting flesh stinging its way up her arms to her throat, stifling her.

Metal jingled. With a dull horror, she stared at the silver links of heavy chain that wrapped the bars. The thick padlock gleamed new from the overlapped ends.

Locked in.

CHAPTER

1 5

Rachel slowly turned away from the locked gate, her heart pounding, panic threatening to overwhelm her. He was out there. Okay, so he was. *Think,* she told herself fiercely. *Think about the situation. Don't panic.* He had locked the gate, disabled her car. Closing her eyes for an instant, she struggled for calm. *Think. What do I do now?* She glanced up at the tall gates. No way she could go over, through, or under. Not without taking a lot of time. She imagined a shadowy figure charging out of the darkness and leaves, lunging for her as she tried to scrambled over the tall gates. Rachel shuddered. She glanced up and down the wet street, praying for a car. As if in answer to her hope, headlights splashed the dusk. They washed her briefly with light, and she waved, arms flailing, her shadow dancing briefly behind her.

The car didn't even slow. For a numb instant, she stared after the red eyes of the retreating taillights. Then she spun away from the gate, half-expecting to find someone behind her. The parking area was empty, but she could feel him out there. Watching her. She looked up the slope, trying to think. That way, dense trees and shrubs blocked her way, heavy with water. She could scramble and slip her way up there, but it would be slow and noisy progress in the thick darkness. She had a flashlight. In her truck. The thought of running back across the parking space to her truck terrified her. Shivering, she shoved her hands into the pockets of her rain jacket.

Her fingertips touched hard plastic, and her heart leaped. Her mother's cell phone! She had answered it when she found out about her mother's cancer. She had put it into her pocket, she remembered now. She had forgotten to give it to her mother, had forgotten about it completely. Hope flooded her, weakening her knees worse than the fear. She moved away from the gate, feeling her way down the path that led to the footbridge and the creekside path. It was almost completely dark, and more rain misted her cheek. She crouched low on the path, lady ferns brushing her cheek with chill wet fronds.

She dialed Jeff's cell-phone number, her fingers moving almost without volition.

"It's me, Rachel," she whispered when he answered.

"What's wrong?" Alarm flared in his voice. "Where are you?"

"I came back to the garden. Eduardo isn't here. Someone locked the gate, and my truck won't start."

"My God." The words exploded over her phone. "Call 911. Get in your truck and lock the door."

"Jeff, the window's already broken." She swallowed. "Anyone could break more."

"Stay there, then. Right where you are. Don't start running and don't hang up. Keep talking to me. I'm calling Spiros on my office line. He'll get over there. Are you there?"

"I'm here. I'm okay." The words came out breathless, as if she'd been running. The early dusk thickened around her, filling the woods with roving shadows. All sound was drowned by the rush and roar of the flooding creek.

It wasn't really pitch-dark yet. Rachel peered into the shadows, watching for any movement, finding a thousand

creeping menaces in wind-shaken leaves, branches swaying, limbs and trash churning along on the creek's swollen
surface. It shocked her how close the water was to where
she crouched. The creek must still be rising. Then she realized that the footbridge had been lowered. Floodwater
surged across the deck, and already a raft of branches, logs,
Styrofoam, and trash piled against the upstream side of the
bridge. A soccer ball whirled in an eddy, caged by branches
and boards.

The bridge hadn't been down that morning. Eduardo
wouldn't have lowered it. Why would he? Why would anyone? The first big log to come downstream on the flood
would destroy it.

"Rachel, Rachel, are you still there?" Jeff's voice jolted
her from her numb thoughts.

"I'm here," she whispered. "I'm on the steps that lead
down to the creek." Was the water getting higher? She
couldn't tell. Holding her breath, she listened intently. Footsteps? She strained her ears. Wind, she told herself fever-
ishly. Wind scraping branches against stone.

Which branches? Which branches were thick enough and
close enough to the steps to make that kind of scrape?

"Spiros's damn phone is off. I called Portland. People
are on the way. Just hang on a couple of more minutes,
and they'll be there."

"I hope so," she whispered. She *was* hearing footsteps.
Not branches, not wind. She bolted to her feet, shrieked as
someone grabbed her. An arm crossed in front of her, under
her chin, pressing hard on her throat, so that air couldn't
go in, couldn't get out. *Like Beck in the clearing,* she
thought giddily. Only this time the touch wasn't light.
Strangling, she clawed at it, nails digging at fabric and muscle beneath, doing no damage. Her knees were buckling,
and black specs danced at the edges of her vision, turning
the night darker. Her feet slipped, and she realized dimly
that she was being dragged downward, backward. Her nails
touched bare skin, and she dug them in. Her attacker exhaled sharply and jerked her backward hard. Her fingers

slipped, all strength draining from her muscles, leaving her limp. Metal banged her hip, and then shocking cold bit her ankles.

The sudden cold revived her. She reached up, flooded with a last surge of desperate strength, and this time she clawed her attacker's face. With a hoarse cry, the man jerked his head back, and for a moment the arm choking her loosened. Rachel wrenched free, staggering, clutching for support as she started to fall. Her groping hands struck metal, and she clung to it, her legs trembling, her vision clearing slowly. She was on the footbridge, and the rush of icy floodwater surged around her ankles.

Paul Claymore crouched in front of her, blocking her path back to the bank.

"You," she croaked, her eyes widening. "I thought so."

"You're really not too smart, you know." Claymore spoke calmly, almost casually, although his eyes blazed with a frightening light. "Working by yourself, you walk out onto a footbridge in the middle of a flood. I guess you didn't realize how easy it is to slip between those struts on the rail. Too bad you fell in upstream and got caught under the bridge by all the flood debris. It only takes a few moments to drown. What a shame."

"Another accident." Rachel found herself seized by an eerie calm. "Just like Linda, right? Fall off a cliff, fall into a flooding creek. No family picnic this time. Did you expect the coroner to think that Eloise had overdosed on her heart medicine?" She tried to keep her voice steady. "Do you really think people won't put two and two together?"

"They can do whatever arithmetic they choose," Claymore said coldly. "Linda's long dead and cremated, and no one can ever prove anything. I didn't mean to kill her. It really was an accident, you know. And I was exonerated. In any case, she deserved whatever happened. She got pregnant on purpose. She just wanted to get married, and I couldn't do that. I'd already met Claire, and I meant to marry her. But Linda wouldn't understand. She said she'd tell. That would have ruined everything." For a moment his voice got higher, pitched in the aggrieved tones of an angry teenager. "Claire had money. I didn't have anything. It takes money to go into politics, and that's where I meant to go. As for tonight"—his voice returned abruptly to normal—"my maid will testify that I'm home in bed. She saw me go into my room in my bathrobe, and there's no way she could hear my car from her quarters. There will be no other evidence that I was ever here." He lifted a hand to show her the black gloves that covered them and waggled his fingers at her. "The only one who's likely to bother me is that crazy detective, and everyone knows he's obsessed about me. I've filed a dozen complaints against his behavior over the years. Nobody will take him seriously."

Rachel's heart sank. "I wouldn't count on having fooled your housekeeper," she said defiantly. "She's dating my assistant, and from what he tells me, she sees a lot more than you think. She tells Julio about it," she said, thinking fast. "She told him you went to visit Eloise on Monday."

"I didn't." Claymore's lip curled. "Nice try, but you missed. Anita's not that bright. In fact, I think she'll run off with some of Claire's jewelry and disappear."

His icy tone chilled Rachel. "Don't." She gasped. "I was lying. Anita doesn't know anything."

"You know, I have no idea why Eloise decided to confide in you," Claymore went on in the same cold tone. "She guessed, you know. She suspected me, but she kept it to herself because of Carl. He's a distant relative of mine, and he had a fit the one time she said something about the accident to him. I know because I was listening at the bedroom door." He smiled mirthlessly. "I could see that she thought I'd done it, every time she looked at me. I don't know why she decided to do these crazy memoirs after all these years, or why she told you, or why you got Spiros started on me again." He sounded aggrieved. "I've been a good politician. I've done a lot to help the farming industry around here. Why did she want to punish me like this? Why now? She could never prove anything. But she told you."

"You killed her daughter," Rachel said softly. The horror

in her chest chilled her more than the floodwater swirling around her feet. "You stole the manuscript, and then you killed Eloise."

"I didn't kill her." He sounded genuinely surprised. "That former drug addict she thought she could rehabilitate did that. It's obvious. If that damn detective wasn't so obsessed with getting me, he'd still have her in jail. He let her go just to spook me. As for the manuscript, I figure you have it," he said coldly. "You've been stirring up the media, like that jerk Balfour of the *Bee*. What do you plan to do? Produce it and get yourself a whole lot of publicity? Is that the idea? Too bad."

Without warning, he lunged, and before Rachel could turn to flee, his hands closed on her arms. She screamed, struggling as he dragged her closer to the upstream side of the bridge, terrified by his strength. If he pushed her over, the powerful current would indeed sweep her under the bridge. Entangled by the brush and snags caught there, she would drown. Rachel clutched at the rail, but he tore her free, leaning against her like a lover, levering her body up and over . . .

"Police! Let go of her, or I'll shoot!" Spiros's harsh voice rang out so close that both Claymore and Rachel started. A flashlight beam stabbed through the darkness, splashing Claymore's face with white light. For a moment, he didn't move, and Rachel struggled to hang on to the rail, afraid he'd throw her over anyway. Then she felt a tiny tremor run through Claymore. His whole body slumped suddenly, and he let go of her, his face turning from the light. She fell to her knees, hip-deep in cold muddy water, her head swimming.

"Rachel, get up." Spiros snarled. "Move away from him. Now!"

"Relax, I'm not stupid. You'd love an excuse to shoot me, wouldn't you?" Claymore said in a soft bitter voice.

"Yes." The single syllable carried no inflection. "Put both hands on the bridge rail and step back. Rachel, come this way."

She scrambled toward him on hands and knees, then hauled herself upright, dizzy, her head pounding as she stumbled toward the safety of the bank. The cold water surged and tugged at her, as if disappointed at her escape. The flashlight beam speared past her, pinning Claymore with light. The water's strength frightened Rachel. It sucked away what was left of her strength, until she feared she would fall facedown and not be able to get up again. A knot of alder twigs covered with green spring leaves wrapped around her leg, then slipped on downstream, vanishing into the darkness. Her foot came down on the bank, jarring her teeth together. Gasping with relief, she stumbled onto the bank, past the dark, upright figure of Spiros. Shaking all over, she collapsed onto the welcome, muddy ground.

Out on the bridge, Spiros's flashlight beam spotlighted the branches of a cedar as he waded out to handcuff Claymore. The red bark and dark green foliage glowed jewel-like against the darkness. A bird fluttered, speared by the light, its eyes blinking. Then the beam swept down to light the brown, foamy torrent as Spiros shoved Claymore ahead of him toward the bank. The man fell once, going down on his knees and onto his face before Spiros hauled him upright again. Water dripped from his chin as he stumbled blindly through the water.

Out on the road, red-and-blue lights flashed. Voices sounded, and metal scraped loudly. Uniformed officers appeared on the path at the top of the bank. It was over. The detective and the two officers spoke together briefly, then Spiros and one of the men began to escort the wet and muddy Claymore up to the parking area, while the other man helped Rachel to her feet.

"Are you all right?" he asked with genuine concern. He wasn't even as old as she, Rachel thought with a small twinge of surprise. His round face and blond hair made him look like a teenager.

"I'm just cold," she said through chattering teeth.

"I'll get you a blanket." He helped her up the slippery

path and left her sitting on the mossy stone bench near the parking area while he returned to the two Portland Police cars that stood in the driveway, their lights twirling slowly. Red-and-blue light slid across the bent form of Claymore as he limped over to the rear car and was helped into the backseat. The young officer returned with a plain brown blanket which he wrapped around Rachel's shoulders. "We'll need to get a statement from you," he said. "I've got some coffee in my car. Would you like some? It's hot."

"Thank you," Rachel said. She was watching Spiros, who stood beside the car that held Claymore, one elbow on the roof, talking to the other officer. His face might have been carved from stone, she thought as she watched him. *Justice,* she thought. *That would be the title of the scuplture. Harsh and cold. Relentless justice.*

Someone had said something about Lieutenant Spiros, Rachel remembered suddenly. About how he had moved to Blossom because he was in love with a cousin. It wasn't a cousin, Rachel thought with sudden comprehension. It had been Linda Johnston. He had been in love with her, and she had been in love with Claymore, and then she had died.

Obsessed, Claymore had said. Oh, yes.

She looked at Spiros again, just as he approached, carrying the cup top from a thermos. Fragrant steam rose from the cup. As he handed it to her, their eyes met. Beneath the hard, cold triumph in his eyes lurked an empty darkness.

"We're going to have to get your statement tonight." Spiros looked down at her as she sipped at the blessedly hot coffee. "We'll make it as fast as we can. I let Price know what's going on. He said to tell you he's on his way."

"Thank you," she said. "I need to call my mother, too. I was supposed to go back to the hospital to see her tonight. She just had surgery." She was still having difficulty getting the words out, but the coffee was helping.

"Here." He handed her a cell phone and stepped back. Soaked to the skin, he stared fixedly at the creek, seemingly oblivious to the water that dripped from his hair and ran down his face.

At least the rain had stopped. As Rachel dialed the number that Joshua had given her, she realized that a few stars had appeared. The Chinook had finally ended, she thought as the phone began to ring. Joshua answered her on the first ring.

"We were worried," he said anxiously. "Did something happen?"

Did something happen? Rachel took a deep breath. "A lot," she said. "I'm fine, and I'll tell you all about it. But it'll be a while before I can get over there. I don't know how late you're going to be at the hospital."

"What happened?" Her mother's voice came over the phone. "I can tell by Joshua's expression that something did." Her voice sounded almost normal. "Tell me right now."

"Oh, Mom, you sound great." Her voice trembled. "I'm so glad. And it's too long a story to tell you right now. How late can I come by?"

"You come over here as soon as you can. I don't care if it's one in the morning. I'll tell the nurses that they'd better make sure you come up here no matter what time it is, or I'll be the worst patient they've ever had! Joshua is laughing at me." She said something to him that Rachel couldn't quite catch, then her voice returned. "You're sure you're all right? You're not sparing me because I'm in the hospital?"

"I really am all right, and Jeff is going to come over there with me, so don't worry."

"Of course I'm worrying! I'm your mother. I'm not going to be able to relax until I hear what is going on from you, right here in front of me, so that I can be sure you're in one piece."

"Do I have to strip to prove it?" Rachel asked.

"You just might, young lady. You just might."

"We'll be there." Rachel smiled, in spite of her shivering. "Just don't blame me if you're sound asleep and I wake you up."

"I won't be alseep. I'll be waiting." Her mother hung up.

The brief interchange—so typically Deborah—had lifted some of the darkness from Rachel's spirit. She raised her head as the lieutenant came over to take her statement, and spoke calmly and coherently as she recounted the events of the evening. "I think he must have found a way to send Eduardo and his crew home," she told the detective. "I couldn't figure out why they had left when I told them I'd be back. And there was no note. If there had been some kind of emergency, Eduardo would have left me a note."

"I'll need this Eduardo's phone number and last name."

Rachel gave it to him. "Just be sure you make it clear why you're calling him," she told him. "He had a brother who came here illegally, and the INS arrested him last fall. Eduardo's a little afraid that he'll be arrested, too. He has his green card," she added hastily. "He's here legally. But if you scare him, he might decide to disappear."

"I'm not the INS, and I really don't care whether he's here legally or not." Spiros wrote down the number. "The only way he'll get in trouble is if he doesn't cooperate."

Rachel sighed, hoping that translated. Tact didn't seem to be the lieutenant's long suit, and Eduardo was a bit jumpy when it came to uniforms and the legal arm of the government. She hoped she could get Julio to talk to him before Spiros came knocking. Spiros finished taking her statement, recording her words carefully in his notebook in small, meticulous writing. As he closed it finally, a dark car came roaring down the road outside the gates, pulling over on the muddy shoulder with a crunch of gravel. Jeff. She recognized the vehicle and felt a rush of relief.

"One question," she said, as Spiros pocketed his notebook. "How did you end up out here tonight to come to the rescue?"

"Aren't you glad I did?" He didn't smile.

"Very," she said fervently. "I just wondered how you knew this might happen."

Spiros shrugged. "Claymore's been following you." He looked down at her, his expression unreadable. "I've been following him." He pocketed his notebook and walked across the parking area to intercept Jeff.

The two men spoke briefly, then Jeff shouldered past the older man and strode over. Without a word he lifted her into his arms and hugged her so hard she could barely breathe. "Hey, easy, I'm fine." She gasped. "Unless you break a couple of ribs."

"Actually, I'm tempted to shake you." He held her at arm's length, worry, relief, irritation warring on his face. "You promised you wouldn't come here by yourself."

"Turns out I wasn't by myself at all," Rachel drawled. "I'm sorry, Jeff." She bent her head. "It really was a stupid thing to do—but Eduardo and the crew were supposed to be here. I should have left right away, but I just thought it was a mistake, and I only meant to stay a few minutes, and then . . . It was too late." She shivered again, remembering the moment when she realized that the gates had been locked and she was inside with her stalker. "I'll never do something that stupid again."

"I sure as hell hope not." He hugged her again and kept his arm around her this time. "I don't think my heart can take many more episodes like this one."

"Can I go?" She was wet, cold, muddy, and feeling utterly exhausted as the last of the evening's adrenaline evaporated from her system. "I need to stop by the hospital," she said in a small voice. "I'd better change clothes." She looked down at her soaked jeans and mud-stained shirt. "I'll leave puddles on the floor like this."

"I'll come with you," Jeff said grimly. "No way I let you out of my sight tonight." He kept his arm around her as they walked back to the truck, and waited while she got the clothes she'd worn to the hospital from her truck box.

She let them back into the house, changing in the dark, goose bumps prickling on her arms as she stripped off her wet clothes. The dry clothes felt wonderful. Jeff bundled her wet things up without a word and carried them out to her truck, putting them on the floor of the cab. "Why don't you ride with me? We can come get your truck in the morning." He brushed the hair back from her face. "You don't look as if you're up for a drive back to Blossom tonight. Or do you want to stay here, like you planned?"

"I don't think I want to," Rachel said slowly. "I just want to go home. But I need to see Mom and Joshua first. I really worried her."

"Sweetheart, you really worried me." Jeff's light tone sounded forced, but he touched her face gently. "Let's go reassure your mom, and then let's go home."

"It's going to be a short night for you. I'm sorry."

"I'll live."

They walked out to his Jeep together. Spiros was still there, but the car with Claymore in it had left. Jeff went over to speak briefly with him, then returned to Rachel. "He'll make sure somebody keeps an eye on your truck tonight. He might need to talk to you tomorrow, when we come back to get it. He'll call."

They drove over to the hospital, through a downtown full of restaurant neon and strolling couples out for a late supper or on their way to watch a movie or a play, or to listen to music. The normal bustle of casual nightlife seemed eerie, after the dark cold moments on the bridge. When they walked into the lobby, Joshua was waiting for them. "Just to make sure you get up there," he said cheerfully, although a hint of worry lurked in his eyes. "Your mother is in a bit of a state," he told Rachel. "She does do the Jewish mother thing when she needs to." He chuckled. "I guess it's genetic."

"I hope not," Rachel said, and rolled her eyes.

"Well, you've got your dad's genes, too," Jeff drawled as he ushered her into the elevator after Joshua. "You could be an Irish mother just as easily."

"I'm not sure that's any better." Rachel found herself blushing. Fortunately the elevator reached their floor, and the doors opened, saving her from further comments. They exited onto her mother's floor, to find her standing in the doorway of her room, peering anxiously into the hallway.

"Well, I see she's up and around, at least." Joshua sighed.

"Rachel's right here. She's fine. You can relax now."

"Not yet." Deborah seized her daughter by the arm and looked searchingly into her face. "What is this? I can't even go into the hospital without you getting yourself into trouble?"

Her mother's smile reached her eyes, in spite of her tone. Rachel bent and kissed her on the forehead. "You're doing a marvelous job," she murmured. "Aunt Esther couldn't do it better."

"Oh, come now." Deborah laughed. "She's the ultimate walking stereotype. I couldn't do her act justice if I studied for the part for years." She kissed her daughter, her relief evident in the pressure of her lips. "And thank you, Jeff, for coming out here to take charge of her." She gave Jeff a bright smile. "Now I can get back into bed and relax. Thank heavens they at least took the darn IV out. It was truly a nuisance, especially when I had to use the bathroom." Still clutching Rachel's wrist, she went back into the room and let Joshua help her onto the bed. "Actually, I'm amazed at how many nerve endings are attached to my chest," she said cheerfully. "Reminds me of when I had the C-section when you were born. I thought every muscle was attached to my belly back then. I guess they relocated. Whew." She settled back on the pillows, looking a bit pale in spite of her light tone. "I think I had my exercise for a while." She smiled at Joshua and reached for his hand. "So now I'll behave, and you can relax and stop playing watchdog."

"I just didn't want you to harass the nurses," Joshua murmured. "They're no match for you."

"Like mother, like daughter," Jeff said with a wink.

"Ha. At least *I* have some common sense." Deborah sniffed. "So, young lady." She fixed Rachel with a pointed stare. "Tell me right now what happened."

"It's a long story," Rachel began.

"I have time," her mother said pleasantly.

Rachel recounted the events of the evening, trying to downplay the danger on that flooded footbridge, struck by guilt as her mother's face paled.

"Paul Claymore did this?" Her voice trembled. "I just . . .
It's almost hard to believe. Maybe the rumors were right."
She looked at the night-dark square of window, her face
drawn. "I always chalked it up to small-town gossipmon-
gering. But maybe . . ." She shook her head. "How ironic
that the officer who suspected him all those years ago finally caught him."

"It is ironic, isn't it?" Jeff said.

Rachel glanced at him quickly, but his eyes were on her
mother's face.

"What if he hadn't been there?" Deborah drew a shaky
breath. "Rachel, you were really in danger."

"It's fine now, Mom. He's in jail." Rachel took her
mother's hand and leaned down to give her a kiss. "Jeff's
going to drive me home, so I'll even have a bodyguard.
I'm perfectly safe."

"Yes, you are." Her mother gave her a wan smile. "I'll
try to keep that in mind, even though I'd love to lock you
in your bedroom." She made a face at her daughter. "Just
wait until you have kids. See how calm, cool, and rational
you are then!"

"I'm sure I'll be yelling for help every time you turn
around." Rachel squeezed her mother's hand and gave
Joshua a kiss on the cheek. "I need to go home," she said.
"I'll stop by tomorrow." A new worry crossed her mind.
"I hope I still have a crew," she said as they left the
room. "I hope something awful didn't happen. And I hope
Spiros's questions don't send them all running."

"He can be tactful when he needs to be," Jeff said as
they waited for the elevator. "Hard to believe, but true. He
did better than a lot of cops in LA."

"I hope so. Eduardo always brings me a good crew."
Rachel sighed. "I'd hate to see him move up to Wenatche
or something, just to get away from Spiros."

They crossed the lobby and went out into the spring
night. Stars sprinkled the sky, and it felt chilly. Rachel
found herself keeping close to Jeff, feeling threats in the
shadows in a way that she hadn't before. The memory of

Claymore's strength as he dragged her onto that flooded bridge would haunt her dreams, she suspected. She felt vulnerable in a way she never had before.

Jeff insisted on stopping for hamburgers before they started the drive back. She protested that she wasn't hungry, but when he handed her a big burger, stuffed with lettuce and tomato and fragrant from the grill, she discovered in an instant that she was ravenous, and ate every drippy bite and every last one of her french fries, calories be damned. Licking her fingers, she sat back with a sigh. "Glad you're driving," she said. "I'd have food all over me by now."

"Glad you forced yourself to eat," he drawled. "You did pretty well for somebody who wasn't hungry."

"Yeah, well, I guess I wasn't listening to my stomach." She yawned, suddenly sleepy.

"I stopped by and talked to Julio today," Jeff remarked as they left Portland and its environs behind. "I got to meet Anita, who is a very nice girl and obviously very taken with Julio. Which didn't seem to bother him at all." He grinned. "She did tell me—with Julio translating—that Claymore sneaks out quite a bit. Apparently he would leave from his private patio and walk across the lawn to where he parked his car. I don't think he realized that Anita frequently sits outside at night until very late."

"So he really could have killed Eloise." Rachel watched the red-and-gold lights of the trucks ahead of them on the dark highway. "Lieutenant Spiros was right."

"Oh, no." Jeff sighed. "He really does have an ironclad alibi for Tuesday night. He and his wife were at a fancy fund-raiser dinner party in Portland, and they spent the night as guests of the host—who are old friends. Much as Carey would love to nail him for Eloise's murder, he can't pull it off. He was definitely at that house all night. Carey has known about that from day one." He shook his head. "That's why I was a little surprised when he let Beck's new girlfriend go."

"So April might still be a suspect." Rachel blinked at him.

"I think she is," Jeff said slowly. "I think he only released her to pressure Claymore. I don't know who else
he's got. The sons are both clear. And so is Roger Tourelle.
He has a solid alibi." For a while he drove without speaking, his frown intermittently revealed by the headlights of
oncoming cars as they curved along the river. Finally, he
shrugged, smiled, and reached over to touch her knee
lightly. "I think you must have been a cat in a previous
existance," he said. "You seem to have nine lives. Which
is a good thing. Just don't push it, okay?"

"Okay," she said. "I won't."

It was late by the time Jeff parked in her driveway. They
went up the stairs together, to be met by Peter on the landing. He stalked in ahead of them, and took up position on
his couch-back perch, reminding them continuously that he
wanted to be fed, thank you very much.

"I am going to take a shower," Rachel announced to him.
"You'll have to talk to Jeff about food." She went into the
bedroom, thinking that she might very well fall down and
go to sleep in the shower if she wasn't careful. She couldn't
remember ever feeling so tired and shaky.

The rush of hot, hot water helped wash some of the evening's chill echoes away. She dried off, hearing Jeff talking
to Peter in the kitchen, and sat down on the bed for a moment. April was still a suspect. Rachel yawned, thinking it
was silly even to suspect her, leaning back just for a moment. Something tickled her brain—something that was important, something that mattered a lot . . .

She woke to darkness, covered with the bed's quilt,
emerging from a dark dream of rushing water and the hiss
of wind in cedar boughs. Jeff slept next to her, and the
sound of his even breathing drove away the echoes of her
nightmare. She snuggled closer to his warmth, closed her
eyes, and thought as she was falling asleep that she had
remembered something in her dream. "It'll come to me,"
she mumbled under her breath. "In the morning . . ."

CHAPTER

16

Rachel woke late to bright sunlight across her face. She smelled coffee and heard Peter's soft *rrowp* from the front of the apartment. She smiled at the empty side of the bed and got up, stretching luxuriously as she donned her cotton robe. "How nice to have somebody else do the morning stuff," she said as she went into the kitchen. "Wow!" She peered through the windows. "What a perfect day. Do you think that this time summer is here to stay?"

"I hope so. Your cat has been criticizing my housekeeping." He handed her a cup of coffee. "The weatherman is predicting a heat wave. It'll actually be in the eighties and might even hit ninety. How's that for a weather change? And the flooding isn't as bad as the media predicted. We got off easy out here." He kissed her lightly on the cheek. "Much as I don't want to let you out of my sight, I have to go down to City Hall. Lyle's out sick." He frowned slightly. "I can't take you back to Portland for your truck this morning."

"I need to talk to Eduardo." Rachel glanced at her watch. "He should still be at home. I'll get him to give me a ride out to Beck's. I'm going to ask him to get started on the benches, at least. I bet the sons don't fight the contract, after all the publicity over Eloise's murder." She nodded. "Beck should be able to take me to Portland."

"I can run you out to Beck's," Jeff said. "If we leave right now, we can grab a couple of rolls at the Bread Box. You need to make a trip to the grocery store, girl."

"I know." She made a face. "I'd better go have lunch with Mom and Joshua today. I don't think I have enough stuff here to make a sandwich. Ten minutes, and I'll be ready to go." She picked up the phone and dialed Eduardo's home.

His sister answered, her voice raised to be heard over the sound of children's voices in the background. She greeted Rachel cheerfully and went to find her brother. Rachel heard her admonishing various children on her way to the back of the house. She took care of six children—her own four and Eduardo's two from his first marriage. The one time Rachel had been there, she had been impressed with the order that existed in the midst of the chaos of six children between the ages of two and twelve occupying a small frame house. Toys lay everywhere, but the house and children were clean, and the older kids helped look after the younger ones. Eduardo's sister, a small sturdy woman with a ready laugh and short black hair, had a friendly smile and a lively sense of humor, but Rachel had the feeling that she kept her younger brother firmly in line.

"Senorita?" Eduardo's worried voice came on the line. "There is trouble? The job is not good?"

"No, the job is good." She spoke slowly, because her Spanish was about as rough as his English. "I will be late. You start without me. I am coming with Beck—the man who makes things."

"Oh, *sí, Senorita Boss*. The crazy one." She could almost hear his rolling eyes. Beck amused her crew. "We will be there," Eduardo went on. "And I am happy that your *madre*, she is not more sick," he added in English.

"She's doing very well," Rachel told him, wondering where he had heard that her mother was in the hospital.

Well, Blossom was a small enough town. Probably everyone had heard by now. "Eduardo, why did you leave the job before I got back yesterday?" She finally asked the question she had been dying to blurt out with her first breath. "Did something go wrong?"

"You say for us to leave." Eduardo sounded puzzled. "The man came there to us from the hospital, and said to us that we go home, that your *madre*, she was more sick. You would stay with her, he said. You not come. The job is finish for that day."

"I see." A finger of cold, like a trickle of icy floodwater down her neck, chilled her. Claymore had set the scene carefully. She shivered. "If you saw the man again, could you recognize him?"

For a few moments Eduardo was silent—weighing the risk of getting involved with the law against wanting to help her. "I . . . think it would not be so easy." His tone was cautious. "The man, he wore a coat for the rain, you know? And a hat. And he had a big moustache—lots of hair. What was under all that—I do not know."

In other words, it was a disguise, and even Eduardo knew it. Rachel made a face. Combine a disguise with her crew's reluctance to draw any attention from the police, legal immigrants or not, and an identification wasn't all that likely. She sighed, told Eduardo that a policeman would come and ask him questions, and he should tell him about the man. He was not in trouble. The policeman did not think he had done anything wrong.

Eduardo agreed to talk to the policeman. He did not sound thrilled at the prospect, but neither did he sound like a man on his way to Wenatche. Which was something of a relief.

"Eduardo said a man told them to leave," Rachel told Jeff as she hung up. "He pretended he was bringing a message from me. I wish he'd called me on my cell phone to check."

"Claymore." Jeff reached out suddenly, touching her as

if to reassure himself that she was real and not a phantom. "Can he identify him, do you think?"

"Maybe," Rachel said doubtfully. "He was wearing a disguise."

"If he set things up ahead of time, his lawyer is going to have a hard time pleading the attack as a crime of momentary insanity," Jeff said grimly.

Rachel shivered again. "Let's get going," she said. "I want to have time to go see Mom while I'm there."

"Give her my love when you talk to her." Jeff looked around the apartment. "I'll get down there tonight, for sure. I'll bring her some flowers."

"Bring her snapdragons if you can find them." Rachel smiled. "They're her favorite flower."

"Snapdragons." Jeff held the door open for her. "Will do."

Peter stalked through the door with his nose in the air, as if humans bowed him through doors every day. Jeff laughed at him, and the nose tilted more sharply toward the sky. "Better watch out." Rachel chuckled. "Last time I laughed at him, I got a good scratch on the ankle."

"Better not try it, cat." Jeff glared at him, but was utterly ignored by Peter, who ran lightly down the stairs ahead of them, his tail at attention.

They drove over to the Bread Box, to find Joylinn sitting on the deck with a cup of coffee. "Taking my break," she told them as they joined her. "I finished the baking early this morning." She shook her head. "I woke up at four and couldn't go back to sleep. So I figured I might as well walk on over and get started with the day." She made a face. "I've never seemed to need much sleep."

"I'm jealous." Rachel heaved a theatric sigh. "Eight hours would be lovely. Seven gets me by."

"So what's new?" Joylinn asked as the waitress set two steaming mugs down in front of them. "Bring us some of the cinnamon rolls, will you, Celia? How's your mom?"

What's new? "Where do I start?" Rachel murmured. She caught Jeff's eye and rolled her eyes.

"All right, spill it." Joylinn sat up straight. "Something happened. You don't leave here until you tell."

Rachel took a deep breath and launched into a truncated account of the previous day. Joylinn's eyebrows rose higher and higher, and when she finally reached the horrible minutes on the bridge, she pushed her chair back with an exclamation.

"Girl, you are so lucky to be alive! Our revered politician did this?" She shook her head, her eyes round. "Well, I must say, my mother will be happy to know that Linda didn't commit suicide. I think that always haunted her—that her friend might have done that." She sighed. "And your mother's really doing okay?" She searched Rachel's face, then nodded, apparently reassured by what she read there. "I'm going to take the afternoon off and go down there." She nodded decisively. "Want to come with me?"

"I'm on my way in to Portland right now. Well, more or less." Rachel made a face. "I've got to meet Eduardo and the crew there."

"You're not going on with that job?" Joylinn sounded appalled.

"Claymore is in custody," Jeff broke in. "There's no reason to think anybody else has any interest in harming her. Believe me, she wouldn't be going there if there was." He gave her a quick, lowering glance.

Rachel made a face at him, then turned to Joylinn. "I really am safe. I have Eduardo and his crew there." She winced and gave Jeff an apologetic look, because this was exactly what she had told him yesterday, when he had worried about her. "And like Jeff said, Claymore's locked up," she continued hastily.

"I'm still going to worry about you." Joylinn glared at her. "You call me the minute you're back here safe, okay? I'm going to chew my nails down to the quick by tonight."

"I promise," Rachel said meekly. "And speaking of work, we'd better go. You're going to be late getting in by the time you run me out to Beck's," she told Jeff. "I let time get away from me. You should have kicked me."

"I was winding up to." He bent to kiss the top of her head. "I won't be that late."

"I'll run you out to Beck's." Joylinn finished the last of her mocha and stood up. "I'm tempted to come into town with you, just to make sure you're all right. But I'd better not." She sighed. "We have quite an order for tomorrow—this couple who moved into that new condominium project—you know, the gated one where you have to have a card to get past the driveway? Well they ordered a flan, dinner rolls, and some appetizers. I guess they're having an anniversary party," she said happily. "It's going to make this month a record-breaker for income."

"I'm so pleased." Rachel squeezed Joylinn's hand, knowing how close her friend had been to the edge of failure as she struggled to establish her bakery and catering service. "I bet you see a lot of this kind of business, after that great affair you catered for Herbert Southern."

"Let's hope. So you can go ahead and go be official," Joylinn told Jeff. "I'll run her out to Beck's. I want to meet this new girlfriend I keep hearing about. I want to know what kind of person could put up with our local crazy." Joylinn untied her flour-streaked denim apron as she called, "Celia! I'm taking off. I'll be back in less than an hour, okay?"

"Okay." Celia raised her voice to be heard above the hiss of the espresso machine. "No problem. Take your time."

"What would I do without her?" Joylinn scooped the rest of the cinnamon rolls into a white sack and handed it to Jeff. "A donation to the force."

"Accepted with thanks, ma'am," Jeff drawled. "You two have a nice gossip. At least I don't have to worry about Rachel for a little while."

"Oh, I'll take good care of her," Joylinn said. "I promise."

"And if Eduardo isn't at the garden, I'll leave so fast you'll find tire marks on the pavement."

"This time you do that," Jeff said, and didn't smile. He lifted his hand as he left them.

"He's serious about you, girl." Joylinn looked thoughtfully after him. "He's really worried. Oh, yes, he's serious."

"I know he's serious." Rachel didn't look at her friend as they walked to the car. She felt Joylinn's attention like a prodding finger in her spine even as she refused to look.

"Well?" Joylinn skipped around her and planted herself against the passenger door, facing Rachel. "I mean . . . you two have been diddling around for two years plus now. Never mind your high school romance. So if this is all so serious, what's with you?"

"What's with me, what?" Rachel managed an innocent look. "Eduardo's waiting for me. I'm a working girl, remember?"

"Hey, if you don't want him, just let me know." Joylinn lifted one eyebrow. "I've been practicing serious self-restraint, but I could stop."

"How do you do that?"

"Do what?" Joylinn looked perplexed.

"Lift one eyebrow and not the other. You read that in books, but no way can I do it."

"I practice in front of the mirror," Joylinn said dryly. "Honestly, Rachel . . ."

"Don't." Rachel held up a hand. "Just don't. Please."

For a moment, Joylinn was silent. "All right," she said quietly. "Let's go out to Beck's. I can at least satisfy one prick of curiosity."

They pulled onto the county road and headed up into the hills toward Beck's lonely cabin. The silence started out tense in the small car, then stretched like bread dough, softening and becoming gentle. "I'm sorry I snapped," Rachel said. "It's just . . . I don't think I can explain this to myself, much less anyone else."

"That's okay." Joylinn shot her a quick sideways look. "Is your mother really all right?"

"I think so." Rachel watched the spring orchard rows swing past. "I think it's going to be tough, but she has Joshua, and that's important."

"You know, when I found out . . ." Joylinn paused. "I

thought . . . I was afraid that she might . . . you know . . . just end it. I mean, she seemed so *distant*."

Suicide? Her mother? Rachel shivered, holding herself as if Joylinn had just turned on the air conditioner. "She couldn't! She wouldn't!" Rachel drew a deep breath. "She has Joshua. She wouldn't do that to him."

"And you!" Joylinn shook her head. "That was stupid of me to even think it." She reached for Rachel's hand and squeezed it gently. "You're right. She would never do that to you."

"No." Rachel stared through the window, utterly unaware of the scenery beyond the highway. "Eloise has the same doctor as my mother." The words tumbled out. "When I met him, I mentioned that Eloise was dead. He wasn't surprised to hear that, Joylinn. He . . . expected it. But he was shocked when I told him she was murdered."

"Well, murder is shocking, isn't it?"

"That's not it." Rachel twisted on the seat to face her. "He knew she wasn't about to die of natural causes, don't you see? He was her doctor. That's what felt weird about the conversation. He thought I was telling him that she'd suicided. And then he hurried to assure me that my mother didn't have the same kind of cancer. So it must have been bad—what she had. So she did it."

"Did what? I thought Claymore killed her," Joylinn said cautiously.

"No, no, he has an alibi for the night. He was at some fund-raiser thing. He admitted to killing Linda, but he said he didn't kill Eloise. He was really surprised that I even thought it. And I know April didn't do it. But why didn't Eloise leave a suicide note?"

"Good question." Joylinn sounded doubtful. "I thought all suicides did that. And I mean—wouldn't she guess that they'd suspect the woman who worked for her first?"

"Yes." Rachel frowned, because it was such a great theory. Except for that.

"Tell me where to turn," Joylinn said. "You know, at least I don't think Beck's dangerous, like some of the people around here. But seriously . . . I mean, this girl's not even from around here. Does she know what she's in for, living with him?"

"I hope so," Rachel said. "Turn right here."

"I should have driven a tank. Honestly, Rachel, does he really live out here?" Joylinn peered through the windshield, wincing as branches whispered against the sides of the car. "So much for my nice, unscratched paint job. Holy cow." She halted the car at the end of the driveway. "I'd heard he lived in a cabin . . ."

A thin curl of smoke drifted from the stone chimney. At least a dozen black cats lounged in the sun in front of the big metal-sided shop, and their eyes—in all shades of agate, gold, and green—turned as one toward the car.

"Jeez, girl." Joylinn sounded spooked, although she laughed. "Are you sure it's safe to leave you here?"

"Yes, it's very safe." Rachel laughed at her friend, opening the car door, although Joylinn hadn't yet turned off the engine. The cats instantly streaked for the shelter of the woods. In less than three seconds, not a cat could be seen in the clearing. "You can take off if you want."

"No way. I want to meet the crazy girl who's willing to live here." Resolutely Joylinn reached for the key and turned off the engine. It ticked loudly in the sudden silence. With a muttered exclamation, Joylinn thrust the door open. "Okay, so let's go knock on the door," she said with forced cheerfulness. "Or does Beck take off with his cats?"

"Sometimes." Rachel crossed the trampled dust of the yard, heading for the split-log steps that led up to the porch. The cabin door opened as she approached, and April stuck her head out.

"Hi." Her glance traveled a bit warily from Rachel to Joylinn and back to Rachel again. "I didn't expect to see you," she said hesitantly. "If you're looking for Beck, he's in the shop." Dark circles shadowed the pale skin beneath her eyes.

"Are you all right?" Rachel held out a hand, concerned about the girl's drawn face. "Did something happen?"

"That police jerk came back out here late last night." She looked toward the shop from which emanated the rasp of sandpaper on wood. "I guess . . . He made it sound like they suspect me again. I guess . . . I guess Eloise left me money." April swallowed. "From her life insurance or something. I didn't know. I told him that—that I didn't know—but he didn't believe me, I don't think. Who are you?" She looked at Joylinn. "You're not from the police?"

"I own the Bread Box—a little bakery in town." Joylinn smiled at her with sympathy. "I'm sorry you're getting harassed. I'm just Rachel's ride today."

"She's a friend of mine. April, I'm so sorry." Rachel thought of Jeff's guess that Spiros had pretended to accept April's innocence only in order to provoke Claymore. A slow anger kindled in her chest. "Have you talked to Gladys?"

"Oh, yeah." April sat down on the top step. "I told her. She told me not to talk to him unless she was there. Which I knew anyway. Mostly I think she was afraid I'd take off again."

"Will you?" Rachel looked down at her bent head. The sun struck sparks of bronze and gold from her fine, light hair as she lifted her head sharply.

"No. Not this time." Her chin jutted defiantly. "I did that, I know. I've done it a few times, if you want to know the truth. Not anymore." She shook her head until her hair shimmered like a curtain of light in front of her face. "If I ran, Beck would go with me. Or he'd . . . he'd try to protect me. Isn't that crazy?" But her smile lighted her face in spite of her head shake. "He believes me. He knows . . . all about me. And he still believes." She met Rachel's eyes, her own eyes clear. "I guess I have to believe in me, too. What else can I do?" She shrugged. "I don't want him to have to leave here. I want us both to stay. So, no, I'm not going to run."

"I bet Gladys is happy."

"She grunted. Is that what she does when she's happy?" April bounced to her feet. "I'll go tell Beck you're here." She crossed the yard, moving lightly, the flowered shift she wore wrapping around her lean, muscled legs.

"She's gorgeous." Joylinn sounded stunned. "Hair a mess, no makeup, dressed in a muumuu, and she's still gorgeous. She could be a model." Joylinn stared after her, shaking her head. "What in the world does she want with him?"

"Ask her."

"No, thank you." Joylinn shook her head. "You know, she could make me think there's more to Beck than I guessed."

"I think there's a lot more to him than we'll ever know." Rachel raised her eyebrows as two of the black cats appeared from nowhere to rub briefly and luxuriously against the girl's ankles as she vanished into the shop. "Well, I guess she's really moved in here." She lifted her hand to wave as Beck stuck his head out of the shop door. He bent his head gravely as April spoke to him, then brushed a lock of her hair lightly from her face before turning toward the cabin.

"Hello," he said gravely as he reached them.

"Beck, this is Joylinn," Rachel said. "She owns the Bread Box."

"I know." He nodded.

"Can you come to Portland with me, to the garden?" Rachel asked. "I'd like you to start working on the benches. You still want to do it, don't you?" she asked anxiously.

"I'll come." He turned to April, who had come up behind him.

"We'll both come along." She took his hand. "I want to go there and . . . I guess say good-bye to Eloise. I think she's waiting for me to come by."

Beck nodded.

"Well, I'll be getting back, then," Joylinn said brightly. "I guess you're all set for transportation." Taking Rachel firmly by the arm, she walked her back to the car. "She's sweet and stunning," she whispered in Rachel's ear. "But she's as nuts as he is. Oh, they're a matched pair, all right. Are you sure you're okay here?"

"Oh, go bake more cinnamon rolls." Rachel laughed and closed the door on her friend as Joylinn slid behind the wheel. "Just be glad Beck wasn't talking to his cats today."

"I could believe it," Joylinn said darkly. Then she smiled. "I trust your judgment, dearie. Just call me when you get back, okay? Or drop by if I'm still at the shop. I'll save you a pecan roll," she wheedled. "I'm baking a batch this afternoon."

"I'll call you." Rachel smiled at her friend. "Believe me, I'm safe."

She waved as Joylinn left the clearing, but beneath her smile, she was worried. Spiros again. Frowning, she went over to Beck's truck. He had already loaded his small tool-box into the bed. Today, Rachel knew, he would simply look at locations and create the benches and gazebos in his head. Then he would come home and start working. She had never seen him draw a sketch or use a blueprint once. But everything fit perfectly. April emerged from the cabin with a canvas bag and a plastic milk jug full of water.

"Lunch," she said. "Let's go."

It was a tight fit for the three of them in the cab of Beck's big truck, and the noise from the engine made conversation nearly impossible. But April, peering out the window, kept asking about the Columbia River and the Gorge cliffs as they drove. "I grew up in Portland—over in the northeast. But I never really paid attention to stuff like the Gorge. It was just something we learned a little bit about in school. It's . . . beautiful."

To Rachel's surprise, it was Beck who answered her questions, speaking in an easy if spare manner that silenced Rachel for the entire trip. She had gotten so used to Beck's one-word conversations that she had begun to believe that he had no more language than that. It was like discovering that someone you thought was blind could see after all. It jolted Beck out of his usual space in the landscape of the universe and made her see him with new eyes. Her mother had remarked more than once that he had changed a lot, Rachel remembered. He laughed once, and she realized with a start that she had never heard him laugh before. In that moment of unbidden mirth, he looked young—late-teens young, as if the brief syllables of laughter had transported him back across a bleak gulf of years to a point in time long ago, when he had last laughed.

Rachel found herself wondering if he could still craft wood the way he used to. The change in him was that profound.

The drive passed quickly, but as 122nd Avenue narrowed and curved down to the creek beneath its canopy of firs, Rachel found herself growing tense. The day had turned out to be lovely—blue sky dotted with puffy clouds, warm the way it was supposed to be warm this time of year, even in Portland. But as they drove between the iron gates that stood crookedly ajar, the light seemed to dim for a moment, as if a cloud had passed in front of the sun. The chain—cut by an officer's bolt cutters, she assumed—still dangled from one of the gates, the padlock hanging from the severed links like an oversize charm on a bracelet.

Eduardo's car stood at the end of the parking lot. Her truck stood where she had left it, dappled with shade and glistening with water from the previous night's rain. The sun touched it, making the water droplets sparkle, and birds sang riotously as they climbed out of Beck's truck. A pair of squabbling jays tumbled across the parking lot, totally oblivious to the human company. The sound of voices laughing and conversing in Spanish came to them faintly—Eduardo and his crew at work already. Rachel walked slowly over to the top of the stairs that led down to the creek. The water there had gone down rapidly overnight. The bridge cleared the brown water now. A basket-weave mat of branches, grass, and bits of trash clogged the upstream rails. Those branches and roots would have snagged in her clothes, held her under last night . . . Rachel shivered.

"Who put that down?" April came up beside her, outrage in her tone. "It's way too early. Look at that mess! One big tree trunk comes down on the water, and the bridge is wrecked. Eloise said we shouldn't put it down at all until

June this year." Her eyes strayed eastward, toward the spot along the bank where they had found Eloise. "I wish," she faltered, and fell briefly silent. "How can they think that?" she whispered.

Beck had come up behind them. He put a hand on their shoulders, one hand each, light as the touch of a visiting moth, not speaking, his eyes full of sympathy.

"Okay." Rachel drew a deep breath. "Let's go get to work." She led the way back up the steps to the asphalt, wondering if Spiros was going to show up here to arrest April. She also wondered what Beck might do.

Beck had fallen into his working mode—utterly oblivious to all, his gaze seemingly inward as he created decks and benches and gazebos in his head. He crossed the lot and started up one of the overgrown trails that led to the upper garden. "I put together a lunch," April told Rachel. "Can we get into the house? Can I put it into the refrigerator?"

"I have a key." Rachel and April crossed to the house. Rachel unlocked the door, and they went on into the kitchen. Already the house seemed to have a musty, abandoned feel. "I'm glad this is going to become a public garden." April sighed. "I'd like to be able to come back and visit sometimes."

If Eloise Johnston had committed suicide, she would have left a note. She would have made sure that no one would suspect April. Rachel waited while April put the sack of lunch that she'd brought into the refrigerator, then the two of them climbed the path to where Eduardo and his two crew members weeded among the Oregon grape and camellias of the upper slope. He grinned at her and nodded, then pointed down the slope to where Beck stood with his head bent, contemplating the small flat terrace where Eloise had wanted a bench, and rolled his eyes. Rachel put on her leather work gloves and shrugged, which earned her a wink and a grin. "You certainly don't have to help me weed," she told April.

"Do you know . . . ?" April hesitated. "Is it okay for me

to get some of my stuff from the house? I . . . left just about everything here."

"I never thought of that." Rachel straightened up. "I don't know. I mean . . . if it's your stuff, how could anyone argue? It's not a crime scene anymore. They let me in here, and I'm sure they've gone through your stuff as much as they wanted. They got a search warrant, didn't they?"

"Oh, they sure did." April made a face. "I bet my room is a mess. But I'm tired of wearing the same clothes. And . . . I'd like to collect my journal. I'd hate to think that a cop read it." She blushed. "Or anyone else. But I hid it pretty well, so I don't think they could have."

Slowly Rachel pulled off her gloves, her heart pounding. "Did . . . did Eloise know where you kept your journal?"

"Oh, yes," April said. "She saw me writing in it one day and told me about this neat place in the outdoor fireplace across the creek. It was their secret safe-deposit box. She told me that Carl, her husband, built the fireplace. It's got petrified wood in it, and agates, and a few fossils even. They kept money there. And her jewelry. And the notes for their books. Just in case the house burned. You take out this pretty piece of petrified wood, and there's a big space behind it. Plenty of room for things. I put my journal in it."

"Show me," Rachel said softly. "Eduardo, I'll be right back. When you're done here, start there." She pointed across the slope to a grove of firs and native shrubs that was being engulfed by weedy wild geranium. "I'll be right back. Come on, April. Let's see this secret place!" Holding her excitement in check, she followed April back down the slope and down the stone stairs to the driveway.

April led her over the footbridge. It cost Rachel a moment of hesitation before she could bring herself to set foot on the slimed planks of the bridge. Mud was drying to a powdery tan in the warm sun, and she kept her mind firmly on the moment as she made her way across the rush of the still-swollen creek. She smelled the dank odor of flood and caught a whiff of something dead. A nutria, maybe, or a beaver, swept to its death in the churning rush of the flood. She tried not to think about last night.

Then they were across and climbing a needled path through dense shade. The fireplace dominated a stone-flagged patio that had been terraced into the creekbank. Stone tables provided space for picnic dishes, and the cool shade would make this a lovely spot in summer's heat. The faintly acrid scent of old ashes clung to the cavernous opening of the fireplace as they knelt on the blackened and smoke-stained hearth. April counted over from the edge of the chimney, then tugged at a stone that looked like any other stone. It resisted her a moment, then slid easily out of its space. She reached gingerly into the dark cavity behind it. "I'm always afraid that some kind of spider is going to be in there," she began, then fell silent, frowning. "What's this?" She pulled out a small spiral-bound notebook and a plastic rectangle. "A tape recorder." She stared at it, confused. "I didn't put a tape recorder in here."

Rachel took it from her. The machine had a tape in it. She clicked it on.

"This is Eloise Johnston," the familiar voice spoke from the machine. "It's very late. Today I signed a contract with Rachel O'Connor to restore the grounds of my property, and paid her in advance. It is my will that she finish this job for me. I intend to hand over this property that Carl and I so loved in the condition in which it was maintained when we were both capable of caring for it. My sons, you have sufficient money, and the stock that your father left you. So forgive me for disposing of this property to suit myself."

Both Rachel and April sat spellbound and silent as Eloise's voice continued.

"I spoke to my doctor yesterday. The breast cancer—which we might have at least delayed for a few more years—has spread into my bones. It is a virulent form, my doctor tells me. It will kill me shortly, and it will not be a pleasant death. I will not be able to watch the garden become the lovely place we once made it. I will linger briefly and painfully in a hospital and then die. So I see no reason why I should not meet death halfway. I have taken care of all the necessary details to hand over the garden to the Northwest Garden Conservancy, under Roger Tourelle's guidance. I have left my life insurance to April Gerard, my caregiver, so that she will have the means to go to college and perhaps do with her life what she wishes. I have for a long time kept some dried foxglove on the shelf—ever since I first discovered the cancer. Considering the medication I'm taking for my heart, a cup or two should suffice. I find a heart attack to be a more acceptable way of dying. I will put this message where April will be certain to find it, where it will be safe from my ghost, who has been lurking about lately. Then I will make my tea. Then I will go for a last walk in our garden, and I will ask Carl to join me. I think he will accept.

"I wish you a wonderful life, my sons. I love you both very much, and you have been very successful. Your father and I have always been proud of you."

"April, I wish you a good life—I hope you, too, are able to find what you love and pursue it."

The voice ended. The small reel of tape turned, and a tiny hiss emerged from the speakers. Numbly, Rachel clicked it off. Across from her, April knelt on the hearth, her hands covering her face. Rachel touched her lightly on the arm, got stiffly to her feet, the recorder in her hand. Swallowing, she went into the kitchen to call Lieutenant Spiros's cell-phone number.

Lieutenant Spiros arrived at the garden quickly—very quickly, in fact. He listened without speaking to Rachel's explanation of how April had remembered the secret hiding place, and how they had checked it. Taking a handkerchief from his pocket, he wrapped the recorder without touching it and put it in his pocket. "So it just occurred to you to look there?" His dark eyes pierced her.

"It didn't occur to me, it occurred to April," Rachel said acerbically. "Perhaps you kept April a bit too distracted to think of it before today."

"What else was in that space?"

"Dust." She met his gaze, held it until he finally shrugged. "Show me," he said.

They took him across the bridge to the picnic patio, and April removed the stone again. Spiros shone a small flash into the space, frowning, then took out the recorder again and carefully rewound it. They all listened without speaking. When Eloise's voice finally ended, he rewrapped the recorder and dropped it back into his pocket. "I'll be talking to you again." He spoke to April. Then he turned on his heel and started for the bridge.

"Lieutenant Spiros?" Rachel waited until he had paused and looked back. "How did you manage to get here so fast?"

For the first time, he looked almost embarrassed. "I . . . drove by and noticed that you were here. I thought I'd keep an eye on you, considering yesterday." He gave a jerky shrug, turned on his heel, and stalked out of the house.

"What was bothering him?" April sent a glare after him. "He looks guilty about something."

"I don't know." Rachel shook her head.

"What a grouch." April tossed her head. "I bet he's afraid the guy he busted will get off. Lots of people do, and they're not even politicians like this guy. He must have lots of judge and lawyer friends."

"That's a thought." Rachel hunched her shoulders briefly, wondering what it would be like at night to go to bed knowing that Claymore was out there somewhere, wondering if he would decide to get even with her one day. It was not a pleasant line of thought. What evidence did Spiros really have beyond an overheard conversation on a bridge in a storm?

"He sure won't get off if that cop has anything to say about it," April reassured her. "That guy scares me. I'm sure glad you found that tape. I think he was going to keep after me until he found a way to prove I did it. You know, I wonder." She tilted her head, chewing thoughtfully at her lip. "When they let me go, I kind of wondered what was

going on. Because he sure seemed to think I did it, and I
was there, and the poison was there. I wonder if he didn't
let me off just to worry that politician guy. What do you
think?"

"Jeff think's that's possible," Rachel said slowly.

Obsessed, Claymore had called Spiros. She caught a
glimpse of Beck's lanky figure above on the far slope. He
was staring down at the lawn on the north side of the house,
imagining the benches he would build there, choosing wood
and fingering grain in his mind. A small anger began to
smolder inside her. Lieutenant Spiros hadn't much cared
who got hurt, as long as he got Claymore.

"Thank you so much for not telling him about my journal." April patted her pocket. "He's the last person I want
to read it."

"That personal?" Rachel smiled.

"That personal." April nodded. "I started it while I was
here. Eloise suggested it. She said it had always helped
her—to write things down. She said it settled her mind
better than just thinking. I guess that's where she got the
material for her memoir."

"So somewhere in her papers, there might be her account
of her daughter's death." Rachel looked after the vanished
Spiros. Not that it mattered now, she thought. Claymore's
career in politics was over once the media got hold of his
arrest. Never mind what happened in the trial. "Actually I
was surprised that Spiros wasn't a lot more suspicious
about why we suddenly decided to check that hole—or why
Eloise might have put the recorder there."

"I don't think he cares," April said. "He has what he
wants, doesn't he?"

"I suppose so." But perhpas what he had really wanted
was gone forever, since that day Linda Johnston had fallen to
her death. The unattainable thing could seem so perfect. . . .
Rachel shook her head, pierced by a brief and unexpected
pang of sympathy for the man. She picked up her gloves
and climbed the hill once more, up to where Eduardo and
the crew were taking a cigarette break. The men jumped

up quickly, putting out their cigarettes, picking up hoes and
digging forks.

They worked together until lunch, moving slowly across
the face of the hill, excavating huckleberry, duck's-foot,
hellebore, and the spent stems of trilliums from the rampant
weeds. An amazing variety of native and nonnative species
lurked beneath the jungle of weedy growth. Rachel mar-
veled at the way the Johnstons had utilized the small individual microclimates of sun, or dry shade, or wetland
down along the creek. This garden represented a lifetime
of combined knowledge about plants and their habitat, and
years of collecting. Rachel hummed to herself as she extri-
cated struggling plants from their burden of weeds. Sometimes, when the sun moved behind one of the high clouds,
she felt as if Eloise looked over her shoulder, casting a brief
shadow on the vanilla leaf she knelt among, or shaking the
branches of the mock orange that grew along the upper
meadow.

As they descended the hill for lunch, April met them to
tell Rachel that she and Beck were returning to Blossom.
"He's ready to start working." She smiled, but she seemed
a little awed. "He's really kind of dedicated when he's
working, isn't he?"

"Oh, honey, he sure is." Rachel chuckled. "I hope you
don't get ignored."

"He's teaching me how to work wood." April smiled
shyly. "He says I have talent."

"If he says that, you do." Rachel felt a quick flash of
relief. She, like Joylinn, had wondered if April knew what
she was in for. "Good for you. I hope you have fun."

"Oh, I will." She turned and ran lightly down the path
to where Beck waited for her beside his truck.

"I'm going to go visit my mother again. In the hospital,"
she told Eduardo as they reached the patio behind the
house. "I'll be back in an hour or two. If anyone comes by
to tell you to go home, ignore them. They're lying."

They both laughed, but then Eduardo sobered. "Senorita

Boss," he said hesitantly. "Before, the man who came—he is a policeman, yes?"

"Yes." Rachel nodded. "His name is Lieutenant Spiros."

"I think . . . I am not certain, but I think so. That he came here yesterday. That he is the one who said for us to go home. That you would not come back here. He had a . . ." He made a gesture at his mouth.

"Moustache?" Rachel said.

"*Sí.*" He nodded. "And I cannot be certain. Like I say. But I think it may be him."

She had assumed that Claymore had sent away her crew. For a moment, she said nothing, simply stared blankly at the slabs of stone that made up the entry path. Finally, she shook herself. "Well, today you keep working." She forced a smile. "No matter who says what."

"*Sí*, Senorita Boss." Eduardo grinned briefly, then disappeared into the kitchen to wash his hands. The scent of chilis and onions drifted through the open window. Somebody was heating up their lunch on the elderly electric stove. The power was back on. She wondered if Claymore had simply thrown the master switch. It hadn't occurred to her to look for an electrical panel.

Rachel's stomach rumbled as she hurried out to her truck. If she hurried, she could visit her mother and be back here in a little over an hour.

At the hospital she was surprised to find her mother dressed and drinking tea with Joshua. "I'm going home," she announced gaily to Rachel as she entered. "I start my chemotherapy and radiation as soon as the surgery heals—which is happening so fast that they've kicked me out."

"I'm so glad." Rachel hugged her mother. "You look great."

"I look a lot more great than I thought I would." Her mother touched her chest lightly. "They've got a new procedure. You'll hardly be able to tell when it's all healed." She smiled at her daughter. "Maybe my hair will grow back in red. I've always wanted red hair, you know. My mother

had lovely auburn hair. I've always been jealous that I
didn't inherit it."

"Maybe it will." Rachel laughed, feeling better than she
had in days. "You can always help it along a bit."

"That occurred to you, too, did it?"

"Not on your life, lady." Joshua leaned over to kiss her.
"I like those dark curls of yours. I've never been one of
those men who swoons over red hair."

"Oh, well, I guess I'll just have to stick to the natural
look." Deborah kissed her husband back. "Ah, here's my
transportation." She nodded at the nurse who had appeared
at the door with a wheelchair. I guess I can't walk to the
door, can I?" she asked plaintively.

"Nope. The insurance company would have a fit." Joshua
picked up her small suitcase. "Are you going back to
work?" he asked Rachel. "You're not over at the garden
again, are you?"

"Well, Claymore's in jail," Rachel said quickly. "And
Lieutenant Spiros seems to feel that he owes me personal
bodyguard service. So I'm perfectly safe."

"I'm going to worry anyway." Deborah looked alarmed.
"I didn't realize you'd go back there."

"I'm safe, I'm safe." Rachel lifted her hands, laughing.
"I have Eduardo and his crew to protect me. And I'll call
you as soon as I'm back in Blossom, okay?"

"Come out to eat dinner with us," Joshua suggested.
"We're going to celebrate. Your mother needs to recover
from hospital food."

"If you're cooking, I'll be there." Rachel smiled. "Although I'll have to stop eating for two days to make up for
it, I bet. What can I bring?"

"Yourself." Her mother sat gingerly in the wheelchair.
"That's more than enough. Joshua has been planning this
meal for days, I think."

"Just one day." Joshua held his wife's hand as the nurse
wheeled her down the wide corridor. "It should be edible."

"Oh, I bet so!" Rachel smiled as she joined them in the
big elevator. She walked with them to the entrance and

waved as they pulled away in Joshua's MG. She had a feeling that they would have a fun drive back to Blossom, even if it cost them a speeding ticket. "They're never going to completely grow up," she remarked out loud.

"They're a sweet couple." The nurse who had wheeled her mother out smiled after the departing car.

"They are," Rachel said. "They surely are."

EPILOGUE

Rachel worked at the Johnston Public Garden on her birthday. It fell on a Wednesday this July, and since the grand opening of the garden was set for the weekend, Rachel didn't feel that she could take the day off. She found Beck's truck already there. He was finishing the gazebo he was working on, adding the last finishing touches to the structure. He had crafted it without nails to match the construction of the old stone cabin on the far side of the creek. The benches and casual shelters—also built with wooden pegs— were already in place. A painting contractor's van stood beneath the thick clump of black bamboo at the edge of the parking area. He had been cleaning and refinishing the wood paneling in the main house.

Roger Tourelle hurried out of the front door as Rachel climbed out of her truck. She had meant to bring Julio with her today, but he hadn't been able to come. His finals were over, but his growing landscape-maintenance business had forced him to become only a part-time assistant. Although Rachel was delighted to see his business grow, she missed her cheerful and canny assistant. Eduardo filled in when he wasn't busy with orchard work, but she was beginning to realize that she needed a new full-time assistant. Her business was growing, too. In fact, she had received several queries from Portland residents who had seen a feature article in the paper about the garden restoration. One of the offers involved restoring the extensive grounds of an historic mansion. It tempted her. Jeff teased her that she was going to have to move to Portland to keep up with her fans.

"I'm so glad to catch you," Roger said breathlessly. Small and rotund with prematurely thinning hair, he indeed fit his telephone persona. "I just wanted to tell you how lovely everything looks up on the hillside. I really hadn't had a chance to go up there this last week or two—since your man got all the benches set in place. I took some media people on a tour last evening, and it's just stunning! I'm sure Eloise would be thrilled with what you've done." He beamed at her. "You can't tell anyone ever tried to damage the plantings here."

Claymore had finally admitted to the vandalism after Anita/Chankina had told Spiros that he was gone that night. The damage had been repaired, and few of the plants had been damaged beyond recovery. Rachel had done some creative pruning and planted new items to fill in a few holes. A few weeks of growth had done the rest.

"Everything is actually finished," she told him. "I'm just here to do a little summer pruning in spots, and to finish that last bit of path up in the trillum bed."

"I didn't even notice that anything needed to be done. You've done such a fine job. The grand opening is going to be wonderful. Several very well regarded nurseries will have display tables here, along with environmental groups and nonprofit organizations. We're welcoming some local crafts people to set up booths, too. And several local wineries will be doing a tasting. We should attract quite an upscale crowd," he rushed on. "The publicity has been wonderful. Listen, I've got to get back inside. I hope you can make it this weekend!"

"I'll be here," Rachel promised, and gratefully fled his flood of words. Roger Tourelle never seemed to run out of energy or speech. She smiled as she climbed the path. He had certainly managed to put the garden project on the Portland media map. She had no doubt that the weekend opening would be a success.

As the gazebo near the crest of the slope came into sight, she paused to watch. April was working with Beck, dressed in a sleeveless jersey and cutoff jeans that revealed a lot of new muscles. She was rubbing a last coat of oil finish into the gleaming golden wood. As usual, the grain of each individual post or plank worked with every other piece to form a subtle unity. Rachel sometimes thought that Beck didn't so much do carpentry as he painted in wood-grain. April brushed her hair back from her face with the back of a rubber-gloved hand, then straightened as she spied Rachel.

"Nice, isn't it?" She waved a proud hand at the shelter. Octagonal, the radiating rafters fit together so closely that you had to look to see the join. The grain merged as if the pieces had grown together. "It's yellow cedar," she told Rachel. "It's old wood that Beck says cured just right. It's lovely, isn't it?"

The finish had added no additional tint to the yellow-gold wood, but it intensified the gold light of the afternoon sun. "It's beautiful," Rachel agreed, "but your work is always beautiful, Beck." As he grinned at her, she looked at the string of wooden beads he wore around his neck. Sure enough, one carved, polished orb glowed with the same intensity as the gazebo. Its twin hung around April's neck. No, not its twin, Rachel realized. The carving wasn't quite as fine, but it was close. April had carved her own bead. She was going to be as fine a woodworker as Beck, Rachel guessed. Perhaps talent called to talent.

"Have you been to the clearing lately?" Beck spoke softly as he dipped his rag into the plastic bucket of the finish he had mixed up.

"Not for a long time."

"Would you stop by?" he asked.

"Of course," Rachel said, more than a little surprised. "I would love to see what you've done."

"Why not stop on your way home?" April went back to polishing finish onto the railing of the gazebo, a secret smile on her face.

"Fine. I'd love to." Intrigued, Rachel left the two to their work and continued on her tour of the garden. There really wasn't much to do. She and her crew had been thorough, and the job was truly over.

She always had a mixed sense of triumph and a little bit of sadness when she ended a job. Unwilling to leave, she continued to pull a weed here or there, and to trim a few dead flower heads until past noon. She finally made her way down to the main house, but Roger had vanished. Detouring down to the creekbank, she made her way along the path. This time of year, the creek was low, and ferns, stinging nettle, and salmonberry grew lush along the path. She picked a few ripe golden salmonberries as she reached the bridge and the stone steps that led back up to the new parking area. She no longer shivered when she crossed the bridge. It was merely a bridge. Claymore would go to trial soon, and she would have to testify. She wasn't looking forward to it but no longer had nightmares about that night. She hadn't seen Spiros since the day after the attack, when he had arrived to take charge of Eloise's suicide tape.

Eloise would be happy with the garden, Rachel thought. She would be pleased. She climbed up to the parking lot and got into her truck. She would swing by Beck's clearing and have plenty of time for a shower before she and Jeff went out for the birthday dinner he had promised her. Her mother had called this morning to wish her happy birthday, and had asked them to drop by for dessert after their dinner. She was tired and sometimes sick from her chemotherapy but had sounded cheerful and full of energy that morning.

Rachel drove back to Blossom with the windows open, enjoying the summer heat. The summer following the wet spring was turning out to be a cool one. The temperature had been down in the eighties most days lately. The night

would be warm tonight. Maybe she and Jeff would take a
walk down along the river after dinner. The stars would be
out, and there would be a breeze. She turned off the freeway at the Blossom exit and passed through town, heading
out to Beck's clearing.

The lane that led to his cabin had hardened into concrete-
hard ridges with the drying weather. She pulled over near
the entrance from the county road and walked along the
verge, listening to the sound of birds and wind in the trees.
The path to the clearing was so faint that it might have
been a deer trail. One of Beck's black cats darted across
her path, vanishing into the shadows beneath a clump of
young firs. If she was superstitious, Rachel thought, she
would have a hard time visiting Beck. As usual, she stepped
into the clearing before she realized she was there.

The thick trunk of an old-growth cedar stood in the center of the clearing, a good four feet in diameter. The roots,
thick as her thigh, twisted into the ground, exposed as if
the tree had strained to pull itself free from the loam. In
the three years since she had discovered it, she had watched
Beck's face slowly emerge from the wood. For a long time,
she had had the feeling that Beck was predicting his future
in this piece—revealing not who he was or had been, but
who he would become.

So it was with a mix of both excitement and apprehen-
sion that she had hurried down the path that led to the
clearing. Last time she had been here, the forehead and part
of one eye was visible. Not enough to enable her to deci-
pher his expression. That was what she was waiting for—
to discover the expression on his face. She sometimes had
the eerie feeling that Beck was waiting, too.

She halted just inside the periphery of young cedars, her
shoulders brushed by their scales. He had worked on the
sculpture a lot, obviously. Nearly the entire face had been
carved, eyes, nose, and mouth.

He smiled from his log, his eyes full of warmth.

Rachel felt a small knot of worry unravel inside her—a
knot she had never really acknowledged. Beck would be

okay. Beck would be fine. An object caught her eye—
something at the base of the carved face. Rachel went over
to look. It was a pair of nested wooden bowls, with a slip
of paper stuck between them. *Happy Birthday* had been
scrawled on the paper in Beck's spiky writing.

Surprised, Rachel picked them up, wondering how on
earth he had ever discovered her birthday. The bowls were
stunning—gracefully shallow, carved from maple wood.
One bowl was pale, and the other had almost a red cast to
it. As she turned them over, she realized with a sense of
awe that they hadn't been turned on a lathe. Beck and April
had carved them by hand, had sanded them mirror smooth.
They were unfinished. She could use vegetable oil on them,
she thought, and use them as salad bowls. Smiling, warmed
by this totally unexpected gift, she went back to her truck
and drove home to shower, lounge around, and finally to
get dressed for dinner.

As she drove through town, she saw her mother on the
street outside the Bread Box. Her mother waved, and Rachel pulled over.

"Well, I guess you know where your cake is coming
from," her mother said cheerfully. "Not that you expected
otherwise, I'm sure."

"Of course I expected it. What kind? Her double chocolate fudge cake?"

"You'll just have to wait." Her mother grinned. "Just
don't eat too much dinner."

"I'll save room." Rachel laughed. Her mother wore a
sleeveless cotton blouse and jeans that highlighted her slim
figure. Her shoulders and arms were tan and firm, if a little
on the lean side, and it was only the bright scarf she wore
on her head to hide her hairless scalp, and the dark circles
the chemotherapy left beneath her eyes, that hinted at the
cancer she battled.

She would win, Rachel told herself. It would take a lot
more than a few rogue cells to stop her mother, which certainly seemed to be Deborah O'Connor's attitude. She
reached through the window to take her mother's hand. "I'll

see you tonight," she said. "Maybe we can all go for a walk on the river afterward."

"Sounds good to me, sweetheart." Her mother blew her a kiss, then went on into the Bread Box, her bright scarf jaunty in the summer sun.

Rachel drove home, still smiling. She found her door open to the screen and Peter lounging in the afternoon shade on the landing.

"See what happens when you give people your key?" Jeff sprawled on the sofa, one of her nursery catalogues open on his lap. "I'm thinking about landscaping the front yard, up at the house," he said. "I need a consultation."

"There's a fee." Rachel put the bowls down on the low table and went into the kitchen. "Want a beer? I think I've got a couple."

"I brought some. Yes, I'd like one. I'm officially off duty, gone home for the day, thank you."

This being a special day, she got down two beer mugs from the cupboard and filled them with foamy gold ale. Carrying them into the main room, she handed one to Jeff and sank down beside him with the other. "Here's to a finished job." She touched the rim of her glass to his. "And to Beck, who made me these." She reached for the bowls and handed them to him.

He whistled softly. "What a present." He ran a finger lightly around the rim of one of the bowls. "He really is quite the artisan, isn't he?"

Rachel nodded and licked foam from the rim of her glass. "And April's good for him," she said. "I think they are a solid pair. You know, I've meant to ask you for a long time—is Lieutenant Spiros married?"

"Long ago, I gather. I get the impression it didn't last very long." He stared thoughtfully into his glass. "By the way, I found out who was there, on that first day you visited Eloise Johnston."

"Claymore?"

"Carey." Jeff raised his eyes and grimaced. "I guess he'd been visiting her—pressuring to make her suspicions about

Claymore public, instead of including them in her memoirs. He thought he could reopen the case if she did."

"Her ghost." Rachel shook her head. "Why did he sneak in and out like that?"

"He had been told to leave her alone after she complained once before," Jeff said soberly. "He really was obsessed with Linda Johnston's death. But in the end, he was right."

Rachel wondered what would drive him after Claymore was convicted. "I feel a little sorry for him," she said.

"Don't." Jeff's tone was cold. "Carey went over the top on this. Claymore couldn't have taken that manuscript. I think it was Carey. Maybe he was trying to make Claymore nervous, because there wasn't really anything about him in it. I suspect he suggested to Balfor that you knew something about the memoir that implicated Claymore. He set you up as bait from the day Eloise Johnston died. Then he shadowed you, waiting for Claymore to get desperate and make a move. He sent your crew home so that you'd be at the garden alone." His eyes were hard as polished agate. "He didn't give a damn if Claymore killed you, as long as he was there to catch him at it."

Rachel looked away, remembering her anger that Spiros had been willing to let Beck be destroyed. "That bar fight you said you broke up in Portland last month? When you got that black eye." She looked at him sideways. "That wasn't from a bar fight, was it?"

"Carey understands what he did," Jeff said stiffly. It was his turn to look away. "We got some things straight."

Once upon a time, Jeff had put his career on the line to back Icarus Spiros. Rachel wondered if Spiros realized what he had lost these past weeks. Maybe not. Maybe there had only been one thing that had ever mattered in his life. She touched Jeff's hand lightly. "I didn't get hurt. It's okay."

"He's lucky you didn't," Jeff said very softly. But he smiled as he turned back to take her hand. "To change the subject—I didn't have time to go shopping for a present for you. That rash of burglaries kept us hopping this last couple of weeks."

"The price of the tourist trade." She sighed. "Out-of-town crime. And you don't have to give me a present." She made a face at him. "You know that."

"Oh, I have a present for you." He sat up suddenly and set his glass down on the table. "I bought it over a year ago. But then I thought it maybe wasn't appropriate. Maybe I'm wrong about some things." He looked at her sideways, unexpectedly serious. "But I think I understand you a little better than I did. I hope so, anyway."

"You're being really cryptic," Rachel said, but her heart began to beat faster. "Whatever are you saying?"

"Happy birthday." He laid something gently on her jeans-clad knee.

It was a ring—white gold with a small square-cut emerald in it.

"It's not traditional," he said, "but you aren't either. And an emerald—green—seemed right somehow."

Rachel looked down at it, unable to speak, emotion tumbling through her.

"I'm giving it to you as a birthday present," he told her gently. "If you want, that's all it has to be. But if you want it to mean more—I'd like that." His voice faltered. "It means a lot more to me."

She picked up the ring and held it on her palm, watching the slanting beam of afternoon sun from the window strike sparks of light deep in the heart of the emerald. "This scares me to death," she said, and watched his shoulders slump a bit. "Which is a good thing, I think." She picked up the ring slipped it onto his palm, then offered her left hand. "Will you put it on?"

"Girl, you had me scared." He gave her a crooked smile and slid the ring onto her fourth finger.

"So we're both scared." She took his face between her hands. "Like I said, that's probably a good thing. Beat it, cat," she said as Peter leaped onto the sofa between them. "Three's a crowd right now."

L A N D S C A P I N G   T I P :

Go native! When you're considering new plantings,
consider native species. There are many lovely trees,
shrubs, and ground-cover plants that are native to your
area. They are adapted to your climate and generally need
less care than nonnatives or exotics. Many of them
provide lovely blossoms, fruit that attracts wildlife, or a
show of dramatic fall color. Consult local nurseries that
specialize in species indigenous to your area.

BETSY DEVONSHIRE
NEEDLECRAFT MYSTERIES
by Monica Ferris

FREE NEEDLEWORK PATTERN INCLUDED
IN EACH MYSTERY!

EARLENE FOWLER

introduces Benni Harper, curator of San Celina's folk
art museum and amateur sleuth

❑ **FOOL'S PUZZLE**   0-425-14545-X/$6.50
Ex-cowgirl Benni Harper moved to San Celina, California, to
begin a new career as curator of the town's folk art museum. But
when one of the museum's first quilt exhibit artists is found dead,
Benni must piece together a pattern of family secrets and small-
town lies to catch the killer.

❑ **IRISH CHAIN**   0-425-15137-9/$6.50
When Brady O'Hara and his former girlfriend are murdered at the
San Celina Senior Citizen's Prom, Benni believes it's more than
mere jealousy—and she risks everything to unveil the conspiracy
O'Hara had been hiding for fifty years.

❑ **KANSAS TROUBLES**   0-425-15696-6/$6.50
After their wedding, Benni and Gabe visit his hometown near
Wichita. There Benni meets Tyler Brown: aspiring country singer,
gifted quilter, and former Amish wife. But when Tyler is murdered
and the case comes between Gabe and her, Benni learns that her
marriage is much like the Kansas weather: bound to be stormy.

❑ **GOOSE IN THE POND**   0-425-16239-7/$6.50
❑ **DOVE IN THE WINDOW**   0-425-16894-8/$6.50